Mouse-wolf

To Yvonne

Mouse-wolf

by
Elisabeth Hallett

love & thanks

from

Elischeth

Anglepoise
Books

Anglepoise
Books

Anglepoise Books
46 Hayfield Road, Oxford, OX2 6TU
www.oxfordfolio.co.uk

Typesetting by Michael Ward
www.mikewarddesign.co.uk

Set in 13/17 pt Goudy Old Style

Printed by Biddles Books Ltd., King's Lynn, Norfolk, UK

ISBN: 9780995679498

British Library Cataloguing-in-Publication Data

A catalogue record for this book is available from the
British Library

10 9 8 7 6 5 4 3 2 1

www.mousewolf.co.uk

To Ning and Bao

'Imagination is the best pathway through troubled times.'

Malcolm Bradbury

Pronunciation and Glossary

The language spoken by the characters in the story is Mandarin Chinese.

Names

huangshulang [*hwahng-shoo-lahng*] weasel, literally 'yellow-mouse-wolf'

Xiao Mei [*Shiaow May*] a name

Nainai [*Nigh-nigh*] Granny (paternal grandmother)

Old Wang [*Wahng*]

Tong [*Toong*] a surname

Yeye [*Yeh-yeh*] Grandpa (paternal grandfather)

Guanyin [*Gwahn-yin*] the Goddess of Mercy

Long Xian Ping [*Loong Shyen Ping*] 'Long' is a surname and 'Xian Ping' is a given name.

Yuan [*Yüen*] a surname

Miaoshan (*Meeow-shahn*)

King Yan [*Yen*] king of the underworld

Words

hutong [*hoo-toong*] alleyway

chai [*chy* – rhymes with 'why'] demolish

jinghu [*jing-hoo*] a two-stringed musical instrument played with a bow and used in Beijing Opera

ganbei! [*gahnbay*] cheers!

wei! [*way*] what you say when you answer the phone

kuai [*kwigh*] unit of money

yuan [*yüen*] unit of money (formal name for *kuai*)

taiqi [*tigh-chee*] Tai Chi (a kind of physical exercise with slow controlled movements)

qilin [*chee-lin*] a mythical creature with a beard, cloven hoofs and antlers like a deer, and scales like a fish

Places

Tiantan [*tyen-tahn*] - Temple of Heaven (and surrounding park)

Beihai [*Bay-high*] - a lake in Beijing

Houhai [*Hoe-high*] - a lake in Beijing

Hebei [*Her-bay*] – a province in the north of China near Beijing

Sichuan ['Si' as in 'sit'; *Si-chwahn*] - a province in the southwest of China

Xi'an [*Shee-ahn*] capital of Shaanxi [*Shahn-shee*] province in the northwest of China

Harbin – capital of Heilongjiang [*Hay-loong-jeeang*] province in northeast China

Guilin [*Gway-lin*] - city in Guangxi Zhuang [*Gwahng-shee Jwahng*] Autonomous Region, a province in south China.

Urumqi [*Oo-room-chee*] capital of Xinjiang [*Shin-jeeang*] Autonomous Region, a province in northwest China

Lhasa – capital of Tibet

Putuo [*Poo-tor*] mountain – a holy mountain on an island in the East China Sea, south of Shanghai

1.

White Paint

Xiao Mei heard the shouting, the creak of the wheels, the banging of wood on metal before she saw the men from her rooftop perch.

She climbed higher and, carefully straddling the roof ridge of the low building where she lived, looked down into the hutong below. They had come with buckets of whitewash on a handcart and were moving down the hutong from house to house, painting the big white sign on the outer walls.

A man in shorts and a dirty white t-shirt was standing outside the door of their courtyard, a dripping paintbrush in his hand. Ma and Old Wang were arguing with him. Nainai was banging the side of the cart with a stick.

Xiao Mei shinned down the ladder, ran across the yard and out into the alley. On the wall of their house the men had painted a large Chinese sign enclosed in a circle. The paint was still wet and white trickles were running to the ground. She looked down the hutong. The white sign had been painted on every single house. The sign was 拆, (chai) - the word for 'demolition'.

She looked up at Ma.

'What's happening?'

But Ma was too busy shouting at the men.

'Where's the official notification? We haven't been told anything! You can't go painting on people's walls like that!'

The man with the paintbrush laughed.

'It's my job,' he said. 'I'd paint the same sign on the Forbidden City if they paid me enough!' He spat on the ground.

The other man lit a cigarette.

'Let's go. There's still another couple of streets to do.'

And they pushed the cart away down the hutong.

He would dare paint a big white chai sign on the imperial palace, right in the heart of the city? Xiao Mei pulled at Ma's arm.

Ma turned slowly back into the yard. Old Wang gave a deep sigh.

'So, it's finally going to happen.'

Xiao Mei pulled her arm again but Ma shrugged her away. Her face was white.

Xiao Mei's heart beat hard in her chest.

'They can't knock our house down! Where will we live?'

Ma 's voice was harsh with emotion.

'Old houses are being knocked down all over the city. You know that. Have you forgotten about the Olympics? They're beautifying the city. Who knows where we'll go.'

She glanced at Nainai, then said, more gently than usual, 'Go back inside. There's no point standing out in the street.'

Nainai was muttering to herself. She shuffled back into the house, re-emerging a few moments later with a shopping bag.

'If I don't buy food today, then who will?'

Xiao Mei turned to her mother. 'Doesn't she understand what's happening?'

But Ma just stared at the receding backs of the men and said nothing.

Xiao Mei hovered on the threshold of their house. Then she walked down the hutong to the little hole-in-the-wall shop on the corner. The shopkeeper was leaning out over the counter and staring down the street, shaking his head. She bought a packet of bubble-gum, broke off a piece and chewed it miserably as she walked home.

Back in the courtyard, she climbed the ladder and sat on the roof, looking up at the sky. She sat there for a long time, her absence unnoticed by Ma or Nainai, until she heard the slam of a door and Ba's voice, yelling for Ma. He was back home and had seen the white paint.

Xiao Mei was in a daze. Where was the Goddess of Mercy to protect them now? Her benign presence had vanished. She – Xiao Mei – should have taken better care.

2.

The Inheritance

The great summer heat oozed into every corner, wrapping the city like a bug trapped in a steaming damp towel.

Some days before the white paint incident Xiao Mei had been lying on her bed fanning herself to keep cool. The sun had been up barely an hour but already the heat was unbearable and tempers were fraying.

A commotion erupted in the courtyard. Ma's shrill voice, going on and on. Ba's voice, cajoling one moment, swearing the next. Nainai's feeble screeching. Xiao Mei fanned herself even harder. She could hear pedals going round, Ma still shouting as she pushed her bike out into the hutong. A scrape of a stool as Ba sat down, swearing under his breath. No sound at all from Nainai.

Then all was still, except for the pulsating whine of the cicadas. With a flick of her wrist she snapped the fan shut, sat up and wiped the sweat from her face.

The first thing she saw when she went out into the courtyard was a blackened saucepan lying on the ground under the pomegranate tree. Nainai was in the kitchen. Ba was sitting on a low stool, smoking, a green bottle of beer by his feet. His trousers were rolled up to his knees and he was wearing an old white vest. Xiao Mei knew what that meant. He didn't have any work that day. He looked round.

'What are you staring at? Go and get dressed,' he said, taking a gulp from the bottle.

Xiao Mei was about to open her mouth, but seeing the expression on his face thought better of it and went inside. Her green t-shirt and white shorts were hanging over the back of a chair. She dressed, then splashed water over her face from the basin in the corner of the room. Her hair was short. She didn't bother to comb it.

When she went out into the courtyard again, Ba had gone. She ran over to the kitchen to find her grandmother.

'Nainai,' she said, 'where's Ba?'

The old woman was bent over the gas ring, stirring something in a pan. She didn't reply, just stirred more vigorously.

'Where's Ba gone?' said Xiao Mei again, raising her voice.

'Gone out,' said Nainai, muttering under her breath 'useless, good for nothing'. She ladled some rice porridge into a bowl and gave it to her.

'Steamed buns on the table. Don't eat them all.'

Xiao Mei took her breakfast outside and sat on Ba's stool. Good, she thought. They had both left. Ma was at work, and Ba? ... She frowned, where had he gone to? Nainai was at home, but soon she'd go out to do the shopping. That left Ba's best buddy Old Wang. She tended to avoid him these days. Like Ba, much of his day was spent sitting in the yard smoking, a bottle of beer by his side, or feeding the pigeons that he kept in a cage on the roof. Why couldn't they all go out and leave her alone?

She looked towards the kitchen. Nainai was scraping at the burnt pot. Seeing that her grandmother would be preoccupied for quite some time, she slurped down her breakfast, sidled towards the ladder leaning against the wall, then climbed up and onto the roof.

She lay against the slope, felt the heat of the grey tiles warm her back, shut her eyes and sensed the sun shining through her eyelids. Then she spread out her arms and her legs. Her fingers brushed the tufts of grass that grew in the cracks between the tiles. She liked to think of the grass seeds finding a home on their roof, sprouting so easily in friendly little clumps of green, in winter turning a dry, dusty yellow.

But the noise of the cicadas was deafening, drowning out thought. She could hear nothing else, see nothing but an orange haze, feel nothing but the warmth of the sun. It felt like flying.

Not for long. Now Nainai's shrill voice and a shaking of the ladder. She sat up, her head spinning, turned over onto her stomach and slid down the tiles until she could feel her feet touching the top rung of the ladder, Nainai scolding her all the while.

'What if you fall off, what then? You'll split your head open and who will pay the hospital bills? Don't think your Nainai has that sort of money!'

Then half-complaining to herself, 'and as for your father, that useless son of mine, you won't find much in his pockets, I can tell you.'

And on and on, all the way down the ladder, until she could feel Nainai's thin little monkey-like hands pulling at her bare feet.

'You're tickling me,' said Xiao Mei, wriggling her foot. Nainai snorted, but she let go and shuffled back into the house.

'Come with me,' she said sharply, without looking round.

~

The old house that Xiao Mei and her family lived in consisted of four low buildings constructed around a central courtyard. Each of these wings was painted grey outside and each had a grey, tiled, sloping roof. Over the years many houses like this one had been divided up between different families.

Xiao Mei's family lived in the sunny, south-facing north wing. It was divided into four small rooms: a living room with a small extension for the kitchen, and three bedrooms. They didn't have a bathroom. When they needed to they used the public toilets down the hutong, though Nainai kept a chamber pot under her bed. Baths and showers were taken in the public bath-house several streets away, otherwise a flannel and water poured into a basin resting on a metal wash stand in a corner of the living room sufficed.

Nainai's room had two doors. One led into the living room and the other opened directly onto the courtyard. Nainai disappeared through this second door into her room. Then she put her head out and beckoned.

'Quick, before he comes back.' She retreated into the gloom.

Nainai's room contained a narrow bed along one wall and a wardrobe against another. On top of the wardrobe were a suitcase and several boxes covered with an old blue sheet. Under the bed were bundles of newspapers tied up with pink plastic string. Stuffed between the end of the bed and the wall was a shopping bag on wheels filled with neatly folded plastic bags. The walls were papered with yellowing newspaper.

'Shall I put the light on?' Xiao Mei looked up at the dusty fluorescent light strip that dangled from the ceiling. The room was dark and not much light came in through the high small window facing onto the street and covered with the shrivelled little bodies of mosquitoes that Nainai had squashed against the netting.

'No, leave it alone,' Nainai snapped. She was sitting on the bed clutching a large cushion that lay in her lap.

'Sit here. Next to me.' She patted the bed.

'But first,' she spoke in a hoarse whisper, 'bolt the door behind you.' Her face had a strange expression on it, of craftiness mixed with fear.

'Why?' said Xiao Mei.

'Never mind why, just do as you're told.'

Xiao Mei bolted the door and sat on the bed.

'Shh,' said Nainai, her head on one side, 'can you hear anything?'

Xiao Mei listened. All she could hear were the voices of passers-by in the hutong, the distant noise of traffic and the incessant shrilling of the cicadas.

'Nothing,' she said.

Nainai held the cushion tight and rocked backwards and forwards. Her lips moved silently as though she were chewing a tough bit of meat. Then she slid one of her hands under the cushion. Xiao Mei put out her hand but Nainai slapped it away.

'Don't touch!'

She stopped swaying and looked hard at Xiao Mei.

'Ten years old,' she said, half to herself. 'How quickly time passes.'

She sighed and from under the cushion drew out a little square box made of dark wood. She put it into Xiao Mei's hand.

Xiao Mei looked at the box then looked at Nainai.

'Go on,' said Nainai impatiently. 'Open it.'

Xiao Mei opened the lid. Inside, resting on a bed of red silk, was a small figure carved out of shining white jade.

'Go on, take it out,' said Nainai, prodding Xiao Mei's arm.

Xiao Mei picked it up. It felt cool and smooth to the touch.

'What is it?'

Nainai peered at the figure, then said, 'That's Guanyin, of course.'

Xiao Mei turned it over in her hands. A tiny statue of the Goddess of Mercy. She was standing, dressed in flowing robes, one hand raised, palm facing outwards, and a slim vase balanced on the upturned palm of the other.

'It belonged to my grandmother,' said Nainai, 'and her grandmother before her.'

She went on, as if reciting a well-known verse:

'Now it's yours, the next girl in our family. I don't have many more years to live so I am giving it to you before it's too late. Keep her safe and she will keep you safe.'

She sniffed and wiped her hand across her face.

'Several times in the last hundred years she was lost and very bad things happened to us all.'

Xiao Mei barely took in what Nainai was saying. She held the little figure in her palm. It glowed with an inner light.

Nainai sighed. 'Keep it in a safe place, she repeated, 'and don't tell anyone that you have it.'

'Not even Ba and Ma?'

Nainai grasped Xiao Mei's hand so tight that she winced in pain.

'What did I say just now? No one. Understand? Just hide it somewhere safe and think no more about it.'

Xiao Mei put the jade back into the box and put the box deep into the pocket of her shorts. But....? She had a thousand questions.

Nainai stood up as fast as she could and pushed her towards the door.

'Go, go.'

As Xiao Mei drew back the bolt she heard a familiar whistling outside. Nainai cleared her throat, shuffled to the door and spat into the courtyard. Ba was home, sitting on the stool smoking and looking pleased with himself. He had changed into a pale yellow, short-sleeved shirt and a pair of grey trousers, and his hair was slicked back.

'Where've you been?' Nainai asked, giving him a keen look.

'Out and about,' said Ba, flicking some cigarette ash off his shoes. 'Out and about.'

Xiao Mei sidled to her room, the box bulging in her pocket. She shoved a large white plastic crate full of winter clothes against the door, sat on it, then took the little wooden box out of her pocket and opened the lid.

The little jade Guanyin glowed with a faint pinkish light. The silk cloth on which she was cushioned was faded and torn. The wood was very dark, almost black. Xiao Mei held the box to her nose and breathed in its musty odour.

Then she stood up, hauled the bed away from the wall and, lying on her stomach, reached her hand down so that it nearly touched the floor. Feeling along the wall, her fingers soon detected a roughness on the surface. The brick came out easily. She sat up, picked up the little wooden box, lay down again and carefully slid it into the cavity. Then she replaced the brick.

Just as she was pushing the bed back against the wall, she heard Ba come into the living room. He was walking around, talking on his phone.

'OK, OK,' he said, 'I'll be there first thing tomorrow.'

She heard his hand turning the handle of her door. She pulled the crate away and opening the door a crack, shouted, 'Don't come in, it's private!'

Ba laughed. 'You putting your make-up on?'

'Go away,' said Xiao Mei. 'I'm busy.'

Ba laughed again. 'Are you sure you won't let me in?'

'No,' said Xiao Mei, 'just leave me alone.'

At that moment Ba's mobile phone rang. She could hear him going out into the courtyard. With a sigh of exasperation she pushed the plastic crate back under the bed.

~

That night the air was hot and close. Xiao Mei tossed and turned, unable to sleep. After a while she turned over onto her stomach, felt for the loose brick in the wall and took out the box. Then she climbed out of bed and crept into the cool yard. All was silent. She sat on the step and opened the lid. The little white jade Guanyin shone in the dark.

She wanted to talk to someone, but who was there except Nainai? You never knew where you were with her. Sometimes she'd look at you if you were a ghost from another world.

She glanced up and saw a thin dark shape scurry across the yard. The huangshulang? A faint moan came from Old Wang's room. She put the jade figure back in its box and returned to her bed.

3.

The Goddess with a Thousand Arms

Ma kept her most precious possessions - a porcelain dancing girl, an exquisite embroidered butterfly in a frame, a sandalwood fan, and a small model of a terracotta warrior a relative had given her after a trip to Xi'an - in a glass-fronted cupboard in the living room. On the bottom shelf was a small pile of recipe books and books about health. Xiao Mei flicked through them and soon found what she was looking for: a dog-eared little book that Ba had given her in her first year at school.

It was an illustrated storybook with black and white drawings on each page and a few lines of text underneath. The title on the cover was 'The Legend of Miaoshan – the Guanyin with a Thousand Arms,' and the picture, which was in colour, showed a serenely smiling goddess in a long white gown, waving her many arms.

Xiao Mei climbed up to the roof, lay on her back and leafed through the pages. Gradually the story came back to her.

~

"There was once a king and a queen who had three daughters. The youngest one was called Miaoshan. At the moment of her birth, flowers fell from the sky and a wonderful fragrance filled the land. Miaoshan grew into a beautiful and virtuous young woman. She needed nothing more in life than fresh air and a place to pray. This angered the king greatly because he was greedy and wanted to marry her off to a rich prince in order to increase his wealth and prestige. But Miaoshan was not in the least interested in being married to anyone and told him so.

The king went on and on at her and finally, exasperated by his constant nagging, Miaoshan made a suggestion:

'I will get married only if you free humankind of the three misfortunes.'

The king, who believed he had boundless power, agreed on the spot.

'Make preparations for the wedding!' he called to the queen. 'Our daughter will soon be married!' Then turning to Miaoshan he said:

'Quick, tell me what these three misfortunes are so that I can rid humankind of them as soon as possible.'

'The first,' Miaoshan said looking directly into her father's face, 'is the suffering when someone loses their youth and becomes old. The second is the suffering when someone who is healthy becomes ill. The third is the suffering when someone dies.'

Upon hearing what Miaoshan said, the king flew into a rage, for who on earth, even if he were a king, could ever have the power to relieve human suffering? Miaoshan said nothing, but just stared at the ground.

'Lock her up in the tower!' the king roared.

'There is no need to use force,' Miaoshan said quietly. 'I am happy to go.'

So the guards led her away and she stayed in the tower, content to pray and eat no more than a bowl of rice while the king waited for her to come to her senses and get married. He waited and waited but Miaoshan did not change her mind.

The king could not contain his fury at her disobedience. After pacing up and down, he decided there was only one thing to do.

'Kill her!' he ordered his soldiers.

Like everyone in the palace, the soldiers loved and respected Miaoshan. But they feared the king even more, so with great sorrow they bound Miaoshan's wrists and led her out of the tower, through the palace grounds and into the forest. Here, in a grassy clearing, they surrounded her and drew their swords from their sheaths, ready to pierce her through the heart. Miaoshan took a deep breath and prepared herself for the next life. With a terrifying swish the blades cut through the air.

At the very moment the swords were about to pierce Miaoshan's skin, a huge tiger leapt out from behind the trees and knocked the swords from the soldiers' hands. Seizing Miaoshan in its giant jaws, it made off with her into the dark forest.

The tiger ran and ran until it came to a great hole in the ground. By the hole's deep mouth it opened its jaws and Miaoshan drifted down and down, as light as a feather, until she landed on soft ground. Ghosts wafted around her like smoke. She had arrived in the place of dead souls.

Suddenly, a huge figure of a man appeared before her with flames darting out of his head and bulging eyes. Miaoshan stood her ground bravely.

'Who are you?' she cried.

The flames on the giant man's head blazed even more fiercely.

'I am King Yan, the god of death and ruler of the underworld!' he roared, gnashing his teeth. 'None who enter my kingdom can ever escape from this place.' All around him the ghosts floated mournfully on their everlasting journey through hell, never to be reborn, never to atone for their past misdeeds.

Miaoshan said nothing, but stood quite still, her hands folded before her in prayer. Around her head hovered a radiance that penetrated the cavernous gloom. The drifting ghosts were drawn towards the light like moths to a flame.

When King Yan saw the strong, young woman standing unafraid before him he knew he had met his match. He watched helplessly as Miaoshan blessed each lost soul one by one and they floated out of the cave into the light, ready to be reborn in a new body and live their life again. Then Miaoshan..."

~

A loud clattering sounded in the courtyard below. Xiao Mei sat up, looked down and saw Nainai vigorously scrubbing out an old tin bucket. She placed the book face down, and clasped her hands round her knees.

For a moment she sat lost in thought. Then she felt in

her pocket and took out the jade Guanyin. The little figure sat calmly on her outstretched palm. Xiao Mei looked at her carefully. As another heavy earth-moving machine shuddered past in the hutong below, the Goddess of Mercy seemed to smile, but Xiao Mei couldn't be sure. She turned her round in her hand. From one angle the Guanyin looked happy, but from another she looked sad, and from another she gave no sign of any emotion at all. It must be hard to carve jade, Xiao Mei thought. She held the little figure to her cheek for a moment, so cool and smooth, then slipped it back in her pocket.

'Xiao Mei, Xiao Mei! Come down at once and help!' Nainai was shaking the ladder.

Xiao Mei sighed, stuck the book into her waistband and climbed down. She'd finish the story another time.

4.

Tiantan

'I told you I'm not going,' said Nainai, plumping herself down on the step. 'My legs are bad today. All those people and noise. And who will buy vegetables if everyone goes out? '

A little too quickly, Ma said, 'Yes, it'll be too hot in the park. You stay here and rest.'

Ba winked at Ma.

Good, thought Xiao Mei. Whenever she went out with them, Nainai made sure she looked especially decrepit, shuffling along, complaining all the while. It was embarrassing.

Ma was wearing a new navy blue skirt with a narrow white belt. She wore it with a short-sleeved white cotton blouse, on her feet she wore white sandals and on her head she had a new white sunhat. Just as they were on their way out she said she'd forgotten something and turned back into the house. When she came out again Xiao Mei saw she had put on some lipstick.

'Ma's very beautiful today,' said Ba.

'Hmmph,' said Ma, with a toss of her head. 'You're talking nonsense!'

Then she turned to Xiao Mei and said sharply, 'What are you dawdling for?'

Xiao Mei was squatting in the shade of the wall.

'Let's go, 'said Ba.

Although it had been Ma's idea to go on a picnic in Tiantan park, it was Ba who set the pace once they were out of the house. Ma followed behind Ba with a picnic bag, and Xiao Mei followed behind Ma, one hand in her pocket.

'Bus or metro?' said Ba.

'Metro,' said Xiao Mei.

On the escalator down to the platform she shut her eyes. If she could count to fifty before the steps levelled out and propelled her off, it was a lucky sign. Forty-eight, forty-nine. Her eyes flickered open just as she felt the steps become shallower. Fifty. It was cheating really. She was half-lucky, she told herself. Did half-lucky mean that she would have just a small amount of luck? Like getting fifty cents instead of a whole yuan? Or did it mean that half her luck would be good and half bad? She started counting again. If three of the people standing on the platform were holding a mobile phone, then it would be all right. She looked around. Ba – that was one, and there was another - a young guy in tight black jeans, leaning against a pillar and playing a game on his phone. And a smartly dressed middle-aged woman with a phone in her hand. Three people with phones. So it was OK. But just then a man walked past. He had a phone, too! That made four people with mobile phones. Did that mean she was more lucky or less lucky? But just as she was trying to work out what it might mean, there was a whoosh of air and the train drew alongside the platform.

'Quick,' said Ma, as she pushed against the other passengers trying to get on. 'Get a seat.'

But all the seats were occupied and the three of them had to stand, Ba and Ma holding on to the straps above their heads and Xiao Mei holding on to a support pole. Her other hand she kept deep in her pocket.

The sun was high in the sky when they arrived in the park and there were crowds of people.

'Follow me,' said Ba. 'I know a good place.'

'Oh,' said Ma, 'I can't even remember when we were here last.'

They skirted the Temple of Heaven with its red walls and circular, tiered blue roofs. Soon they were in a large grove of ancient pines planted in rows. The earth below the pines was trampled flat by people doing early morning exercises. But there were also patches of grass and it was at one of these that they stopped for their picnic. From one of the trees came the insistent tap-tapping of a woodpecker. Just beyond was the grey curved outer wall of the park. Ma spread out some newspaper to sit on and unpacked the picnic. Ba lit another cigarette. Xiao Mei looked up at the trees.

'What are you doing?' Ma shouted, 'you want to go to the toilet or something? Come and help.'

Xiao Mei scowled and took her hand out of her pocket. But when neither Ba nor Ma were looking, she put her hand in her pocket again and half pulled out the little wooden box. She had struggled with herself about taking it away from its hiding place in the wall. Just this once, she thought, and slipped the box into her pocket. The beautiful little Guanyin would accompany her to the park, just this once.

Ma brought out hard-boiled eggs, some little cakes, four red sticks of sausage, several cucumbers, two packets of crisps, a packet of coconut biscuits, three large peaches and a big bottle of coke. She poured the coke into plastic cups. As Ba sat down he knocked over one of the cups, splashing coke onto Ma's new skirt. That was enough to set them off again. Ma told Ba he was a clumsy idiot and Ba told Ma that she should have warned him that the cup was full. When the shouting had finished Ma sat with her back to Ba, and Ba lay on the grass. After a while he gave her a little shove with his toe.

'Nice picnic,' he said.

'Hmmph,' said Ma.

Then she stretched out next to him, put her new sunhat over her eyes, and before long they were both asleep.

Xiao Mei wandered off. She found a patch of grass between two small cypresses that concealed her from view, and lay down on her back looking up at the sky. Apart from distant noises from the crowds of visitors around the temple and the faint rumble of traffic beyond the park walls, everything was still. She held her breath and listened. Not a sound. Just the sun beating down. She felt dizzy so she wriggled herself backwards so that her head was in the shade of one of the trees.

But soon, in her drowsy state, she became aware of small noises all around her. The whine and buzz of innumerable tiny insects; the liquid call of the bugu bird: four falling tones, over and over again. A faint rustling and a grasshopper springing up, just brushing the hairs on her arm. She turned over on her stomach and looked into the grass. It smelled fresh and damp.

As she raised her head, she saw, at least she thought she saw, the glint of a pair of eyes – or was it broken glass? – under the branches right at the bottom of the tree, and a twisting black shape that could have been just the shadows of the branches, lifted by the slightest of breezes. She held her breath but all was still except for the cicadas and the mournful bugu bird.

She sat up and glanced at Ma and Ba. She could just see them. Ba was lying on his back, his chest moving up and down. Ma lay on her side next to him, her mouth half open. When she had reassured herself that they really were asleep, she drew the little wooden box from out of her pocket, opened the lid and took out the jade.

It was the first time she had seen it in daylight. It glowed as before, but this time with a warm, rose-pink colour. She turned the figure over. The Guanyin's robe fell in folds to her feet. Then she turned it over again. The goddess's eyes were almost closed and there was a faint smile on her lips. She tossed the little statue into the air several times to see how it shone in the sunlight and to feel its weight, surprisingly heavy, as it landed in her hands.

And then, she tossed it too high and it dropped a little way away into the long grass. She raked her fingers through the grass but could not find it anywhere. Her heart in her mouth, she stood up, thinking that it might have fallen into her clothes. Nothing. She took off her sandals and shook them. Nothing. Then she bent down and scrabbled through the grass again. Nothing. The Guanyin had completely disappeared.

Xiao Mei stood, rooted to the spot. Ma was waking up, looking over towards the cypresses.

'What are you doing?' she called.

Ba gave a final wobble of a snore and sat up.

'Time to go,' he said, looking at his mobile phone. 'Xiao Mei, let's go.'

But Xiao Mei had gone very quiet. She squatted down under the cypresses and again dragged her hands through the grass.

'Come on, come on,' shouted Ma, 'time to go home. What's the matter with you?'

Xiao Mei said nothing, there was no way she could tell them. When Ba walked over to her she didn't move. 'Let's go,' he said again.

'The child looks ill, her face is quite white.' Ma glanced at her. 'Better get back home quickly.'

'Must have eaten too much sausage,' said Ba.

There was nothing Xiao Mei could do and she followed them miserably back, through the park, to the station, down the escalator, onto the train, up the escalator, out of the station and down the street until they turned into the hutong where they lived. When they got home she was told to go straight to bed.

She turned from one side to the other, unable to sleep, a taste in her mouth of something like dust and burning plastic. She drifted into sleep, imagining a return to the park to do a proper search. Because otherwise something bad would happen, she felt sure of it, just like Nainai said it would.

Two days later the men arrived with the white paint. And the little jade goddess was about to embark on a long, long journey.

5.

Nainai and the Huangshulang

Xiao Mei waited in an agony of unease, convinced that any day soon the family would be turned out onto the street with all their possessions and nowhere to go.

But after the commotion caused by the white chai sign, everything went quiet. When she begged to know what would happen now, Ma and Ba changed the subject, though at night after she'd gone to bed, she could hear them talking in low, anxious voices. When she went outside and looked down the hutong nothing had changed; everything seemed exactly the same.

The days became hotter and hotter. The air was as clammy as a wet rag. It was too hot to sit on the roof tiles, too hot to do anything. She stayed inside, lying on her back on the sofa and watching television. Nainai pottered about the yard or rested on her bed waving the air around with a fan. Ma left early for work at the department store. Ba went off on mysterious expeditions or hung out in Old Wang's room, drinking beer and playing chess.

It was only when the sun began to go down that Xiao Mei ventured into the courtyard. Nainai brought out an old white enamel basin of peapods and the two of them sat on low stools shelling peas into a yellow plastic colander.

For a moment Nainai stopped what she was doing and cocked her head in the direction of a pile of boxes covered by a tarpaulin in the corner of the yard.

'Pestilential creature,' she grumbled. 'I thought I heard it scratching.'

'The huangshulang?' said Xiao Mei, as she dropped an empty pod on the ground. 'She never does anything.'

'You can never be too careful,' said Nainai. 'Even if they kill your chickens, it's better just to let them be.'

'But we don't have any chickens!'

Nainai looked at her, then said, 'Let me tell you a true story about a huangshulang that lived in our yard a long time ago.'

Xiao Mei picked up another peapod. Nainai was always coming up with crazy stories. At least it would make the time pass more quickly.

Nainai began.

'Many, many years ago, before I came to live in this house in the middle of Beijing, I lived in a small village a long way north of here. Of course that was before it was built over with new houses and roads. When I lived there the village was surrounded by fields and trees and streams. I was just married and we lived together with your great-grandmother. Your grandfather was out in the fields every day and I stayed at home helping great-grandmother cook and clean. This is a true story that she told me about something that happened when she was young and lived in the very same house.

'Next door, great-grandmother said, all those years ago, lived a young man with his wife and young son. Our two houses shared an outer wall and the families knew each other well. In our yard was a great haystack. It had been there for generations, with dried straw added each year to use as fuel. Inside the haystack, right at the bottom, lived a family of huangshulang. Every now and then they would steal eggs and sometimes kill a chicken by grabbing it by the comb and sucking the blood from the neck. When this happened, great-grandmother would stand by the haystack and curse the huangshulang, but she would never do any more than that.

'One day, the young man rushed over in a great rage, saying that the huangshulang had sneaked into his yard, stolen three eggs and killed two of his chickens. Great-grandmother commiserated with him and gave him a pile of buns she had just steamed. By dusk, the young man was still simmering with rage. He waited until it was dark and tiptoed into our yard to set traps for the huangshulang. Then he went back home to wait. Just before dawn he returned. To his great frustration he found that the traps were sprung, but no huangshulang. All he could see was a little heap of sawdust where the huangshulang had gnawed at the wood.

'The next night he set more traps, but again, no huangshulang. On the third night, when the moon was high, he set traps all around the haystack. When he returned just before daylight, he discovered, to his great satisfaction, a big fat huangshulang, dead, with its neck broken. He took the body and hung it in his yard. When great-grandmother saw what he had done, she started cursing him for an ignorant fool. But he just laughed at her and told her not to be so superstitious.'

'What a horrible story,' Xiao Mei said, wrinkling her nose in disgust. 'I bet it's not true.'

'I haven't finished yet,' said Nainai sharply.

'Soon it was Chinese New Year's Eve, the time when families make dumplings to celebrate. The young man's wife was busy kneading the dough, rolling it out into small circles, placing a spoonful of meat filling in the middle of each circle and folding the dough over to make a small crescent-shaped, delicious-looking dumpling.'

'I know how dumplings are made,' said Xiao Mei impatiently. Nainai glared at her and continued.

'She made about fifty dumplings. Then she put a great pot of water on to boil. When the water was churning and bubbling she dropped the dumplings in. Then she gave the water a stir, peered down into the pot, and screamed. The young man came running in alarm.

'The dumplings! The dumplings!' she shrieked.

The young man looked into the pot and found, to his horror, that each dumpling had turned into a big brown dog-turd. He grabbed the pot, rushed outside with it and threw the contents into the pigsty. As the turds tumbled out, they turned back into snow-white dumplings. Still screaming, the young man's wife grabbed her son, rushed out of the house and ran all the way back to her parents.

'Several days later the young man was sitting alone in the

house overcome with misery and fear and not daring to go out. A man arrived at the house with a terrible message. The young man's wife and son had been walking outside when they fell into a ditch and froze to death. His mother-in-law was so overcome with shock that she collapsed and died. A fearful look came over the young man's face and he rushed around the room, not knowing what to do.'

Nainai leant forward so that her face was just inches away from Xiao Mei's and, putting her hand in front of her mouth, said in a hoarse whisper:

'And from that time on, great-grandmother told me, the young man became stranger and stranger. His hands and feet became thin and agile and his behaviour tricky and sly. He started stealing chickens and developed a great fondness for eggs, which he would never cook but eat raw. Sometimes you would see him sitting on top of the haystack, scratching himself. Then one day he disappeared, and we never ever saw him again.'

'That's horrible,' Xiao Mei leant back with a shiver. 'I'm glad we live in the city.'

There was a noise behind them. Ba swaggered in with a bag of shopping, followed by Ma pushing her bike.

'What's the old lady on about now?' he said, slapping Nainai on the back.

Nainai recoiled, pursed her lips and said nothing. She stuck a peapod in her mouth and ripped it open with her teeth. Then she knocked the pod against the side of the bowl and the peas bounced out.

Ma propped her bike against the wall and stepped wearily inside. She turned to Xiao Mei.

'Put the shopping away. Why do I always have to ask you?'

Nainai ripped open another peapod. She glared at Xiao Mei.

'What are you hanging about for? And take these peas with you.'

Xiao Mei gave a huff of irritation. Why was the older generation always so rude? She took the bowl of peas, stood up as slowly as she could, and stomped back inside. When she had put the shopping away, evading Ma's eye, she disappeared into her room.

She sat on her bed pondering Nainai's huangshulang story. It was all just ...what was that word she had been taught in school? ...superstition. It was science that had all the answers, not fanciful stories from feudal times. That's what her teachers said. But when she thought about the lost jade Guanyin, the Goddess of Mercy, and the men with the white paint a hard, tight, anxious feeling came into her chest. Things were going to get worse, weren't they?

6.

Mouse-wolf

The last of the visitors had left Tiantan park. The park-keepers did their rounds, locked each gate, and went home. The light of the setting sun illuminated the golden tear-shaped dome on the top of the blue roof of the Temple of Heaven. A small breeze rustled the pine trees and cypresses where earlier in the day the family had had their picnic.

From under the cypresses where Xiao Mei had played with the little jade figure emerged a slender shape with small, round, erect ears and a quivering nose. It hesitated, then raised itself up on two short legs to sniff the air, its long thick tail curled round behind. Reassured that all was well, it rolled over and over in the grass, the golden fur on its long sleek body catching the last rays of the setting sun. Night fell quickly, but a full moon was rising and the golden fur turned silver in the bright moonlight.

The huangshulang was hungry and began to search for food. Soon he found a fat cicada on a tree-trunk and crunched it between his sharp little teeth. He rolled in the grass to disturb other insects, snapping at them as they flew up. He knew that mice lived under the trees, and scrabbled under a cypress, looking for the entrance to a burrow. But the mice were wise to the huangshulang and remained hidden in the sun-warmed earth.

The huangshulang worked quickly, not waiting for other huangshulang to snatch what he was looking for. He tended to avoid his kind. Not that they were enemies, it was just that, like most huangshulang, he preferred to be alone. All he wanted was to eat and sleep and live in peace. There was enough space in the big park for all of them. Of the chaotic, changing world beyond the park's grey walls he knew nothing at all, had never given it a thought.

As he clawed at the earth his paw touched something smooth and firm, an egg perhaps, dropped from a nest or left behind by human visitors. He scraped at the earth some more until the object revealed itself, white and glowing in the darkness. It wasn't an egg, for sure. It was smooth and cool like an egg, but the shape was irregular and it was hard, like a stone. He sniffed it, bit it, took it in his paws, tossed it in the air and caught it in his teeth. Then he set it down on the grass and looked at it. The thing seemed to look at him. He backed away, disconcerted. It looked almost like a human. He sat back on his haunches, not knowing what to do.

The Guanyin gazed at him, an inscrutable smile on her lips. He stretched out his neck and sniffed her again, then licked her face. Did she blink? He couldn't be sure. He yawned, and in that split second between his eyes closing and opening again she seemed to glow with a golden radiance and grow a thousand arms. He backed away in alarm.

He blinked again. The little jade figure sat next to him, inert. He stood up on his four feet and sniffed the warm night air. Muscles tensed, ears erect, nose quivering, he crouched low to the ground. Some unseen danger threatened but he had no idea what. He stood like this for a while, as motionless as the Guanyin sitting next to him. But then his stomach reminded him that he was hungry and he turned to scrabble in the earth once more. After a few minutes, he stopped, feeling uneasy, but not knowing why. He glanced at the Guanyin, then swiped at her with his paw. The little figure toppled over onto its back. He returned to his digging. After scraping half-heartedly at the earth for another minute or two, he stopped to look round. The Guanyin was bathed in a softly glowing pool of light, a slight smile on her lips. His unease turned to fear. What was this strange inanimate thing that seemed to be alive? What had it to do with him?

Though he scarcely knew it, he was waiting for a sign, a signal. When it came, it overwhelmed him in a great shuddering wave, dragging him forward, one slow reluctant paw at a time. It was something stronger than instinct, powerfully insisting that he go, drawing him away out of the park and into the wild encircling city. He felt afraid. He understood what he had to do, but not why.

He had to reunite the jade Guanyin with the one who had lost her. Like so many in the city, uprooted and powerless, Mouse-wolf had no choice at all over his destiny.

~

The sun had not yet risen but there was a glimmer of light in the sky and the birds were stirring. Mouse-wolf was leaving Tiantan for the first time in his life, carrying the little jade figure in the pouch of his cheek.

He slipped under the park gate and stared at the wide road in front of him. Even though the sun was scarcely up, cars and buses were streaming past. He stood bewildered, keeping close to the park wall. A short way beyond was a footbridge that led over the road to a long, multi-storeyed building with a grey roof and upturned eaves. Taking a deep breath, he ran up the ramp of the bridge, over the top, and down the ramp on the other side.

The main doors of the building were open. Many people were going in and out: delivery men wheeling carts stacked high with boxes, stall-holders arriving to arrange their wares, security guards and cleaners. The noise and commotion was frightening and disorientating.

Just ahead of him he saw a rat, reclining against a wall and chewing on a stale crust of bread. It stared at the bulge in Mouse-wolf's cheek, sneered, then, either in jest or out of malice, lunged at him. Mouse-wolf bared his teeth and, scarcely knowing what he was doing, raced into the building, shot onto an escalator, and crouched in panic on the moving metal steps as he was borne up to the next floor.

When he arrived at the top, he was dazzled for a moment by a bright shaft of early morning sunlight that streamed in through a large window. As his eyes adjusted to the brightness, he looked about him in confusion. Stretching in front of him were hundreds of stalls selling jades of every shape, size and colour: loose jade beads, jade necklaces, jade bracelets, jade earrings, carved jade mountains, creamy white, rose-pink, peach-coloured, pale-blue and green-grey jades. He stopped and took the jade from his mouth. It glowed with an intense inner light. Then he looked at the other jades and they seemed dull and lifeless in comparison. He realised that he had come to the wrong place entirely.

At that moment, one of the stall-holders caught sight of him, shrieked, and in her panic knocked over a basket of jade beads that rolled all over the floor. A cry went up: 'Huangshulang! Huangshulang!' A woman threw a stool at him, everyone was pointing and running and shouting. Tables were upturned and jade scattered everywhere. Frightened out of his wits, Mouse-wolf fled. He pelted helter-skelter down the escalator, past the rat who grinned at him through bared teeth, and out into the street where he crept exhausted into a cardboard box that was lying half-flattened on the pavement. Here he hid, panting and trembling all over.

From inside the box, he could hear the sound of traffic and the footsteps of passers-by. As he turned himself round in the confined space, there came a patter of small feet and a loud snuffling noise, which was followed by a watery, malodorous trickle that seeped into the box. It was not safe to come out.

Some minutes later, he heard something rattling and, before he had time to guess what it might be, he felt his box being heaved up and slung roughly on top of something. When the box had settled, he peered out through the top to discover that he was on a three-wheeled cart piled high with other boxes, broken sheets of white polystyrene and plastic bottles. A small, wiry, bare-backed man in shorts and black cloth shoes leapt onto the seat and as he began to pedal, the box swayed from side to side. Mouse-wolf cowered low in a corner, looking out through a tiny hole in the cardboard. It was unbearably hot in the box but at least the jade was still safe in the pouch of his cheek.

After a while, the man stopped pedalling. Mouse-wolf could see him getting off his seat and walking round to the back of the cart. Then he could see no more. The cart shook, there was a noise of something flat hitting the pavement, and then silence. After a few moments Mouse-wolf peered out once again through the top of the box. The man had spread a sheet of cardboard on the ground underneath a scholar tree, and was using it as a mat to sleep on. A stream of ants moved busily along in the gutter. Unseen in the trees, in the heat of the day, the cicadas were stridulating as if their lives depended on drowning out any other sound.

Mouse-wolf crawled cautiously out of the box. They were parked in a narrow lane. On either side stood empty, half-demolished houses. Walls had been knocked down, exposing beams and interior paintwork, and everywhere were piles of bricks and rubble. At the far end of the hutong was a large orange digger, its claw raised in the air. Nothing stirred in the intense midday heat.

I can't stay here, he thought. He eased himself down and hesitated before the threshold of one of the condemned houses. A large white character had been painted on the wall. Stone lions guarded each side of the wooden door. It was open a crack, allowing Mouse-wolf to squeeze through. For a moment the stone lions came to life, growling and extending their claws, but they were too enfeebled to retain their spirit and quickly returned to stone. Then, in a strange little puff, they crumbled to dust behind him.

But Mouse-wolf was already in the empty courtyard, clambering over the piles of rubble, broken beams, fragments of glass, plastic bags and scraps of paper. On one remaining wall of a room was an old poster of a plump man in a khaki-green uniform, arm outstretched and standing in front of a large red sun.

One room on the north side of the courtyard was still intact. Mouse-wolf stopped and listened. Sounds of voices came from within. He drew closer. Four workmen were sitting around an upturned box, playing cards. Mouse-wolf drew back in haste but in doing so knocked over an empty can on the ground. The workmen looked up, saw Mouse-wolf and leapt to their feet.

'Huangshulang!' cried one of them and threw the can at him.

In his fright Mouse-wolf opened his mouth. The jade dropped out and tumbled into a corner of the room where it winked and glowed in the shadows. One of the men swore in surprise and stooped down to pick it up. Mouse-wolf rushed at him and bit him on the hand. The man yelped and dropped the jade. Mouse-wolf raced off, the jade back in his mouth.

In the ensuing commotion the card table was overturned and cards flew everywhere. The men cursed and tumbled out of the house into the hutong, convinced that they had been attacked by an evil huangshulang spirit. Mouse-wolf cowered in a corner of the courtyard, trembling all over. Some minutes passed before he stopped shaking.

And then came a different sensation, a familiar smell that told him he was not alone.

7.

The Old Aunts

Xiao Mei sat sulkily on the step in the courtyard. She knew she was expected to go, but why, she asked Ma, did she have to?

'But you always liked going to see them,' said Ma as she packed up their lunch. They were going to visit the great-aunts.

Ma had packed a bag with three plastic containers: one of rice, one of red-cooked eggplant, and one of meatballs. It was true, in the past she had not minded going. But Ma had become irritating and embarrassing to go out with. It was the way she walked, always in a hurry with her head poked forward and a cross look on her face. Other mothers were more smiley and relaxed and didn't drag their daughters to places they didn't want to go to. All she wanted, Xiao Mei, thought, was to be left on her own.

She thought about Old Auntie and Second Auntie and how, not so long ago, they too had had to move. Until last year they had occupied a ramshackle old house built around a courtyard with a persimmon tree in the middle. In the yard was a single tap. When they needed the toilet they stepped over the threshold of the house with its stone lions guarding either side of the door, and walked a short distance down the hutong to the public conveniences. In winter, a single coal stove provided heating for one of the rooms. They would sleep with most of their clothes on, under piles of cotton quilts.

Second Auntie did most of the cooking while Old Auntie sat in her room painting delicate scenes of beautiful young women holding fans, or mountains and rivers with little boats floating downstream. On warm summer evenings they would sit outside in the courtyard listening to local opera on the radio.

One day, a big white chai sign appeared on one of their walls and a short time later the demolition men arrived. With the help of Ma and Ba the aunts gathered their few possessions and moved to the southern outskirts of the city where they had been assigned a small, third-floor flat. The number on the side of their building was 10. There were twelve other tall buildings in their compound.

As Ma and Xiao Mei walked down the street towards the bus stop, Ma said, 'I wish Laolao was still alive to see how much you've grown.'

Xiao Mei said nothing. She barely remembered her grandmother, Ma's mother, her great-aunts' younger sister.

Ma went on, half to herself, 'I don't know what she would think of the way they are living now.'

'Better than before,' Xiao Mei said, kicking a stone into the gutter and remembering the derelict courtyard. 'At least there's an inside toilet.'

'That's not what I mean,' said Ma. 'I mean compared to when they were young.'

Here we go again, Xiao Mei thought. The old story about books and paintings and goldfish and everything.

Ma went on.

'We were an educated family, you know. Father was a history teacher. Mother was a beautiful woman in her youth. She was an artist and an excellent calligrapher. When she was little she lived in a lovely courtyard house, with books and paintings and a little goldfish pond. That's not where I grew up. Our rooms at the school where father worked were bleak and sparsely furnished. "Where are all those things now?" I asked her once. But she would not tell me. She just waved her hand and said, "That was all long ago. The world is different now." '

Ma glanced at Xiao Mei. 'She was certainly right about that, wasn't she? Look at everything that's going on these days.'

Xiao Mei nodded.

~

The windows were wide open when they arrived at the aunts' flat. A stiff warm breeze buffeted through, rippling the thin cotton curtains and a pile of papers on a table. Ma went round shutting them.

'It may be hot outside but you'll catch a cold if you sit in a draught,' she admonished them.

Old Auntie said, 'We miss the air. We're suffocating.'

Ma knew they were pining for their open courtyard, but said, 'Everything is so convenient now. You've got water in the kitchen and an indoor toilet. And a fridge too.' The fridge was a present from Ma and Ba.

But Second Auntie repeated her sister's words, 'We're suffocating here.'

Xiao Mei sat on a chair. She wanted the windows open.

'Ma, it's so hot.'

'I've brought a few dishes for lunch,' said Ma, going into the kitchen.

'No need, ' said Old Auntie, rising slowly from her chair. 'We made some pork and cabbage dumplings yesterday. They're on the counter, just waiting to be heated up.'

Ma picked up one of the dumplings from the plate, sniffed at it and took a bite. It tasted strange. Then she opened the fridge. A sour smell wafted out. She looked behind the fridge. The electric cable wasn't connected to the power supply. The fridge was off – and so was the food inside.

When she asked the aunts about this, Old Auntie grumbled, 'Why would we want a fridge anyway? It just costs us money!'

Second Auntie said, 'We managed without one all these years. What do we need one now for?'

'Never mind,' said Ma, in a conciliatory voice. 'I've brought some food I cooked this morning.'

Xiao Mei kicked her heels against her chair. Couldn't they just hurry up, eat their lunch and go?

Ma undid the catch on the round fold-up table and snapped it open. Before they sat down to eat, Old Auntie switched on the radio. It was their time to listen to Beijing opera. The volume was turned right up. The shrill, high-pitched female voice, the relentless sawing of the jinghu, the rapping of the clappers, and the clanging of the cymbals made Xiao Mei wince.

'The neighbours complain,' Second Auntie said. 'They don't understand opera like we do.'

Old Auntie nodded sadly, 'Our live opera group is too far away, so all we can do is listen to the radio.'

Bang, bang, bang, went the cymbal. Ma stood up and turned the volume dial. 'Perhaps it's a little too loud, ' she said. 'We can hardly hear each other talk.'

But the aunts were enjoying Ma's food too much to make further conversation. When they had finished, Second Auntie belched loudly and said that it was time for a nap. Old Auntie laid her chopsticks neatly by her bowl. Then she stood up and without another word made her way to the bedroom. Second Auntie washed her hands under the kitchen tap. Ma stood up and turned off the radio.

'Don't worry, Xiao Mei and I will wash up,' she called, looking at Xiao Mei and indicating with her hand that she should go to the kitchen.

Xiao Mei stood up reluctantly. By the time she and Ma had washed the dishes, the only sound in the flat was the rhythmic snoring coming from the aunts' bedroom. At last they could leave.

~

When they got back home Ma said to Ba, 'It seems as if they've lost all their spirit. They're not looking after themselves.'

Ba said nothing. He had enough to think about without concerning himself with Ma's elderly aunts and their idiosyncrasies. They, at least, had moved and got a new flat sorted out. That was more than could be said about their own situation.

That night, Ma lay wakefully in bed, worrying about them. Her stomach felt queasy and uncomfortable. Eventually she fell asleep and dreamt troubled dreams.

She dreamt of two beautiful sisters who lived in a house with many courtyards. One of them was wielding a large pair of scissors, cutting up silk dresses and fur coats that she snatched from a heap on the floor. The other stood next to her, wringing her hands and saying 'hurry, hurry, they are outside, can't you hear them banging on the door'. There was a great sound of many people shouting and chanting in unison.

'Gone, gone' said the one of the sisters, 'everything gone', as she swept the scissors along a shelf full of porcelain, which shattered to fragments on the ground. Next they dashed to the bookshelf and ripped the pages from the books, one by one. Now they were throwing lit matches at the pages and wailing and swaying like mad things, but the noise outside drowned out their voices, and everything became a mass of swirling colour and sound, and then, louder and louder came what sounded like the tinkling of a thousand bicycle bells rushing down the hutong.

The bells went on and on. Ma opened her eyes. It was daylight, the alarm clock was ringing and it was time to get up and go to work. She was covered in sweat. Ba was standing over her, looking at her with concern.

'Are you all right?' he asked.

Ma nodded. She got up, splashed water over her face from a basin in the corner of the room, and pulled on her clothes. Then she brushed her teeth. In the kitchen she drank a glass of hot water.

'Aren't you going to eat anything?' said Ba, following behind her.

Ma made a face and shook her head. She glanced into Xiao Mei's bedroom. She was still asleep. Then she went into the courtyard and looked at her bicycle. Would she cycle or take the bus? The thought of the crowded bus was too much to bear. She needed air, if not fresh air, then at least air. She pushed her bike over the threshold and cycled down the hutong, and as she cycled she thought about the aunts and the strange dream she'd had about the things that had happened to them in the time of chaos all those years ago.

~

Xiao Mei woke up, poured herself a glass of milk, took a peach from the yellow colander, and climbed up onto the roof before it became too hot. She looked down at the courtyard and thought of the great-aunts and their new flat. Was that the sort of place they would have to move to?

Her thoughts turned to the little jade Guanyin, the Goddess of Mercy. Was she still lying hidden somewhere in the long grass? Or had someone picked her up and carried her off, all alone with no one to protect her?

~

Ma brooded over the aunts for some days. As soon as she had a free half-day she returned, again taking Xiao Mei with her.

It took a while for the aunts to answer the door.

'They've probably gone out,' said Xiao Mei hopefully. 'Let's go.'

But after a few moments they heard footsteps and Second Auntie let them in.

'Thank goodness you're here.' Her hair was unkempt and her apron askew.

They followed her into the living room. It was in chaos. The table stood in the middle of the room with chairs stacked on top of it. The bookcases were empty and the books were lying in piles on the sofa, which had also been dragged to the centre. A plant pot lay shattered, earth and leaves spilled all over the floor. Old Auntie was sitting on the sofa, wheezing and wrapped in a blanket.

'What on earth are you doing?' cried Ma.

Second Auntie plumped down next to her sister. The two of them had complexions as grey as unbaked clay. When Old Auntie got her breath back she explained to Ma what had happened. In between pauses for breath and Second Auntie's frequent interruptions and elaborations, they discovered what had been going on.

Everything had seemed fine when the aunts first moved in. But recently strange things had started happening in the night when a creature took up residence. This creature would take on different forms, sometimes becoming a young woman with long red hair, other times an old man with dry papery skin and bald gums. But whatever shape it took, it always performed the same evil deed.

Old Auntie shivered and drew the blanket tight around her.

Xiao Mei sat up wondering what would come next.

'It squats on our chests and tries to stop us breathing!' cried Second Auntie.

'And whatever we do we're unable to move even a finger to push it off!' added Old Auntie, pushing out with both her hands. 'We're paralysed!'

'And then....,' Second Auntie's voice dropped to a whisper, 'and then....'

'It breathes foul air into our nostrils!'

Xiao Mei leant forward.

'Then we shout at the tops of our voices and the creature gnashes its teeth and vanishes!'

'And then we wake up.'

'But the next night it is back again! And the next!'

They had been to the temple, made a donation and burnt incense, and they had consulted a geomancer. The geomancer had come to the flat. After they had paid him he told them that it was no wonder they were plagued by ghosts. The fengshui was all wrong. The flat was inauspiciously situated and the furniture was in all the wrong places. They couldn't do anything about the position of the building but they could move the furniture around and that was what they were doing when Ma arrived.

Ma sighed. Why hadn't they at least phoned her for help?

There was no way she could leave the two old ladies in such a state. Putting down her bag, she and Xiao Mei moved the furniture into position according to the aunts' tremulous directions.

When they had finished, Xiao Mei went into the kitchen. The fridge was still switched off. There was nothing inside. On the windowsill were two covered bowls. She lifted the lids. In one bowl were some cooked noodles. In the other were some pickled radishes. Ma came in and looked around. Was that all they were eating? The women were starving themselves. No wonder they were having nightmares. Ma took out the food that she had brought for their lunch – some rapidly melting frozen dumplings - and filled a pan of water to boil.

As they walked back to the bus stop, Xiao Mei said, 'Why do they believe all that stuff?'

Ma shrugged her shoulders and said, half to herself, 'How else can they explain everything that's happened to them?'

'Superstition,' Xiao Mei said firmly. 'It's just superstition.'

A few days later Second Auntie phoned. The creature had become less aggressive but it hadn't disappeared completely. They had consulted the geomancer again and he had told them that they must hang up a gong which they should strike every morning and evening. Would Ma be able to get a gong for them in her shop? She must be sure to buy a gong made of copper and not of any other material.

The next day Ma went to the musical instruments department. Hanging behind the counter were seven or eight copper gongs. The salesman said he didn't know why there was such a demand for copper gongs these days. He gave her a good discount and that evening she dropped in at the aunts' place to deliver it. They greeted her with cries of relief. She hung the gong in the kitchen doorway, and as she left she could hear it boom as it was repeatedly struck before the aunts lay down for their afternoon nap.

Some weeks passed before Ma saw them again.

8.

Old Wang

Most of the families in the hutong had now moved. All Xiao Mei's friends had gone. Why should her family be almost the last to leave? There was no one to talk to, Ma was at work, Ba always had better things to do, and who in their right mind would want spend time with Nainai? As for Old Wang...

For as long as she could remember, Xiao Mei had fallen asleep to the gentle cooing of Old Wang's pigeons and the soft pattering of their little claws.

Old Wang lived opposite them in the sunless north-facing south wing. He had constructed a cage on top of his roof, made of bits of board and wire-netting, with perches and trays of seed placed inside. Most days he would climb up to the cage to let the pigeons out to have a 'fly around', as he called it. He would watch as they hopped to the edge of the cage, stretched and fluttered their wings and, one after the other, soared up and over the courtyard. He had tied bamboo whistles to their bodies, and as the birds swooped and swirled over the city, they trailed an unearthly windy music in the still air.

Xiao Mei liked to imagine what the pigeons saw as they flew up. Spread out below them they would surely look down on a crisscross of wide roads and narrow hutongs, dark green patches of trees, the red walls and golden roofs of the Forbidden City, and the still grey waters of the lakes of Beihai and Houhai. Shimmering new tower blocks soared up alongside the low courtyard houses. Orange cranes on dusty grey-yellow construction sites swung their arms over vast caverns, from whose depths rose spiky columns of steel and concrete. In the distance, on the city's outskirts, stretched the blue-grey Western Hills.

After a while, the pigeons would descend in slow spirals over the fourth, third, and second ring roads that encircled the city, dancing down between the kite strings pulled by old men standing on flyovers, down over the hutongs, until they came back home to roost on top of Old Wang's roof.

Old Wang was almost old enough to be Xiao Mei's grandfather. For as many years as she could remember he had lived by himself in two rooms on the south side of the courtyard. His wife had died or run away - no one was quite sure. He had a daughter, he said, but she was working in the south of the country and he hadn't seen her since she was a child.

Old Wang was strong and lean, though his face was lined and several of his teeth were missing. Those that were left were stained yellow from years of smoking. Sometimes he would go out to do odd carpentry jobs and his hair, still mostly black, was often dusty with sawdust. When he wasn't working he would sit out in the courtyard smoking and chatting with Ba, or else he would be up in the pigeon cage, feeding the birds and cleaning out the mess.

When Xiao Mei was little she used to sit on his lap and he would stroke her hair. She liked the smell of wood that always clung to him and she would ruffle his hair in return, sending little clouds of dust up into the air.

But the past few months she had taken to avoiding him.

One day, she had been sitting in the courtyard after school. Ma and Ba were out and Nainai was in the kitchen preparing the evening meal. She was just about to go inside when Old Wang emerged from his room in the south wing. He was carrying a basin piled high with washing. As he stepped across the courtyard to the washing line a wet towel fell to the ground.

'Xiao Mei', he called, 'pick it up for me.'

She turned back and put it in the basin.

'Help me hang this lot up,' he said, grinning at her. 'A big girl like you will have a home of her own in just a few years.' He took a sheet from the basin and spread it across the line, so that the north wing where Xiao Mei lived was obscured from view by the big rectangle of stripy cloth.

'Good girl,' he said, putting put his face close to hers. Then he reached down and pinged the elastic of her shorts. Xiao Mei looked up at him, confused. He had been drinking and she recoiled from his beery breath.

'Good girl,' he said again, moving his hand around her waist and squeezing her bottom.

Without thinking, she pushed him away and dashed through the sheet, in her haste pulling it off the line so that it trailed behind her. She sat on the step feeling hot and flustered.

Old Wang said nothing, picked the sheet up, pegged it back on the line and went back to his room. 'Huh', he muttered to himself, 'huh'.

She hadn't said anything to either Ma or Ba and after all nothing had really happened. Not that they would have taken much notice. Ma was always so tired and preoccupied. And as for Ba, Xiao Mei thought ruefully, he was much more interested in listening to what Old Wang had to say than to his own daughter. The two of them – at least according to Nainai – were as 'thick as thieves'.

~

Xiao Mei sat on her rooftop perch observing Old Wang and Ba, unseen by either of them. They were squatting on low stools under the pomegranate tree. Ba tapped the bottom of a pack of cigarettes to loosen them and offered one to Old Wang, then took one for himself. They were talking in low rapid voices. Something was afoot and Xiao Mei slid down the roof so she could hear them better.

'And it would only take ten thousand, twelve at the most,' Old Wang was saying.

They were talking money again. The more they talked about it the less there seemed to be. It was always about giving money away and nothing happening in return.

Ba nodded and stared thoughtfully at his feet.

'And you think that would work?'

'Of course. He's completely reliable. You could move in right away.'

Ba exhaled a long plume of smoke.

'It's really far out, beyond the Bird's Nest, but at least it's near the metro.'

Old Wang leant back.

'You just think about it. Take your time.'

Ba opened his mouth to reply but his voice was drowned out by the rumble of heavy machinery passing by outside in the hutong.

That evening over supper, Xiao Mei asked, 'What were you and Old Wang talking about?'

'What?' Ba was taken aback.

'You and Old Wang ...'

'Just discussing pigeons,' he said airily, 'buying more pigeons.'

'But ten thousand......?' said Xiao Mei, widening her eyes and waving her chopsticks in the air.

Ma's attention was alerted. Like a rabbit, with her ears pricked right up, Xiao Mei thought.

'What's she talking about?' Ma said.

'Nothing, nothing, I don't know what she's on about. As I said, Wang is thinking of getting more pigeons, from way out near Sandy River.'

'But, you said Bird's .....'

'That's enough,' said Ba quickly.

He picked up his bowl, shovelled the remaining noodles into his mouth with his chopsticks and refused to say anymore. Ma glared at him for the rest of the meal. Nainai, who had been concentrating hard on her food, gave a large burp of satisfaction and left the table.

Later that evening, Ma drew Xiao Mei aside and said in a low voice, 'Ba doesn't always tell me everything. He doesn't want to worry me, but if you hear him and Old Wang talk about something, you'll tell Ma, won't you?'

Xiao Mei nodded but said nothing. How would she know what the 'something' was that she ought to tell Ma? As Ma herself was fond of saying, Ba was always full of nonsense. And as for Old Wang, she'd just keep out of his way. She glanced at Ba, sprawled on the sofa. The television flickered in a corner of the room. He looked round.

'Come here,' he called. Xiao Mei hesitated, caught like a line being pulled back and forth between two opposing forces. She looked up at Ma. But Ma was already turning her back, bending down to sweep the floor.

'Come here,' Ba insisted again. 'Come and watch this. You'll learn something about our country's history.'

Xiao Mei gave a huff of irritation and plumped herself down. It was boring stuff about some old tombs outside the city and some massive statues. She stared at the screen for a while, slumped against Ba's shoulder. Then her head nodded, and before long she was fast asleep.

9.

The Boy

Bang! Crack! Bang!

Xiao Mei sat up with a start and pressed her face to the small window that opened onto the hutong. A man sitting on the roof of the house opposite was prising off the tiles and throwing them down to another man who was stacking them in a pushcart. This house also had a big white chai character painted on its wall. The door of the house was wide open. Through the door Xiao Mei could see into the courtyard. The people who lived there had left weeks ago and the house was deserted. Litter was blowing about and weeds had begun to sprout. She stared out, biting her lip.

Most of the houses along Xiao Mei's hutong were empty. Some were already half-knocked down. Every now and then a motor-driven cart passed by, piled high with furniture and household goods. Another family was leaving. The door to the street would be left open, the courtyard empty. Everything worth taking away was taken away and the houses abandoned to rats, cats, and human scavengers. The scavengers would move in for a few nights, rummage around for anything useful and depart. There was a rank smell in these courtyards and lush grass grew on urine-soaked patches of ground. Ma told Xiao Mei not to wander out by herself.

Xiao Mei rolled off the bed and went out of her room. She crossed the courtyard, stood on the threshold of their house, and looked down the hutong. The men had finished their work and were pushing a cart loaded with roof tiles, their bare backs glistening with sweat. Soon they turned a corner and were out of sight and the hutong was silent.

Xiao Mei stepped back into the courtyard and glanced towards Nainai's room. There was no sound. She must be having her afternoon nap.

She turned and walked back to the porch. She paused for a moment to check that no one had seen her and then walked slowly down the sunlit alley, keeping in the shade of the overhanging eaves.

At the end of the hutong was a house that had been evacuated only recently. The door was swinging open. She stepped over the wooden threshold and gazed across the courtyard at the empty rooms, the piles of litter in corners, and the broken, discarded furniture. An empty birdcage hung from a beam.

She walked across the courtyard towards the main wing of the house. Like in her own home, the wing had been divided into several small rooms. She looked inside one of them. It was very dusty. There were piles of newspaper in a dark corner and a cupboard with broken doors. A small red vest hung from a nail on the wall.

Then she heard something, a small whimpering noise

coming from beneath the cupboard. She stopped to listen, then squatted down to look. There, in the darkness, she saw a small white dog. It gave a feeble bark and emerged slowly, dragging one leg. It seemed that the dog had also been discarded as useless.

Then came a second sound, a scuffling from an adjoining room. She caught her breath and listened intently. The dog whined and limped through the doorway. Hesitating for a moment, she followed, stepping carefully over piles of bricks and rotting planks of wood. There was a sudden movement in a corner. A low voice called out 'here' and the dog disappeared into the darkness.

'Who's there?' Xiao Mei called out, sounding bolder than she felt.

There was no reply, just the deafening shrilling of the cicadas. Perhaps she had imagined it. It was so hot. The sun beat down, the heat shimmering off the outside walls. The shadows in the rooms were black. For a moment she felt faint and she closed her eyes. Points of light danced in front of her eyelids. Then all seemed to go dull for a moment as if the brightness in her eyes had drained away.

When she opened them she saw that a cloud had moved across the sun. And she saw a boy, just a little older than her, standing in the doorway, staring at her fiercely, cradling the white dog in his arms.

'Who are you?' Xiao Mei took a step back, ready to run if necessary.

The boy stared at her for a moment. Then he said in hoarse

voice, 'Have you got anything to eat?'

Xiao Mei shook her head. It was just a beggar. Ma's words came to her 'keep away from vagrants' and she turned to leave.

But the boy called out again, 'Have you got any food? Something to drink?'

She looked back and saw how bright his eye was in his thin face and that the other eye was closed up. In fact, it was not so much an eye as a scar across the skin covering the socket. She stopped and felt in her pocket.

'Here,' she said, and threw a packet of bubble-gum at his feet.

He dropped the dog, picked the bubble-gum up, stripped off the wrapping, and stuffed the gum into his mouth.

'Oh,' said Xiao Mei curiously, 'you're hungry. When did you last eat?'

Yesterday, a banana that he'd found on the ground.

'I could get you a steamed bun,' said Xiao Mei, thinking of the ones Nainai had steamed that morning.

The boy nodded his head.

She ran home, no one was about. Nainai was still sleeping. Ma was still at work. Where Ba was was anyone's guess. She went quietly into the kitchen, lifted the lid covering a pile of steamed buns and slipped two into her pocket. Then she grabbed a can of coke from a shelf, and ran back to the demolished house. The boy was squatting on the step.

'Don't sit there,' she said, 'otherwise someone will see us.'

The boy followed her inside and almost snatched the buns and the can out of Xiao Mei's hand. He broke off a morsel of bun and threw it to the dog, who snapped it up in one gulp. He took the bubble-gum out of his mouth and stuck it carefully under a windowsill. Then he pulled the ring off the top of the can and sat down. He ate all but a third of the buns, which he put it into the pocket of his tattered shorts. But he drained the can to the bottom.

'I've got to go.' Stumbling over the high wooden threshold of the old house Xiao Mei ran as fast as she could down the hutong and back home.

She was so quiet over supper that Ma suspected that she was going down with something again. She could not get the thought of the hungry boy out of her head.

~

The boy had been hiding in the derelict house for over a week, venturing out from time to time to scavenge for food or any object that might come in useful. Apart from Xiao Mei, no one knew he was there. He knew no one at all in the city, except the uncle who had brought him, and he had disappeared. The little white dog had become his closest friend, both of them abandoned and lost. This was the second derelict house he'd taken refuge in. The first one had been knocked down and he had been lucky to escape unhurt before the great yellow excavator moved in and started tearing down the walls. The little dog had not been so lucky as a brick had fallen on his paw, half crushing it.

After that he had slept in doorways and under flyovers. One rainy night, the dog under his arm, he crept past the sleeping guard into the lobby of a newly built luxury block of flats, barely occupied. Concealing himself behind a pillar he watched as a lone man came out of the brightly lit lift and walked through the lobby and out through the main entrance, the lift doors closing silently behind him.

Then he had walked over to the lift and pressed a button. The doors had opened and he had gone in. He had never been in a lift before. Before he knew what was happening, the doors closed and he felt a sensation of movement and held the dog tight. The illuminated panel above the door flashed numbers. At number 21 the door opened and he stepped out into a dimly lit corridor.

No one was there but he could hear the silent whirring of the second lift as it descended. Hesitating for a moment, he turned right not knowing what he might find, but desperate for a warm, dry place to sleep. Some way down the corridor a door stood ajar and he went in. The room was in darkness but the light from the pale night sky was enough for him to make out a large new sofa and two armchairs covered in plastic sheeting. He stripped off his wet vest and lay down exhausted. The dog curled up next to him. He closed his eyes.

~

As he fell into sleep, he felt a great wind rushing past his ears and found himself being twirled around, floating high above the rooftops. The sky was the blackest night could get around these parts, a dull orange, fading into pale. Far below were the highways with their criss-crossing ribbons of red and white light. He tumbled over clusters of tall, shadowy buildings thrusting upwards and patches of black emptiness containing pinpricks of light.

The wind was gentler now and he felt himself descending, down, down until he was hovering over a tall white block of flats. A draught of air drew him down the side of the building until he was level with a balcony on one of the upper floors. His feet brushed the balcony wall and for a moment he felt as if he were about to fall backwards down into the darkness below. But a little breeze nudged him forward and he tumbled down onto the balcony floor.

As he picked himself up he saw that the door was open, and he stepped inside. Immediately he pulled himself back, gasping, overcome with a sickening feeling of vertigo in his stomach. Breathing hard, with both feet planted firmly on the balcony floor and both hands grasping either side of the door frame, he forced himself to look – and gave a little gasp of astonishment.

The floor and the walls were quite transparent, emitting a pale ghostly light, like an ice cube, except that the ambient air was so warm the ice would have melted in no time. When he touched the floor with his toe he could feel that it was, in fact, quite solid.

He took a deep breath and stepped through the door and just for a second glanced down. Once more, there was a rush of vertigo to his head and a falling sensation, but he shut his eyes tight and steadied himself with outstretched arms. Eyes still shut, he lowered himself to the floor and lay there, spread-eagled on his stomach. Then he opened his eyes again and dared himself to look down.

With a gasp he saw that the entire building was transparent, each luminous floor visible through the glass ceiling of the one above it. It was like looking into the depths of a deep lake, the water clear and pale green near the surface and becoming darker and blacker towards the bottom. He could just make out the outline of rooms and corridors and the shapes of furniture.

Then far below, on the ground level, was something different. He rubbed his eyes to see better. Occupying the same space as the tower block, was a ridged roof – no, several ridged roofs - set in a square, and in the middle a courtyard and in the middle of that, a tree, all so faint and misty grey they hardly seemed to be there at all. He rubbed his eyes again. And saw a small figure crossing the courtyard and disappearing into a side building.

The more he looked, the clearer the vision became, so that now he felt he was floating in air high above the courtyard house, and the glassy floor that supported him and the tower block were fading away. Higher and higher he floated, up through the flat roof of the block and out into the sky. When he looked down he saw hundreds and hundreds of tall luminous buildings, some clustered together, some standing by themselves, rising out of the darkness below. And within each one was enclosed the memory of what had been there before, an older house, an older street, a tree, a rack of bicycles, a factory chimney, a line of washing.

Once again he was overcome by dizziness and he felt himself tumbling down, turning over and over through the warm air, knowing that soon he would hit the ground hard and shatter into a million pieces.

But as he kicked his legs and flailed his arms, he found himself back on the sofa, covered in sweat, and the little white dog standing beside him, nuzzling his neck.

~

Ma was back late that evening. She had had to work overtime and on top of that the traffic was terrible and the bus was so full she had to stand all the way. She went into the kitchen and found that Xiao Mei had forgotten to hang up the washing, which lay in a damp pile in a basin on the floor by the sink. It was the last straw. As soon as she saw Xiao Mei she began to shriek, 'Lazy, useless! What did I do wrong in my last life to have a stupid daughter like you?'

Then Nainai shouted at Ma, that her son had married a bad-tempered shrew, no wonder he was never at home. It went on and on. Old Wang stuck his head round his door, wondering what the noise was about this time.

In the middle of the commotion an acrid smell wafted out from the kitchen. Nainai had forgotten to check the pot of savoury rice porridge that she had put to simmer on the gas stove. It had burnt to a cinder. Ma gave a howl. She sat down on the step, her head in her hands. Then, wiping her tears and blowing her nose, she felt in her pocket.

'Come here,' she said, without looking at Xiao Mei. 'Go

and get some packets of instant noodles.'

Xiao Mei took the money in silence.

'Go, go, go. At least try and do something for this family.'

Xiao Mei turned and left. It's not fair, she thought as she walked to the corner shop.

There was no one around. Before families had begun to move out, the hutong had been a lively place at night. There had been street vendors with carts piled high with peaches or squatting on the ground selling combs and socks and cheap jewellery, or snack stalls selling peanuts or pancakes or toffee apples. But now there was no one selling anything, just the hole-in-the-wall shop with its bubble-gum, cigarettes, cheap alcohol and instant noodles.

Xiao Mei walked slowly down the hutong preoccupied with the unfairness of life. If she had more to do, if she wasn't so bored, then she wouldn't forget things so easily. Everything was going wrong. Ma was angry all the time and Ba always had his mind on some mad scheme or other. He was 'totally unreliable'. That's what Ma had said to him. And Nainai, well she was just a crazy old woman. But when Xiao Mei thought of the little jade goddess and how she'd lost it, it seemed that perhaps Nainai really did know something about bad luck.

Out of the corner of her eye Xiao Mei saw something, a movement in the shadow of the wall. She looked over her shoulder and walked faster. Not a soul was on the street. There was a noise, like cardboard boxes falling over, and footsteps. She caught her breath. No, it was probably only cats.

A hoarse voice behind her whispered, 'Hey, little sister.'

Xiao Mei turned, her heart in her mouth. It was the boy.

'Do you have any food, little sister?'

His one eye glistened. The other half of his face with its closed up eye socket was in shadow. Xiao Mei looked at him.

'Where's your dog?'

The boy darted back into the shadows and re-emerged with the dog in his arms. The dog and the boy stared at Xiao Mei.

'Wait there,' she said.

When she got to the corner shop she counted out the money Ma had given her. There wasn't enough. The packets of instant noodles were lined up on a shelf next to the counter: red-cooked beef noodles, chicken and mushroom noodles, seafood noodles. She picked up two beef packets for Ba and Nainai, a seafood one for Ma, and a chicken one for herself. The shopkeeper was busy on his mobile phone so she took another beef one, stuck it in the waistband of her shorts and pulled her t-shirt down as far as it would go. The shopkeeper took her money with barely a glance and gave her a few loose coins in change.

The boy had retreated into the shadows again, but she could see the little white-haired dog sniffing amongst the boxes. When she came close the boy appeared.

'Here, 'Xiao Mei said, giving him the packet. 'You'll have to eat them dry.'

The boy's mouth stretched in a crooked smile which, in the dim light of the hutong, made it seem as if his bright good eye had moved to the centre of his forehead.

'That's good,' he said.

She was about to ask him if the dog was hungry but there was a shout from down the hutong.

'Xiao Mei! Xiao Mei!' It was Ma.

'I've got to go,' she said. And she turned and ran back home.

~

The huangshulang from Xiao Mei's courtyard felt her run past, stirring up a little wind as she went. The huangshulang flattened herself to the ground and crawled along the dark side of the wall. When she reached the familiar crack where the cement had split and the bricks had parted, she slipped through to the other side and waited till the footfalls had faded away and it was safe to continue her foraging.

~

The next morning Xiao Mei woke up with a start as she recalled the hungry boy and the noodles she had stolen.

She sat up, pulled on some clothes and went to the kitchen. Everything was silent. A nectarine and a steamed bun had been left for her on the table. She ate these quickly. She opened the fridge, took three meat dumplings from a plate, and wrapped them in a cloth. On the windowsill was a bowl of peaches. She took one. She filled a bottle with water, found an old enamel bowl, and put everything in a bag. Then she ran across the courtyard and out into the hutong.

The sun was blazing down and the hot surface burned beneath her flip flops. She ran down the hutong to the empty house. No sound came from the courtyard, except for the incessant whining of the cicadas.

'Hi!' she called out in a low voice.

There was no answer. She stood motionless, apprehensive. It was too silent. But then she heard a pattering noise and there was the little white dog standing in the shadows.

'Here,' she said, stretching out her hand, 'here, doggie.'

She took the bottle of water and the bowl from the bag. She poured out some of the water and set the bowl down. The dog lapped it up, glistening drops spluttering all over its muzzle. Then she pulled out one of the dumplings and broke it into pieces which she put on the ground next to the bowl. She squatted next to the dog while he ate.

When she looked up she saw, with a start, that the boy was standing next to her. He had come up so quietly she hadn't heard a thing. She stood up quickly. He was barefoot and dirty and a faint musty smell came off his skin. He grabbed the bottle of water and drank in one long thirsty gulp.

'Have you brought anything to eat?' he asked, wiping his mouth with the back of his hand.

She took out the remaining meat dumplings and the peach. The boy took them and sat down on a pile of bricks. She watched as he ate, cramming the first dumpling into his mouth so that the meaty juice ran down his chin. He ate the other more slowly. Then he stood up and put the peach in his pocket.

'That was good,' he said.

'That's OK,' said Xiao Mei. 'You were really hungry.'

The boy sat down again and, after a moment's hesitation, Xiao Mei sat next to him.

'I saw you come out of your house,' he said after a while.

'Where's your family?' asked Xiao Mei.

'In the countryside,' he said briefly. Xiao Mei looked at him expectantly. After a pause, he went on, 'My uncle is in Beijing. I don't know where. I can't find him.'

'Oh,' said Xiao Mei. 'You're lost.'

They sat in silence. After a while the boy said, 'I need some money. Then I could get the bus back home.'

Xiao Mei didn't have any money. She stood up, feeling uncomfortable.

'I must go.'

The boy looked up at her, pleading.

'Just ten kuai?'

She shook her head, turned, and ran home. At the wooden threshold, she stopped and listened, then peered round the corner into the yard.

Ma and Ba were having a row. Ma slapped Ba and Ba pushed Ma. Nainai shrieked at both of them. Neither of them took any notice of Xiao Mei. Then they both went out. She sat down in the courtyard feeling angry and miserable. It was hotter than ever and the air was thick with moisture. She could hardly breathe. If only it would rain.

Everything was bad.

An idea came to her. As she turned it over in her mind she began to feel excited and hopeful. If she went in the afternoon when Nainai was asleep no one need know she had even left the house. Ma would be at work and Ba was always out. But she didn't want to go on her own.

She would ask the boy to go with her.

10.

Foxy Woman

The plan had come to nothing. And it was all because of Ba and that foxy woman.

Dawn broke and Beijing awoke. The sky was grey and heavy with moisture. The roads filled up with cars and buses and bicycles as people made their way to work. The two ring roads that circled the centre of the city were jammed with traffic.

Xiao Mei, dressed in white shorts and a green t-shirt, was standing glumly on a footbridge over the second ring road and looking out over the parapet at the scarcely moving traffic and the tall buildings, misty grey in the early morning light. Far to the west were the faint shadowy shapes of the Western Hills. Far to the east the ring road curved round and disappeared among dense groups of tall buildings. The sun was already quite high, a glowing white disc in a platinum sky. Next to Xiao Mei stood Ba, smoking a cigarette.

'One day, we'll have a car,' he said, 'it'll make life much more convenient.'

Xiao Mei said nothing, she'd heard that before. Like one day they'd move to a new luxury place to live. When she looked down at all the people in the cars below her and all the buses and taxis and bicycles it seemed as if the whole of Beijing was on the move and her family too was getting swept away in the rush to get somewhere. But where to? Xiao Mei thought, with a stab of anxiety. No one was telling her anything.

It was Saturday and they were on their way to visit Mrs Chen. Mrs Chen and Ba used to work in the same factory together. For some reason Ma didn't seem to like Mrs Chen and she always pursed her lips whenever her name was mentioned. But if she didn't like her why did she always insist that Xiao Mei accompany Ba on his visits? Xiao Mei didn't mind Mrs Chen too much. She usually came away with some small trinket or other. But this time she really didn't want to go.

She had decided that morning to ask the boy to go to Tiantan with her. Ma was working weekends so would be out all day, and Ba and Old Wang nearly always went fishing in the canal on a Saturday. She would tell Nainai that her teacher needed to see her about some extra holiday homework. As soon as the boy had agreed to go they could set off together and be back before it got dark. She had even found some money for the bus in Ba's trouser pocket. He should have emptied his pockets before putting his clothes in the basin to be washed.

But Ba told Old Wang that he would be busy that day and Old Wang had gone fishing by himself. It was very frustrating.

She leant over the parapet, thinking about the boy. She hadn't seen him for several days. Each time she tried to slip out of the house someone would call her back, reminding her to do her homework, tidy her room, clear the dishes. She hoped he would still be there.

~

Mrs Chen lived in a small modern flat filled with family photos, framed certificates, a portrait of Chairman Mao, and all sorts of little ornaments. Her husband, Old Song, worked abroad and there were no children. Mrs Chen looked like a film star. Her hair was rolled in a coil and fastened at the back of her head with a large tortoiseshell clip. Her face was powdery white and as soft as a freshly steamed bun. She wore bright red lipstick and her nails were neatly filed and polished. Mrs Chen was plump all over, like a cushion, and the flesh of her small fat feet was squeezed by the narrow black straps of her sandals.

Ba sat down on the cream-coloured sofa and lit a cigarette. The smoke drifted lazily upwards.

'What a cute child,' said Mrs Chen, as she always did when she saw Xiao Mei. 'I am sure you would like an ice-cream. Why don't you just pop down to the shop and buy yourself whatever you like.' She pressed a five-yuan note into Xiao Mei's hand.

So off Xiao Mei went, leaving Mrs Chen and Ba on their own. When Xiao Mei got back, Mrs Chen beamed at her. Ba looked annoyed.

'That was quick,' he said, smoothing down his hair with one hand.

'Such a cute little girl,' Mrs Chen sighed, the tortoiseshell clip askew on her head. 'Here, I have something for you. Lift your chin up.' She clipped a necklace around Xiao Mei's neck.

'Green jade beads,' she said, 'and very precious.'

'Say thank you to auntie,' said Ba as he lit himself another cigarette.

'Thank you,' said Xiao Mei.

She glanced down at the necklace. The beads were perfectly round and even in size and colour. But they didn't glow like her jade. Ba and Mrs Chen looked at her. Ba's cigarette smoke swirled around the two of them.

'Oh,' said Ba, patting his pockets. 'Where's my bus pass? I must have dropped it as we came in.'

He gave Mrs Chen a sly look. Mrs Chen leant forward.

'Xiao Mei, just pop downstairs for a moment and have a look around the yard to see if it's there. But go quickly before someone picks it up.'

They want to get rid of me for some reason, Xiao Mei thought. Well, she didn't care. She'd have a look around the yard and see if there was anything interesting going on.

Out on the communal landing she found herself in the middle of a great commotion. Two small dogs on leads were snapping and snarling at each other. Their respective owners, a fashionable young woman in heels and an elderly woman in a shapeless cotton dress, were shrieking at each other.

'A person can't come and visit this block without being attacked,' the young woman screamed.

'It's not safe to set foot out of one's own home these days!' shouted the old woman, her heavy braless breasts swaying from side to side in her agitation. 'Just look at his ear, you better pay for this!' A small bead of blood had formed on her dog's floppy ear.

'And my dog's frightened out of her wits,' cried the young woman. 'She's a pedigree and very delicate. I shouldn't be surprised if she has a heart attack tonight!'

She pressed the lift button.

'People like you know nothing about dogs,' snorted the old woman, regaining her composure. 'You don't understand their characters. People like you shouldn't even be allowed to own a dog! People like you ...'

But before she could say any more the lift door opened, and cramming her dog under her arm, the young woman flounced into the lift without a backward look. Xiao Mei followed her in quickly, leaving the old woman glaring at the doors as they slid shut. So many crazy people around, Xiao Mei thought. Almost as crazy as her own family.

When the lift door opened again she went out into the yard. An old man was picking through an overflowing rubbish bin and there were bits of paper and vegetable peel everywhere. There was no sign of the bus pass. She wandered about but nothing was happening. Apart from the old rubbish man the only other person to be seen was a young woman pegging a sheet onto a wire stretched between two trees. She was looking over her shoulder and yelling to someone standing in a doorway. She doesn't talk the way we do, thought Xiao Mei. A bit like the way the lost boy spoke. But it was too hot to think about anything much and she turned and went back into the building.

The door of the flat was locked and she rang the bell. The door opened almost immediately. Ba and Mrs Chen were standing in the hallway.

'Ah, there you are,' said Ba, 'we better be going now. Say goodbye to auntie.'

'Come again soon.' Mrs Chen smiled benignly and patted Xiao Mei on the head. 'Give my regards to everyone at home.'

There was a spring in Ba's step as they left the building. It seemed that he had completely forgotten about the bus pass. Xiao Mei couldn't quite understand Ba's high spirits. He told her jokes all the way home.

Ma, who was in the kitchen, ignored them both when they got back, except to say 'What's that thing round your neck?'

Ba sat down on the stool in the courtyard and lit another cigarette. On the ground next to him was a bottle of beer. Ma was clearly not happy. She followed Ba out, muttering words under her breath that sounded like 'that insatiable fox woman'. Ba cast a sideways look at Xiao Mei, who was sitting on the step, and said nothing. He took another swig of beer. Ma hesitated, gave a sigh of exasperation and went back inside.

Seeing that everyone was busy, Xiao Mei sidled towards the door to the street but Ma called her back sharply and told her to wash some spinach leaves for supper. So Xiao Mei took a bowl of water and a bag full of spinach out to the courtyard and sat on the step washing the mud and bits of grass off the bright green leaves.

Suddenly tears were rolling down her face. This might be the last summer she would ever sit outside in the courtyard, with a little breeze rustling the branches of the pomegranate tree and the bright stars coming out one by one in the pale sky of the evening.

~

The next morning, Xiao Mei went to Nainai's room and asked her some questions that she felt she couldn't ask Ba or Ma.

'What exactly is a fox woman? And what does 'insatiable' mean?'

Nainai was sitting on her bed, fanning herself. 'Shut the door, she said. 'You're letting all the hot air in.' She looked at Xiao Mei and snorted. 'You're too young to know about such things. Go away and do something useful.'

But Xiao Mei stood her ground.

'Please, Nainai,' she said choosing her words carefully. 'You know so much and you've lived so long.'

Nainai was pleased. It was not often that her age and wisdom were properly acknowledged. However, she did not reveal her pleasure on her face. Instead she said, 'Hmmph.'

'Please?'

'Very well,' said Nainai. 'There is a story about this that I was told when I was not much older than you are.'

'Who told you the story? Xiao Mei made herself comfortable on the bed next to her.

'Who?' replied Nainai impatiently. 'Who is not important. Why do you always interrupt?'

So Xiao Mei kept her mouth shut and listened.

~

'There was once a clever young scholar. One Lantern Festival a beautiful young woman appeared whom he had never seen before. Her name was Yingning. She was always smiling and laughing and when she dropped a sprig of plum blossom at his feet he was totally captivated. But Yingning vanished into the crowds and try as he might the young man couldn't find her. He returned home feeling both on top of the world and in the deepest despair. Although he asked everyone if they had seen her, no one knew anything, even denying that such a young woman had ever been there. The young man felt he was going mad.

'One day, his cousin said that he had heard about a beautiful young woman with a tinkling laugh who lived in a village on the other side of the mountain. The young man immediately packed his bags and set off to find her. Over the mountain he climbed and down into the fertile valley below. There were many villages and the young scholar visited every one of them, but no Yingning. He was just about to return home in despair, when he saw a group of little houses at the end of the valley. It was his last chance. There, to his utter delight, he found the laughing young woman and took her back with him to be his wife.'

'But did he ask her if she wanted to go with him? What if she didn't want to leave?'

Nainai glared at Xiao Mei and continued.

'Yingning laughed and laughed all the way home. Although the young scholar's parents were delighted that he had found a wife, her constant laughing and giggling drove them mad. That first night, as they lay in bed together, the young scholar felt he was in heaven. But, as he was drifting off to sleep, a pain, as sharp as daggers, struck his body. He was dreaming that he had stuck his hand in the hollow of a tree and at the bottom of the hollow was a scorpion, who gave him a vicious bite. The young man sat up screaming in pain and terror. Yingning sat up next to him and laughed and laughed and laughed.

'When the young man looked at her, he froze in terror. The beautiful young face had become narrow and the eyes long and green. He leapt out of bed, shouting 'fox woman, fox woman!' But when his parents rushed in to see what the matter was, all they saw were two sleeping figures. The next day, Yingning was as sweet as anything and from that day on she was a dutiful wife and daughter-in-law. But the young scholar never forgot his encounter with the fox woman and always treated Yingning with respect, just in case.'

'And then what happened?'

'And then what happened?' snapped Nainai. 'How should I know? That's all they told me.'

'But was she insatiable?'

'She was,' said Nainai slyly. 'She could never get enough.'

'Oh,' said Xiao Mei.

'She wanted everything and a whole lot more as well. Fox ladies are never satisfied.'

'Oh,' said Xiao Mei again. She stood up.

'Thanks,' Nainai, she said. And she went out into the courtyard, closing the door behind her.

No one was around so she climbed up on to the roof to have a think. She thought about Mrs Chen and her plump round arms and smiling, lip-sticked mouth. Was she really a fox woman? Then she thought about Ba. He certainly was extremely cheerful when he was in Mrs Chen's company.

Still, she couldn't really be a fox woman like Yingning because she had a husband somewhere or other. And Ba had Ma.

Nevertheless, it did seem as if foxy Mrs Chen had some sort of hold over him. Perhaps it would be better if she didn't accompany him on his visits. On the other hand, it might be just as well to keep an eye on things.

She remembered the jade necklace. She had taken it off last night and put it in the pocket of her shorts. She took it out and looked at it. The beads were no more than bright green glass. Not jade at all, even she could see that. Stupid fox woman. As if she could be bought off with cheap jewellery!

She caught sight of Ma crossing the courtyard with two heavy bags of shopping. Without a second thought, she hurled the necklace up and over the roof. For a moment it seemed to hang in the air, the green beads glinting in the sunlight, before falling into the hutong below. The string snapped as it landed and the beads bounced and scattered in the dust and debris, and would lie there until they were swept away, or until someone, passing, would pick them up and wonder whose they were and how they had got there.

11.

Big Yellow and Little Yellow

Mouse-wolf stiffened and sniffed the air. Several shining eyes were observing him from a dark corner of the room. Slowly, from out of the darkness crept two small and very dusty huangshulang. They looked at each other cautiously. Then the larger of them whispered:

'You're not from around here, brother. Where do you come from? What are you doing here?'

Mouse-wolf breathed a sigh of relief. He was glad to see faces of a familiar kind.

'I'm from Tiantan,' he said.

'Ah,' said one of them wistfully, 'I've heard that is a beautiful place.'

The two huangshulang related the sad story of the demolition of their courtyard house and the departure of the humans, even though their families had lived there for decades. Mouse-wolf told them about the trees and grass where he had come from and they begged him to take them there. Mouse-wolf scratched his thigh.

'No,' he said, 'I can't. Not yet.' Feeling that the two could be trusted, he showed them the little jade figure. 'Somehow, I don't know how, I've got to find its owner.' He put it back in his mouth.

'I'm Big Yellow,' said the bigger one, 'and this is my sister.'

'I'm Little Yellow,' the smaller one said. 'Please, let us come with you.'

Mouse-wolf looked from one to the other. It would be good not to be alone.

'It won't be easy,' he said. 'Are you sure?'

Big Yellow twisted round to bite at his tail.

Mouse-wolf understood. 'Then I'd be happy for you to help.'

Upon hearing this the two leapt into the air with joy and chased each other round and round the courtyard. Butterflies flitted in the warm air and a breeze sighed through the trees. Two magpies flew into an old pomegranate tree. Cicadas chirruped. Finally, in the heat of the day, the three huangshulang curled up into three tight balls and fell asleep till dusk descended and the stars began to come out.

~

By the time they awoke the moon had risen. All was still apart from the rumble of traffic in the far distance. They were hungry. Big Yellow found a fat mouse to eat and offered it to his new friend. Mouse-wolf placed the jade on the floor next to him while he ate. The two young huangshulang set off in search of more food, scampering over the debris of the half-demolished house. When they returned to where Mouse-wolf was sitting, licking his paws, Little Yellow gave him something.

'We found this under a pile of old rags,' she said.

It was a tiny red silk bag with a golden drawstring that might once have contained a pair of earrings.

'Your jade will be safer in here,' said Big Yellow, and he hung the little bag around Mouse-wolf's neck. Mouse-wolf put the jade inside and fastened the bag.

'Thank you,' he said. Wearing the bag made him feel that his mission to find the jade's owner was more urgent than ever.

When the huangshulang had caught and eaten several more mice, Mouse-wolf said they must leave at once and continue the search. With tears in their eyes the two huangshulang said goodbye to the house they had lived in since they were born.

'It is best to leave now,' Big Yellow said, 'before the big machines move in.'

Mouse-wolf comforted them, saying, 'When we have returned the jade I promise I'll take you to Tiantan and you can make your home there.'

The three of them clambered over the wooden threshold and out into the hutong. Out of habit they kept close to the wall of the houses, one in front of the other, pressing their elongated bodies close to the ground. The shattered houses cast strange shadows in the moonlight. Not a single light burnt in any of the windows. Every family had left. Broken masonry lay in the courtyards and jagged walls exposed rooms with dangling lampshades and faded curtains. Moonlight glinted off shards of glass. Piles of bricks were heaped up against the pomegranate and persimmon trees. The huangshulang did not know where they were going yet instinct told them to keep moving. They would not find what they were looking for in this place of devastation. A night bird warbling its clear liquid notes gave them courage.

Mouse-wolf led the way with Big Yellow and Little Yellow following behind. Every now and then he paused to sniff the air for some sign of where to go. All three were alert to the faintest of sounds. Things rustled in the dry grass, twigs snapped, water dripped from a hidden tap. All the time the cicadas buzzed unseen. The huangshulang moved swiftly, alive to any danger.

When they came to the end of the hutong, they paused. Mouse-wolf took a cautious look around the corner - and froze. All three animals pricked up their ears. From some way off came a peculiar, high-pitched sound like the twittering of a great flock of small birds.

'Don't move,' breathed Mouse-wolf.

The noise grew louder, and before more than a minute or two had passed a strange sight appeared at the end of the hutong. The huangshulang stared, aghast. Approaching them was a multitude of squeaking mice, flushed out of the old buildings no doubt, and a large grey rat that appeared to be driving them before it. As the rat passed by it seemed to smirk at them, as if to say that though the demolition might not suit the humans, it suited him very well indeed.

Little Yellow shuddered. Something was not right in the world when a rat, a huangshulang's normal prey, struck fear into a huangshulang.

'Let's go,' Mouse-wolf said, barely able to conceal the

agitation in his voice. Keeping near to the wall, he set off, Big Yellow and Little Yellow once again following close behind. They crept forward in silence. From time to time Mouse-wolf looked back to check that they were still with him. Big Yellow seemed to be finding it hard to keep up. Mouse-wolf stopped.

'He hurt himself,' Little Yellow explained. 'He can't go very fast.' Some days before, when they were out looking for food, a wall had collapsed and a falling brick had bruised his foot.

Big Yellow twisted round, licked his injured foot, then shook himself all over. Little Yellow ran back, touched her nose to his, then the two of them rejoined Mouse-wolf. 'It's nothing much,' said Big Yellow. Mouse-wolf looked at them enquiringly, but they said nothing more, and so the three of them set off again, one behind the other.

12.

Sacred Animals

Xiao Mei assessed the situation.

Nainai was squatting on the stool outside, murmuring to herself and fiddling with a long red paper packet that she held on her lap. If she could pass behind her without her noticing there might be a chance she could get as far as the doorway and out into the hutong to see the boy.

'Where do you think you're going?'

'Nowhere, Nainai.'

'Sit down, here. Where I can see you.'

Xiao Mei gave up. She took a peach from the kitchen and sat on the step next to her. She bit into the juicy flesh.

But as soon as she had sat down, Nainai stood up and drew several long thin sticks out of the packet. Then she reached into her pocket and pulled out a cigarette lighter, which she clicked several times before a flame appeared. She touched the flame to the tips of the sticks and when they were glowing she waved them around the courtyard. Soon the air was filled with a sweet, pungent, jasminey smell.

'Why are you burning incense, Nainai?'

The old woman said nothing and waved the sticks around

harder than ever. Then she lit several more and stuck them into the ground beneath the pomegranate tree. When she had done this, she sat down, breathing heavily and murmuring to herself. Xiao Mei opened her mouth to say something, but Nainai waved her away impatiently. Xiao Mei waited.

After a few minutes Nainai wheezed, 'Dead huangshulang in the hutong this morning. Squashed flat.'

'Not our huangshulang?' Xiao Mei's eyes went wide.

But Nainai was coughing so hard that the tears ran down her cheeks.

'Nainai?'

'Listen.'

A few nights before when the moon was full she thought she had seen the huangshulang, squatting on the ground with its front paws pressed together in front of its chest, staring at the moon with blazing red eyes. Now someone had killed it. No wonder they'd been plagued with so much bad luck.

'Red eyes staring at the moon? That's just superstition, Nainai. No one believes in that crazy old stuff anymore. It was probably just some car lights.'

Nainai gave Xiao Mei a sharp look.

'There are a lot of things you don't know about. Nainai's lived a long time and seen and heard many strange things. Sit down next to me.'

Xiao Mei sighed. There was no way she was going to be able to get out of the house. She sat down, propped her head in her hands, feeling bored and cross.

'When I lived in the countryside,' said Nainai, sitting up

straight, 'not so far to the north of here, everyone knew about the four animal families: foxes, huangshulang, hedgehogs and snakes.'

A bright look came into her eyes. 'Are you listening?' she said. Xiao Mei nodded.

'Normally they are timid and hide away from people, keeping out of trouble. But some of them become immortal and have special powers. You can hunt an ordinary animal but it is absolutely forbidden to kill a sacred one.'

Xiao Mei thought of the huangshulang that lived under the tarpaulin.

'How do you know which are ordinary animals and which are sacred ones?'

'The sacred ones,' Nainai leant forward, 'stroll around as bold as anything. Their eyes shine. If you treat them with respect they will bring you good fortune. But if you insult them or hurt them then bad things will happen to you and your family. They might even enter your body and drive you mad.' She leant back, a look of satisfaction on her face.

'Like that horrible story about the dumplings and the young man who killed the huangshulang?'

But Nainai had fallen silent, her eyes seeming to mist over. She stood up slowly shaking her head, and without saying another word shuffled back into the house.

There she goes again, thought Xiao Mei. She's getting more and more weird. She walked over to the tarpaulin and lifted a corner, then picked up a broom leaning against the wall and poked the handle into the dark space behind the box. There was a faint sound of scurrying. The huangshulang was still there. She thought of the dead huangshulang, its body squashed flat. Who would do such a thing? What if something happened to their huangshulang? Despite the heat, she shivered. How could Nainai talk about evil spirits when real evil things happened just outside their door?

13.

The Fox Spirits

One morning, some days later, when Ba went out to buy a paper, he saw Nainai standing all by herself in the middle of the street, a bag in either hand. He was about to call out when she turned round and walked away from him.

'Where are you going?' he called. She stopped and turned to look at him.

'I'm going home,' she snapped. He was about to say, 'you're going the wrong way', when he saw an expression of confusion cross her face.

'Let's go together,' he said. He turned her round and slowly they walked home.

Later, Ba said to Ma, 'The old lady's really losing her memory. Better keep an eye on her.'

'As if I had the time!' Ma retorted, 'it's your mother, after all.'

Xiao Mei looked from one parent to another and thought, why is Ma always so mean to him?

Late that afternoon, Nainai sat in the courtyard, hunched up on a little wooden stool. She was squinting at something in her hands. Every now and then she would give it a jab. 'Stupid,

stupid, stupid,' she muttered to herself. Xiao Mei was sitting outside on the step drying her hair. When Nainai saw Xiao Mei looking at her, she stuffed the thing into her pocket and gave a snort.

'What are you doing, Nainai?' asked Xiao Mei.

'Useless thing,' Nainai said out loud, looking at Xiao Mei out of the corner of her eye.

'What's useless?'

'Your grandmother, that's what's useless!'

Xiao Mei went over to her.

'What did you put in your pocket?'

Nainai sat tight, swaying a little on her stool and saying nothing.

'Show me,' Xiao Mei said, her curiosity aroused.

'It's nothing to do with you,' said Nainai. 'Go inside and help your mother.'

'Go on, Nainai, show me!'

Grumbling, Nainai pulled the thing out of her pocket.

'Useless,' she said again. In her gnarled hand was a mobile phone. Then she added, 'your father gave it to me.'

Xiao Mei laughed.

'Shall I show you how to use it?'

But Nainai glared at Xiao Mei and stuffed it back in her pocket.

'Don't bother me,' she said. 'Go and help your mother.'

Xiao Mei gave her hair a comb and went into the house. When she looked out Nainai had the phone in her hand again, jabbing at it with her forefinger and talking to herself. Then she put the phone in her pocket, picked up her stick from the ground, stood up with difficulty, and shuffled towards the door and out on to the street.

'Where are you going?' Xiao Mei called after her.

'Buying vegetables. I told you already. Don't bother me.'

Xiao Mei hardly heard her. She was looking at herself in a small mirror, combing her hair first one way, then the other. Was it better with a side parting, or a middle parting or swept back from her forehead entirely? But her hair was too short and it kept flopping back down in a fringe just above her eyebrows. One day she'd have long hair like one of those celebrities and do whatever she liked with it, whatever Ma said about it being easier to keep clean if it was short.

Nainai turned left out of the door and walked slowly down the hutong, tapping the ground with her stick as she went. In her hand she carried a cloth bag for vegetables and in her pocket were the mobile phone and some money. It was early evening and a little cooler. She followed the wall of their house with its large white chai sign. Whatever the men who had painted it had said about it being knocked down soon, their house was still standing. But further along the hutong the demolition work had already started. One house had been completely levelled and all that was left was a large pile of bricks and debris and a single persimmon tree that for some reason had been left standing.

On the other side of the hutong were several still intact houses, only recently evacuated by their occupants. By the wooden threshold of one of them lay a small white dog, sleeping in the shade of the porch. Nainai poked at it with her stick as she went past. Abandoned by its owners when they moved, she thought. The dog yapped, stood up and retreated inside the courtyard.

She thought of the half-wild dogs that she'd grown up with in the countryside. Ugly misshapen scabby scrawny creatures, always hungry, always prowling around the village looking for scraps, tail between their legs, alert to assault from sticks and stones. Not like this little white dog, that had once been someone's cherished pet. But this little dog wasn't her business, wasn't anyone's business anymore.

A large orange excavator was backing out of one of the courtyards a little way down the hutong, its upraised claw bearing a load of earth, bricks and broken tiles. A man stood next to it, shouting and waving his arms. The excavator was half way across the hutong but Nainai kept going, oblivious to the noise and the dust, tapping with her stick as she went. The man moved towards her, took her by the arm and walked her round the machine. Nainai said nothing, just shook her arm free, and carried on down the street.

The vegetable stall was a little way ahead, not so much a stall as a few sacks spread out on the street. The vegetable seller, a sinewy old man, squatted by the side. For sale there were a few bundles of green cabbage leaves, some potatoes, five or six overripe tomatoes, bunches of carrots, heaps of shiny green peppers and purple-black eggplants, and some garlic and ginger roots. Once there had been five or six vegetable sellers but all of them had left when the demolition work started, apart from this one stall. Nainai bought three peppers, two potatoes, a large eggplant and a bunch of green leaves.

The excavator was making its way towards them. The vegetable man swore, leapt up and pulled the sacks away from the road. Nainai stood transfixed, not knowing which way to turn. Now the excavator was passing them, deafening them with its roar. The old man dragged her to the side and they were enveloped in a cloud of dust and diesel fumes. As the air cleared and the noise disappeared round the corner, Nainai shook her head in irritation and set off for home.

As she walked, the hutong looked less and less familiar. All the houses on either side had been knocked down or half-knocked down. She stood there, puzzled. Had she really been out for so long? Had they come with their big machines while she was away buying vegetables? Had everyone gone and left her on her own?

She had a sudden memory of long ago standing alone in a huge field, clutching a cloth bag, and in the far, far distance a line of people digging and shouting, and a small red flag planted on a hilltop nearby. But she couldn't remember what she had been doing there, except that she hadn't been able to keep up with them and that she was completely on her own, tears streaming down her face, and so, so tired.

She sat down on at entrance to one of the courtyards to rest. The light was fading fast. One side of the hutong was in deep shadow, but the other was bathed in a soft golden light. High above her the sky was a deep dark blue. Bats flittered and swooped through the air. All was quiet. The light was almost gone. Nainai sat still. She had learnt that if she waited long enough she would know what to do next.

A light or several lights were coming towards her. Someone with a torch, perhaps. But no, the lights were moving swiftly along the hutong, three or four small red balls of fire, surrounded by pale-blue flames and bouncing up and down. They sped past, oblivious to her presence as if she were no more than a brick in the wall. And then, as suddenly as they had appeared, they were gone. Nainai stood up. Despite all the destruction, not everything was lost, after all.

Slowly she became aware of a noise, a tinkly metallic tune, repeating itself over and over again. From a restaurant in a distant street, probably. But as she walked the noise followed her and, to her consternation, she realised it was coming from her pocket. She put her hand in and pulled out the mobile phone. The noise became louder. It was ringing like crazy. She jabbed at the buttons with her finger, not remembering what she was supposed to do.

And then a voice, 'Ma, is that you Ma? Where are you, Ma?'

They had found her after all.

'Everything's gone, all knocked down.'

'What are you talking about, Ma? We are all here worrying about you. Don't move. Tell me what you can see near you.'

She looked ahead. There was an old tree, with several plastic bags caught in its branches. Then she turned round and looked the other way. There was a big heap of rubbish and a pile of old cardboard boxes. There was also a huangshulang that scurried across the hutong in front of her. She told all this to Ba.

'Wait there, don't move,' he said. 'I'll come and find you.'

So she sat down on a pile of bricks and waited for him to come. It was quite dark now. Not a light shone in the hutong for every house was deserted.

Her head nodded onto her chest, her eyes closed.

She was back home, in the village. On the edge of a field, near some graves, was a deserted house occupied by fox-spirits. Some villagers said that they had seen one once when they had passed by at dusk. The red balls surrounded by pale-blue flames were its soul that it was repeatedly spitting out and swallowing in its attempt to become immortal.

She was ten years old again, sitting on a stone, waiting for her father to come back from the fields, her head full of magical thoughts.

14.

Fire and Rain

Mouse-wolf, Big Yellow and Little Yellow walked until dawn. Forced to abandon their old territorial instincts that bound them to one familiar place, they knew that to survive in this strange new world they had to keep moving.

All around them were half-demolished houses and piles of broken masonry and litter. As the sun moved high in the sky and the air heated up, they found at last an opening at the base of a pile of broken wooden window frames. One by one, they squeezed themselves in and there found enough space to rest. Mouse-wolf clasped the little red bag to his chest as tight as he could. The three of them soon drifted into an uneasy sleep.

Big Yellow woke first. His foot was hurting but that wasn't the problem. It was the intense heat. He wrinkled his nose. Above him floated a strange acrid smell and a crackling, pattering noise. In an instant, knowing at once that they were in great danger, he nipped at Little Yellow and Mouse-wolf and, dragging his injured foot, darted towards the gap through which they had come. Thick choking smoke was snaking in through the narrow passage. The huangshulang coughed and covered their eyes with their paws.

Mouse-wolf stared up in panic and saw flames licking at the wooden frames above them. Little Yellow and Big Yellow were rooted to the spot in fear. In a moment the whole pile would be on fire. Then came men's voices. And a sudden crash behind them as a large, flat, metal object smashed down on top of the pile. And another crash as the men tried to beat out the fire with spades.

Blinded by the heat and the smoke, Mouse-wolf and Little Yellow dashed out, sparks singeing their fur. A man shouted 'huangshulang!' and raised his spade. He brought it down hard, just missing Little Yellow, who raced down the street, not knowing where she was going. Eventually she crouched in the gutter, concealing herself behind an empty cardboard box. Mouse-wolf and Big Yellow were nowhere to be seen.

Little Yellow remained motionless in the gutter, not stirring until the sun began to go down in the sky and bats appeared, darting in the twilight. She was not hurt, only her eyes were sore. As the light faded into darkness she peered fearfully around the cardboard box and sniffed the air. The smoky smell had almost gone. The flames were out, and all that was left was a charred heap of timber. There was no sign at all of Mouse-wolf or Big Yellow. The buzzing and whining of the cicadas was so loud she felt as if her head would burst. She felt frightened and alone.

Something stirred by a pile of bricks. Out of the corner of her eye, Little Yellow saw a thin black shape. She rubbed her eyes and it was gone, perhaps it had been just a trick of the darkness. But there it was again, and this time she pricked up her ears and stood to attention, one paw lifted as she listened hard. A dark shape limped slowly towards her. It was Mouse-wolf, the little bag still hanging round his neck. But Little Yellow was staring past him; surely Big Yellow would be following behind.

Mouse-wolf stopped a little way from her and shook his head.

'Big Yellow, I can't find Big Yellow. He's gone.'

'Gone?'

'He was right behind, following me out of the wood pile, but when I turned round he wasn't there.'

All he had been able to see were the blackened window frames against the fierce orange flames, and the men shouting and beating down the fire and showers of sparks shooting high into the sky.

The two huangshulang looked at each other, hardly daring to believe what surely must have happened. Then Little Yellow stood up on her hind legs and gave a high-pitched cry of grief. Mouse-wolf crouched next to her, clutching the little red bag with the jade, saying nothing.

~

For several nights Little Yellow and Mouse-wolf remained where they were, sheltering in the cardboard box, hoping against hope that somehow Big Yellow would return to them. They said little to each other and spent much of the time sleeping, trying to erase from their minds the dreadful sight of the flames and the men with spades.

On the third night, instinct told them that they had to move on. Neither of them mentioned Big Yellow's name; he was already a distant memory. Mouse-wolf held the red bag tight to his chest. He could feel the jade through the cloth. How many more terrible things might happen to them? Such thoughts troubled Mouse-wolf, though he said nothing to Little Yellow.

In the relative safety of the cardboard box he took the jade out of the bag and held it up to the light. Tell me what I should do, he said to himself. The jade was smooth and cool in his paw and glowed with a faint, bluish light. It felt almost alive. As Mouse-wolf turned it over in his paws he began to feel stronger and braver. Much had happened but at least he still had the jade.

'Come,' he said to Little Yellow, 'let's go'.

But Little Yellow didn't move. After a while she said in a whisper, 'But what if he comes back?'

Mouse-wolf took a deep breath.

'He's gone, Little Yellow. It's not safe to stay here. We must move on.'

Little Yellow sat for a moment with her head bowed and then followed Mouse-wolf out of the box.

The hutong was dark and no one was about except for a large rat that skulked past them, intent on its own business. Every house was deserted, the occupants long gone; the human voices that once filled the hutong all blown away as if by a great wind.

Little Yellow sniffed and wiped her eyes. She knew Mouse-wolf was right.

'If he's not...., If he's not hurt,' said Mouse-wolf, 'he will surely have a way of finding us. Let's go a little further and find a place to sleep.'

The sky was lightening in the east and a little breeze blew up.

'But where are we going?' said Little Yellow. 'After we wake up, where will we go then?'

Mouse-wolf stopped and looked at her.

'I don't know,' he said. 'I just know we have to keep moving.'

What sort of journey was it where neither the way nor the destination were known? A thought crossed his mind. The strength that he had felt a short while ago was ebbing. Why should he not just throw the jade away and then they could both return to the safety of Tiantan? No one would be any the wiser. The idea grew in his mind and he saw himself racing through the pines to the grassy bank that was home. He felt the jade through the cloth of the bag. It was only a piece of coloured stone, after all.

He glanced at Little Yellow. She had set her nose to the wind, an expression of determination on her face he had not seen before. No, this was not the time to give up, not just yet.

~

Ahead of the two huangshulang lay a wide expanse of grass and debris. On the far side of this were the grey shapes of a few low shacks and beyond them, silhouetted against the dawn sky, rose three high-rise buildings, with lights on in some of the windows. There was a faint rumble of traffic and the occasional hoot of a car. Soon the city would be awake and the sun would be beating down again. Little Yellow and Mouse-wolf crept through the grass, alternately running and stopping still to listen, ears pricked, before hastening on again.

They were not half way across this open space when a huge rat appeared from behind a pile of earth, and stood in front of them, snarling and barring their path.

The two huangshulang stopped in their tracks and looked about. Not far off were two more rats, lounging against a low brick wall, eyes half-closed.

Teeth bared in a grin, the rat made a sudden move towards Mouse-wolf and stretched out a claw towards the little red bag. Mouse-wolf recoiled in alarm. The rat turned and jerked his head towards his accomplices, who straightened up, their long tails swishing back and forth. Mouse-wolf crouched close to the ground, baring his teeth, Little Yellow crouching behind him. The rat came closer, so close that its stiff yellow whiskers brushed Mouse-wolf's cheek and he could smell its foul breath.

In an instant the huangshulang were running as fast as they could across the empty site, round piles of bricks, planks of old wood, bushes festooned with torn plastic bags, through clumps of grass and up and over mounds of earth. The rats gave chase for a while, and then turned back in boredom, laughing nastily as they retreated.

When the huangshulang finally stopped to catch their breath, they found they were at the edge of the site. Just ahead of them was a wide road jam-packed with cars crawling along at a snail's pace. The sun was a pale disc high in the sky. The morning rush hour had begun.

~

Mouse-wolf and Little Yellow rested in the shade of a wall, exhausted by their encounter with the rats. The hot, steamy air sapped what remained of their energy. By the wall was a pile of old bricks. They squeezed into a gap. There was no point doing anything till the sun went down and that was many hours ahead. Mouse-wolf touched the little bag around his neck and felt for the jade through the cloth. Little Yellow found a couple of woodlice under one of the bricks, not her favourite food but they would stave off hunger for a little while at least. Mouse-wolf gulped some down as well. Soon they were both asleep.

The air was still and heavy. The sun disappeared behind heavy black clouds that hung low over the city. The sky darkened, suffused with a strange yellowish light. Cars switched on their headlights. A small wind blew up, rustling the branches of the gingko trees that lined the road. Unable to contain itself any longer, the sky broke, first a few large drops of rain that spattered down, creating patterns of irregular black spots on the pavement. Then more and more drops, falling faster and more heavily until they lost all individuality and merged into torrents of rushing water. Soon the gutters were overflowing and the trees tossed and bent in the wind. Cyclists pedalled as hard as they could, heads down, protected to some extent by coloured plastic capes, pink and green and blue. Pedestrians scurried to find shelter, umbrellas turned inside out.

And then, directly overhead, a lightning flash that tore through the sky, and an enormous clap of thunder, and then another and another. The rain beat down, obliterating all from view. Huge puddles formed on the waste ground near the road.

The rain that hit the pile of bricks sprayed out and streamed down in rivulets, seeking out every gap so that it could flow down into the earth beneath. The bricks shifted and the pile partly collapsed under the force of the water.

Mouse-wolf and Little Yellow awoke at the same time, aroused not so much by the wet as by the noise of the thunder and the grinding and slipping of the bricks. Soon the dry earth where they had been sleeping turned to mud, and when the water had nowhere else to go, it started to rise up the side of the bricks that contained the space where the huangshulang were sheltering.

Mouse-wolf spun round desperately, looking for a gap to escape through. There was a single narrow space, the width of two fingers. He looked over his shoulder to Little Yellow. She was crouching low, paralysed with fear. Mouse-wolf bit her hard on the shoulder. 'Move, move now,' he said urgently. Flattening himself, he squeezed through the gap.

Little Yellow followed close behind, dragging her tail out of the pool of water that had collected in their sleeping space.

Then the bricks shifted again, catching her tail and pinning it to the ground. She was trapped. Not realising what was happening behind him, Mouse-wolf kept moving ahead. Little Yellow twisted and turned and pulled as hard as she could, but to no avail. She was completely stuck. The water was creeping up behind her and now a trickle was forming in the dark space ahead where Mouse-wolf had gone.

She pulled again at her tail and felt a spasm of pain that shot the length of the tail and along her spine.

Then she blacked out.

In that brief moment of complete darkness, she saw, just in front of her, a pair of red eyes, bright and sparkling like jewels. As the vision faded, she regained consciousness. With renewed strength she pulled as hard as she could. Another spasm of pain and she wrenched the tail free.

Scraping with her back paws and pulling with her front paws she heaved herself through the gap and kept going with all her strength till she glimpsed a chink of light ahead. The water was now a solid stream. Half scrabbling, half swimming she reached the end and tumbled out into a puddle.

To her relief, the first thing she saw was Mouse-wolf, trembling under a clump of grass. She dragged herself over and collapsed next to him, gasping for breath. Then she twisted round to look at her tail. A drop of blood was congealing at the end of it. The tip of the tail was gone. Taking it in her mouth she licked it all over. Then she shook herself hard, sending a fine spray of water into the rain-fresh air. She remembered the red eyes, sparkling like rubies. Something, she knew not what or who, had given her the strength to save herself.

The rain was lessening; the rumbles of thunder were far away. The sun came out. The drops of rainwater on the blades of grass sparkled like diamonds. Mouse-wolf lifted his nose to sniff the air, one paw grasping the little bag around his neck. He didn't know where they were or where they should go next but at least they were still alive.

15.

The Expedition

And then, finally, came the day Xiao Mei had been waiting for. But first of all there were the usual, early morning family arguments.

Ma had taken time off work to take Nainai to the hospital for a check up. The old lady had spent the entire morning getting herself ready for the event. In her anxiety not to be late, she had lunch soon after breakfast and then sat on the step in the shade, her bag next to her, waiting to go out.

Ma said, 'You don't need to sit there; we don't have to leave for an hour.' But Nainai just glared at her and said nothing. Ba, as usual, was out.

Last night Ma had argued with Ba about who should go with Nainai. Why should she have to take his mother to hospital? But Ba said that he had something important to do and anyway it wouldn't be suitable for him to go to a hospital for women and have to talk about 'women's problems' with the doctor. Ma said it wasn't 'women's problems' it was her memory that was the problem. Didn't men have memories too? Ba said nothing. 'Obviously not,' said Ma.

Then, in a sudden unusual moment of generosity, Ba

pulled out some notes from his pocket and said, 'Take a taxi there, it might rain.'

Ma looked at him suspiciously. Where had he got the money from? They never went anywhere by taxi. Nevertheless, she took it, counted the notes, and stuffed them in her purse.

'And here's a few kuai for you,' he said to Xiao Mei.

'What are you giving the child money for?' said Ma even more suspiciously.

Ba grinned. 'I like to treat my daughter sometimes. Anything wrong with that?'

Xiao Mei took the money quickly before he changed his mind and slipped it into the pocket of her shorts.

'You stay here and do your homework,' Ma said to Xiao Mei before she and Nainai left.

When they had gone, Ba said, 'Old Wang and I have some business to attend to. We'll be out for a while.'

She was in luck.

As soon as the coast was clear, she went into the kitchen, grabbed a steamed corncob, a handful of apricots, some coconut biscuits and a bottle of cold lemon tea that she found in the fridge door, stuffed them into a plastic bag, closed the door, filled a small bowl with water from the outside tap, quickly crossed the courtyard and stepped over the wooden threshold into the hutong.

It was midday and there was no one about. The air was moist and heavy. Walking outside was like wading through hot, sticky syrup. The water splashed over the sides of the bowl onto her flip-flopped feet.

The boy was lying on his back under the eaves of the old house. He had found a dusty old palm-leaf fan and was fanning himself with it. The little white dog was lying next to him, its nose on its paws. When it saw Xiao Mei it jumped up and gave a small bark. Then it came towards her, delicately lifting its feet as it walked over the hot ground. She put the bowl down and the dog drank thirstily. She threw it a biscuit, which it sniffed at before picking it up and carrying it into the shade of the eaves to eat. The boy was now sitting up. He leant forward.

'Did you bring food?'

'You have to do something for me first.' Xiao Mei kept her distance, holding the bag of food behind her back.

He came closer. Xiao Mei moved back. Then he darted out his hand as if to grab the bag, or to grab her.

'Keep away,' she said. 'You can have some food if you do what I say.' She half-turned towards the courtyard door that led onto the hutong. Maybe her plan wasn't such a good idea after all. She turned back to look at him. He was standing with his arms by his side, his one eye bright in his dirty face.

'Please,' he said hoarsely. 'You gave the dog something.'

Xiao Mei stopped and thought for a moment. He was right. He needed food and drink as much as the dog did. She'd give him some of it.

'Sit down,' she said. 'Over there.'

The boy sat down. Then she pulled out a corncob and a biscuit.

'Thirsty,' said the boy.

She gave him the plastic bottle of lemon tea.

While he was drinking it she told him what she wanted him to do. She didn't tell him about the jade, just that she'd lost something and wanted to go back to look for it. They would take the bus from the stop on the main road beyond the hutong. It went all the way to Tiantan. The boy listened. Then he shook his head.

'I can't go. I can't leave the dog.'

Xiao Mei hadn't thought about that. Of course, dogs weren't allowed on buses.

'We could tie the dog up here,' she said.

'No,' said the boy. The dog wouldn't like being left on its own. It would bark and someone would hear it and come and take it away.

Xiao Mei thought for a while. Then she said, more boldly than she felt, 'We'll have to walk.'

It couldn't be that far. When she and Ma and Ba had gone by metro it was just two stops. If they followed the bus route surely they'd get there before too long.

'All right,' said the boy.

He tied some pink synthetic string around the dog's neck to make a collar and lead. Xiao Mei took four apricots out of the bag, gave two to the boy, and they set off.

To begin with the little white dog resisted being dragged, but Xiao Mei dropped biscuit crumbs on the pavement and soon it was trotting along beside them, limping a little because of its injured paw.

As they walked, the boy kept bumping into her. After a minute he said, 'stop a moment.' He moved from Xiao Mei's right side to her left.

Xiao Mei looked at his good eye. Yes, it was his right eye. So of course he needed to be on her left side.

After that they said nothing to each other for a while. Xiao Mei concentrated on finding the right way to go. The boy ate one of the apricots, noisily.

At the end of the hutong was a junction with another short hutong, which bent round to join another longer one that was shaded by leafy scholar trees. Here were several carts selling peaches and grapes and pineapples, and people with shopping baskets. At the end of this hutong was a wide road with cars and buses and bicycles. They turned right and there was the bus stop. At that moment a bus came. People stepped out and more people got on.

'That's the Tiantan bus,' said Xiao Mei. 'We just have to follow all the buses that say 'Tiantan' on the front.'

She looked at the sign that listed the bus stops along the route.

'Look, we're here,' she said, pointing to the name of the stop. Then she counted. Five stops to Tiantan. It was quite far after all.

The road was long and straight. On either side were grey office blocks, some with blue plate-glass windows. Department stores displayed their names horizontally in big red characters on top of the roofs or vertically down the front. The road was so wide that a white metal barrier had been erected down the middle of it, separating the traffic.

Ahead of them was a footbridge that you reached via a long

ramp - if you wanted to push your bike up - or by climbing up a flight of shallow steps. The Tiantan buses turned left just beyond the footbridge. They would have to cross the road. Xiao Mei ran up the ramp, the boy and the white dog following behind.

A man was on the footbridge, lying on his side, his hand stretched out. By his hand was a cap with several coins in it. As they passed he lifted his face. A big jagged scar ran across his cheek ending where his ear should have been, but instead of an ear was a little petal-shaped flap of skin. Xiao Mei walked passed quickly, averting her eyes, but the boy stopped for a moment. The man stretched out his other arm. Where the hand should have been was a smooth round stump. Then he rolled over a little. One of his legs ended at the knee.

The boy stared at the man and touched his own empty eye-socket. He still had the other apricot. He placed it by the man's good hand. The man closed his fingers around it but said nothing. Had he lost his voice as well?

Xiao Mei stopped at the end of the footbridge and looked out over the railing. Black clouds were gathering in the distance. The air was very still and close. She looked back and when she saw the boy give his apricot away she felt cross. She'd brought it for him, not for any old beggar.

'That was your apricot,' she said when he caught up with her.

'Yes,' said the boy,' but he was hungry.'

Xiao Mei tried to work this out. 'But you were hungry too,' she said after a while.

The boy said nothing.

They walked slowly down the ramp, stopping for the little white dog to lift its leg against the railing, and for a few minutes they continued in silence.

Then Xiao Mei said, 'What happened to your eye?'

'Accident,' said the boy. 'Near my village.'

'How?'

He told her that he had been working at a brickyard where he came from, a long way from Beijing. A wall of loose bricks had fallen on top of him, burying him for many minutes. He was lucky only to have lost the sight of an eye. The eye had become infected and so they had had to remove it.

'Oh,' said Xiao Mei. She didn't know what else to say. She thought for a moment. 'But don't you have a school you go to?'

The boy said nothing.

'But I don't even know your name.'

The boy looked at her.

'Back where I come from they call me Stone.'

'Why?'

'Because I liked to play with the pebbles in our yard.'

'Aren't you going to ask me what my name is?'

'What's your name, then?'

'Xiao Mei.'

And for the first time Stone smiled at her.

Another Tiantan bus clanked past them. It was two buses joined together really, with a bendy bit in the middle, like Old Wang's accordion. They were still on the right route and had been walking nearly twenty minutes. The road they were on was narrower and lined with shops. But there were no trees and it was hotter than ever. Xiao Mei kept pushing damp strands of hair away from her face. Stone trudged along beside her. The little dog kept stopping to sniff and lift its leg. In the end Stone picked it up and carried it under his arm.

Just ahead of them was a man with a cart selling bottles of cold water and ice lollies. Remembering she had money, Xiao Mei bought two orange-flavoured ices and two bottles of water. Stone's face lit up in a smile.

'I haven't had one of those for a long time,' he said.

Xiao Mei stood next to him dreamily, licking the orange ice. The air, which had been so still, moved in a little breeze. There was a faint rumbling noise in the distance, like heavy furniture being moved in a faraway building. A feeling of anxiety came over her. They still had a long way to go. No one knew she was out, and what if they didn't get there? They could just turn back now and forget the whole thing. After all, it was only an old piece of jade and Nainai was always talking a lot of nonsense.

Stone said, 'Come on, let's go. Didn't you say that you'd lost something really important? You can't give up now. Tiantan can't be that far away.'

Had she been speaking her thoughts aloud? Or did they just show in her face? People's emotions sometimes did, like when Ma was unhappy or Ba had a guilty secret. You could see what they were feeling just by looking at them. Xiao Mei looked at Stone. But his face had gone blank and she couldn't tell what he was thinking or feeling at all.

A gust of wind blew up. A cardboard box whirled past them and a sheet of metal propped outside an ironmonger's shop clanged flat on to the pavement just missing Xiao Mei's foot. She jumped and, grabbing her arm, Stone pulled her away just in time, dropping the little white dog to the ground as he did so. The sky overhead had darkened, though in the distance, at the end of the street, a band of bright sky illuminated the buildings, golden rays of sunshine reflecting off the windows. Big, heavy drops of rain spattered on the pavement.

'Rain, rain!' cried Xiao Mei as she threw back her head and spread her arms wide.

Stone looked up at the sky with his one eye. Raindrops streamed down his dirty face. He rubbed his hair with both his hands. It was a long time since his hair had been near water.

There was a mighty clap of thunder, followed almost immediately by a lightning flash and then another clap of thunder and another, all the thunder claps rolling into each other as if there were some great engine reverberating through the sky above them.

The little white dog barked and strained at the lead. Stone picked it up and put his hand over its eyes to calm it down. The more it wriggled the tighter Stone held it.

The rain fell harder and within minutes it was one great sheet of water. They dashed into the doorway of the ironmonger's shop. A thin young shop assistant was standing there and told them they could step inside and wait until the rain had passed. They were both soaked to the skin.

'Where are you going to?' asked the shop assistant curiously, as he looked at the bedraggled girl in her shorts and t-shirt soaked to the skin and the boy with his one eye, dirt-streaked face and sticking-up hair, a dog under his arm. The other shop assistant, also thin but a little older, sat on a small stool at the back of the shop, picking his nose and staring glumly out at the rain.

Xiao Mei was about to reply when there was another enormous clap of thunder and next to where the shop assistant was sitting a small back door, which had been shut, blew open and the wind rushed through, blowing a box of little nails off the counter, scattering them, bouncing, all over the floor.

The little dog wriggled out from under Stone's arm and tumbled to the ground where it stood barking furiously. The shop assistant leapt up but before he could close the door the dog had rushed out into the yard behind the shop, where Xiao Mei and Stone could see it racing round and round in circles, terrified by the thunder. Then it disappeared behind a pile of boxes and vanished from sight.

The rain began to ease and the rumbles of thunder became more distant. Stone and Xiao Mei ran to the door and looked out. The rain had almost stopped. The air smelled fresh and earthy and clean.

They could hear the little dog scrabbling underneath the boxes. The pile tottered and fell. The little dog turned tail and fled. A flash of dark yellow fur streaked past and disappeared into a dark corner of the yard. Stone rushed out, picked up a stone lying by the door and hurled it at the corner. The two shop assistants looked out and one said, without expression, 'huangshulang'. The dog stood barking wildly but the huangshulang had gone.

Then Xiao Mei heard a strange hiccupping, whooping noise next to her. Stone was squatting on the ground, his shoulders heaving.

'Stone,' she said in alarm. But when he looked up she saw that he was laughing. He leapt to his feet, grabbed the little dog and stuck it back under his arm.

'That was a laugh,' he said, grinning. 'The best thing that's happened today.'

But Xiao Mei wasn't thinking about the huangshulang. She had gone back into the shop where one of the shop assistants was picking up the nails that had scattered on the floor. She had caught sight of an advertisement on the wall behind the till. A beautiful smiling young woman was holding on her outstretched palm a little white jade statue.

'Let's go,' she said urgently.

But when she saw the clock next to the advertisement, and the time – nearly five o'clock - she panicked. Nainai and Ma would be home by now and wondering where she was. All hell would break loose if they discovered she'd gone out by herself. She ran into the yard and grabbed Stone by the arm.

'We've got to go. Now.'

She hesitated, feeling bad about what she was going to say next.

'I've got to go home. It's too late. I'll take the bus back and you'll have to walk with the dog. Sorry. Here.'

And she gave him the rest of the food that she had been

carrying in the bag.

Stone shrugged his shoulders. He was used to the unexpected. Xiao Mei turned and ran to the nearest bus stop, all the while wondering what excuse to come up with when she got home, and when she would ever find another chance to go to Tiantan.

~

Xiao Mei ran all the way back from the bus stop and arrived panting at her house. She pushed the door open gently and, holding her breath, crept into the porch, There she paused and listened. Not a sound from the courtyard. She peered round the corner. Ba was sitting on a low stool smoking and reading a newspaper. No sign of Ma or Nainai. As quietly as she could she tiptoed round behind him, intent on reaching her room before he saw her. Too late. Without looking up, he said:

'Ah, there you are. Fill this up for me.' He held out a jam jar with soggy green tea leaves at the bottom of it. Xiao Mei hesitated for a moment. Was he going to say anything else? No.

'Where are Ma and Nainai?'

'Not back yet.'

She breathed a sigh of relief, ran inside, filled the jar with hot water and went back out. Ba was laughing and pointing at the paper.

'Look at this,' he said. 'The crazy things that happen down south. Billions of them, it says here. Swarming all over the hillsides, eating everything up, the munching noise so loud it keeps the villagers awake at night. Flushed out of their holes by the floods.'

Xiao Mei set down the jar of tea and looked over his shoulder. 'Ugh,' she said, giving a shudder. 'Billions of rats, that's horrible.'

'Good business for some, though,' Ba said. 'People are making a fortune selling them to restaurants.' He did some calculations on his fingers.

'If one kilo of rats...'

'Ba,' Xiao Mei said sharply, 'you wouldn't do anything like that, would you?'

Ba sighed and stared ahead wistfully.

'No, I guess I wouldn't. Even so....'

Xiao Mei fell silent.

'Good thing we've got a huangshulang here,' Ba went on. 'It'll sort the rats out if they ever give us any problems.'

Xiao Mei felt doubtful. Their huangshulang seemed pretty lazy. But then she thought of the fierce huangshulang that Nainai had told her about. Walking on its hind legs with glowing red eyes. Everything was more complicated than it seemed. She sat down next to Ba to think about it all. Ba carried on reading his newspaper and for a short while all was quiet.

Quiet, at least, until Ma and Nainai arrived back. Nainai clattered in, tapping at the ground with a brand-new aluminium walking stick that Ma had purchased for her at a medical supplies shop near the hospital. Ma did not look happy.

'So,' said Ba, scarcely looking up from his paper, 'what did they say?'

'Cost a fortune,' said Ma crossly. 'Hospital registration, tests for heart, blood pressure and everything. Walking stick. Medicine.' She held out a large bag. 'And all they said in the end was that she was getting old and losing her memory. As if we didn't know that already! Just make sure she doesn't get ill or fall over or wander off and get knocked down by a car, they said. Because then it'll cost us even more.'

Ba stood up and went over to Nainai. 'Ma?' he said. 'You OK?'

Nainai looked up at him. 'This stick is really good, much better than the old one,' she said with a sly smile. 'Now I can go anywhere I want without worrying about falling down.'

Ma sighed. 'She'll be gadding about all over the place. You'd better look out for her. And don't blame me if she ends up flat on her face under a bus.'

No one took any notice at all of Xiao Mei. She had gone to her room and was sitting on her bed, tired, hungry and disconsolate. She hadn't even managed to get to Tiantan, let alone look for the jade. She'd gone half way there, all that way in the heat, got caught in a thunderstorm, and then turned back, empty-handed, because she thought that they'd be worrying where she was. But Ba hadn't even noticed she'd gone out. Ma hadn't said a single word to her. And Nainai was just a crazy old woman. None of them cared about her, not a single one of them. She sniffed. Well, she didn't care about them either.

At supper, she refused to say a word to any of them. She ate her bowl of noodles as fast as possible and left the table. Then, while they were still eating, she climbed the ladder to the roof and lay on the warm tiles, hating the whole world and feeling sorry for herself.

She scarcely thought about Stone and whether he had got back all right.

16.

Flying

When the two shopkeepers saw that the rain had stopped, and after Xiao Mei had gone, they threw Stone and the little white dog out of the shop. Who knew what a one-eyed ragged boy from the countryside would get up to if they let him stay? They eyed him suspiciously as he left, making sure that he hadn't pocketed anything.

In fact, Stone had taken something, a half-eaten packet of crunchy spicy beans that had been lying on the counter and which he tucked out of sight under the dog under his arm. As he walked down the street he ate them one by one. Where was he going to go now? He didn't have to go back to the hutong. He could go anywhere. But Xiao Mei was a source of food. He thought of the steamed buns and his mouth watered. And she needed his help, to go with her to Tiantan. She needed him. Someone needed him. He would go back.

It was dark by the time he arrived in his courtyard house. The yard was full of puddles and the rain had gusted into the room where he usually slept. But he found a dry corner and lay down on the floor, the dog by his side. His stomach felt sore after the spicy beans and for a while he tossed and turned, unable to find a comfortable position. He was exhausted after the afternoon's expedition and after some time he fell into a deep...

~

...but now he was wide awake! Hovering above the courtyard, beating the air with his arms to keep aloft! The dog was running round in circles below, leaping up on its hind legs, frantically trying to reach him.

'Jump,' he said, 'jump!'

The little white dog jumped as hard as it could. Stone leant over and, still beating the air with one arm, stretched out with the other and pulled the dog up by the scruff of its neck. The dog scrabbled onto Stone's back where it lay panting for breath.

Stone beat hard with both his arms and they rose above the yard and out over the hutong. By scooping the air back with one hand or the other he found that he could change direction. Out they sailed over the houses, the silent dark hutongs and the wide, lamp-lit roads. Every now and then there would be an uplift of moist warm air from below and Stone could stop paddling and float, resting his head on the warm airy cushion.

Apart from a few cars - mostly taxis - and a few late-night cyclists and pedestrians hurrying home, the streets were deserted. A dull orange glow hovered above the city, light trapped in the dense air. Below him were dark patches, which were clumps of trees, and small enclosed unlit courtyard spaces. He flew on through the muffled air, the sound of the city a faint and constant hum like a vast glass, vibrating.

Night noises floated up to him. The four falling notes of the bugu bird. A yowl of cats. The grating of ten thousand cicadas. He paddled on, dipping up and down as he navigated the currents of rising air. He was travelling south now, following the line of a hutong that ran parallel to a well-lit wide road, flying very low, just over the roofs of the houses. The little white dog looked down. Every now and then a lovely fragrant whiff rose up from a pile of discarded takeaway boxes next to a small restaurant and it would breathe in deeply.

They flew up and across the wide road and over to the other side. Here was a barren piece of open land. Shiny black puddles of water reflected light from nearby street lamps. Weeds and piles of earth and old bricks were everywhere, a site waiting to be built upon.

The dog stood up on Stone's back, balancing precariously as it looked over the side. Then it gave a little yelp of surprise and almost fell off. Stone looked down to see what had attracted the dog's attention. A squeaking, twittering noise rose up through the still air. Below them was a swiftly moving column of mice - hundreds of them - driven on by two unusually large rats with long snaky tails that lashed this way and that.

Stone stopped paddling, quickly losing height, until he was hovering just a few metres above the rodents. Then, rowing hard with his hands, he swooped up again and the rats and mice scattered in all directions, just like the nails that had bounced around the floor of the ironmonger's shop. He laughed and dived down again, aiming for the two big rats. But they stood their ground, baring their teeth and angrily swishing their tails.

While the two rats were occupied with snarling at Stone on the one hand and rounding up the dispersed mice on the other, they failed to notice that a small flat-bed truck had appeared in a far corner of the wasteland. Two dark figures jumped out and rushed towards the rodents. Each was carrying a large bag and a shovel. Using the shovels, the men scooped up as many mice as they could, stuffed them into the bags and when each bag was full, zipped it up and ran back to the truck with their squirming, squeaking bundles. They threw the bags onto the back of the truck, jumped in and sped off. Stone laughed again. Served them right, nasty vermin.

The two big rats dropped to all fours and scurried off angrily across the wasteland.

Stone, the little white dog on his back, flew upwards and on. Soon they had crossed the wasteland and were flying along a narrow road that followed a railway line. Between the road and the railway was a wall. In the dark shadow of the wall was a small bluish light. The dog yapped and Stone dipped down to see what it was.

Something was moving and when it moved the light moved too. Two long sinuous shapes were twisting and turning in the darkness, the point of light leaping between them. When the light came to rest for a moment, Stone saw to his surprise what they were. He craned his neck to get a clearer view and could just make out that the light came from a small, irregularly shaped object. He kept very still, with only his hands moving as he beat the air to maintain height.

~

Mouse-wolf had taken the jade out of the bag. He and Little Yellow were tossing it between them, and as the jade arced through the blackness it left a thin pinkish-blue trail of light just bright enough to illuminate them. The huangshulang did not see Stone hovering above them but they froze, alert to some hidden danger. Mouse-wolf stuffed the jade back into the bag around his neck.

A sudden gust of wind blew up. In the distance, on the other side of the wall, came a dull rumbling clanking noise. As the noise grew to a deafening roar, the huangshulang flattened themselves against the wall. Then came a powerful shriek, and a train shunted slowly past, panting and screeching as it went.

~

The displacement of the air above as the train passed by blew Stone and the dog up and away till they lost sight of the huangshulang hiding in the shadows. They spun past the railway, the little white dog digging into Stone's back with his toes to keep himself from falling off. Stone paddled wildly with his hands as he tried to steer a steady course but it was no good. The dog lay flat on his back, scrabbling with its feet and snuffling in his ear. He was losing control and falling fast, spinning as he went, the ground rising up to meet him with terrifying speed, about to slam into him and knock him out for ever.

He opened his eyes. The little white dog was standing up, pawing at his back. The sun was shining into the room. The stridulation of the cicadas was deafening. Stone rubbed his eyes and sat up. In the intense heat of early morning, the bugu bird called over and over, over and over again.

17.

The Spirit Way

Xiao Mei lay on her back on the roof and stared up at the dark, orange-grey sky. Her eyelids felt heavy but her mind was spinning as she thought about Ma and Ba and Nainai, and Stone, the crippled man on the bridge, the thunderstorm, the two shopkeepers, the huangshulang, not getting to Tiantan, and the little jade Guanyin lost somewhere in the grass. She wriggled from side to side, trying to get comfortable on the hard tiles. At last she lay still, her eyelids fluttered and her muscles relaxed. She gave a deep sigh.

And then her body contracted in a sudden violent spasm and she flung up her hands in self-protection. But from what?

Through the cracks between her fingers she saw a great bird. The eagle owl swivelled its neck to look at her with its yellow eyes as it balanced on the roof ridge, its strong wings beating the air. As if it was the most natural thing in the world, she climbed onto its back, holding tight to its mottled, tawny feathers, and they soared up, higher and higher until she could see the whole of the moonlit city spread out below them. Soon they were beyond the city's edge, flying over the hills, lower and lower until they alighted on a pine tree by an ancient red arch with heavy wooden doors. She slid off the bird's back and scrambled down to the ground.

The doors gave way when she pushed against them, and creaked open. She peered through. A long straight path led from the archway, flanked on either side by huge stone statues, stretching as far as the eye could see. Pairs of elephants and horses and men in armour and strange mythical creatures cast black shadows on to the path in the moonlight. Hadn't she seen them before somewhere?

She stepped forward towards the first pair of statues, two elephants caparisoned with tassels, saddles and embroidered cloths carved in the stone. But as her foot touched the shadow something happened that made her rub her eyes in bewilderment and dart back into the shadows.

Again she moved forward, dipping her foot into the elephants' shadows and again it happened. The greyness of the stone drained away, revealing a kaleidoscope of colour and, even more extraordinary, two living elephants that waved their trunks and stamped their feet and shook the bells on their harnesses.

She took several steps back, and again a grey film descended and the elephants turned back to stone, first their heads and backs, then their trunks and last of all their stamping feet. Xiao Mei moved in and out of the shadows several times, each time feeling braver and even more astonished.

When she realised that she could control what was happening she stepped forward boldly into the next pair of shadows, cast by Qilin monsters that bared their teeth, paddled the air with their cloven hooves, and shook their tails. She grimaced at them, stepped away and turned them back into stone. Pair by pair she transformed into living, breathing, vividly coloured creatures, returning each to stone as she passed between moonlight and shade.

Then she came to the last pair, two stone soldiers in armour who, when she stepped into their shadows, raised their shields and flashed their weapons. But when they roared, 'Who are you?' she took fright and turned them back into stone again. But again she gathered her courage and stepped forward. Again they roared the same question, but she shouted back at them 'I am Xiao Mei – who are you?'

The soldiers stared at her, eyes bulging in fury, and roared, 'We are the guardians of the tombs' and before she could step back into the shadows, one of them bent down, seized her in his enormous hand and held her aloft as she kicked and screamed to be let down.

'Stop that noise at once,' growled the soldier, 'and tell me why you are here.' Xiao Mei wriggled and whimpered but the soldier scowled even harder at her and finally, in a whisper, she told him about the flight on the eagle owl's back and her search for the lost jade Guanyin. 'Do you know where she is?' she asked.

When the soldiers heard what she had to say their eyes widened even more and they gazed on her in awe. Then, the soldier who was not holding her took the spear from his side, drew his arm back and, with a grunt of exertion, hurled it as far as he could, following the line of the Spirit Way.

The spear flew up and landed some distance away, its head piercing the ground. The shaft quivered for a moment and then, in a sudden burst of light, transformed into a tree with brilliant green foliage unlike any tree that Xiao Mei had ever seen before. The soldier set her down and, sticking one huge finger in her back, gave her a push, saying 'That's what you're looking for'.

As Xiao Mei ran towards the tree, buds appeared and soon flowers of all colours blossomed on it, peach and cherry and hibiscus, rose and peony. The Guanyin's flowers! thought Xiao Mei, as she ran towards the tree, inhaling the mysterious sweet aroma. But before she reached the tree the petals shrivelled and fell, fruits and pods appeared and ripened and dropped to the ground, and the leaves turned gold and russet and brown.

A wind came up that almost blew Xiao Mei off her feet and whipped the leaves from the tree so that they danced and whirled over the ground. By the time she had reached the tree it was completely bare.

She looked up into the branches, black and spiky against the moonlight, and felt distraught, tears running down her cheeks. When she looked down at the ground she saw, with an overwhelming feeling of relief, pods, pips and stones of every shape, colour and size. She knelt in the grass, picked them up one by one, and placed them in the little wooden box that she carried with her in her pocket.

Then she stood up and walked back down the Spirit Way, but even though she walked through the shadows of the stone figures they remained silent and grey in the moonlight, not heeding her at all.

She stepped through the red arch to the pine tree and climbed up through its branches. When she reached the topmost branch she stood up and looked out over the tree's crown. Before her on the hillside stretched groves of walnut trees and a few dark shapes of farm houses and, far beyond on the plain, like stars scattered over the earth, were the lights of the city of Beijing.

A dark shape floated towards her. With a soft flutter of wings and a low hoot the eagle owl glided down. Once again she climbed onto its back, where she lay, her face resting on the bird's soft feathers.

~

When Xiao Mei next opened her eyes she found herself back home in her very own bed and the sun streaming in through the window. She lay quite still. A spider hung in a dusty web in a corner of the room. She watched, wondering if it was alive or dead. The spider did nothing, just biding its time. The events of the night came slowly back to her. She sat up in bed, reached down for the loose brick and pulled out the little wooden box. The jade Guanyin was not there, of course. Neither were the pods and seeds and stones. It was only a dream after all. What did it all mean? She tried to remember everything that had happened. But already the dream was fading like an early morning summer mist dissolving in the heat of the sun.

Ba came in, carrying a glass of milk and a steamed bun on a plate, a worried look on his face.

'Good thing I was there, just in time.'

Xiao Mei sat up. Of course, she'd been on the roof. And then the eagle owl...and the statues....and everything..... She yawned. How had she got down again and into her bed?

Ba was talking all the while.

'One of your flip flops was on the ground by the ladder. So I climbed up and there you were, fast asleep. A moment later and you would have rolled off. I carried you down and put you to bed. Poor Ma, she was beside herself just thinking about what might have happened.'

'Ba,' Xiao Mei said, 'Ba.....?' Ba looked at her. But she forgot what she wanted to ask him and instead said, 'Can I have a boiled egg as well?'

Ba gave a broad smile. 'Of course you can,' he said and went off to the kitchen. Xiao Mei lay back down again. She could hear the voices of her parents talking softly. Nainai was crooning to herself in the yard. When Ba returned with the egg, Xiao Mei had fallen asleep again. He put the egg down on the little table next to her and left quietly, closing the door behind him.

18.

People in the Sky

Xiao Mei lay on her back on her bed while the cicadas outside droned on and on. She made spectacles of her thumbs and forefingers and stared up at the dusty white ceiling. The spider hung in its web, motionless. The afternoon air was thick with silence. There was nothing to do, absolutely nothing.

She turned over onto her front, then hung her head over the side of the bed, so that the blood rushed to her face and her scalp felt tight. Stretching out her palms, she placed them flat on the cool concrete floor, wriggled a little, tucked her head in and somersaulted clumsily off the bed. Then she leapt up, shook herself like a dog, and scratched her fingers through her hair so that it stood up in spikes all over her head.

~

Further along the hutong, Stone was also lying on his back, eyes closed, stretched out on a mat in the shadiest part of his room. The dog was spread-eagled on the floor, softly panting, trying to keep cool. A shadow passed in front of his eyes. The dog scrabbled to its feet. Stone sat up.

It was Xiao Mei. She sat down on the step between the

room and the courtyard. 'Here,' she said. She'd brought two cans of Sprite and a bag of salted peanuts.

Stone sat down next to her, opened one of the cans and, tipping back his head, slurped noisily. Xiao Mei stared ahead of her, absent-mindedly running her hands through the dog's rough coat. She hadn't seen Stone since their failed expedition to Tiantan, hadn't given him much thought at all. She felt as if she was constantly wrapped in hot cotton wadding, sapping all her energy and stifling all thought.

'Stone, she said after a while, 'are you homesick sometimes?'

Stone shook his head. But he said, 'I miss the food we eat back there.'

Xiao Mei went on, 'I feel homesick sometimes.'

Stone gave a short laugh.

'How can you be? Your home's just over there.'

'I know. But it feels as if it's gone already. It's almost not there anymore.'

'But your parents are.'

Stone took a peanut from the bag, licked the salt off and put it in his mouth. Xiao Mei reached into the bag as well.

'One day soon, none of this will be here anymore. Can you imagine? They'll come with big machines and dig big holes and build all over our hutong and there'll be an enormous building like an office block, and there'll be people sitting at their desks way, way up in the sky above us.'

She closed her eyes and tilted her head up. Stone did the same. He closed his eyes.

'Let's wave to them,' she said, stretching out her arm and

fluttering her hand. 'Hey, people of the future, look down, look at us, we're here! It's me and Stone and the little white dog. How do you like it, being up in the sky so high?'

She waved harder.

'You're sitting on top of my hutong, you people up there. Who gave you permission to do that? Who?'

Stone opened his eyes. Xiao Mei was still waving. Her voice was hoarse, her eyes were still shut and tears were running down her face. He stretched out his hand and touched her knee. 'Don't cry, don't cry. It will be all right.'

'It won't be all right,' Xiao Mei wailed. 'Everything is so horrible.'

Stone squatted back on his haunches. He didn't know what to say. He took a handful of peanuts. He gave one to the dog who snapped it out of his hand.

'Everything changes,' he said at last. 'Nothing ever stays the same.'

'But why does it have to get worse?' Xiao Mei wailed again.

'I don't know,' Stone said. 'It's just the way things are. Some people say that everything is getting better and better.'

'But I don't want things to get better and better. I want things to be like they've always been. Ma and Ba and Nainai and me and our house, and the rooftop and the hutong and the pomegranate tree and the huangshulang....'

The words tumbled out in a rush.

'Well,' said Stone, 'I don't want to stay here forever.'

'But when they knock this house down then you'll have nowhere to go,' said Xiao Mei, her voice rising again.

Stone looked at her.

'It's not my home here. I want things to change. It's no good being here like this.'

'But I don't want you to go either!'

Stone looked away with a strange expression on his face.

'No one has ever said that to me before,' he said.

'I've never said that to anyone either.'

Xiao Mei sniffed back her tears. The little dog sat down between them and licked the salt off Stone's fingers. Xiao Mei stretched out her hand. The dog turned its head and began to lick her fingers as well. They sat there saying nothing for a while.

Then Stone began to sing.

'Don't ask me where I come from, my hometown is far, far away, why do I wander, wander so far...?'

His voice was clear and strong.

'Like the birds, like the white clouds in the blue sky, like the little mountain streams, I wander, wander so far...'

Her eyes still glistening, Xiao Mei listened, then quietly began to hum along to the familiar tune.

'Stone,' she said after a while, 'you know when we went to Tiantan?'

'Except we didn't get there.' He leaned back on his elbows.

'No, but I didn't tell you why I wanted to go.'

'To look for something, you said.'

Xiao Mei turned to look at him. She wanted to be able to trust him.

'When my Nainai gave it to me she told me not to lose it.'

'Lose what?'

Xiao Mei took a deep breath.

'The little jade Guanyin.'

'Oh,' said Stone, 'was it worth a lot?'

Ignoring what he said, Xiao Mei went on. 'She told me that if I lost it, it would bring bad luck.'

She sat up straight.

'But I don't really believe all that superstitious stuff.'

The word sounded familiar but Stone couldn't quite remember what it meant.

'Believing in bad luck and things like that,' Xiao Mei went on.

'Well, she's right, your Nainai.'

'And that animals have spirits and humans can change shape.'

Stone thought about this for a while.

'Things like that could happen in the countryside but maybe not in the city,' he said doubtfully. 'Did your Nainai say anything else?'

'She said that the jade had been lost before and all sorts of bad things had happened to the family.'

'Bad things happen in all families. There's always a reason somewhere.'

'And I'm worried something bad will happen to it as well.'

'She's Guanyin, the Goddess of Mercy. She can look after herself.' Stone smiled at this thought.

'Will you come with me next time?'

Stone nodded.

A voice floated down the hutong.

'Xiao Mei, Xiao Mei...'

She leapt up.

'I'm going to be in trouble again.'

Waving goodbye, she turned and ran to the porch just in time to see Nainai's back disappearing into the house. If anyone saw her, she could just pretend that Ba had asked her to buy something at the hole-in-the-wall shop.

19.

The Evil Brushes

The railway track with its rushing clanking trains was too dangerous to be near. The last train to speed past had almost blown Mouse-wolf and Little Yellow off their feet. They raced off in panic not knowing where they were going but keeping always in the shadows, and then scrambled, exhausted, into an old dry water pipe where they hid, dozing in and out of sleep. The little red bag, now dirty with soot, was still around Mouse-wolf's neck. The jade inside was covered with a thin black film of dirt.

The huangshulang slept deeply all through the next day. When they awoke it was dusk and the bats were flittering in the darkening sky. Mouse-wolf put his nose out of the pipe, sniffed the air and darted out. He returned almost immediately with a limp mouse between his teeth. Little Yellow was ravenous and fell upon the mouse with relish. When they had both eaten, they emerged from the pipe and surveyed their surroundings.

They were in the shadows, on the corner of a brightly lit pedestrianised little street with many people coming and going in the warm evening air. On either side were old-looking, single-storeyed shops, with steps and red pillars, green lattice-work windows and big red lanterns. In the windows were displays of porcelain vases of all different sizes, scrolls of calligraphy, paintbrushes, and paintings of birds and flowers, mountains, clouds and waterfalls.

On the corner of the street stood a man selling skewers of barbecued mutton. The delicious aroma was mouth-watering. The huangshulang peered round the corner, noses quivering. Just at that moment two young women in high heels clattered past, each gnawing at a skewer of meat. They were talking animatedly to each other as they ate. The huangshulang were in luck. One of the young women squealed in irritation as a large chunk of juicy meat dropped to the ground.

Scarcely waiting to check that it was safe to enter the busy little street, Mouse-wolf and Little Yellow dashed out and carried the mutton back into the shadows. It had a strange spicy flavour. 'Fresh mouse is way better than this,' said Little Yellow. Mouse-wolf agreed, but they devoured the entire chunk all the same.

It wasn't safe to be near the bright lights. The huangshulang retreated down a narrow alley that led into a small yard behind one of the shops. One side of the yard led into the back of the shop; on the other side was a small, dimly lit store-room lined with shelves. The space under the bottom shelf was dark and dry. It was a good place to hide.

The huangshulang knew that what they most needed were food and places of safety. But food might be poisoned and dangers might lurk in hiding places. They had been lucky with the mutton. Keeping close to the wall, Mouse-wolf and Little

Yellow, now running, now stopping to sniff the air, made their way into the store-room. Little Yellow put her nose under the shelf and sneezed. Although there was a thick layer of dust and bits of dead insect, there was enough space to lie low for a while.

Mouse-wolf, meanwhile, was standing on his hind legs surveying what lay above. The shelves were stacked with dozens of shallow boxes. Some of these were open, revealing their contents: thin bamboo sticks, with furry tufts sleeked into a point at the end of each one. Mouse-wolf felt uneasy. He put his nose to one of the tufts. The smell was overwhelmingly familiar. A great shiver went down his spine. He spun round, looking for Little Yellow who was now curled up under the shelf.

'This is a bad place,' he said urgently. 'We can't stay here.'

The musty, musky smell from the brushes was overpowering.

'Can't you smell it?' Mouse-wolf said in a low voice. Little Yellow looked puzzled for a moment. Then she smelled it too.

Without waiting another second, the two huangshulang turned tail and bolted out, rushing past the stacks of shelves. On each one of the dozens of boxes was a bold red label declaring 'Calligraphy brushes – finest yellow weasel hair'.

After this incident the two huangshulang said little to each other. It was hard to comprehend that hundreds, even thousands of huangshulang had contributed their lives to those brushes.

'What are they for?' whispered Little Yellow, her heart still beating.

'I don't know,' said Mouse-wolf. 'It's impossible to think of a reason.'

After a while, the ghastly image of the evil contained within the store room retreated to the back of their minds, just one more terrifying event that proved to them yet again that they needed to be constantly on their guard.

~

A few days later, when Mouse-wolf and Little Yellow were hiding out in some dense foliage behind a rubbish bin, Little Yellow brought up a subject that both of them had been avoiding. Mouse-wolf was busy scratching himself and Little Yellow was lying on her back, grooming her whiskers.

'We don't know that he didn't escape. He might be out there looking for us.'

Mouse-wolf stopped scratching. He said nothing, turning his head away.

'But he might have, mightn't he? After all, the two of us escaped, and Big Yellow could always run much faster than we could. He's probably looking for us at this very moment. He's got to be ....'

Little Yellow's voice trailed off. She looked at Mouse-wolf. Then she said, more loudly, 'We're just trying to live, like anyone else. We're not doing anyone any harm.'

She thought for a while.

'This place is no good for huangshulang anymore.'

Mouse-wolf thought of everything he had experienced in the last few days: the shrieking women in the jade market, the derelict houses, the wicked rats, the fire and men with shovels, the disappearance of Big Yellow, the thunderstorm, the clanking trains, and the terrifying bamboo sticks with their pointed tufts of weasel hair.

He felt for the little bag round his neck. Was it something to do with the jade? He took it out of the bag and held it in his paw. Through the grime on its surface it winked and shone with a pale bluish light. Could such a beautiful thing be the cause of so much misfortune? Hadn't life been better before he had set out on this journey? He thought of his home in Tiantan, the trees and grass and birds, all living undisturbed, in safety.

He clasped the jade, hesitated for a moment and swung back his paw.

'But at least we are still alive,' Little Yellow said, not taking in what Mouse-wolf was doing. 'Maybe it's the jade, protecting us in some way.'

He was about to swing his arm up over his head and unclench his paw to let the jade go flying high in an arc far, far away to who knew where. He stopped.

'I don't know,' he said. Then he brought his paw slowly down and put the jade back in the bag. 'I really don't know.'

Though they spoke rarely of him, Big Yellow was never far from their minds. It was hard to draw breath, have space to think up a plan about how to find him. That is, if Big Yellow was still there to be found at all. Fate swept them along in a relentless rushing torrent. As for returning the jade to its owner, it seemed to Mouse-wolf that he was no nearer to accomplishing that task than he had been right at the very beginning. Life, scary and unpredictable, just kept getting in the way.

20.

Ma's Secret

If Xiao Mei had to choose between her parents, she might choose Ba, she thought. He was crazy and unreliable but at least he had a sense of humour. Ma was always tense and tight-lipped, ready to snap at anyone at the slightest provocation. Ba would sit for hours in the yard, laughing over something he'd read in the paper, swigging back bottle after bottle of beer, singing snatches of old songs, or rushing in to tell them about some mad new scheme that would make them rich any day soon.

But Ma would leave early for work and come back late, tired out after an hour of standing on a crowded bus, and then spend the rest of the evening cooking and cleaning. Or else re-cooking and re-cleaning if Nainai had taken it into her head to do the household chores, always a recipe for total disaster. On evenings like that they all knew better than to cross her as she was more than ready to fly off the handle, shouting and wailing that she wished she had never been born.

But there was one evening in the week when Ma came back late because she had to work overtime. That evening the rest of the family would have to fend for themselves with food because as soon as Ma came back home she would go straight to bed, barely saying a word to any of them. They all knew better than to disturb her.

Nevertheless, strangely enough, the next morning she would often be in a better mood, her face wearing an absent-minded, almost happy expression as she bustled around the kitchen getting ready to go to work. Xiao Mei thought this quite odd, though it never occurred to her to ask Ma what was going on. Not that Ma would have told her anyway. Ma kept her secrets firmly to herself.

It was incomprehensible to Xiao Mei that Ma might be doing something that they didn't know about. Wasn't her life just going to work and keeping the house in order? What else would there be? Mothers like her all seemed to be the same. They worked, they chopped vegetables, cooked and cleaned, they nagged and shouted at their husband, child, mother-in-law. Xiao Mei knew of some mothers who went out dancing in the community areas, but Ma wasn't interested in dancing. And now that the hutong houses were being pulled down and everywhere was such a mess there wasn't any public space to dance in anyway.

~

But Ma had something that no one knew about. Something she kept entirely to herself, her own private passion. Early evening, every Thursday, after her shift in the department store had finished, she would walk in the direction of the bus stop. But instead of waiting for a bus she would go quickly down the road and then turn left into a dark little alleyway. Over her right shoulder she carried her usual shoulder bag, but in her left hand she carried a dark canvas holdall. This holdall she kept in her locker at work and never brought home.

Halfway down the alleyway, she stopped in front of a metal gate. She pushed it open and walked across a small yard surrounded on each side by low blocks of flats, five storeys high, each block with five dark entrances. She entered the furthest doorway, climbed an almost pitch-dark stairway (since the light-bulb was broken and the windows were tiny and covered in years of grime), and stopped, on the third floor, outside a grey metal door with the numbers 3-5-31 stencilled on it in red. A weak light came from a naked bulb screwed into a fitting above the door. Next to the doorframe were several dusty cardboard boxes stacked one on top of the other. Still panting with the effort of climbing the stairs, she rang the bell.

A dog yapped. There was a sound of footsteps and keys turning in the lock. Then the door opened and Ma stepped inside.

The man moved aside as Ma entered. He said nothing. She stooped to pat the dog, which jumped up at her, wagging its tail, and she stood in the dimly lit corridor while the man disappeared into the kitchen. He reappeared with a chipped cup of tea in his hand. Ma followed him into the small living room.

'Have a rest first,' said the man. 'You can't do anything until you are relaxed.'

He handed her the cup. The sofa against the wall was covered with piles of books and magazines. Every inch of the wall was lined with bookshelves that went right up to the ceiling. Ma sat down on a chair and placed the canvas holdall by her feet. Her feet and back ached from standing all day. If the sofa hadn't been covered with stuff she would have just kicked off her sandals, stretched out, and fallen fast asleep there and then. Instead, all she could do was sit on the hard wooden chair and sip her tea. The man was at a desk, clearing off the books and spreading it with newspapers. Above the desk hung a fluorescent light strip, dangling on two wires from the ceiling.

The man returned to the kitchen and came back with a jam jar of water and several white enamel plates. She watched him: thin, a little stooped, hair greying, long, lean face and large eyes, long slender hands. As always, he was wearing a white vest, and round his neck, threaded onto a narrow red silk cord, was a small carved green jade Buddha.

'Let's start,' he said, after a few minutes.

Ma stood up, unzipped the holdall and brought out her things. These she placed on the desk: a sketch pad, a roll of white paper, some pencils, some tubes of paint and some brushes. Then she sat down at the long end of the desk and the man sat down at the short end.

'Mountains and water,' said the artist. 'Clouds and craggy rocks. Pine trees on precipices. A little pavilion. A rushing torrent. Three tiny people walking in the valley, dwarfed by the majestic peaks.'

Ma's imagination soared. It was like poetry. For a moment she could almost smell the pure mountain air.

Teacher Fu picked up a brush, dipped it into water, dabbed it on his stick of black ink and swept the brush boldly across the paper.

Ma watched him. Then she spread out her own sheet of paper, picked up a brush and did the same. Soon she was absorbed in her task, far away from home, from work, from the city with its endless traffic and noise. She was in the mountains, with the sound of waterfalls and little streams and the great river rushing in the valley below. And there would be only one figure in her painting, not three. She wanted to be completely alone.

When her hour was up she packed away her things in the canvas holdall, everything except her painting. This she pegged up to dry on a wire line stretched between two bookcases. Teacher Fu looked at it.

'Very good,' he said.

He opened a drawer of the desk and took out a small narrow box.

'For you. You are making progress.'

He placed the box in Ma's hand. She opened the lid. Inside was a thin bamboo stick with a sleek tuft of the most beautiful golden weasel hair, a little darker at the tip. She took it out and drew the tip of the brush over the back of her hand. It felt soft and springy and full of energy. She placed the brush back in the box and put the box in her holdall.

'Thank you, thank you,' she said, clasping her two hands in front of her and giving a little bow. And for the first time that week a small smile broke across her face.

21.

Luck and Fate

Ba and Old Wang were sitting together in the courtyard. Ba was doing most of the talking and from time to time Old Wang would nod his head and open another bottle of beer. Xiao Mei was sitting on the roof, reading a magazine and listening with half an ear to what they were saying.

Ba was confident that he would make it big one day soon. It was just a matter of finding the right connections, people you could trust and who had influence. Loads of people were making loads of money these days and there was no reason why he couldn't be one of those lucky people as well. You just had to be in the right place at the right time.

'You see,' Ba said, 'every man has his own value. What I mean is, it's not just a question of hard work, it's a question of ....' His voice trailed off and he scratched his head as he searched for the right words. 'Luck! It's all about luck, and Fate! Some people are destined to be lucky.'

He fell silent, contemplating a small brown ant that was hauling a dried leaf past his feet.

Meanwhile, Old Wang was saying, 'Just three weeks to go. That's what I heard. If it doesn't work out...'

Ba looked up quickly.

'What do you mean "if it doesn't work out"'?

Old Wang held up both his hands.

'No need to get rattled. Of course it will work out. But we just have to look at the situation from all angles, that's all I'm saying.'

Ba fell silent again. Xiao Mei put down her magazine and peered over the edge of the roof. Ba looked worried and offered Old Wang a cigarette. For a while neither of them said anything.

'Ba,' she called down. 'What did he mean, "three weeks?"'

Ba jumped. He looked up in irritation.

'That's when they start the demolition work. In three weeks' time. So we'll have to be out of here before then. Don't worry about it.'

'But where will we go?'

'Don't you worry about that. Ba's got it all in hand.'

Xiao Mei climbed down the ladder as fast as she could, her feet scarcely touching the rungs. She rushed over to Ba and stood shaking, her hands clenched into fists.

'Why doesn't anyone ever tell me anything? You think I'm an idiot!'

Ba leant back. He laughed nervously.

'You're much too young to have to worry about these things. It'll all be fine, just fine. A nice new flat, high up, with a balcony and a view and a proper toilet.'

'But where, where?' Xiao Mei's voice rose in agitation. Then, 'Does Ma know?'

Ba went quiet. 'Yes of course she knows...kind of. She knows we have to move, of course she does. But at this point we're not exactly sure where to.'

Old Wang interjected.

'But it will all be sorted out very soon. As your Ba said, it's all in hand.'

'Yes,' said Ba impatiently. 'This is not stuff for children to worry about. Stop asking questions.'

'Go on,' he said raising his voice as Xiao Mei stood there, staring at him. He flapped his hand in the direction of the kitchen. 'Go and do something useful.'

Xiao Mei looked from Old Wang to Ba and from Ba to Old Wang. Neither of them was telling her the truth. They never did. They said one thing and meant something else. Or they just told you half the truth and then changed the subject.

She brushed her arm over her face to wipe away her tears, or was it sweat? She could hardly breathe, let alone think straight. Old Wang stood up, murmured something, and shambled off back into his room.

Ba opened another bottle of beer. Then he said, inconsequentially, 'I wonder what's for dinner tonight?'

When Ma came back from work, Xiao Mei confronted her with the new information. Ma looked tired.

'Yes, I know. The rate things happen I shouldn't be surprised if we end up on the street. Or in one of those basement rooms where migrants live.'

But when she saw Xiao Mei's expression she said, 'We just have to trust to Fate. They said we'd be rehoused so we just have to trust that they'll do what they said.'

'Who's 'they'?' said Xiao Mei.

Ma gestured wearily with her hand.

'Oh everyone. The local officials, the developers, the building contractors, everyone you can think of. So many of them.'

Xiao Mei was on the point of asking another question but Ma said sharply, 'Stop pestering me with all your questions. Go and put the water on to boil. Do you think the porridge will cook itself?'

Xiao Mei gave an audible sigh of frustration. What was the point? she thought. She couldn't get any sense out of any of them.

Nainai shuffled into the room carrying a string bag full of vegetables.

'Look what I've got,' she said happily. 'Lovely red tomatoes. Just lying on the ground, waiting to be picked up.'

Ma snatched the bag from her and tipped the tomatoes out onto the floor. Some were squashed and some were mouldy.

'Stupid old woman!' she shouted. 'You expect us to eat rotten vegetables?'

Nainai looked at the tomatoes slyly. 'Specially for you. You like tomatoes.' And she took herself off outside.

Xiao Mei followed her out into the yard. It was almost dark. She climbed the ladder up to the roof and sat looking out over the rooftops and listening to the sundry voices, the ringing of a bicycle bell down the hutong, the growl of a car engine starting up, and beyond, the ever-present low hum of the city settling down for the evening.

~

Ba was lying low in Old Wang's room. Old Wang had opened a bottle of spirits which they were drinking from little white cups. There was also a plate of salty boiled peanuts. Above their heads could be heard a gentle cooing and papery scratching of little claws as the pigeons settled down for the night. What would happen to them when they had to move? Old Wang's face drooped.

'It will be one of the biggest tragedies of my life,' he said, dramatically. 'I love my pigeons. I can't give my pigeons up, but I can't take them with me either.'

His eyes watered. Ba nodded sympathetically, helping himself to a peanut with his chopsticks.

'And they love you! Those pigeons are like your children. Better than children! However far they fly away they always come back to you! There's nothing more loyal than a pigeon!'

'I'll drink to that,' said Old Wang raising his glass. 'Ganbei!'

'Ganbei!' said Ba, downing his cup in one gulp.

Old Wang refilled the cup and then refilled his own. Ba took another peanut. Old Wang did the same. For a while they sat there in silence. Ba gave a deep sigh. Old Wang did the same.

'You've been a good mate to me over the years,' Old Wang said. 'The only one I've got in the world. There's no one in my life. Just you. Only you.'

'And the pigeons,' added Ba, raising his cup.

'And the pigeons,' said Old Wang, knocking back another measure of spirits. He hiccupped loudly. They sat in reverie contemplating the hardships of life.

Ma's voice called across the yard.

'Come and eat!'

Ba stood up slowly, swaying a little on his feet, and stumbled back home. Ma, Nainai and Xiao Mei were already sitting at the table. Ma ladled out a bowl of millet porridge for each of them.

'If I'd known you'd eat so many buns while I was at work, I would have bought more,' she said in irritation. 'You'll just have to eat what there is.'

'I didn't eat any of them,' said Ba. 'I had that left over rice.' Nainai slurped noisily.

'Greedy old woman,' Ma muttered under her breath.

Xiao Mei bent low over her bowl and said nothing.

In his room across the courtyard, Old Wang slumped in his chair, head thrown back, snoring loudly, his smooth naked belly shiny with sweat. He would wake up an hour or so later, eat two cold steamed buns with red-bean filling washed down with a bottle of beer, and then collapse into bed to sleep a deep sleep devoid of dreams.

~

The huangshulang slid out from behind her box in the corner and sniffed the air. Then a dash across the courtyard, a clamber over the wooden threshold, and into the dark hutong. The little white dog in the derelict house yapped as it dozed. The mice hid themselves as well as they could as the huangshulang resumed her nightly search for food.

22.

The Man on the Building Site

Stone, bored with sitting around in the derelict courtyard house, had wandered out to see what was going on. He didn't want to go too far away as he had come to rely on Xiao Mei bringing him food most days. Yet he knew that he couldn't stay here forever. One day Xiao Mei had lent him Nainai's mobile phone to try and phone his uncle. But he must have remembered the number wrong because the voice said the number didn't exist.

He tried to remember what his uncle looked like, but the image kept sliding around in his mind. His uncle had been a big man, with a square face and hair cropped short to his scalp. The main thing he remembered was an overpowering smell of garlic and the folds of skin on the back of his uncle's fat neck. He didn't really know him very well. Though he called him 'uncle' he had only met him once or twice. He didn't think he was a blood relative. But then Stone knew very little about his own family. Everything was all mixed up in his mind, ever since his grandmother had died. No one seemed to know what had happened to his mother after she had left to find work in the city. She had never come back. He didn't miss her because he didn't remember her at all. She had left him when he was just a few months old.

Nothing stays the same, everything changes. That's what he told himself. It was the only thing in his life that he could be certain of. So he bided his time and waited to see what would turn up.

With Stone was the little white dog with the length of pink string tied around its neck for a lead. Not that the dog would have strayed far from Stone's side. The thought crossed Stone's mind that if his uncle had tied a string around his – Stone's – neck then he wouldn't have got lost. When his uncle had disappeared into the crowds he would have just followed him. He would make absolutely sure to keep the dog, who depended on him, safe.

Together they walked down the hutong, past the large white chai sign painted on the wall of Xiao Mei's house. 'Demolish' and then what? Where did people go? He stepped aside as a large truck piled high with broken doors and window frames rumbled past him. The whole world seemed to be on the move.

He remembered the great dusty building sites he had seen from the window of the crowded long-distance bus he and his uncle had taken from the village. Where once there had been fields of wheat or plots of vegetables, now there were mountains of earth and half-built high-rise buildings looming out of the ground like new-born giants. A whole new world was being created. It was scary, but exciting as well.

He didn't know exactly what his uncle had planned for him. His uncle had told him that he'd find him a job so he could 'get some experience'. Perhaps as a little guard outside one of those smart new villa compounds, where rich people lived in big houses. Though it might be difficult, his uncle had said, on account of his having only one eye. It might put those rich people off. They liked everything to be perfect. Not to worry though. Something would be found for him.

But now none of this would happen. He thought back to the moment when he realised that his uncle had disappeared. They had just arrived at Beijing's long-distance bus station and were sitting on a step eating some corncobs that his uncle had bought from a stall. His uncle kept looking round uneasily, as if he were waiting for someone to turn up. Stone sat staring at the hundreds of people streaming out of the bus station, many of them staggering under great cloth bundles of bedding, clothes or goods to sell. Taxis honked their horns, men riding little three-wheel motorbikes with awning-covered seats touted for passengers.

His uncle stood up. 'I'll be back soon,' he said, a strange look on his face. And before Stone could say anything his uncle had vanished out of sight into the milling crowds. Stone had waited for him all night. But his uncle never came back. Hungry, frightened and exhausted he had made his way on foot into the city, looking for food and shelter, half-hoping his uncle would miraculously appear, yet knowing, deep in his heart, that the greater probability was that he would never see him again.

~

Stone walked down the hutong, the little white dog trotting ahead of him, every now and then stopping to sniff at something interesting and lift its leg to leave a message. Most of the houses here had been abandoned and many of them were half demolished. Several men with hand-carts were picking through the debris, recovering whatever could be reused or recycled.

On the ground, lying on its back in the dust, was a cloth monkey with long red arms and legs and a red-and-white striped body. The monkey grinned up at Stone. Stone picked it up, shook it hard to remove the dust, looked at it and, just for fun, stuck out his tongue. The little white dog danced up on its hind legs, yapping and snapping at the monkey's long limbs. Stone tucked the monkey under his arm and carried on down the hutong.

The further he went, the more destruction there was. Soon there were no houses at all, just a level stretch of waste land, scattered with odd bricks and tiles, and here and there a persimmon or pomegranate tree that for some reason had been left standing. On the far side of this wasteland was a solid metal fence, dazzling white against the blue of the sky. Behind the fence were four tall orange cranes, slowly revolving, swinging dangling loads of concrete blocks, like giant leggy birds engaged in some mysterious dance.

Stone pressed his one eye to a hole in the fence and looked through. Below him was an enormous pit, as wide and as long as an entire neighbourhood of houses and as deep as .... Stone tried to think what it was as deep as. As deep as Coal Hill was high, perhaps. He had never seen such a massive pit. And the men moving around the bottom were like so many ants, he thought, ants in yellow helmets and orange jackets.

A man's voice called out behind him, making him jump. He swung round, in his haste tangling the dog's pink string around his legs. The monkey grinned at the man from under Stone's armpit.

'Hey!' said the man. 'What are you doing?'

Then, when he saw Stone's one eye staring at him, muttered something under his breath. Stone picked the dog up and started to move away.

'Not so fast,' said the man. He was wearing a stained brown suit and dusty black, slip-on shoes. A cigarette dangled from one hand. Stone took another step back.

'That dog,' said the man, 'that's a nice-looking dog.'

He took a step nearer and stretched out his hand to pat the dog on its head. The little white dog bared its teeth in a snarl. The man laughed, and bent down, bringing his head close to the dog's.

'Boo!' he said in the dog's ear. 'Boo!'

The dog barked in fright and wriggled frantically in Stone's arms. Stone stepped back in alarm.

'Just a joke,' said the man, drawing on his cigarette. 'I just wanted to see how lively it was.'

Stone turned, thinking that he needed to get away as fast as possible, but the man put out his hand.

'How about I give you ten kuai for the dog? You look as if you're in need of it. I'd be doing you a favour.'

Stone shook his head and held the dog even more tightly.

'Twenty kuai then. Think what you could do with that'.

Stone paused and thought. Twenty kuai would get him back to the long-distance bus station and might even buy him a ticket back to the village. At least he thought it might. He couldn't be sure.

'A nice meal of meat and rice and vegetables this evening,' the man was saying, 'and money left over for tomorrow and the next day as well.'

Stone's mouth watered at the thought. He felt very hungry. And, as if reading his thoughts, the dog began to lick his hand with its rough little tongue. If he had twenty kuai he could feed the dog as well....except...except... he wouldn't have a dog anymore! The little white dog looked up at Stone, tail wagging.

'So, that's settled then,' the man was saying. 'Here's the money and you pass me over the dog.'

He waved a twenty-kuai note in front of Stone's face. But Stone had taken another step back, had taken a decision, and before the man could say another word he turned and ran as fast he could, the little white dog under one arm and the red monkey under the other.

The man stood there, not bothering to follow them and, after a few minutes, turned and walked slowly away in the opposite direction. When Stone had reached the far side of the wasteland he turned to look back. The man was gone.

Stone made his way back to his house. A packet of instant noodles and a bottle of water had been left just inside the porch. He looked back down the hutong, but no one was around and the door to Xiao Mei's courtyard was shut.

23.

The Great Fat Panda

One morning, Nainai called to Xiao Mei from her room. Xiao Mei was sitting under the pomegranate tree, doing nothing in particular, drawing patterns in the dust with the end of a stick. She was waiting for a chance to sneak out and see what Stone was up to.

Reluctantly she stood up and shouted back, 'What is it?'

Nainai stuck her head out.

'Come here at once.'

So Xiao Mei went inside and saw on Nainai's bed an empty box and a tangle of clothes. Nainai grabbed her hand.

'The Guanyin. Where's the Guanyin?'

Xiao Mei froze. 'It's in a safe place. Don't worry about it.'

Nainai grunted, then her eyes glazed over.

'Who are you? Do you live here?'

'Of course I live here, Nainai.' Xiao Mei was startled. 'It's me, Xiao Mei.'

'Where's my son?'

'Ba's out.'

'Will he come back?'

Xiao Mei looked at her anxiously.

'Soon, Nainai, soon. Don't worry.'

But Nainai had already turned her back and was rummaging amongst the clothes on her bed. Xiao Mei was unsure whether to stay or to go. After a minute, Nainai turned round and said sharply, 'What are you doing here? Stop bothering me! Go away and do something useful!'

Xiao Mei gave a huff of irritation and went back outside. Nainai was getting worse and worse by the day.

This short incident, however, brought the little jade figure back into Xiao Mei's mind and a wave of anxiety swept over her.

~

Then, something unexpected happened. Ba rushed in from the hutong, shouting 'Quick, get your shoes on. We're going out.'

Where? Xiao Mei wasn't going anywhere, not without knowing.

'Tiantan. But hurry, the car's waiting.'

Car? Tiantan? Xiao Mei leapt up. Ba shouted something to Nainai and rushed out, Xiao Mei hopping behind him as she pulled on her sandals. Outside in the hutong was a small grey car, its engine running. A chubby young man was at the wheel and, sitting on the back seat, scrutinising her eyebrows in a small mirror, was Mrs Chen. Ba opened the back door.

'Sit next to Auntie Chen,' he said. Xiao Mei hesitated before climbing in. The driver leant over, opened the front door and Ba climbed in, too.

'Oh, so cute!' said Mrs Chen, beaming at Xiao Mei who

scowled and looked at her feet.

'But shy too,' she added, beaming less vigorously.

The driver revved the engine and they drove off. Xiao Mei wound down the window and put her head out.

'Careful,' warned Mrs Chen, 'you'll lose your head.'

'Shut the window,' shouted Ba, 'we'll lose the air-conditioning.'

Xiao Mei rolled up the window reluctantly and pressed her face to the glass. The car turned left and right and left and right and after a short while they came to the inner ring road round the centre of the city. Cars were crawling along. The driver entered the slipway and joined the sluggish flow. Ba and Mrs Chen were talking and laughing. Ba lit a cigarette. Xiao Mei felt sick, put her hand over her nose and closed her eyes.

She must have fallen asleep because when she opened then again the car had stopped and Mrs Chen and Ba were getting out. They were parked next to a pedestrian overpass by a multi-storeyed department store. Xiao Mei started to get out of the car as well but Ba said quickly, 'We've got some business to attend to. You wait here with the driver and we'll be back soon.' He looked across the road. 'He could take you to play in Tiantan, if you like.'

Xiao Mei looked across the road as well. Yes, there was the grey arch leading into the park and the ticket office next to it on the right-hand side. Ba and Mrs Chen went off and the driver drove the car round the corner into a small street and parked alongside the pavement.

'What's your name?' Xiao Mei asked the driver as they

walked over the footbridge.

'Just call me Brother Tong,' the driver said.

'You look very young, 'said Xiao Mei boldly.

Tong flushed. 'I'm nineteen,' he said. 'At least ten years older than you.'

'No, you're not,' said Xiao Mei. 'You're only nine years older.'

Tong smiled. A man selling kites called out to her. She shook her head. They stood in the middle of the bridge looking over towards the park. Above the pine trees rose the blue-tiled roof of the Temple of Heaven. Somewhere, below a cypress tree, was the little jade Guanyin.

Tong bought two entry tickets to the park and Xiao Mei raced ahead, Tong following lumpily after her. She sped past the brightly decorated walkway where people were singing and playing musical instruments, past the amateur dancers whirling in pairs to loud music from loudspeakers, away from the noisy people to the quiet of a grove of low pine trees. She stood to catch her breath and looked around. The ground was trampled flat by the feet of early risers walking round and round the trees, practising taiqi or singing snatches of local opera. The bark of some of the trees was worn quite smooth.

Then she remembered. When Ma and Ba had fallen asleep she had gone off and sat on a grassy patch between two small cypresses near a wall. She stood and looked around her. Through the trees she could just make out the grey outer wall that circled the park. She set off on her own, Tong trailing some way behind her and playing with his mobile phone.

When she reached the wall, she hesitated. It curved away on either side of her. She touched one of the grey bricks, warm from the sun, as if it might give her a sign. Someone had carved their name in three clumsy, angular characters: Long Xian Ping. Someone had stood there, like her, also waiting for some sign as to what to do next.

She turned and leant her back against the wall's warm surface and looked around. To her right, a gnarled old pine, to her left a raggedy bush with small yellow flowers. Two azure-winged magpies swooped down chattering from the pine, skimmed the ground and flew up again into the branches.

Then she saw what she was looking for - the two slim cypress trees and near them a patch of bright green grass, the very patch where she had sat and played with the jade figure on the day of their picnic.

Tong was sitting nearby, his back to a pine, his eyes closed, his mobile phone in his hand. Careful not to attract his attention, she walked slowly towards the trees.

The phone rang, an ear-splitting, jangly noise. Tong leapt to his feet.

'Wei!' he shouted into his phone. 'Wei! Right away!'

Xiao Mei was already running towards the cypresses. Tong ran after her, panting.

'That was Mrs Chen. They're waiting for us. We've got to go.'

Xiao Mei turned to confront him, her eyes blazing.

'Just a few more minutes!'

He shook his head.

'Quick, they're in a hurry. I'll get into trouble...'

He looked desperate.

'Mrs Chen will get angry. You don't know what she's like when she's angry.'

The two of them were facing each other, each bent on fleeing in the opposite direction. The phone jangled a second time.

'Yes, yes,' said Tong, beads of sweat forming on his temples. 'Two minutes. We'll be there in two minutes.'

He grabbed Xiao Mei's hand but she shook him free. She turned to run towards the cypresses, looked back at Tong, and saw the sweat – or was it tears? – dripping down his chubby face.

'Please, Xiao Mei, I'll lose my job!'

She hesitated for a moment, then shaking her head, protesting under her breath, she ran with him, through the pine grove, past the amateur dancers and the decorated walkway with the musicians, back through the main gate and over the footbridge until, panting with the exertion – and in Xiao Mei's case, frustration – they arrived back at the car where Mrs Chen stood glaring at them from under the shade of a lacy white parasol, and Ba skulked nearby, puffing anxiously on a cigarette.

No one was happy. They climbed into the car in silence, this time Mrs Chen in the front and Ba and Xiao Mei at the back.

'It's a very important meeting. I'm going to be late,' said Mrs Chen, pointedly.

Ba looked miserable.

As they entered the slipway back onto the ring road, the car stalled. Tong sweated more than ever. He revved the engine several times. Finally, with a violent jerk, the car lurched forward.

'Heavens!' said Mrs Chen. 'On top of everything else are we all going to die today?'

Tong held tight to the steering wheel and stared straight ahead.

Xiao Mei looked at Ba. Then she took his hand and held it all the way until the car stopped at the end of their hutong since Mrs Chen said there was no time to take them to their door. When they got home, Ba sighed deeply, fetched a bottle of beer from the kitchen and sat down on his stool in the courtyard.

'Well, you really messed things up today,' he said.

Queasy from the car ride, unable to control her frustration, angry with Tong, with Mrs Chen, with Ba, with everyone, Xiao Mei, who very rarely cried, burst into tears. Ba was taken aback.

'Don't cry, don't cry. You were late but ....,' he hesitated for a moment, 'this afternoon didn't go smoothly. That business I mentioned .....we didn't quite manage to complete it. It really didn't go well. Never mind. Don't think about it. Auntie Chen is very fond of you.'

Xiao Mei stopped crying. She hated Mrs Chen. She was a stupid, dressed up woman. But all she said to Ba was, 'Brother Tong is too fat. He can hardly run. He's like a great fat panda.' Ba smiled and agreed. Tong was like a great fat panda, come to think of it. He had a good heart though.

'Yes,' said Xiao Mei, remembering Tong's sweaty, tear-stained face. 'He's a great fat panda, but he's OK.'

24.

Melons

Nainai lay on her back on her bed, eyes open, looking up at the ceiling. Despite the midday heat she had pulled a cotton quilt right up to her neck. Her feet in their white cotton socks stuck out from under the quilt. Her arms were by her side. I might as well be in my coffin, she thought. She closed her eyes to see what it might feel like to be dead. They'll all be sorry, when they see I've passed away. She chuckled. That would teach them.

Earlier that day, Ba had staggered home with five large water-melons, given to him, he said, by an old friend. He cut one of them open and he and Xiao Mei sat in a shady part of the courtyard eating wedges of the bright red juicy flesh, spitting out the black seeds on to the ground in front of them. From her bed Nainai could hear the spitting and slurping.

As she dozed, a picture came into her mind, something from long, long ago, something her own grandmother had told her when she couldn't have been more than four or five years old. The two of them were sitting in their yard and, like now, it was the height of summer. The men were out in the fields, her mother was in the kitchen. She and grandmother were eating wedges of musk melon and spitting the seeds into a bowl.

These would be dried and saved for later. Grandmother was a big, strong woman with a lined, weather-beaten face and there was nothing she loved better than eating melon and telling stories. And so she began:

'Way over there, not in the next village, or the next village, or the next village, but in the one after that, lived a family by the name of Yuan. Now, one of these Yuan people told me that when he was a boy, two large huangshulang appeared in their yard completely out of nowhere. They were enormous – quite as big as cats. They settled in under a haystack and each evening they would come out and chase each other round and round the yard. Some people try to drive huangshulang away or even kill them, and indeed the family were somewhat alarmed by the presence of these two strange residents, but they decided that it was better to do nothing and just accept that they were there. Because as everyone knows, it will not do to upset a huangshulang. However, once the huangshulang had settled down and everyone had become used to their presence, strange things began to happen.

'Just like us, the Yuan family owned a small plot of land on which they planted musk melons. The crop was poor and each year they would harvest no more than a dozen or so. That season, Old Yuan went out into the field with his melon basket. As usual, there were only a few melons worth harvesting. Many were rotten and worm eaten. Old Yuan sighed. He collected just five melons in his basket, left a few unripe ones to be harvested the following week, and trudged back to the village.

'The next day he went back to the same field with his

hoe, intending to get rid of the weeds and any worms intent on attacking the few remaining unripe melons. But when he got there, he found, to his amazement, that the melons were already ripe, and not only ripe but perfect and unblemished. How could the melons have ripened in just one day? He picked the beautiful melons, just five of them, and in delight put them in his basket and ran back home to show his wife. Now all the melons had been harvested. The next day he would return to dig the plot of land over.

'Back he went the next morning and saw, to his astonishment, that the plot was completely covered with strong, healthy melon plants, each bearing a ripe, perfectly unblemished musk melon. Throwing down his hoe, Yuan tore back home to tell his wife. She dropped what she was doing and together the two of them rushed back to the melon plot. His wife gazed in wonder on the melons. There must have been at least fifty of them. She turned to her husband and said:

"Our luck changed once the huangshulang came to live with us. Surely we have been visited by the Gods of Wealth in huangshulang form."

'Husband and wife looked at each other, scarcely able to believe their good fortune. Quick as they could they rushed back home, lit incense and kowtowed before their shrine. Their good luck continued for many years.

'But one night, the two huangshulang came out from under the haystack, sniffed the air, ran across the yard and out into the fields. They were never seen again. But the Yuan family continued to prosper. Their protection of the huangshulang for so many years had ensured that their lives would always be happy and peaceful and that their melon crop would be the best in the village.'

Nainai smiled to herself and then felt a little sad. It was all so long ago. Now she was a grandmother, with a grand-daughter who at this very moment was sitting on the step eating water melon. But Xiao Mei wasn't interested in those old stories. What did she call them? Superstition. Nainai lay dozing on her bed, trying to work it all out. Where would all the birds and animals go once the hutong was destroyed? Their own huangshulang under the pile of boxes? The world was being turned upside down and surely there would be retribution. But what exactly? She fell asleep, dreaming of hurricanes, droughts and dust-storms, and a giant golden huangshulang that stood on its hind legs, flashing its ruby-red eyes.

~

When Ma came back later that day she saw the four enormous water-melons that Ba had deposited on the kitchen floor. Why did he always go over the top with everything? She liked water-melon as much as the next person but there was a limit. There they were, taking up space, and if they weren't eaten soon they would start to rot.

She sighed, but when Ba came in looking as pleased as anything with his latest acquisition, she said nothing. There were some things that weren't worth arguing over and melons were one of them. And when Ba cut her a slice she thanked him and went outside with it and sat dreamily on the step for a few minutes slurping the sweet red juice and spitting the black seeds out on to the ground before it was time to return to the kitchen and prepare their evening meal.

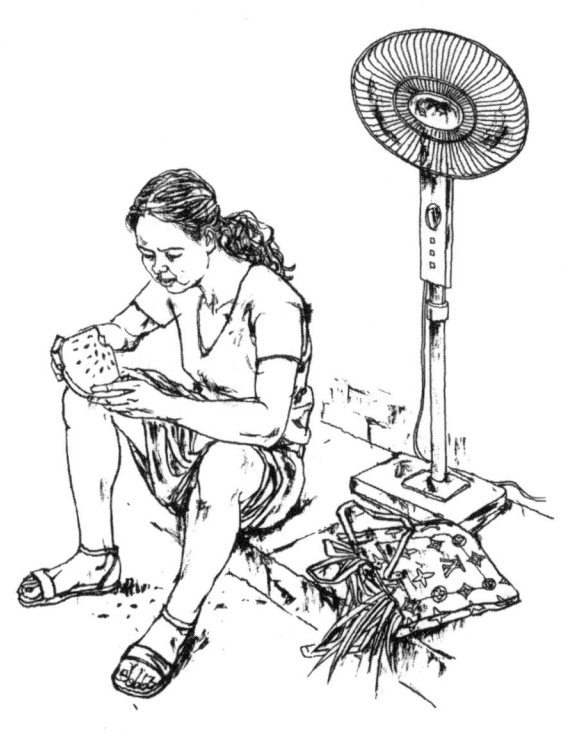

25.

The Bird's Nest and the Chickens

Mouse-wolf put his paw into the bag and felt for the little jade goddess. For a moment he thought he must have dropped it for he seemed to be holding nothing more than air. It was some hours after midnight and raining hard and he and Little Yellow were sitting behind a shoe shop, concealed in a small cardboard box. Other boxes were stacked up in a corner nearby.

When he looked again more carefully he could see that the little jade was there after all, winking with a feeble blue glow, as if covered in a thick film of dirt that prevented its inner light from shining through more brightly. He held the figure in his paw and licked it all over. The goddess regained her spirit for a few seconds but then seemed to lose energy, like the light bulb of a small torch gradually running out of battery. He looked anxiously at the little figure, then put it back in the bag. Little Yellow was lying next to him asleep.

An engine revved. A truck backed slowly into the yard.

'Don't let them get too wet!' shouted a man standing on the back of the truck.

Then another voice: 'What's the hurry? Just leave the stuff there till the rain stops!'

'And the truck?' cried the first man. 'What about the truck? We've only got it till dawn. Just get the cardboard up here as quick as you can. But try to keep it dry.'

A man was standing right next to the box in which the two huangshulang were concealed. Mouse-wolf could feel the man's leg pressing against him. The man on the truck leapt down and begun chucking the cardboard onto the truck. Before either Mouse-wolf or Little Yellow could escape they felt their box being lifted up and swung through the air. It landed at the back of the truck, tilted over, and settled at an angle. The huangshulang slid helplessly into a corner.

'Last box!' shouted one of the men. 'Quick, get the tarpaulin over!'

Again, the sound of a great wind as a tarpaulin descended over the back of the truck. Silence for a moment before it revved its engine and inched its way out of the yard. The rain drummed down, drowning out all other sounds, leaving the huangshulang utterly disorientated as to where they were going. There was nothing they could do, except huddle together.

Out of habit, Mouse-wolf put his paw to the bag to feel the jade through the cloth. It was there, but he did not dare take it out to see whether it was still glowing or whether its energy had run down completely.

The truck bumped along, stopping and starting at traffic lights, swinging round corners, spewing out exhaust fumes into the air and up under the tarpaulin. The box rocked from side to side with every bump. The tarpaulin flapped noisily in the wind.

And then, one corner flapped loose and the warm night air rushed in. Mouse-wolf saw an opportunity.

'Quick,' he said, 'roll this way!' He and Little Yellow rocked backwards and forwards till the box slipped, teetered on the tailgate of the truck, toppled off and fell – fortunately for them – right into the low hedge planted along the central reservation of a dual carriageway.

Shaken to the bone, they peered out of the top of the box. The sky had lightened. The rain had stopped. The sun was rising. Cars, headlights still on, whizzed past. They crept out of the box, into the low hedge and looked out across the other side. Cars sped past in the opposite direction, red taillights glowing in the dim dawn light.

Mouse-wolf looked across the road to try to get his bearings. One thing was clear, they were in strange territory. No alleyways, no little shops, no people. Just a huge sky and open space and sticks of trees planted at regular intervals along the road. And looming up in the twilight, a massive circular structure made up of criss-crossing beams of steel, like a vast untidy bird's nest dropped into the human world by a mischievous crow.

'What's that?' said Little Yellow, gazing at it.

Mouse-wolf felt uneasy.

'I've no idea.'

They were stranded. Even if they could cross the road without getting run over, the world on the other side with its wide-open light-filled spaces was no place for a huangshulang. Who knew what fresh dangers lay under the vast dome of that pale-blue empty sky? They sat down and began to groom themselves. That, at least, was something they still had control over. Little Yellow took her damaged tail in her paws and licked it. Mouse-wolf scratched his haunches. The sun was now fully up. The low hedge provided little shade.

Approaching them from the right, walking alongside the central reservation, came a woman pushing a small handcart and carrying a long-handled dustpan and brush. She was wearing a bright orange vest and old leather gloves. A blue headscarf was tied under her chin. Across her nose and mouth was a white cotton mask. From time to time she would stoop to sweep up litter: empty crisp packets, aluminium cans, the butts of cigarettes. Sometimes she would stop and beat the hedge with her brush to release whatever had become trapped in its scrubby foliage. She swept the litter into the pan and tipped it into the handcart. Occasionally she would pick something up, look at it, and shove it into her pocket. Sweep, beat, sweep, beat, sweep, beat. Slowly and methodically she made her way down the road, oblivious to the cars speeding past.

Immediately, the huangshulang stood still, whiskers quivering, ears twitching. The narrow hedge would provide little or no protection.

Sweep, beat, sweep, beat. The woman was nearly upon them.

'Now!' cried Mouse-wolf. Without thinking, without looking to left or right and closely followed by Little Yellow, he dashed into the stream of traffic and ran for his life.

The woman stopped sweeping. She saw the two slim shapes darting between the cars. Poor things, she thought. Then she picked up her brush and moved on. Sweep, beat, sweep, beat all the way along the highway until she was just a small orange speck on the horizon.

~

The car swerved and screeched to a halt. The car behind crashed into it. The occupants jumped out, gesticulating and shouting at each other. Vehicles travelling in the opposite direction slowed down, the drivers sticking their heads out of their windows to take a better look at the chaotic scene. A cacophony of horns swept down the line of angry cars, taxis and trucks.

Oblivious to the commotion they had caused, Mouse-wolf and Little Yellow reached the other side of the highway and cowered in a shallow ditch, a whisker's breadth away from death.

There was no shade, not a blade of grass to shelter them from the heat of the sun hanging high in the pale yellow sky. The sticks of trees planted at wide intervals sprouted only a few useless leaves. The two huangshulang scrabbled at the dry earth, hollowing out a small burrow to hide in while they waited for some sign as to what to do next. When the depression in the earth was deep enough they curled themselves up and fell half-asleep, senses alert to any dangerous sounds or smells.

It was a strange place they found themselves in, so silent, light and open, not like the narrow hutongs they had come from with their shady corners and familiar noises. On the far side of the empty wasteland rose a great white metal wall on which were painted five linked circles of different colours. The writing below the circles – a message for the human world - announced: 'One World One Dream'. To one side of the white wall was the huge tangled pile of steel struts as tall as a large building and round like a flattened doughnut. Workmen in hard hats scurried around beneath, pushing wheelbarrows or pulling on pulleys. Faint banging noises of metal on metal resounded through the hot air.

All day the huangshulang remained motionless in their hideout, their dusty yellow fur providing camouflage against the powdery yellow earth. Then, as the sun set below the horizon in a huge red orb, Mouse-wolf raised his head and sniffed the cooling air. Little Yellow stretched her back and yawned. They were both starving.

Once again Mouse-wolf raised a paw to his neck to feel for the little red bag and the jade inside. For a moment he thought he had lost it. The bag seemed to have shrunk and become embedded in the matted fur under his chin. He took out the figure, a pale greyish little lump in his paw, barely glowing at all. For a moment, in his exhausted state, he couldn't remember why he had it and what he was supposed to do with it. And then, when he did remember, it was accompanied by the now familiar tremor of anxiety.

The jade in the bag around his neck was beginning to feel more like a nagging irritation, a pimple under his skin, than a precious jade goddess. It had brought nothing but trouble. Little Yellow peered at it.

'It's still glowing,' she said. 'Just a very little. It's still alive.'

'And so are we,' murmured Mouse-wolf, returning the Guanyin to the bag, 'but only just.'

As the twilight faded, the huangshulang left their shallow hiding place and set out in search of food. Little Yellow caught a grasshopper singing in a clump of dirty grass. Mouse-wolf explored the contents of a paper bag that had a large yellow M against a red background printed cheerfully on one side. Inside he found some minced meat sandwiched between two halves of a soggy bread roll. A crescent-shaped bite had been taken out of the side of the roll and then someone, for some reason, had thrown the whole thing away. The bag was sticky inside. Mouse-wolf ate the roll and licked the sweet red gooey paste off the bag. It wasn't an ideal meal but it would do for the moment.

The two huangshulang looked around them.

'Where now?' said Little Yellow, glancing back over her shoulder. Behind them was the highway with its endless stream of traffic.

Mouse-wolf looked ahead. Beyond them and to their right was the huge pile of metal rods. To the left, the white wall with its curious linked rings. Ahead was wide-open space and beyond, far in the distance, were clumps of sheltering trees, black against the fading sky.

'We'll make for the trees. Over there.'

They set out, keeping as close as possible to the ground, stopping now and then to smell the humid air, darting between loose masonry and clumps of grass. There had once been houses here, it seemed.

And then, a different smell, of wood smoke. The huangshulang froze. Mouse-wolf sat up on his haunches to take a look, Little Yellow crouching by his side. Just ahead loomed two large tents, lit from within. Shadows moved inside. Music drifted from a radio, men shouted.

Cautiously, the huangshulang skirted the tents. On the one hand it felt safer keeping close to the canvas walls rather than being exposed to danger on open land. But on the other, there was the risk of being seen by the humans.

But now came a rank odour, the smell of dog, and then the dog itself, a skinny beast tethered to a stake not far from the entrance of one of the tents. As they approached, the dog set up a furious barking, pawing at the ground and straining to free itself. A shoe was flung from inside the tent, hitting the dog on the side of its head. It whimpered for a moment, then continued its frenzied barking. The huangshulang flattened themselves against the side of the tent, scarcely daring to breathe. The dog knew they were there and was beside itself with rage that it couldn't get at them. A man emerged from the tent, bowl of noodles in one hand, chopsticks in the other. He aimed a kick at the dog and yelled at it to 'stop that filthy noise'. The dog whined and yelped. The man gave it another kick for good measure and went back into the tent. The dog lay down with its nose between its paws, whimpering with pain and frustration.

With the dog silenced, keeping as low as they could to the ground, the huangshulang raced past the tents and out into the open space. The clumps of trees were only a field's length away.

Exhausted and fearful, Little Yellow trailed behind Mouse-wolf. Mouse-wolf felt no better. He just wanted to disappear into a safe place and sleep forever.

The deafening barking of the dog was still ringing in their ears, but now came another sound. The two huangshulang stood still, straining to listen.

'Sounds like a huge swarm of insects.' Mouse-wolf was puzzled.

Little Yellow shook her head. 'No, listen. Don't you recognise it?'

Of course. Mouse-wolf caught his breath as a gust of warm air floated the familiar, high-pitched twittering in their direction.

In the darkness they could just make out a moving black mass, an oil slick of rodents, passing across the surface of the earth and then disappearing out of sight. Little Yellow put her paws in front of her eyes. Mouse-wolf shivered. They said nothing to each other and moved on.

At last, they reached the far side where they found, concealed within the clumps of trees, two low houses and next to these a vegetable patch with neat rows of carrots, beans and onions. Here were many places they could hide, amongst the vegetation, the trees or the walls of the houses.

Then, as they skirted the wall of one of them, they came across another welcome sight: a wire-netting cage containing two chickens and in the corner of the cage a further surprise - two large eggs. The chickens were restless, crooning anxiously to each other.

There was only one thing to do, burrow beneath the cage as fast as possible, gnaw through the wooden base and retrieve the eggs. Mouse-wolf hesitated. There had been no chickens in the park in Tiantan where he'd grown up.

'It's not difficult!' said Little Yellow, 'but we'll have to work fast.' The chickens were becoming agitated and it was only a matter of time before their clucks and shrieks attracted the attention of the houses. Fortunately the earth was soft.

Mouse-wolf stood guard while Little Yellow burrowed a tunnel. The wooden base was half rotten and easy to gnaw through. The eggs dropped through the hole, and Little Yellow rolled them one by one out through the tunnel. The chickens clucked and beat their wings in outrage.

'Quick,' said Mouse-wolf, 'before they wake up.'

But nothing stirred in the house. The huangshulang rolled the eggs into the bushes. Then they bit the top off each egg and sucked out the delicious contents. It was the first proper meal they had had for a very long time.

The next morning they were woken by a commotion of voices. A woman was lifting up the cage and a man inspecting the base was saying:

'Huangshulang! Nothing else would have done this except those evil huangshulang!'

But the woman shrieked:

'I told you to reinforce the base! Didn't I tell you it was rotten? But would you listen?'

The man dropped the cage. The chickens squawked in indignation.

'What are you making so much noise about? It's only two eggs!.'

'Only two eggs, only two eggs?' The woman pushed the man. 'You think we can afford to lose two good eggs?'

The man grabbed her upraised hand.

'Do that once again and I'll hit you well and good!'

The woman let fly a torrent of angry words. Before long the two of them had wrestled each other to the ground. The chickens shrieked in alarm.

The huangshulang watched the scene from their hiding place in the bushes. The ways of humans were very puzzling.

The man and the woman picked themselves up, dusted down their clothes and went back inside the house. The chickens settled, and soon all was quiet.

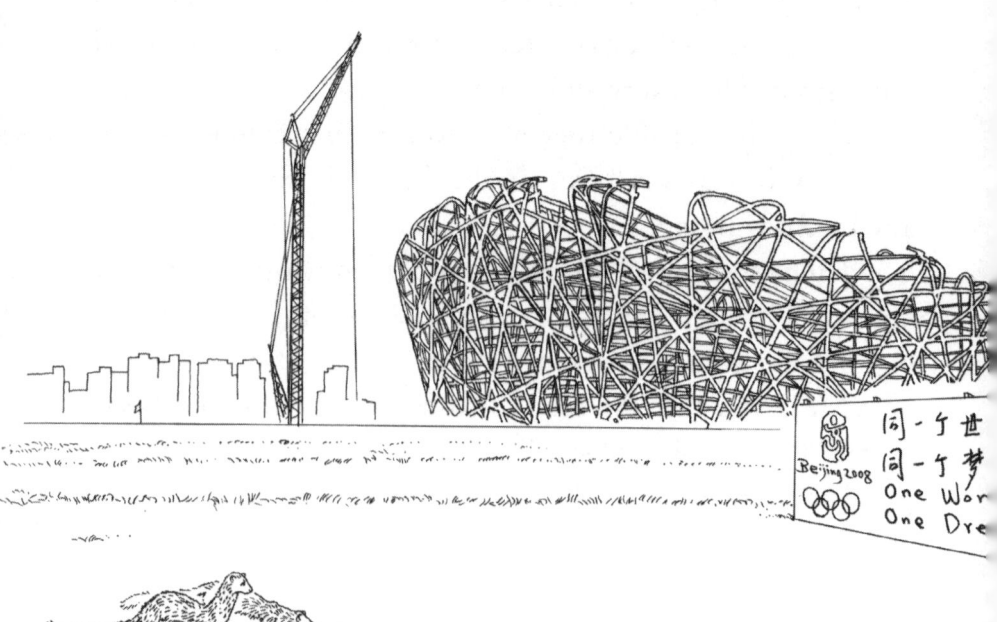

26.

Foreigners

Xiao Mei was worried. She and Stone were sitting on the stone step in the yard of his house. The little white dog lay at their feet.

'What are you going to do? What if you don't find your uncle?'

Stone bent forward, picked up a pebble and scraped it along the ground.

'I've just got to find him.'

'But what if you don't?'

Stone looked grim. 'Then I'll go and look for work by myself. On a building site.'

Xiao Mei gave him a sideways glance. He was so small and skinny. She couldn't imagine him heaving bricks or mixing concrete. As if reading her thoughts he said:

'After all, I worked at that brick factory. I carried bricks all day at that place.'

He held out his arm.

'Look, I've got real muscles.'

Xiao Mei put her hand on his thin arm and felt a small movement under the dusty skin. She looked doubtful. Stone stared at her hand. How soft and clean and white it was, despite the little black crescents under her nails.

'You wash your hands every day,' he said.

Xiao Mei laughed, glanced at her nails, and quickly withdrew her hand. Stone changed the subject.

'There was a man who offered me money the other day. Twenty kuai. I didn't take it, though. But I know I can make money if I try hard.'

'Why didn't you take it?'

Stone looked at his feet.

'Because ...because it was a bad deal. I can't be bought off just like that.'

Xiao Mei looked at Stone with respect. He was talking like a grown up.

'No, you couldn't,' she said. Then thinking of what she'd overheard Ba say to Old Wang, she went on, 'A man has his own value after all.'

'Yes,' said Stone, sticking out his chest. 'That's exactly what I think. A man has his own value.'

He scratched the little white dog's head. Xiao Mei picked up the red monkey lying next to it. She held it up, jiggling its long limbs. The monkey grinned.

'And what are you so happy about?' she said to the monkey, dangling its long legs over the little dog, who snapped at it in irritation. Stone laughed.

The little dog pricked up its ears, froze for a moment, barked, stood up and ran to the entrance of the courtyard. Stone and Xiao Mei looked up. Standing on the threshold were two tall figures, a brown-haired man and a blonde-haired woman. The man was pointing a camera at them. The woman was bending down, hand outstretched towards the dog, who yapped and snarled at her. Over her shoulder she was carrying a long narrow bag.

Stone rushed forward and gathered the dog in his arms, stroking it to quieten it down. The last thing he wanted was to attract attention to him and his hiding place.

Xiao Mei came up behind him. 'Foreigners,' she whispered.

The woman gestured with her arm. 'Can we come in?' she asked with a smile.

The man pointed his camera at the carved wooden eaves over the threshold. He said something to the woman who looked up at the eaves. Stone and Xiao Mei took a step nearer and looked up too. The carved chrysanthemum flowers had once been painted. There were still little flecks of green and red colour. Now the wood was dusty and rotting. They hadn't taken much notice of the carvings before. The woman peered into the courtyard.

'Wow!' she said to the man. She gestured once again, and when neither Xiao Mei nor Stone said anything, she stepped over the threshold into the courtyard. The man followed her. The woman unzipped the bag and took out some metal legs. She opened them up and set them down in the middle of the yard. The man screwed his camera on top of the legs and stood back to survey the scene.

Stone and Xiao Mei stared. The man put his eye to the camera, turned the legs around a little and pointed the camera at them: a girl holding a red cloth monkey, a boy cradling a little white dog, standing in a tumbled down traditional courtyard house. It was a magical picture. He clicked the camera shutter several times. Then he unscrewed the camera, and the woman folded up the tripod and slid it back into the bag.

'Thanks,' the man said. The woman smiled again.

'Here, these are for you!' she said, extracting two lollipops out of her pocket. Stone took them without saying anything and gave one to Xiao Mei.

Just as the man and the woman were leaving, a voice screeched from down the hutong.

'Xiao Mei, Xiao Mei!'

Xiao Mei sneaked out behind the foreigners and sidled back homewards. Nainai was standing at their door, looking to left and right. When she saw Xiao Mei she scolded her, saying, 'Where've you been? Who said you could go out?'

The foreigners were behind her. They stopped and the man raised his camera. The woman smiled at Nainai and said, 'Good morning.'

Nainai stopped shouting and stared at them, her mouth a little open.

Then the woman said, 'Is this your house? Have you lived here a long time?'

Nainai mumbled something under her breath.

'May we come in and have a look? These old houses are so beautiful.'

Nainai looked taken aback. Xiao Mei stood next to her. When Nainai didn't say anything, the foreigners said something to each other and the man put his camera down.

'Goodbye and thank you,' the woman said.

'Goodbye,' said the man.

Xiao Mei and Nainai stood at their doorway as the couple walked down the hutong and disappeared from sight. Nainai turned to go back home, Xiao Mei following behind her. Back in the courtyard, Nainai pulled up a stool and sat down. She was muttering something to herself.

'What are you saying, Nainai?' Xiao Mei asked.

A gleam came into Nainai's eyes.

'I never knew I could!'

'Could what, Nainai?'

'That foreign language. I never knew I could understand a foreign language!'

Xiao Mei looked at her in bewilderment. Then it dawned on her.

'That wasn't a foreign language they were speaking! That was our Chinese language!'

But Nainai wasn't having any of it.

'They were foreigners. They were definitely foreigners.'

'Yes, said Xiao Mei. They were foreigners but....'

She stopped. Nainai was looking at her defiantly.

'You think you know everything,' she said as she shuffled back to her room.

Huffing in frustration Xiao Mei climbed the ladder to the roof and lay there thinking about things. Then she remembered the lollipop the foreign woman had given her. She took it out of her pocket, peeled off the wrapping, and licked the sticky red ball. What would happen to the photos the man had taken of them? Who would he show them to? And what would they tell the other foreigners when they got back to their place, wherever that was? She closed her eyes and tried to imagine that foreign country. America? Europe? Cities full of foreigners and tall modern buildings made of glass and steel. What amazing places they must be!

~

A short while after this incident, Xiao Mei found Nainai in the yard, squinting and chuckling at a colour magazine of Ma's. She was staring intently at a colour photograph.

'Look at those strange huangshulang!'

Xiao Mei snatched the magazine away and looked at the picture and the caption beneath. 'Five meerkats standing in a row. Southern Africa.'

'Those aren't huangshulang, they're meerkats and they live in Africa.'

Nainai took the magazine back and contemplated the image.

'Just as I thought,' she said, 'they are foreign huangshulang. That's why they look a bit different.' She stood up. 'Give me my basket, I've got some shopping to do.'

Xiao Mei sighed with impatience. The sooner she grew up and left home the better.

27.

The Fortune-teller

It seemed to Xiao Mei that despite all Ba's reassurances about where this new place was that they would be moving to, nothing was actually happening.

But then, one morning, she woke up to find a pile of empty boxes on the living room floor and Ma sitting on the sofa holding a cushion to her chest. Ba was standing next to her saying, 'For goodness sake, stop worrying. We'll know for certain in a day or two.'

'But is it definite?' Ma's voice rose. 'Just tell me that!'

Ba squatted down next to her.

'Just get on with the packing. It will all come right in the end.'

Ma hurled the cushion to the floor.

'You and your eternal optimism! What if it's so far away I can't get to work? What about Xiao Mei's school?'

Ba stood up and left the room. Since he didn't have any answers there was not a lot of point hanging about. He went out to the courtyard and sat on his stool staring into space. Xiao Mei stood on the step. The sight of the boxes and Ma and Ba's bickering unsettled her. Best to keep away from both of them, she thought. She'd go and see if Stone was still there. He was better company.

~

Though he wouldn't admit it to himself, Ba felt as anxious as Ma. Of course, in a month or so, it would all be sorted out and then life could get back to normal. What he needed right now was a bit of guidance to get through the next few weeks, to know that they were on the right track. And now he came to think about it there might be one person whom he could turn to, who would point him in the right direction. With a bit of luck this person might still be there. He hadn't seen him for a couple of days, but you never knew with people like that. They came and they went.

He stood up, went inside, washed his face and hands, and combed his hair.

'Just going out!' he called.

Ma was busy dragging out some dusty boxes from under the sofa. She coughed and squatted down to catch her breath.

'Do you need any help?' He hovered next to her for a few seconds, but when Ma said nothing, he turned round and left the room.

He walked down the hutong and out onto the main street. He looked in both directions, then crossed the street and walked south. After not more than five minutes he came to a rack of bicycles. Next to the bicycles was a scholar tree and under the tree, squatting on a low stool, sat an old man with a straggly white beard and wearing a blue cloth cap and an old grey jacket buttoned to the top. Lying on the pavement in front of him was a sheet of paper on which had been printed a large circle, half black, half white, with Chinese characters all the way round the edge. On a stool next to him lay a booklet with a dirty-white, dog-eared cover and well-thumbed yellow pages.

Ba hesitated for a moment, but the old man said, 'Sit down, I've been waiting for you.'

Ba took a step back. If the old man knew he was coming then he must know other things as well. It was a good sign. He sat down, and leant forward clasping his hands in front of him.

'Good morning, Master.'

'Give me your hand,' the old man said. Ba held out his hand.

The fortune-teller bent Ba's hand and scrutinised the lines. Then he picked up the booklet and flicked through the pages, muttering to himself. He ran a bony forefinger down a line of characters, then put the booklet back on the stool. Ba observed him closely. He seemed to be calculating something on his fingers, murmuring to himself all the while. Finally he said, 'Hmmm. There's going to be a big event in your family.'

Ba jumped. 'Yes, yes, you're right. We have to move and if you could give us any advice...'

The old man raised his eyebrows.

'About...about any preparations we ought to make. Anything we ought to be careful about. That sort of thing.'

The old man thought for a while, then said, 'You need to prepare yourself well.'

They sat in silence for a few moments. Ba shifted on his

stool. Was that all he was going to say?

'Master...,' he said.

The old man looked hard at Ba as if reading the lines on his face. Then he picked up the booklet again.

'There is an elderly relative at home. The old one's health is poor and getting worse. Take good care of the old one.'

Absolutely right, thought Ba. The old lady had been pretty bad these last few months.

The fortune-teller went on. 'You have something precious at home. And there is an animal as well.'

Ba thought hard. There were mice in the yard sometimes, and of course there were Old Wang's pigeons. And there was the huangshulang. But there wasn't much that was really precious. The fortune-teller continued.

'Guard them well,' he said, adding cryptically, 'clean air and mountains.'

'Thank you,' said Ba, not really understanding, 'thank you.'

'And one more thing. Red is a propitious colour. Always make sure you and your wife wear red.'

'Outer clothes or underwear?' asked Ba quickly. You never knew, it might make a difference.

'Underwear,' said the fortune-teller. He closed his book and stuck his hands in his sleeves. The session was over. He looked at Ba expectantly. Ba felt in his pocket and pulled out his wallet. He took out a five-yuan note. The fortune-teller narrowed his eyes.

'Many people give twenty yuan,' he said. 'But of course, just give what you can afford.'

Ba hesitated. Then he put the five yuan back in the wallet and took out a twenty-yuan note. He put it on the booklet. It was just as well to be on the safe side. The fortune-teller inclined his head. Ba stood up and thanked him but the fortune-teller seemed to have fallen asleep. Ba turned and headed back home, feeling both richer and poorer for the experience.

Ba said nothing about the encounter with the fortune-teller to Ma. But on the way home he stopped off at a small supermarket to buy some nourishing milk powder. Nainai was sitting on her bed in her room. Ba walked in.

'Don't catch a cold sitting there,' he said, adjusting her jacket.

Nainai looked up in surprise. What was he on about now? It was the height of summer and she was doing all she could do keep cool. She shook his hand off impatiently.

'You need to look after yourself,' Ba said. 'Here, I've got something for you.' He put the packet of milk powder on her lap. Nainai looked at it.

'What's this?' she asked suspiciously.

'Milk powder,' Ba said. 'To give you strength!'

Nainai snorted and said nothing. But she took the packet and stuffed it under her pillow.

'I like milk powder,' she said. 'Haven't had milk powder for a long time.'

'Well,' said Ba, grinning. 'I know how to look after you, don't I?'

Then he thought of something. 'Did we ever have anything precious in our family?' Nainai put her head to one side.

'As if people like us ever had anything of value,' she said sharply. 'Now go away and leave me alone. Always bothering me, everyone's always bothering me!'

Over supper, Ba asked the same question. Xiao Mei sat up and looked at Nainai out of the corner of her eye. But Nainai had her head down in her bowl of noodles.

'Are you sure you don't have anything in those old boxes of yours in your room,' he went on.

'Yes,' said Ma. 'It would be worth looking through those boxes and throwing things out before we move.'

Xiao Mei held her breath. Nainai lifted her head from her bowl, her chopsticks in her hand. She mumbled something.

Xiao Mei stood up, her chair scraping on the floor. 'Any more noodles left?' she said, walking over to the stove.

Nainai's voice trailed off. She looked confused again. Ba's face fell. Stupid old woman, always full of nonsense!

That night, as Ma undressed for bed, Ba saw that she was wearing a white bra and flesh-coloured knickers. He hadn't thought much about the colour of her underwear before, not until today. When Ma was in bed, the sheet pulled up over her head, Ba opened the top drawer of the chest of drawers and took a quick look inside. Ma stirred, and he shut the drawer quietly. Then he went to bed too and lay on his back, thinking about what he needed to do the next day.

~

The next morning when Old Wang came out of his door into the courtyard, Ba, who was passing by, mentioned his visit to the fortune-teller and how impressed he was at the old man's perception. Old Wang was sceptical.

'How much did you pay him?'

Ba told him.

'You were ripped off,' said Old Wang. 'Five is the usual rate.'

Ba said nothing.

'Where is this old man?' Old Wang asked after a while.

Ba told him. Then he said he was busy and had to go out on an errand.

Old Wang went back inside. He washed his face and hands, rubbed a towel over his hair, pulled on a clean t-shirt and left. Pausing on the threshold of the house, he saw Ba at the far end of the hutong. He waited till he was out of sight and stepped out.

The fortune-teller was still there, squatting on a stool under the tree next to the bicycle rack. Old Wang squatted down next to him and held out his hand. The old man took it in his, bent it and scrutinised the lines. He ran his bony forefinger down a row of characters in his book. Then he did some calculations on his fingers.

'Hmm,' he said. 'Prepare yourself for a big event.'

Old Wang nodded and was about to say something when the fortune-teller held up a hand.

'There is more,' he said. 'The imprisoned ones must find their freedom. All will then be well.'

The old man closed his eyes. Was that all he was going to say? But he went on:

'The high ground is propitious. The clean air is cleansing.'

Then he stuck his hands into his sleeves. The session was at an end. Old Wang felt unsettled. What did it all mean? He took out a five-yuan note and handed it to the fortune-teller. The old man narrowed his eyes.

'Most people give me twenty,' he said. 'But of course just give me what you can afford.'

Old Wang hesitated. He pulled out a handful of notes. He took one and stuffed the rest back in his pocket. He handed the note to the old man. The fortune-teller said nothing but inclined his head. Old Wang stood up, hesitated for a moment and then walked slowly back home, pondering the old man's words. If Ba asked, he would say nothing about his visit.

~

But Ba had his own concerns. He had crossed the main road and was walking along a busy thoroughfare lined with little shops and stalls. The shop he was standing at had clothes displayed on an outside rack. By the door, suspended from a series of linked clothes hangers, were underpants of all shapes and sizes, white, pale blue, beige, yellow and pink. Some of them were very large and some were minimal. They couldn't be very comfortable to wear, Ba thought. Mrs Chen's plump backside floated unbidden into his mind but he swiped the thought away. A young shop assistant, hair scraped back in a tight ponytail, came out.

'What are you looking for?' she said, leaning against the doorpost.

Ba hesitated. 'Do you have any of these in red?'

'Is it someone's special year?' She turned her head and shouted into the interior.

'Customer's looking for red knickers. What have we got?'

'Nothing too fancy,' Ba added. 'Just plain red.'

He stepped into the shop. Clothes were everywhere, piled up on the counter and on the shelves that lined the walls. A young man appeared from behind the counter, a large plastic bag in his arms. 'Take a look through these,' he said. 'Red ones, all of them.'

Ba took the bag and pulled out a pair. They were nothing but lace. He didn't think Ma would like them. The second pair was printed with five coloured rings, all linked to each other and the motto 'One World One Dream'. He thought for a moment. The fortune-teller hadn't said anything about writing or pictures so it was probably best to be on the safe side and reject them. The third pair was scarlet, high-waisted and made of cotton. He turned them over. They were completely plain both back and front, apart from a little red heart embroidered on the waistband.

'Five kuai,' said the young man.

'Three,' said Ba.

The young man thought for a moment. Ba had three kuai ready in his hand.

'All right,' he said. He'd make a profit anyway. Back home he'd bought them for only a few cents.

Ba stuck the red knickers in his pocket. As he turned to leave, he noticed a pair of red socks on the shelf. He would take those for himself as well.

When he got home, Ma was kneeling on the floor, packing winter clothes into boxes. He presented her with the red knickers.

'Especially for you,' he said. 'You need something more colourful.'

Ma took the underpants, then looked up at Ba. What was he up to now? But all she said as she inspected the label was 'the quality isn't bad. 100% cotton, it says.'

Ba smiled. At least she hadn't said that she didn't like them.

28.

Ghosts

The encounter with the man in the brown suit two days before had left Stone feeling uneasy. The man hadn't actually done anything bad, only offered him money. But not even fifty yuan would have made him part with the dog. What did he want the dog for? For company? Or would he have sold it at a profit to someone else? Whatever it was, the man had unnerved him and scared the dog as well.

He squatted in a shady corner of the courtyard, thinking. Though Xiao Mei brought him food most days, he couldn't stay here forever. He picked up a little twig and drew a circle in the dust at his feet. Then he drew a line coming out of the circle. That was the village and that was him leaving the village. He made the line longer and drew a little rectangle on the line. That was him on the bus with his uncle. Then he drew a much bigger circle. That was the city. The line stopped at a square on the edge of the circle. That was him getting off the bus at the bus station. He scribbled a lot of crisscrossing lines in the circle and drew a wobbly line from the bus station to somewhere near the middle of the circle. He marked the spot with a cross. That was where he was now. Then he drew two parallel lines. That was the hutong. He drew a rectangle on one side and another rectangle on the other. He marked one rectangle with a cross. That was the house where he was now. The other rectangle was Xiao Mei's house. Then, after a moment's thought, he drew another smaller cross next to his cross. That was the little white dog.

He sat back on his heels. Then he drew some more, smaller rectangles. A pair of shorts. A pair of underpants. Two t-shirts (the white one he was wearing and a red one). A square with two little squares inside to indicate a plastic bag containing a small towel and a sliver of soap. That was everything he had. And the bottle of water and packet of instant noodles that Xiao Mei had brought him. And, of course, the little white dog.

The cicadas were shrilling at top volume, a rhythmic pulsating drone that gave him a headache. It was too hot to think straight. He couldn't make any decisions while the sun beat down. He would wait till evening. Followed by the dog, he went inside, lay down and slept.

The sun was low in the sky when he woke up. The sleep and the cooler air had cleared his head and he knew what he needed to do. He summarised what he knew about his uncle. Number one, he was - possibly - his uncle. Number two, he was quite old, about forty. Number three, he spoke in the local dialect. Number four, he liked eating garlic. Number five, he had a thick neck. Number six, he worked on building sites, or at least he said he did. He put to the back of his mind the seventh thing: that his uncle might have deliberately abandoned him.

Stone considered. It wasn't much to go on but it was

something. He would set out and go to as many building sites as possible. He looked at the marks on the dusty ground, then drew another line, from where he was now to the outer edge of the circle.

But first he needed to eat. He tore open the packet of instant noodles, spread the packaging out on the ground and broke the brick of noodles onto it. Then he ripped the sachet of chilli chicken seasoning with his teeth and sprinkled the contents on top. Next, he twisted the top off the bottle of water and set the bottle down next to the noodles. The little dog stood up and sniffed the packet. Stone pushed the dog away with one hand, and with the other scooped up some of the noodles and placed them on the ground a little way away. Then he put the dog down. The dog sniffed the noodles carefully and began to eat.

He sat down and surveyed his meal. It wasn't too bad, though it would have been even better if he'd had hot water to add to the noodles to make a soup. When he had finished eating and drinking, he gave the packet to the little dog to lick and poured some of the water into a broken bowl. The dog lapped the water with enthusiasm. When the dog had finished he tied the pink string round its neck. He pulled at the string, but the dog sat down on its haunches and refused to budge. So Stone picked it up and stuck it under his arm, and in this way they made their way together down the hutong and out into the city, walking west to follow the setting sun.

When he came to the main road he turned to look back, noting any landmarks that would help him find the hutong when he returned. Across the street were several trees and a rack of bicycles. At the far end of the road was a many-storeyed building with illuminated blue characters on top announcing the name of a hotel. The street-lights were on now. Glowing red lanterns hung outside restaurants. People jostled each other on the pavement in their hurry to get home. Bicycles weaved in and out through the slowly moving cars, taxis and buses. The sky was suffused with yellow on the horizon, the colour merging upwards into an intense velvety blue.

No one took any notice of him as he walked, the dog now trotting along beside him. Every now and then he looked back to make sure he could still see the blue lights of the hotel. But all too soon they disappeared from view. He would need to keep to the straight main roads. If he diverted into the mass of alleyways he would get lost.

Was it because it was cooler, or because his stomach was half full, or because of the cheerful lights of the shops and restaurants, or because he was walking along the street with everyone else, that he felt almost happy? A group of boys, not much older than he was, ran past him, laughing, one pausing to pat the dog, before speeding off.

He passed a little shop selling meat buns that were displayed on a tray on the counter. A young waitress in a pink apron who was standing on the step outside smiled at him and waved. 'Cute!' she called out.

Stone gave a broad grin. He caught sight of himself in the reflection of a window. Hair sticking up, one bright eye, goofy smile, baggy white t-shirt and a little white dog jumping up and pawing at his legs. He put his hand to his head to smooth down his hair. It didn't make much difference. The waitress beckoned to him, looked over her shoulder, and then picked out a bun from the tray.

'Here,' she said with a giggle. Stone hesitated, but she thrust it into his hand. A man's voice called from inside and she quickly turned and went back in. Stone couldn't believe his luck. The bun was almost as big as his palm. He bit into the soft white dough and a delicious meaty juice oozed out and dribbled down his chin. He broke off a small piece and threw it down for the dog, who leapt up and snapped it out of his hand. Life was not bad after all.

He'd been walking for a while when he caught sight of two tall cranes with winking red lights silhouetted against the sky. As he approached, he saw that along one side of the road was a high brick wall that went all the way around a building site. Through a gap in the wall he saw an unfinished building several storeys high, just a shell of concrete at this stage. On the far side of the site, near the wall, were four large tents. Shelves had been fixed to this part of the wall. As Stone got nearer, he saw what they were for. The workmen kept their mugs and bowls there. Men were squatting on the ground by the tents, eating their evening meal.

Picking up the dog, Stone stood still and watched, and listened to the noise of food being slurped. The men weren't talking much, too tired after a day's work to do much more than concentrate on their food. Where had they come from? The accent was unfamiliar. They might have been a group of migrants from faraway Sichuan. His uncle was unlikely to be with them. Nevertheless, he drew a little nearer and then, tired after walking, squatted down in the shadow of one of the tents. The dog lay down quietly next to him, its nose on its paws. Some of the men had finished eating and were rinsing out their bowls in a basin of water. Others were lighting up cigarettes. A group of four men were sitting round a low table, playing cards.

A voice attracted Stone's attention. It was coming from inside the tent, right behind him. In fact, the man talking was leaning against the canvas and was so close that he could almost have touched Stone's arm. Stone stiffened and listened. Another voice spoke and the first man replied.

'If we don't get another delivery soon, we won't be able to get moving tomorrow.'

'You're right,' said the second man. 'I heard there's a hold up on the expressway. The traffic's backed up for at least ten kilometres. And our trucks are right in the middle of it.'

'Nothing to be done about it,' said the first man, 'nothing to be done. Have another drink.' He gave a great yawn that Stone could hear clearly through the canvas wall. There was the sound of tops being prised off bottles of beer. Stone was less interested in what they were saying than in the sound of their voices. These two men, he was sure, came from Hebei, his province.

There was a movement within the tent and one of the men emerged. Stone put his hand on the dog and held his breath. The man hadn't seen them and was lurching to the other side of the tent. Stone could hear a zip being pulled down, then the hiss of a watery stream, and then the zip again. And a warm smell, like boiled cabbage.

But instead of going back inside, the man walked round to the back and squatted down in the shadow of the tent wall. He hadn't spotted Stone, just a couple of metres away. The man was taking something out of his pocket. It was a wad of banknotes, which he counted under his breath, ten, twenty, fifty, a hundred, a hundred and fifty. He was just about to put them back when he glanced to his left. There was a sharp intake of breath and the man leapt up, clutching the notes to his chest. Stone remained motionless, his hand across the dog's muzzle.

'Who's there?' the man called in a low voice.

There was no reply. Stone could hear his breath. The dog moved its head and its eyes glowed green. It gave a low growl from the back of its throat. The man stood rooted to the spot, then turned and stumbled back to the tent.

'What's the matter?' Stone heard the other man say. For a while there was no reply, just heavy breathing. Then a strangled voice said, 'Ghost! Round the back of the tent!'

His friend snorted. 'You've been drinking too much.'

But the man insisted, 'Huge green eyes, staring at me!'

'Impossible!' the other man retorted. 'There aren't ghosts in the city anymore!'

'....and massive' the man squealed, ' like a great sack of sweet potatoes, all lumpy and shapeless!'

'Well,' said his companion, 'best thing is if we go out

together and have a look.'

'No way I'm going out.' The squealer was adamant. 'I'm not going anywhere, not if there are ghosts around.'

For a while there was silence. Then the pop of another bottle being opened. Stone picked the dog up, his hand still over its muzzle and stood up. He was just about to move away from the tent, when something caught his attention. At his feet, just visible in the darkness, lay two bank notes, twenty kuai and ten kuai. He picked them up, stuck them in his shorts pocket and crept away as quietly as he could.

When he was at a safe distance, he turned to look back. The second man was standing by the tent looking around. Then he went back inside. After a little while the first man came out and walked round the back of the tent. Stone saw him squatting down and feeling around with his hands. Then he stood up and looked down at the ground. He squatted down once more, and once again felt the ground. Then he stood up and walked slowly back to the tent. After that neither man came out and all was quiet.

As Stone left the building site, he reckoned that it was unlikely that the two men would have known his uncle. He felt the notes in his pocket. He would not push his luck further by talking to them. First, the big meat bun and now the money. Today had been a lucky day.

He walked towards the gap in the wall and stepped out onto the pavement. Then he sat down on his heels and pulled out the two bank notes, one blue, one brown and both well used. He hadn't had so much money for a very long time. It was more than the man in the brown suit had offered him for the dog.

He thought of the labourer scratching around on the ground. He was probably thinking the ghost had stolen his money. But no, there weren't any ghosts in the city as far as he knew. Perhaps the bright lights and the traffic had driven them away.

He thought he'd seen a ghost in the village once, one pitch-black moonless night. He'd gone out to look at their new-born calf and had seen the woman creeping along the wall, hours after she'd been cut down from the rafters and laid out on their neighbour's bed. He'd banged the bucket he was carrying and the woman had disappeared.

He remembered the four faded red characters that had been painted on a wall at the order of the village head years before, about people being in control, not spirits and ghosts. But that was back then in the countryside and now he was in the city. Where had all the ghosts gone? Even the ghosts had had to move. He had a vision of a multitude of pale vaporous forms streaming out of the city, hundreds and thousands of them, never able to return to a city now covered in concrete.

~

Now that he had money and a full stomach the night ahead was his. He could even get a bus back if he ventured too far. Emboldened by this idea, he stood up and looked down the street. A bus was pulling up at a stop a little way ahead. Forgetting that dogs weren't allowed on buses, he followed the waiting passengers on board, the dog tucked under his arm. No one said anything and the doors closed. When he bought his ticket from the conductor he made sure that the dog was out of sight on the floor. She stared at his one eye, but said nothing.

The bus pulled out into the road. Stone leant by an open window looking out, the warm night air blowing in his face, the dog sleeping between his feet. He didn't know where the bus was going but he would ride for a few stops and then catch the same bus back. And along the way he might catch sight of a fat-necked man from Hebei who smelt of garlic.

29.

Rats

Mouse-wolf and Little Yellow were reluctant to leave the plot of land with the vegetable garden and the chickens. But the man, urged on by his wife, had replaced the base of the cage, sealing the edges with strips of metal. There was no way now that they would be able to gnaw through the wood and extract any more eggs. The chickens had become particularly nervous and would shriek at the slightest movement. The man and the woman knew that there were huangshulang nearby and had come out with sticks to beat the undergrowth. They had escaped by the skin of their teeth.

Wasn't life always like this, Mouse-wolf thought, always escaping danger, always having to move on, with no control over what was happening to you? It was Fate.

He must have been thinking aloud because Little Yellow interrupted his thoughts and said firmly, 'Nothing to do with Fate at all! We worked together to get those eggs.'

Mouse-wolf looked at Little Yellow with respect. Without her, he might have given up long ago.

'You're right,' he said, scratching his neck. 'I guess we know how to survive.' The city was being turned upside down, but there were still huangshulang in the parks and hutongs.

'And woodpeckers and magpies and bugu birds,' added Little Yellow.

'And cicadas,' said Mouse-wolf.

They stopped to listen. You hardly noticed it because the sound was so constant, but the summer air was alive with the vibrating drone and whine of hundreds of cicadas concealed in the trees.

They sat silent for a while. Little Yellow took her tail in her paws and licked it. Mouse-wolf lay on his back, scratching his stomach. The high-pitched insistent buzzing from the trees was overpowering, arousing an unpleasant memory in his mind: the rat driving those dozens of squeaking, twittering mice ahead of it down the hutong. And the black river of rodents they had seen on the horizon before they reached the house with the chickens. He shivered. Once again the thought came to him that it was a scary world when a huangshulang became afraid of a rat.

He felt for the jade figure in the bag around his neck, took it out and looked at it. The Guanyin's features could barely be seen. Had all that rubbing against his skin as he had trekked across the city worn it smooth so that it no longer glowed? He held it up to the yellow sky, where the sun hung concealed behind a thick layer of cloud, but the jade remained dull and lifeless. He glanced at Little Yellow who was now twisted round and busily grooming her back, and quickly returned the jade to the faded bag.

They were concealed in a small depression in the dusty

ground. Far in the distance, white flashes of light glanced off the criss-crossed struts of the shining metal bird's nest building they had seen before they encountered the chickens. Mouse-wolf felt unsafe. Where they were was too flat and exposed. He scrabbled with his front paws to deepen their hiding place. Little Yellow stopped grooming herself and joined in to help. Then the two of them lay down and dozed uneasily as they waited for night to fall.

A familiar, nauseatingly rancid smell, too close for comfort, startled the huangshulang awake.

Mouse-wolf crouched low, nose quivering, sniffing the air. Little Yellow stiffened, not daring to move, yet at the same time ready to bolt. Something was moving stealthily across the ground towards them.

Mouse-wolf shuddered. He knew what was coming before he saw them - the rat and a dozen of its hangers on. In the distance was the trembling, squeaking horde of mice.

The rat skulked towards them. Mouse-wolf remained motionless. Little Yellow held her breath. When the rat was less than a metre away it stopped and grinned, showing its yellow teeth. The smell from its breath was overpowering. It spat on the ground and, as it had done before at their encounter on the derelict stretch of land, stretched out a claw towards the bag.

Mouse-wolf recoiled and covered the bag with a protective paw. Little Yellow glanced over her shoulder. Other rats were positioned all around them. No one moved. Then, after what seemed to Mouse-wolf an eternity of waiting, the rat uttered a string of strange sounds.

Mouse-wolf sat up erect, his ears pricked to catch the unfamiliar dialect.

'I'll do a deal with you,' the rat seemed to be saying. 'You hand over the bag and I'll forget old grievances, my brothers and sisters you killed and devoured without a thought. No profit to be gained in thinking about the past. The past is dead and buried.'

It paused, lashing its tail from side to side. 'I propose a deal, then we'll be quits and' – it spat the words through its teeth - 'all will be harmonious.'

It took a step nearer, its long whiskers just inches from Mouse-wolf's nose.

Mouse-wolf backed away, Little Yellow keeping close to his side.

'It's a cut-throat world out there,' the rat hissed, 'but if you and me do a deal, you'll go away with a cleared conscience. We could even become 'business' partners.' The rat half turned and winked at his followers.

'It's a win-win situation, as I see it. Now hand over the bag and we'll call it a day and all go home.'

Mouse-wolf felt a tide of exhaustion wash over him. The jade had brought nothing but trouble. They were on an entirely aimless, fruitless journey. The rat could have the jade and then it would all be over and they could go back home to Tiantan. He glanced down at the little red bag. The jade was barely even glowing any more. It was just a useless lump of stone.

Little Yellow put a warning paw over his. 'Don't do anything,' she murmured. 'Just wait. Remember, we can run and jump faster and further than any rat can.'

The rat lashed its tail impatiently, eager for a show down.

More rats appeared out of the darkness to join them, and yet more, surrounding Mouse-wolf and Little Yellow with a tightly packed, foul-smelling mass of heaving grey bodies. The rat came closer.

Mouse-wolf took the bag in his paws and began to lift the string around his neck. Little Yellow looked at him aghast.

'No, she said, 'no!'

Mouse-wolf hesitated for a moment. 'It's no good,' he said, drawing the string over his neck.

'But don't you see,' said Little Yellow urgently, 'even if we give them what they want, how do we know that they'll just go away? We're completely surrounded.'

The rat raised itself up on its hind legs and looked out over the assembled rats, who were becoming restless, scratching and biting at each other, their tails whipping back and forth. Then it lunged at Mouse-wolf.

'Run,' cried Little Yellow, 'run!'

But the rats had closed in and there was no way through. The rat grabbed at the bag, but Mouse-wolf spun round and bit it hard on its shoulder. The enraged rat leapt up, hissing with rage. Mouse-wolf, discovering at that moment that there was no way he was going to give up the jade, held on to the bag as tight as he could. But the rat had summoned reinforcements, and while it pulled hard at the bag, another rat nipped at Mouse-wolf's ankles. Out of the corner of his eye, Mouse-wolf saw yet another preparing to leap.

Little Yellow was nowhere to be seen.

Then something happened. The rat let go of the bag. The rat that had been biting his ankles stood stock-still. All the rats were looking in the same direction. To a clamour of angry squeaks and shrieks, the crowd parted to make way for two rats racing in from outside the pack. They came to a halt, panting, just inches from their leader.

'They're gone!'

'What?' said the rat in alarm, 'who's gone?'

'All of them, every last mouse, every single one of them scattered in all directions,' the two rats from outside flashed their eyes, 'while you were otherwise occupied.'

There was a high-pitched outcry. A dozen or so rats pushed themselves forward to defend their leader. It was going to be all-out war. They fell upon each other, biting and snarling and baring their teeth.

Before any of them remembered the original cause of the strife, Mouse-wolf slipped out unnoticed and ran until the heaving grey mass was far behind him. Then he stopped and looked around. He was near the main road. A truck was parked on the verge, and cowering underneath the truck was Little Yellow. He had never before been so glad to see her. But when he reached her, she said nothing, except 'we've got to leave this place. They'll be back for us once they've finished fighting each other'.

The tail-gate of the truck was open. A long wooden ramp had been propped up at an angle against the edge. On the floor of the truck were a few empty sacks, a bucket, several spades and some long-handled brushes. The two huangshulang peered out from under the chassis. A man with a wheelbarrow was coming towards them. He shouted something, and another man, who was sitting in the driver's seat, stuck his head out of the window and answered. The truck was ready to leave as soon as the wheelbarrow had been wheeled up the ramp and deposited at the back. Once it left the huangshulang would be completely exposed.

Mouse-wolf crawled out, making himself as inconspicuous as possible. Then he saw them. Some way behind the man and the wheelbarrow were five rats. They were standing absolutely still, their noses to the wind, staring in the direction of the truck. Then one crouched down and moved slowly forward. One by one the others dropped down on all fours and followed.

The first rat lashed its tail and at this signal the rats spread out and raced, zigzagging towards the truck.

With not another second to spare, Mouse-wolf and Little Yellow dashed out from their hiding place, round the back of the truck and up the ramp with only seconds to spare.

The man pushed the wheelbarrow up the ramp and, with a twist of his wrists, flipped it over to stop it rolling around. Then he lifted the ramp up off the ground and shoved it inside, narrowly missing the two huangshulang who had concealed themselves under one of the sacks. The man bolted the tailgate shut and climbed into his seat next to the driver. The driver revved the engine, drove forward slowly across the bumpy ground, and then joined the traffic on the busy ring road.

~

'Funny thing just now,' the wheelbarrow man said, lighting a cigarette and blowing a puff of smoke into the air. 'Just before I opened the door to get in I turned round to check that I'd shut the tailgate. You know what I saw? A bunch of rats, five of them I counted.'

'Uh-huh,' said the driver, focusing on the traffic ahead. 'What were they doing?'

The wheelbarrow man went on. 'They weren't doing anything, that was the strange thing. They were just crouching there looking at me, or looking at the truck, as if they wanted a ride.'

The driver stuck his elbow out of the window.

'Vermin,' he said briefly. 'Must have been flushed out of

one of those demolished houses.'

The wheelbarrow man nodded his head but said nothing. The world was a strange place, these days. The truck accelerated, and soon the thought was far from his mind.

~

After a while, the truck turned off the ring road onto a broad highway that led north out of the city and into the hills. The smooth motion of the wheels and the drone of the engine was soothing and soon the huangshulang were asleep, exhausted after their narrow escape. Whatever Little Yellow had said earlier, they really were in the hands of Fate now.

They'd been on the move for about half an hour, when the huangshulang sensed a change in the engine as the truck slowed and turned sharply left. They were thrown against the side, and the sack that had been covering them flew off. The spades slid towards them and it was only by sheer luck that they were not hit. The truck was moving very slowly now. Mouse-wolf stood up on the spade handle and, steadying himself against the side of the truck with his paws, looked over the edge.

The sky was bluer than he'd ever seen it and the air was fresh. They were travelling through a broad valley. The road was lined with fruit trees of every sort, apple and pear and peach. In the distance rose a series of blue-green hills. Soon he was joined by Little Yellow. 'It's even bigger than the park at Tiantan,' he said, gazing around.

The truck stopped. The driver got out and headed into the

orchard where he stood behind a peach tree. The wheelbarrow man got out the other side and leant against the truck. He had a jam jar of luke-warm tea in one hand and a cigarette in the other. Mouse-wolf and Little Yellow dropped down out of sight. After a little while, they could hear the wheelbarrow man's footsteps as he walked away from the truck and into the orchard.

Mouse-wolf stood up, climbed on top of the upturned wheelbarrow and looked out over the other side. Parallel to the road they were on and shielded slightly by a row of slim poplar trees stood a great rust-red archway. From the archway led a long straight path, flanked on either side by huge stone statues: elephants, men in armour, and strange creatures, stretching as far as the eye could see. The huangshulang had never seen such statues before, but the red arch was familiar.

'Look,' said Mouse-wolf with a pang of homesickness, 'it's like the red arches at Tiantan.'

The men returned. The huangshulang hid themselves, the truck revved its engine again and they moved off. After a while, the huangshulang sensed that they were climbing. They must have reached the hills for there was a wonderful smell of fresh pine and fragrant walnut tree leaves. They discovered that if they sat near the tailgate they could see out through a crack in the side.

The truck rounded a bend and stopped on the verge. The men jumped out. By the side of the road a woman and her husband had set up camp. They had pitched a small canvas tent, next to which was a cooking stove. Lined up along the road not far from the tent were four little wooden houses, each about the size of a large cardboard box. The huangshulang pressed their noses to the crack.

The truck's engine was switched off, but outside there was a curious sound, like the drone of a small motor. It was the sound of buzzing bees and the little houses were beehives. The wheelbarrow man and the driver were standing by a table next to the tent, well away from the beehives. On the table were jars of rich, golden-brown honey. The driver unscrewed the lid of one of the jars. The woman passed him a little stick. He stuck it in the honey, and then licked it clean. He nodded his head and picked up two jars. The wheelbarrow man did the same. The woman looked at the truck.

'From Inner Mongolia,' she said, glancing at the number plate.

The driver nodded, paid the woman for the honey, then turning to the wheelbarrow man, said, 'Let's go.'

They climbed back in and set off once more. Mouse-wolf was anxious. They were travelling further and further away from the city. The next time they stopped they should find a way to escape. Who knew where they would end up otherwise? Inner Mongolia? Where on earth was that? The huangshulang had never heard of such a place. It must be a very long way away.

The sun was low in the sky and the shadows were lengthening. Soon it would be dark. The mountain road was winding and the truck drove slowly. Hills rose steeply on one side of the road. On the other the land fell sharply away to a pebbly riverbed some distance below. There was little traffic, but occasionally a loaded truck would approach from the opposite direction, flashing its headlights and forcing their vehicle almost to the edge of the drop. Fortunately for the huangshulang, the high sides of the truck prevented them from seeing how close they were to the precipice. Nevertheless, the roar of the oncoming trucks as they rumbled past and the strong smell of diesel fumes were unpleasant and scary. They said little to each other. Hunger and thirst, but above all fear, had driven all thought from their minds. Numbed by the droning of the engine, they dozed fitfully, hyper-alert to any new danger.

And now, not far ahead, a cluster of lights by the side of the road. They were approaching a village. The driver slowed down, turned left down a narrow, unpaved lane between the houses, swung into a silent yard, and stopped. The wheelbarrow man opened his door, got out, and slammed the door behind him. The driver did the same. Then the two men walked into one of the houses. A dog barked furiously from somewhere up the hill. Mouse-wolf and Little Yellow remained motionless, waiting.

After some minutes, the wheelbarrow man returned, opened the truck door, took out two holdall bags, and locked the door shut. Then he walked around to the driver's side, locked that door as well and returned to the house. The two huangshulang heard all this and waited.

The dog was still barking on the hillside. The light from the house window cast a feeble yellow glow over the yard. The lane and the hillside were pitch-black. Mouse-wolf climbed onto the spade handle and looked out. Little Yellow climbed up next to him. Nothing moved. All was clear. Mouse-wolf pulled himself up onto the narrow top of the tailgate and crouched, sniffing the air. Then, with a backward glance at Little Yellow, he sprang down onto the ground below. A second later, Little Yellow was by his side.

They ran as fast as they could, away from the truck, away from the light, out of the yard, into the lane and up into the hills, away from the barking dog - chained up perhaps, since the barking came no nearer – through groves of walnut trees and low pine, until, exhausted and famished, they could run no more. Mouse-wolf felt the pine needles beneath his feet, cool and slippery. The night air was fragrant. Though they had travelled so far, this place felt almost like home.

They were ravenous. Little scratched at some tree roots, dropped a large beetle in front of Mouse-wolf, and darted off to find some more. She returned with some fat white grubs.

'Lots to eat here,' she said. 'We won't go hungry.'

Mouse-wolf set off to do his own hunting. It took him only a few minutes to catch several small mice. When they had both eaten their fill, they slipped into a gap between two stones. Mouse-wolf, as he always did before he slept, felt for the little bag round his neck. Little Yellow was already asleep. Within a few seconds he was, too. The sky above was clear and full of stars.

30.

The Photo

Xiao Mei had spent much of the stifling hot day inside, watching cartoons on television.

After supper, Ma lifted a box of papers and old photographs down from the top of a cupboard, sat down on the sofa and began sorting through them. Xiao Mei lay next to her, head on a cushion and legs over the side, half-watching the television in a corner of the room, listening to the dreamy weather-forecast music.

The magical place names and accompanying photographs scrolled down the screen: Harbin, Guilin, Lhasa, Urumqi, Hong Kong. She thought of the foreigners, the brown-haired man and the blonde-haired woman, she and Stone had seen a few days before. One day she'd go to those places with their different climates and ways of talking and doing things, or even further away to foreign countries. She would travel by plane so she could look down on the winding rivers and mountains and deserts below. But the way things were at the moment it didn't seem possible that she would ever be able to go anywhere. Why did it take so long to grow up? She yawned, arched her back and stretched out her arms.

'Watch what you're doing,' said Ma.

Xiao Mei yawned again and sat up. Several photographs fell to the floor. Ma snatched them up and stuffed them back in the box. Then she stood up, taking the box with her, and went into the kitchen.

One photo lay partly concealed under the sofa. Xiao Mei picked it up.

The photo was black and white with crinkly edges, a family portrait. The older couple sat on chairs and behind them stood the younger couple. The elderly woman sat with her legs a little apart, feet planted firmly on the floor. She was wearing a short padded jacket and padded trousers. The elderly man sat very upright with both his hands on his knees. His face was long and thin. A pretty young woman in a patterned jacket stood behind the well-padded woman, and a handsome young man in a jacket and tie stood behind the long-faced man.

Xiao Mei stared at the photo for a long time. Three of the figures looked familiar, the young couple and the elderly woman. She didn't recognise the old man. But the most puzzling thing about the family group was the baby, who was sitting clasped tight on the old woman's knee, a fat little bundle in padded jacket and trousers and wearing on its head a bonnet with rabbit ears. The longer she looked at it the more puzzling it was. The young couple, surely they were Ma and Ba. And the old woman must be Nainai. The old man was probably the grandfather who had died before she was born. But the baby? Was that her? Except it couldn't be. Because the baby's split trousers, such as babies always wear, revealed quite clearly that it was not a girl, but a boy.

She looked towards the kitchen. Ma was wiping down the gas rings with a cloth. She hesitated before going in.

'Ma,' she said.

Ma turned, saw the photo in Xiao Mei's hand, and went very still.

'It was under the sofa, I just found it.'

Ma said nothing.

'Ma?'

'Put it back in the box.'

'But Ma...'

Ma laid down the cloth and looked away.

'Ma?'

Ma's arms hung limply by her sides.

'Sit down.'

Xiao Mei followed her out of the kitchen. She slumped down on the sofa and Xiao Mei sat on the edge next to her. She took the photo from Xiao Mei's hand and looked at it for a long time.

'Ma,' said Xiao Mei, 'who's the baby?'

Ma said nothing.

'Ma?'

She gave a deep sigh, wiped her eyes and said, 'That's your brother.'

'My brother? I haven't got a brother.'

Ma took Xiao Mei's hand in her own and with the other smoothed the hair away from her forehead.

'No, you don't. Not now.'

'But where is he? What happened?'

Ma looked at the photo.

'He was just eight months old when the picture was taken. That's Nainai holding him and Yeye sitting next to her. Yeye was so proud of his new grandson. We were all so happy. He was such a lovable, healthy baby.'

'But what happened to him?'

Ma turned her face away.

'We lost him.'

She put her face in her hands. When she looked up her eyes were red and watery. Before saying more, she fished a tissue out of her pocket and blew her nose. 'You'll have to know sooner or later. But please,' her voice became urgent, 'don't say anything to Ba or Nainai. They don't want you to know.'

Then Ma told her the whole story and when she had finished. Xiao Mei went very quiet and without saying anything took herself off to bed.

Despite what Ma had told her she slept deeply that night and the morning, when she woke up, seemed like any other. Then, with a start, she remembered the baby. She climbed the ladder to the roof to be on her own and think. She'd had a brother! She tried to remember all that Ma had told her.

~

'Ba and I had to go to work,' Ma began, her eyes reddened with tears, 'and Nainai looked after the baby.'

Nainai and Yeye still lived in the village then, but when the baby was born Nainai had moved into the city to help look after it. She would wheel the baby out in its little bamboo pushchair and meet the other grandmothers in the hutong. Sometimes she would sit on the step of their house and watch the world go by, one hand rocking the baby in its pushchair. Other times she would push the pushchair up the hutong to buy vegetables. These she would put in a string bag which she would put in the pushchair next to the baby. The pushchair was big enough for two babies, one sitting opposite the other, or for one baby and a shopping bag. The baby was growing big and strong and was a favourite in the hutong. 'A big fat baby boy' everyone would say approvingly, pinching the baby's fat cheeks or patting its well-padded bottom. In the summer months, the baby wore nothing more than a little red apron embroidered with dragons.

Was Nainai already becoming forgetful all those years ago? Ma always felt a little anxious, but Ba said she was prejudiced because Nainai was just a simple peasant woman. Nevertheless, Nainai did odd things, even then.

One day, Ma caught her taking a boiled sweet out of her own mouth and giving it to the baby to suck. Ma snatched it out of the baby's mouth. 'He'll choke to death!' she cried.

Another time, she came back from work to find Nainai lying on the bed fast asleep, and the baby sitting in its pushchair in the courtyard, screaming its head off. When Ma remonstrated with her, Nainai had gone off in a huff, saying that if her daughter-in-law was going to speak to her in that tone she would go back to the village and never return.

The worst time was when she had left the baby alone on

the bed, gone out to buy a packet of salt and then got talking to some neighbours, completely forgetting about the baby. It was a good hour before she returned, by which time Ba had come home from work and found the baby lying on its back on the floor, luckily so well padded that no serious damage had been done. It was a miracle that it had fallen on its bottom rather than its head. On that occasion even Ba had to admit that things were getting out of hand.

Nevertheless, there was nothing much Ma and Ba could do since they both had to work at the machinery factory. Though the factory had a nursery, there was no way they wanted to cycle across town with a baby.

But in the end even Ba agreed that Nainai was an impossible liability.

It was Ma's day off and she had taken the baby out for a walk in the bamboo pushchair. She stopped by a stall to look at some mirrors, ribbons and combs. The stallholder was chatty, trying to persuade her to buy a length of red and white ribbon. Ma felt happy and carefree. She stuck one of the combs in her hair and picked up a little mirror to take a look. As she moved her head to get a better look at the comb, the pushchair behind her came into view. Her heart jumped and she spun round. The baby was gone.

She rushed up and down the street shouting the baby's name and screaming 'my baby's gone, someone's taken my baby!' Soon she was surrounded by a crowd of onlookers, some concerned and consoling, others just standing and gawping at the spectacle. She collapsed in a faint and knew no more.

But the baby was found. It was all Nainai's fault. She had picked him up out of the pushchair and walked back home with him.

'But why didn't she tell you?' Xiao Mei's voice rose.

'She said she had but that I had been too busy "tarting myself up." Those were the very words she used.'

'Oh,' said Xiao Mei.

'She always had it in for me, because I came from a better family than hers.'

'But what about the baby?'

'Well, after that, I said to Ba that there was no way she could live with us. She would have to go back to the village and the baby would have to go to the nursery at work.'

Ma went quiet. She picked up a cushion and put in on her lap.

'But what happened to the baby?'

'Some months later there was a flu epidemic.'

Ma looked into the distance. Xiao Mei held her breath.

'And he died.'

Xiao Mei's eyes watered. 'Oh.'

'And later you were born and Nainai came back.'

'Ma,' said Xiao Mei in a small voice, 'how old would the baby be now?'

'Twelve and a half, nearly thirteen. Not quite three years older than you.'

Xiao Mei fell silent for a while. But she had another question.

'What was the baby's name?'

'Ming.'

'Ming.' Xiao Mei mulled this over. 'Ming' was 'bright'. And her own name 'Mei' was 'plum blossom'.

'But it was all so long ago,' Ma went on, 'and now we have you.'

She didn't add something that Xiao Mei would work out for herself in time: we would have had just the one child the government allowed us to have. If we hadn't lost our baby boy you wouldn't have been born.

There was a clattering and rattling in the yard. Ba was back, carrying a bicycle. 'Quick,' said Ma, 'give me the photo.' She slid it into the box and pushed the box behind the sofa. Ba came in, looking pleased with himself.

'I met old Mr Hu down the road. He was going to throw away his bike. Said he was too old to ride it anymore and he won't need it when they move to their new place. He said it wasn't worth selling but I gave him fifteen kuai all the same. The brakes are gone, but they can be fixed.'

He looked at Ma and Xiao Mei, sitting on the sofa. Ma's hair was all over the place.

' Everything all right?' he asked.

'Yes,' said Ma. 'Everything's all right.' She heaved herself up from the sofa and went in to the kitchen.

~

Xiao Mei lay on her back on the roof for a long time, thinking about her dead brother. Why hadn't Ma told her before? Was that why she was always so sad and tired? And why Nainai was so spiteful? And Ba so careless? But one question above all others wormed its way into her thoughts. Had they loved the baby more than her?

Once again Nainai's words of warning about the jade Guanyin rushed into her mind and she felt overcome by guilt. Except of course little Ming had died years before she was born. Nevertheless, she felt somehow responsible, because if the baby hadn't died Ma and Ba wouldn't have wanted another child, and so her presence must be a constant reminder of the tragedy. Maybe that's why they never took much notice of her these days. If she hadn't found the photo would they ever have even told her that she had a brother? Her brother. They were always telling her to go and 'do something useful'. That clearly meant they thought she was useless. And she was utterly useless because hadn't she gone and lost the precious jade? The thoughts went round and round in her head.

She thought of Stone living in the derelict house. He must be about the same age as Ming. She tried to remember what the baby in the photo looked like. But all she could recall was a fat little bundle wearing split pants and a bonnet with rabbit ears. She needed to see it again. Then a second thought came into her mind. She climbed down the ladder.

The box of photos was nowhere to be seen, since Ma had hidden it before she went out to work. But there were few hiding places that Xiao Mei didn't already know about. She went through each room – the living room, Ma and Ba's bedroom, the little kitchen, her own room, and even looked under the tarpaulin that covered the boxes where the huangshulang hid until all that was left was Nainai's room.

Nainai was in the courtyard, a shopping bag in hand. It seemed to take her forever to leave the house, but finally she was gone. Casting a glance over her shoulder, Xiao Mei slipped into her room. The box would have to be here, it was the only place left. In the end it was easy to find. Next to the bed was a wardrobe. The things on top of the wardrobe were covered with a cloth. She stood on the bed and pulled the cloth away. Underneath were two small leather suitcases and two cardboard boxes. She lifted the boxes down carefully. In one there were old notebooks. In the other were old papers and photographs. She put the box of notebooks back, covered everything with the cloth again, and quickly took the box of photos to her room. She tipped them out onto her bed and went through them as fast as she could.

There was one bundle tied up with red ribbon. She pulled at the little bow and there was the photo of the three generations. There were several others, wedding pictures of Ma and Ba, taken in a studio with a background of painted cherry blossom, a painted lake and a painted pavilion. And there was one other studio photo of Ma, Ba and the baby, photographed against a background of sky and balloons. A complete family.

She tucked the first photo into the waistband of her shorts, put the others back in the box, closed the lid and carried it back to Nainai's room, just in the nick of time, since no sooner had she closed the door and come out into the courtyard than she heard the old lady's stick tap-tapping as she crossed over the wooden threshold. Before Nainai could see her, Xiao Mei had shinned up the ladder, onto the roof, and out of sight.

Xiao Mei looked hard at the baby's features. The baby had chubby cheeks, tiny round eyes, and little ears that stuck out prominently from under his bonnet. He was wearing an awful lot of clothes, Xiao Mei thought, maybe that was why he looked peevish and uncomfortable. It was hard to remember ever having to wear so many clothes. It made her sweat just to think about it. The baby looked like any baby. What would he look like now? She looked over the edge of the roof. Nainai was still preoccupied in the kitchen. Tucking the photo back into her shorts, she slid down the ladder, tiptoed across the courtyard and then, with a quick glance behind her, stepped over the threshold and out into the hutong.

~

Stone was sitting in the yard. He'd had a good night riding on the buses and no one had bothered him about the little white dog. Once or twice he'd seen someone who might have been his uncle, but each time he'd been disappointed. The dog was lying on the ground next to him. When Xiao Mei entered, it trotted over to her and jumped up. Xiao Mei patted its head.

'Good dog', she said. 'I haven't got anything for you today.'

The dog scrabbled at her legs with its front paws but she pushed it away and went to sit next to Stone. She pulled out the photo.

'Look!'

'Who are they?' Stone said.

'My family.'

Stone stared at the photo without comment and gave it back to her.

'Did you bring any food?'

Xiao Mei shook her head impatiently and held the photo out.

'No. Look!' she said again, pointing at the baby.

Stone looked at her enquiringly with his one bright eye, round and shiny as a pebble in a stream. He looked at the photo again.

'Who's the baby?' he asked.

Xiao Mei snatched the photo back and burst into tears.

He sat back on his heels, perplexed, then stretched out his hand towards her face.

'Don't cry, little sister, don't cry.'

But his words made her cry even more.

'I'm not your little sister and you're not my brother.'

After a while, when Xiao Mei's sobs had subsided into occasional sniffs, he stretched out his hand and put it on hers.

Eventually, she glanced up. Stone's one eye stared at her. She wiped her eyes with the back of her hand, sat back and told him what Ma had told her. When she had finished, Stone was quiet for a while. She looked at him expectantly. But all he said was, 'So that's what happened.'

Xiao Mei looked down at the photo.

'I wish I'd never found it.'

'Yes,' said Stone. He didn't know what else to say. His stomach rumbled.

'I haven't eaten all day.'

Xiao Mei leapt up, her face streaked with tears.

'All you think about is food! You never think about anything else! You just sit there waiting for me to bring you food!'

She snatched the photo from his hand, stuck it back in her shorts and without another word ran across the yard, down the hutong and back home.

~

Stone stood up. His growling stomach told him to go out and look for something to eat but he sat down again and thought about what Xiao Mei had told him.

He remembered the children in the brickyard where he'd worked. Some of them had no idea who their parents were or where they really came from. He, at least, knew who his mother was, even if she had gone away and left him. If only he'd had a photo. He had never seen a photo of his family. He felt angry with Xiao Mei. She had everything and he had so little.

His stomach rumbled again. Was she going to bring him any food? He stood up and, followed by the little dog, walked across the yard to the gate and looked out down the hot, sunlit hutong. But there was no one there.

He was just about to return to the shade of his room, when he glanced down. A small rectangle of white paper lay in the dust. He picked it up and turned it over. It was the photo. He stared at it. He went back inside the room. He blew the dust off the windowsill, smoothed out a discarded instant noodle packet, placed it on the windowsill, and carefully laid the photo face down on top of the packet. Then he picked up an old brick and placed it on top of the photo. Now they were safe.

Stone was asleep when Xiao Mei returned. She was standing over him, breathing hard.

'The photo, I can't find the photo. I can't find it anywhere.'

Stone looked up and shook his head.

'Just keep looking.'

'But I have!' Xiao Mei was distraught. 'I've looked everywhere. It must be here. I must have dropped it.'

'Well,' said Stone, 'you said you wished you'd never found it. Probably best that it's gone.'

'You haven't seen it anywhere?'

'No,' said Stone. 'No, I haven't.'

Xiao Mei looked at him and then scanned the yard.

'I've got to go,' she said in desperation. 'Ma will kill me if she finds out I've lost it.'

Stone said nothing. She had come to him empty-handed.

Xiao Mei walked slowly back down the hutong. She was angry. He was supposed to be her friend but he didn't seem to care one little bit about her. All he seemed to care about was if she brought him food or not. She hated him.

When she had gone, Stone lay back down. After a few minutes, he stood up and went inside. He lifted the brick and picked up the photo. Mother, father, grandparents, baby boy. His family. Xiao Mei had her own family whom she saw everyday. What did she need a photo for? He lay down again on his mat, the little dog curled up by his back. Dusk was falling. He tucked the photo under his chest. His eyelids flickered. Before it was quite dark, he was fast asleep.

31.

Caught

And then, it was as if a whirlwind had sprung up, rushing in, sweeping them up and away. After weeks of uncertainty, a flat had been found, in the north of the city. The formal demolition notification had arrived and the sooner they moved the better. Ba was energised, dashing about, doing 'God knows what', Ma said. Old Wang was pleased. He'd be moving to the same compound and his drinking days with Ba could continue. Ma began packing in earnest.

Ba kept explaining to Nainai what was happening, but she didn't seem to take it in. On more than one occasion she disappeared down the hutong and Ba had to go out and bring her back before she became completely disorientated like the last time when she'd wandered off in the wrong direction and he had found her standing in the rubble, convinced their house had already been knocked down. One morning, Xiao Mei had gone into the yard to find Ba tying a length of pink twine around her wrist. The other end he tied to the pomegranate tree. So she won't get lost, he explained. Nainai sat on her stool, plucking at the twine in irritation. For once, Xiao Mei felt sorry for her.

A week before the move, Xiao Mei was up on the roof, when Ba called to her to come down. He and Old Wang were sitting in the courtyard. Ma was at work. Nainai was confined to her room. Ba had set a heavy wooden box in front of her door so she couldn't get out and wander off all over the place.

Ba cleared his throat and said, 'We'll be moving soon.'

Old Wang nodded his head and echoed Ba's words.

'Not long before we move now.'

Of course she knew they were moving. Adults had the annoying habit of always stating the obvious.

'Still a lot of things that need to be done,' said Ba, glancing at Old Wang.

'Yes,' said Old Wang looking dejected, 'everything needs to be moved out of here.'

'Everything,' repeated Ba.

Xiao Mei shifted from one foot to the other.

'I've packed my room up,' she said, turning to go.

'Wait!' said Ba.

There was the problem of the pigeons and – Ba hesitated – the huangshulang. Xiao Mei squatted down. What he was going to say next? Ba and Old Wang told Xiao Mei what needed to be done. Tong would be here with a van in an hour or so, there was no time to lose. The pigeons were already in their cages, but the huangshulang...

'What? You want to catch the huangshulang!' Xiao Mei cried. 'She belongs here, in the hutong. What are you going to do with her?'

Ba looked uneasy. It was true, the huangshulang had

always lived here. But over a glass of spirits one evening Old Wang had let slip what the fortune-teller had said to him: 'The imprisoned ones must find their freedom... The high ground is propitious. The clean air is cleansing.' And Ba remembered that the old man had said something similar to him, though he couldn't quite remember what. The huangshulang was not exactly imprisoned, but wouldn't it be better off in the clean air of the mountains, just like the pigeons would be, away from the dust and chaos of the big machines when they came to knock down their home? Huangshulang were tricky creatures, you could never be too careful. It would be wise not to take chances, not when it came to the prophecies of fortune-tellers.

Xiao Mei thought about this for a while. She didn't mind about the pigeons so much, they were creatures of the air and surely one airy place was much like another. But the huangshulang belonged to the earth. She had her little space under the boxes in the corner of the yard. Xiao Mei had seen her as night fell, slipping out into the hutong in search of food. Sometimes she would go into the neighbouring courtyards, sometimes she would explore the nearby streets and alleys, always keeping in the shadows close to the ground. Places with rubbish bins were good, as it was here that scavenging mice or rats might be found. This was her home.

But she had to admit that Ba might be right. How would a huangshulang survive the jaws of a giant excavator and men with sledgehammers smashing up their house? She remembered the dead huangshulang that Nainai had told her about and shuddered at the thought.

The pigeons were already confined in four cages. Old Wang had brought them down from the roof and into his room, where Xiao Mei could hear them softly cooing and fluttering their wings. Ba picked up the box next to Nainai's door, looked into her room to check that she was asleep, and brought the box into the yard. Then he nailed some chicken wire to an old picture frame. Next he nailed two hinges to the frame and fastened the hinges to the box to make a door. Xiao Mei looked inside.

'Wait a moment,' Ba said, pointing towards the foot of the pomegranate tree. 'Pass me that paper bag.'

Xiao Mei picked up the bag. There was something rather heavy inside. Ba tipped up the bag and two dead mice dropped into a corner of the box. He sat back on his heels, satisfied that he had thought of everything.

A car horn sounded in the hutong, then heavy footsteps, and Tong appeared round the corner. Xiao Mei jumped up. It was the great fat panda! Tong wiped his forehead with a handkerchief. He was sweating all over.

'Tong,' said Ba, before Tong could sit down, 'this is a three-man job.'

Ba, Old Wang and Tong moved slowly towards the dusty, tarpaulin-covered boxes. Ba pulled the tarpaulin away carefully, dropped it on the ground, and passed the boxes to Old Wang, one by one. There was a gap between the last box and the wall and it was here that the huangshulang lived. Old Wang lifted up one side of the tarpaulin and Tong held the other. After the last box had been moved, they would drop the tarpaulin down on the huangshulang as it came out, bundle it up, and drop it into the cage. Simple as anything, Ba assured them.

Ba gripped the sides of the box. It was heavier than he thought, full of stuff he had completely forgotten about. He manoeuvred it away from the wall, then lifted it up. But his grip was not firm and the box slipped out of his hands and crashed back onto the ground. He stood up, swearing under his breath. But before he had a chance to bend down again, a dusty yellow whirlwind spun out from behind the box and flashed across the courtyard.

Tong stumbled back, tripped over the cage, and fell heavily on his backside. Old Wang shouted, 'Don't let it escape into the hutong!' Xiao Mei ran to the porch. The huangshulang was nowhere in sight.

Ba looked around the courtyard. Then he saw it crouching below the step just outside Nainai's room. He dashed over, dragging the tarpaulin behind him and threw it clumsily over the huangshulang, who leapt into the air just at the very moment that Nainai opened her door and peered out to see what the commotion was.

The huangshulang bolted past her into the room where it disappeared under the bed. Waving her stick in one hand, Nainai shut the door behind her and stood on the step, glaring at Ba. Elbowing her aside and dragging the tarpaulin behind him, Ba, followed by Old Wang and the perspiring Tong, rushed into the room. He picked up a long-handled broom and poked it under the bed. The huangshulang rushed out, leapt onto the bed and scrabbled up the side of the wardrobe and on to the top where she squeezed herself in between the suitcases and the cardboard boxes. Ba climbed up onto the bed and, helped by Tong and Old Wang, threw the tarpaulin over the top of the wardrobe.

'Now what?' said Xiao Mei. She and Nainai were standing by the door.

Nainai looked anxious. She mumbled something about bad luck.

Something snapped in Xiao Mei. 'It's not bad luck! It's us making a mess of things!' she shouted. The sooner they moved away from this place the better.

Tong came out, picked up the cage, and went back inside. Xiao Mei ran across the courtyard and climbed the ladder to the roof. She'd had enough. She didn't want to see the huangshulang being trapped and humiliated.

Nainai sat on her stool, saying nothing. Shouts and crashing noises came from her room. After a short while, Ba emerged triumphant, with the cage. The huangshulang cowered inside. Old Wang and Tong followed behind.

'This calls for a drink,' said Old Wang. 'It's been a good day's work.'

The three of them sat underneath the pomegranate tree, Ba and Old Wang with a glass of spirits each, and Tong with just a cup of green tea, since he was the driver and would soon be driving them into the hills.

After a while, Ba heaved himself up and said, 'We'd better get going.'

Old Wang went to his room to fetch the pigeons. Ba carried

the caged huangshulang out into the hutong. Tong rearranged the back of the van. Inside were some tools, some old cloths, and a crate of soft drinks that Mrs Chen had given him. Ba climbed onto the back seat and waited for Old Wang. After ten minutes he got out again and went back to the courtyard. Tong followed him. They found Old Wang sitting slumped on the edge of his bed. The pigeons were cooing in their cages.

'Let's go', said Ba.

Old Wang gave a deep sigh and wiped his eyes.

'It's hard,' he said. 'After all these years. It's hard.'

Ba put a hand on his shoulder. 'Best to get it over and done with.'

Old Wang nodded and stood up slowly. He put one of the cages on top of another and carried them outside. Ba did the same with the remaining two. Tong opened the back of the van and they put the cages inside. Old Wang covered the cages with a cloth and the pigeons fell silent. Tong opened the passenger door and Ba sat in the back. Old Wang sat in the front.

Then Tong said, 'What about Xiao Mei?'

Ba hadn't thought about her. He got out again and went back to the courtyard. After a few minutes he came back, shaking his head.

'She's in a bad mood.'

Tong was disappointed but he said, 'Let me try.'

Xiao Mei was still sitting on the roof.

'Xiao Mei', said Tong, 'wouldn't you like to come with us? Into the hills?'

He smiled up at her. Xiao Mei looked down at him. She shrugged.

'Have you ever been to the hills before?'

She shrugged again, then shook her head.

'Won't you come?' His voice was so warm and friendly. 'I'd like you to come.'

He had thought of her, come back to look for her, wanted her to be with them. 'OK,' Xiao Mei said, adding 'As long as I can sit in the front.' She climbed down the ladder and followed him out to the van.

'She's afraid of being carsick', Tong said.

Ba and Old Wang waited for her to climb onto the backseat next to Ba.

'I want to sit in the front,' said Xiao Mei stubbornly, 'otherwise I won't go.'

'OK, OK,' said Old Wang. 'You sit in the front and I'll sit next to your dad.'

'Sorry about that,' said Ba to Old Wang and offered him a cigarette.

Tong started the engine and they set off. Xiao Mei sat very still, gripping the sides of the seat. She felt furious. Ba and Old Wang sat smoking in the back. After a while, she rolled down the window and stuck her head out. When the van came to a halt at some traffic lights she opened the door.

'What are you doing?' said Ba in alarm. 'Shut the door!'

'Stop smoking. I can't breathe!'

Ba and Old Wang looked at each other. Ba said something in a low voice. Old Wang opened his window and threw his cigarette out. Ba did the same. Xiao Mei shut the door, the traffic lights turned green, Tong put his foot on the accelerator, and they moved off.

The pigeons were quiet but the huangshulang scrabbled around in the box, desperate to get out. Gripping her seat with both hands, Xiao Mei stared out of the window.

32.

Pips, Stones and Seeds

They had all fallen asleep, except for Tong, who kept his eyes fixed on the road ahead. Xiao Mei leant against the open window; Ba and Old Wang leant against each other. The van sped along the motorway towards the pale blue hills in the distance. They had left the suburbs of the city far behind them. Large billboards flashed past at intervals, 'One World, One Dream', the five linked Olympic rings announced.

After a while, Tong turned off the motorway onto a single-lane, tree-lined road. Xiao Mei was still asleep. Ba and Old Wang stirred.

'Soon there,' said Ba.

'Not yet,' said Old Wang, 'not till we're in the hills.'

They were driving through a wide green valley, with orchards of peach and pear, apple and cherry stretching as far as the eye could see. A few fruit sellers had set up stalls, piled high with cherries and peaches. A little way to the right and parallel to the road was a row of slim poplar trees. A great oxblood-red archway could be glimpsed through the branches. Tong slowed down. He looked at the peaches longingly but said nothing.

'Stop!' said Ba. 'Call of nature.'

Tong stopped by the side of the road and Ba got out, crossed the road and wandered off into the orchard where he stood behind a peach tree. Old Wang and Tong got out as well. Old Wang followed Ba, and Tong looked at the fruit on one of the stalls. After some discussion with the fruit seller, he bought four peaches and a bag of cherries.

No one was in the car when Xiao Mei woke up. She opened the door, stretched her arms and legs and stepped out. A sweet fragrance wafted on the air. She gazed around her. Peach trees, bearing the most beautiful juicy, red-blushed, pale-gold peaches. Cherry trees weighed down with clusters of large, ripe, shiny, dark-red cherries. She reached out her hand, picked a cherry and put it in her mouth. It was sweet and utterly delicious.

Just as she reached for another, she stopped still. She stared ahead, trying to remember something. The red gate was just visible through the poplar trees. Surely she'd been here before. She glanced across the road. Ba, Old Wang and Tong were squatting on the verge, eating the peaches. They hadn't noticed she'd woken up.

She ate another cherry, then walked through the fruit trees, towards the line of poplars and the red gate beyond. The thought that she'd once been here persisted. She stopped and shook her head from side to side, as if trying to dislodge water from a blocked ear. She probably hadn't woken up properly yet. Perhaps she was still asleep and dreaming.

She ran to the towering rust-red gateway. Two ancient pine trees stood sentry on either side. Then she turned round and gazed down the Spirit Way, lined with pairs of great stone elephants, horses, soldiers, and strange mythical creatures. She stood in the middle of the pathway trying to remember, something that had happened, that she had done to make happen. But the sun was high in the sky and the ancient statues cast no shadows that might have helped her to remember.

She stopped below one of a pair of soldiers. He was wearing a gorgeously carved tunic. In his enormous right hand he carried a club, which he rested on his right shoulder. His enormous left hand rested on a sword hilt. His stern eyes, under their flaring eyebrows, seemed to be looking right down at her. She touched his hand. The stone was as warm as blood. She put her face against it. The soldier stood impassively, as he had done for centuries. She closed her eyes and leant against the warm stone, trying to remember something. The soldier put his hand on her shoulder.

Xiao Mei started, opened her eyes, looked up at the soldier staring down at her from under his fierce stone eyebrows. A cloying smell of sweet peach juice and perspiration enveloped her. She turned round.

'Ah,' said Tong, beaming. 'I was wondering where you were!'

He sat down at the soldier's feet.

'Here,' he said, 'a peach and some cherries.'

Xiao Mei sat down next to him. She ate the peach, and together they ate the rest of the cherries, spitting the stones out on to the ground in front of them.

'Look,' Xiao Mei said. She arranged the stones into a pattern. 'That's you!'

'And that's you!' said Tong, arranging his stones.

Xiao Mei picked up one of them. The cherry stone, a carved, ivory-coloured bead, streaked with red. The peach stone with its whirls and crevasses, a strange sea creature. Would they grow if she planted them? Tong was thinking the same thoughts.

'I planted some apple pips once. But they didn't grow. Fruit trees are too difficult. Flowers are easier. I had some marigold seeds and they came up like anything.'

Pips, stones, seeds. The place of seeds. Xiao Mei frowned. An image came into her mind but she couldn't hold on to it. She shook her head from side to side.

'You OK?' asked Tong.

'It's nothing,' Xiao Mei said. 'Just a thought stuck in my ear.'

Tong nodded. 'I get those sometimes. Not much you can do about it.'

Xiao Mei looked at him. He might be a great fat panda but he understood things. She bent down to pick up the stones and put them in her pocket, just in case. Tong heaved himself off the ground.

'Race you!' Xiao Mei said, jumping to her feet. And with Tong lumbering after her, she sprinted down the length of the Spirit Way, past the stone elephants and horses and soldiers and strange mythical creatures, arms outspread as if she were a bird in flight, winging its way over the hills and over the plain, all the way back to the little courtyard house that was still home.

When they reached the end of the pathway, Xiao Mei said

she would race Tong back again. He shook his head, too out of breath to say anything. But she grabbed hold of his t-shirt and laughing, dragged him back, half-running, half-walking, panting and protesting, till they reached the red archway, where Tong collapsed in a sweaty heap on the ground with Xiao Mei standing over him laughing so much that they didn't hear Ba's cross voice calling them until he was just a few metres away.

'What have you done to Tong?' he said sternly. But a little smile passed across his face. It was good to see Xiao Mei happy for once. 'Let's go. Old Wang is worrying about his pigeons.'

They walked back to the van, where Old Wang was waiting for them. And then they drove on through the valley and into the hills looking for just the right place for what they needed to do.

Xiao Mei started singing, 'like the birds, like the white clouds in the blue sky, like the little mountain streams, I wander, wander so far...'

Soon she was joined by Ba, Old Wang and Tong, all singing at the tops of their voices:

'Why do I wander, wander so far?'

The pigeons cooed restlessly in their cages. The huangshulang slept. It wasn't time to wake up yet.

33.

All Alone

Nainai sat dozing on her stool in the courtyard. From time to time she plucked at the skin on her wrists. The end of the pink twine dangled from the trunk of the pomegranate tree. After a while, she stood up and gazed around her. The courtyard was very quiet. The door to her room was open. She went inside. The tarpaulin lay in a heap on the floor. The bed was all messed up. She bent down stiffly and dragged the tarpaulin into the yard. They had taken the huangshulang away.

They had left her.

She was all alone.

She picked up her stick and walked slowly across the yard, over the threshold, and out into the silent hutong.

Must buy vegetables, she mumbled to herself, though she had no bag or money, must buy vegetables. Tomatoes, green peppers, garlic shoots. Nothing here, must go a little further. She kept close to the wall, walking in the shadows. The bright sunlight on the opposite wall was dazzling. No sounds, except the incessant whirring of the cicadas and the maddening call of the bugu bird.

The little white dog was sitting on the step of the derelict house. As she approached, it gave a warning yap.

'Still here, are you?' she said, poking it with her stick.

The dog yelped, turned, and went back inside. Nainai looked into the yard. Hadn't the Li family lived here once? Now they too had gone. She stood at the entrance looking up at the painted eaves of the wooden doorway. Then she stepped inside.

Stone looked up, startled. He was sitting out in the yard, intent on tying together some lengths of bamboo, two longer pieces and two shorter pieces, to form a small rectangle. Next to his foot lay a small sheet of white card. The little white dog stood nearby. Before Stone had a chance to say or do anything, Nainai poked her stick at the bamboo.

'What's that?'

It was the old woman, he'd seen her before, coming out of Xiao Mei's house. He was just about to snatch the card away, when she flicked it over with her stick and pinned it to the ground.

'What's that?' she said again.

She bent down to look at it. Stone stretched out his hand but she pushed it away and picked up the photo. Then she sat down, slowly, next to Stone and looked at the photo for a long time.

'That's my family,' Stone said. 'They're my family.'

Nainai shook her head. Did she know them? Who were they? The old man and the young couple and the old woman with the baby on her lap? She turned to Stone and pointed, laughing, at the baby.

'I made that little jacket, such a lovely little jacket. It took days to make.'

The laughter faded from her lips and she looked confused.

Then she said, 'That baby is you? And they are your Ba and Ma and your Yeye and your Nainai? Do they live here?'

Stone took the photo from her. 'No, they don't. They've gone away.'

'Ah,' said Nainai. 'They've also gone away. So you're on your own, like me. I'm on my own too. Everyone has gone.' She took Stone's hand in her small wizened one. 'Have you eaten?'

'No,' said Stone, pulling away, 'not today.'

Nainai looked at him, her eyes gleaming.

'We'll eat pork and cabbage dumplings, stir-fried tomato and egg, crushed cucumber with vinegar and garlic, and a meatball soup with bean noodles. And then we'll have watermelon. We'll eat and eat and eat.'

Stone's mouth watered. Nainai heaved herself up on to her feet and turned to leave. Stone stood up too. Would she bring the food to him? As she walked away he called to her, but she did not reply.

'But when are we going to eat?' he shouted in desperation. She turned and stared at him.

'Who are you? What are you doing here? Go away or I'll call the police.'

Then she stepped over the threshold, hesitated for a moment, looked to left and right, and, tap-tapping with her stick as she walked, made her way back in the vague direction of home.

Stone stood in the yard, choked with anger and disappointment.

He was starving. Xiao Mei had not come back; she might never come back. But he could not think about her until he had something in his stomach. The little white dog looked up at him expectantly. The sun was low in the sky now. They would go out into the city and search for food. He felt in his pocket. The bank notes that he had found the other night were still there. He did not want to use them, not for food, not just yet, not if he could get something to eat for free. He would keep them for a real emergency.

34.

More Trouble

Stone and the little white dog walked as far as the brightly lit street with its restaurants and strings of red lanterns. Soon they arrived at the shop selling meat buns. A sullen, middle-aged woman wearing a dirty white apron was serving behind the counter. Stone looked through the door. Inside were three wooden tables and four or five customers sitting on stools eating meat buns and slurping bowls of millet porridge. The smell that wafted out was indescribably delicious.

The young waitress who had given Stone the bun the other day was standing by one of the tables writing down a customer's order. Stone waited, hoping to catch her eye. But when she looked up and out towards the street, it seemed as if she were looking straight through him. Wanting to remain inconspicuous, but at the same time desperately hoping that she would see him, Stone stood outside and waited.

Just at that moment, two men carrying a large white refrigerator staggered out of the electrics shop next door. As they manoeuvered themselves through the door and onto the pavement, a corner of the fridge knocked against the little white dog. The dog gave a yelp and leapt out of the way, tangling its string lead around Stone's legs and toppling him to the ground. The men swore at them for being in the way and, without a second glance to see if they were all right, carried on down the street. As Stone picked himself up off the ground, he glanced up. The waitress was standing by the door.

'It's you again,' she said. She glanced back over her shoulder. 'Wait here.'

But the sullen woman at the counter caught sight of Stone and gave him a hard look. Then she waved her hand, as if flicking flies off a tablecloth, and told him to move away before the customers complained. When Stone hesitated, she came out from behind the counter and stood, arms folded, on the doorstep.

'Go away! Or I'll call the local police!'

It was the second time that day someone had threatened him with the police. He picked up the dog and walked slowly away. All he wanted was something to eat. He sat down on the edge of the pavement and pulled out his precious notes. He would have to use them but he would not go back to the bun shop. He was just about to stand up, when he felt something tap his shoulder. He turned round quickly. It was the waitress.

'Here,' she said breathlessly, handing him a box.

Before Stone could say anything, she had run back down the street. He opened the box. Inside were three cold meat buns, some pickled radish, some chilli pepper sauce, a plastic bag filled with cold millet porridge, and a small white plastic spoon. One of the buns had a bite taken out of it. It looked like the remains of a meal. Had the customers forgotten to take their doggy bag? Stone gave the half-eaten bun to the little white dog and ate the rest himself. He could have eaten the same amount three times over, but at least it was something.

He stood up, unsure what to do next, stay out or go back. He looked along the busy street, with its crowded buses and honking taxis, and the constant stream of people hurrying to get somewhere. The little dog lay at his feet, waiting. Then he turned and walked back the way they had come. He had had enough. His quiet courtyard beckoned. He would go back and sleep.

As he passed the bun shop with its unfriendly saleswoman he kept his head down. Yet, when he was right alongside it, he could not help but glance up at the counter. Would he see the little waitress again? A bamboo steamer full of newly steamed buns had been placed there; the woman was nowhere to be seen. Quick as a thought, he reached up, took a bun and stuffed it in his pocket. There was still no sign of the woman, so he reached for another. But just at that moment, she appeared from where she had been bending down beneath the counter. When she saw Stone with his hand in the basket, she smacked it, swore loudly and rushed out from behind the counter to the shop entrance.

'Thief!' she yelled. 'Thief!'

He dropped the second bun, scooped up the dog and took to his heels, darting between the incurious pedestrians, most of them more interested in finding a restaurant meal or getting home at the end of a long day than in chasing after a one-eyed boy with a dog.

He had barely reached the end of the street, when he felt a heavy hand grab him by the collar of his t-shirt and lift him clean off his feet.

35.

Freedom

Tong drove slowly along the mountain road. Old Wang twisted round and looked back over his seat.

'Hope they're all right,' he said anxiously. The smell of the pigeons and the now wide-awake huangshulang was overpowering. Xiao Mei opened the van window wide and hung out to breathe in the fresh air. Ba did the same. They could hear the huangshulang desperately scrabbling and gnawing at the sides of the box. The pigeons were beating their wings in a futile attempt to break free. Old Wang stared out of the window. 'Just a little further, just a little further', he said. A little way ahead, the road widened.

'Stop! Stop!' Xiao Mei called out, leaning right out of the window.

Lined up on the broad verge were four or five beehives and a green canvas tent. Next to the tent was a table with jars of rich brown honey. A woman stood by the table and looked at them as they approached. Bees buzzed around.

'Not now,' said Ba. 'We've got things to do. We'll stop on the way back.'

Xiao Mei slumped back in her seat. Ba never remembered

things. She turned to Tong and said, 'You won't forget, will you?' Tong, who was keen on honey, said that he definitely would not forget.

They were climbing steadily, following a zigzagging course through the mountains. On one side of the road was a sheer drop down to a narrow valley. On the other was a steep cliff, partly covered in wire netting to prevent rocks hurtling down onto the road if ever there were a landslide. Xiao Mei stopped looking out of the side window and stared ahead. When a heavily laden truck overtook them from behind, she shut her eyes tight. Tong gripped the steering wheel, sweat pouring down his face. Xiao Mei glanced at him nervously, telling herself that Tong always sweated in hot weather. Ba and Old Wang dozed on the back seat.

After a while, the road straightened out. Tong relaxed and picked up speed. Old Wang woke up and looked out of the window. 'Nearly there,' he said.

A billboard advertising farm machinery. Then a few houses, a little shop, and some men standing outside with bicycles. A pile of empty baskets. A child squatting by the roadside. A yellow dog.

'There,' said Old Wang, pointing. 'Turn in there on the left.'

Tong turned into a narrow lane.

Ba woke up. 'Is this where your relative lives?' he said, turning to Old Wang.

Old Wang nodded. 'Turn into that yard over there.'

Tong turned left and stopped next to a small tractor that was parked on one side of the yard under some trees. On the other side was a long low house made of rough brick. In front of it, to provide shade, was a trellis covered in a luxuriant vine from which dangled long, silvery-green gourds. A steep bank next to the house was overgrown with morning glory: deep blue and crimson and purple flower trumpets against lush-green, heart-shaped leaves on slender twisting stems. A basket of tomatoes lay by the door.

A middle-aged woman in a patterned sleeveless dress came out of the house. 'You're here, 'she said, looking in through the window of the van. 'Come in and eat.'

Xiao Mei climbed out of the van feeling slightly sick. They trooped into the house, where the woman set before each of them a large bowl of soupy noodles topped with scrambled egg and tomato. Xiao Mei had not realised how hungry she was. Ba helped himself to a large spoonful of chilli paste, which he mixed into his noodles. No one said anything while they ate. Xiao Mei looked at the woman out of the corner of her eye. She had a long face like Old Wang's. There was a definite family resemblance.

When he had finished, Old Wang stood up and, followed by the woman, went out into the yard. Ba lit a cigarette. He offered one to Tong but Tong said no, he did not smoke. Instead, he drank some hot water, which he poured into his bowl from a large red thermos flask that was standing on the windowsill. Then they went out into the yard and stood around the van, while Old Wang and Ba discussed what to do next.

After some deliberation, Old Wang said they should all get back into the van. The woman sat in the front, and Xiao

Mei squeezed into the back between Ba and Old Wang. The woman directed Tong up the lane and into the hills. They drove for quite some way until the road petered out.

Ahead of them was an abandoned quarry, a stone-strewn yellow basin hacked out of the hillside. Old Wang got out of the van and looked around him. Tong said he would stay behind. Followed by Xiao Mei, Ba and the woman, Old Wang walked up the side of the quarry, along a steep little path lined with scratchy grass and low scrubby bushes. Crickets jumped out of the way in front of them. The path was narrow, so they walked in single file.

When they reached the top of the hill above the quarry, Old Wang stopped and looked ahead. Xiao Mei had not realised how high they were. The side of the hill dropped steeply below them, and beyond stretched ridge after ridge of blue-green mountains. Far, far in the distance, the hills dropped down into a misty plain, scattered with points of glinting white light and plumes of grey-white smoke rising from tall chimneys.

'What's that, over there?' said Xiao Mei, shading her eyes against the sun.

'That,' said Ba, 'is where we've just come from. That's our city. That's Beijing.'

'Oh,' she said, screwing up her eyes and staring at the grey-yellow haze that hovered over the distant plain. 'So that's where we live.'

Old Wang squatted down on his haunches, looking out at the view. Then he stood up and said, 'This place is good. This will do.'

So they walked back down the side of the quarry to the van, where they found Tong fast asleep on the back seat, snoring loudly. Ba rapped on the window and Tong sprang up.

'Open the back,' Ba said.

Rubbing his eyes, Tong lumbered out, and opened up the back door. Xiao Mei covered her nose with the edge of her t-shirt. The floors of the pigeon cages were squelchy with droppings. Old Wang lifted the cages out one by one, and put them on the ground. Then Ba picked up one, Old Wang picked up one, and the woman picked up another. Before Tong shut the door, Xiao Mei looked inside the van at the box containing the huangshulang. She had stopped scratching and had flattened herself against the back wall of the box.

'Shall I carry the huangshulang?' she asked.

'No, not yet,' said Ba. 'We'll do that later.'

Tong picked up the last cage and they set off back up the side of the quarry. When they reached the top, Old Wang told them to put the cages down and wait a little. Tong, panting and sweating, was the last to arrive. He dropped the cage and collapsed in a heap on the ground. 'Careful,' said Old Wang sharply.

For a while they sat there, saying nothing. Xiao Mei glanced at Old Wang. His lined face looked tired and his eyes were watery, but not like when he had had too much to drink. The woman put her hand on his shoulder. Tong lay on his back, chest still heaving. Ba stared out at the view.

Old Wang sighed, stood up and went over to the pigeon cages. He squatted down in front of each one in turn, untwisting the wire that fastened each door. Xiao Mei, Ba, Tong and the woman watched him. There were four pigeons in each cage. He opened the door of one of the cages, reached his hands in and brought out one of the pigeons. It sat quietly, cooing in his hands, its amber eyes looking to left and right. He stroked its head, stood up, raised his hands in front of him, like a priest making an offering at a shrine, and opened them up, like the petals of a lotus flower. The pigeon sat there for a moment.

'Fly,' he said, lifting his hands a little, 'fly!' The pigeon trembled for second, spread its wings, and flew off over the valley.

Then he squatted down again, took out the next pigeon, stroked its head, raised his arms above his chest, opened his hands and released the trembling bird into the air. First one, then two, then sixteen birds, dipping, diving, the light catching on their wings as they swooped and turned, flying ever higher, ever further. Old Wang, Xiao Mei, Ba, Tong and the woman gazed at them until they were no more than faint pencil marks against the pale sky. And then they were gone, erased from sight.

'Let's go,' said Old Wang, picking up a cage and shaking out the dirt.

Ba, Tong and the woman picked up the other cages. They set off in silence back down the path.

Xiao Mei stayed behind for a while, gazing out over the valley and the hills to the grey city beyond, thinking about things, feeling sad but strangely light-hearted as well.

'Xiao Mei!' Ba's voice floated up from the bottom of the

quarry. 'Xiao Mei!'

She turned and ran down the path. The grass scratched her legs but she did not mind, nor the tickle of the little crickets as they sprang lightly out of her way. She spread her arms wide, and ran.

The door of the van stood open. The box containing the huangshulang was on the ground. Tong was squatting next to it, poking a stick through the chicken wire.

'It seems to be asleep,' he said anxiously.

Still panting, Xiao Mei, crouched down next to him. The huangshulang was lying very still, but she could see a slight fluttering movement of its chest.

Ba looked around. On the hillside near the quarry were trees and low bushes, providing shelter from the sun. They all agreed that this would be a good place. Ba picked the box up and, followed by Xiao Mei and Old Wang, began to walk up the hill. Tong said he would stay in the van. The woman said she would walk home as she had things to do.

The hillside had been terraced with stone retaining walls. But the walnut trees looked neglected, with dead branches in amongst the healthy ones. A few scraggy pine trees clung on by their roots to the stones. Perhaps there were just too many trees for the farmers to look after, Xiao Mei wondered. Not many people came here, it seemed. Just as well.

After they had been climbing for some minutes, Ba and Old Wang set the box down by the foot of a tree. Sunlight filtering through the walnut leaves dappled the ground, which was covered with pine needles and small leathery unripe walnuts. The huangshulang started scratching again. Ba began to remove the little sticks that he had pushed through wire loops to fasten the chicken-wire door shut, but Xiao Mei pushed his hand away, saying, 'Let me do it, let me do it!'

'Let her do it,' said Old Wang.

Ba sat back on his heels. Xiao Mei removed the last of the sticks. Then she pulled the chicken wire away and stood up. They stepped back to watch.

Ba threw a walnut at the box. It bounced off onto the ground. Very slowly, the huangshulang put her nose out. She sniffed the air, pricked up her alert little ears, then flattened her chest almost to the ground. Xiao Mei held her breath. The huangshulang crept out. 'Go!' Xiao Mei whispered, 'go!' And then so fast, they scarcely saw her, she disappeared into the undergrowth and was gone. A rustling sound, and then nothing.

Ba turned to leave, satisfied that he had acted on the fortune-teller's cryptic words about an animal and clean air and mountains. He and Old Wang had done the right thing. The huangshulang and the pigeons were free now and would certainly be better off here in the hills than in the dusty hutong with its half-demolished houses. But Xiao Mei was sitting very still on the box. When Ba called to her, she burst into tears. He turned back and put his hand on her shoulder.

'What's the matter?' he asked.

Xiao Mei sobbed even more loudly, wiping the tears from her eyes with the back of her hand. Ba was perplexed. Old Wang squatted down next to her.

'She'll be all right,' he said. 'She'll be happy here.'

Xiao Mei looked up at him, her face wet with tears.

'I know,' she said, choking back another sob, 'but she was our huangshulang in our courtyard. It was her home, and now she's been moved to a strange place. And no one...no one even asked her!'

She was inconsolable. Ba gave an awkward laugh. But Old Wang said quietly:

'Everything is upside down these days. We're just trying to do our best.'

'Let's go,' said Ba. 'Tong will be waiting for us.'

Xiao Mei stood up slowly. Still sniffing back her tears, she walked with them back down to the van.

Tong, having opened the doors to air the van while the huangshulang was being released, had taken the opportunity to have another nap. When Xiao Mei, Ba and Old Wang arrived, he drove them back down the hill to the house in the yard. The van felt odd and empty with the huangshulang and the pigeons now gone. No one spoke as they returned to the van. Xiao Mei stared out of the window. With her emotions still confused and the huangshulang gone forever, she thought of Stone. Was she still angry with him? She did not know, but she needed to see him, to see that he was all right. The little jade Guanyin floated into her thoughts and once again she experienced a tightening in her chest, that by now familiar feeling of impending disaster.

~

Up on the hillside, the hutong huangshulang's every sense was on full alert. What was this place and those unfamiliar smells? What were those spiky things that slid and slipped underfoot? What were those strange rustlings in the trees? Above all, where would she find something to eat?

36.

Disappointment

Ma's shift at work finished early that day, the day Tong drove Ba, Old Wang, Xiao Mei, the pigeons and the huangshulang into the hills.

Her section of the department store was being refurbished and when her supervisor saw that she was sitting around with nothing to do, he said that she might as well go home. She could make up the time some other day. Ma decided that she would look in on the aunts and then, because it was her painting day, go on to Teacher Fu's.

The aunts were surprisingly cheerful. When Ma arrived she found Old Auntie sitting by the window listening to the radio. Second Auntie was in the kitchen cooking porridge. Ma went into the kitchen to say hello to her. Second Auntie was looking for something in the fridge. The fridge light was on, which meant that it was plugged into the electricity.

'Have some tea,' said Old Auntie, pouring hot water into a mug of green tea leaves.

Ma took the mug and followed her into the living room.

'How have you been these past few days?' asked Ma, looking around the room. The furniture had been dusted. The gong was still hanging above the kitchen door. The sun shone in through the window. From the radio came the screechy sound of Beijing opera.

'We're very well,' Old Auntie sat down by the table. 'Everything is good.'

'So you're using the fridge now,' said Ma.

'Of course we are,' said Second Auntie. 'Couldn't manage without it!'

Ma said nothing for a while. Then she enquired, 'And are you sleeping well?'

'Never better,' Old Auntie said. 'We sleep like logs.'

Ma looked towards the kitchen door. 'I see the gong is still there.'

The aunts fell silent and looked at each other. Then, putting her hand to her mouth, Old Auntie said in a whisper, 'The thing has gone. Completely gone.'

'We bang the gong every night before we go to bed ...,' said Second Auntie.

'... and then we go to bed and sleep the whole night through.' Old Auntie sat up straight. 'It's a miracle.'

Ma, who did not believe in miracles, thought it best to say nothing. But she was glad the aunts were happy.

'And what have you been doing recently?' she asked conversationally.

Old Auntie stood up and went over to a small table near the window. 'Look,' she said and, turning round, handed Ma a sheet of paper, the size of a small book page. It was a small painting of a little red pavilion and some pink cherry blossom.

'Oh!' said Ma. 'You're painting again! That's wonderful!'

'Yes,' said Old Auntie. 'I've been feeling like painting again.'

The three of them smiled at each other. Ma looked at her watch and stood up.

'Take the painting,' said Old Auntie.

'Thank you,' said Ma. She put it carefully into her bag. 'I'm going now.'

She made her way out into the dark corridor and down the grimy staircase. When she was outside she looked back up at the aunts' window. For some reason she felt sad. They were standing there, waving at her. She waved back. She unlocked her bicycle, put her bag in the front basket, and cycled off towards Teacher Fu's house, not more than ten minutes' ride away.

~

When she reached the compound where Teacher Fu lived, she locked up her bike again, took her bag out of the basket and went in through the dark doorway, up the almost pitch-dark stairs, to the third floor. She knocked on the grey metal door with its red, stencilled numbers and waited. There was a yapping from within, voices calling, and the sound of footsteps and a key turning in the lock. A young woman opened the door. Behind her stood a small child. It was hard to tell if it was a boy or a girl, since the child wore nothing but a patterned pinafore fastened with straps round its neck and waist. The child looked up at her with wide eyes, its finger in its mouth.

Ma was taken aback. Then Teacher Fu appeared.

'Come in, come in,' he said.

The child pulled at his shirt. 'Play, want to play!'

'Not now,' he said. The child let out a wail.

'Don't do that, or I'll smack you,' said the woman, not unkindly. She picked the child up and went into the kitchen.

Ma followed Teacher Fu into the living room. The room seemed to have shrunk to half its size. The desk with its paints, pencils and brushes had been pushed into one corner of the room. Books were piled up on the floor next to it. The sofa had been opened up to make a bed and on top of it were two neatly folded quilts and some pillows. Clothes hung on hangers from the bookshelves and toys were scattered all over the floor. Teacher Fu looked around him as if seeing it all for the first time.

'Sit down,' he said, waving in the direction of the bed. Ma sat down.

The woman appeared from the kitchen with a cup of tea. The child followed her.

'My daughter,' he said, 'and my grand-daughter.'

'Oh,' said Ma. She stood up. 'You are busy. I should go.'

'No, no,' said Teacher Fu quickly. 'Sit down, sit down.' He looked embarrassed. 'There's something I have to tell you.'

His daughter and granddaughter had moved in with him. She was getting divorced. In fact, her husband had thrown her out. 'Another woman' he said in a low voice, putting his hand in front of his mouth. Their flat was in her husband's name, so she didn't have any rights. What else could she do but come and live with him? Ma looked sympathetic. Life was difficult.

But the thing was, Teacher Fu said, there was no room, no room to teach. His voice rose, there was not even any room for him to do his own work, the child got into everything, and there was always so much noise. He was very sorry. Ma would have to find another teacher, he was really very sorry indeed. She was a promising student and he hoped that she would continue her interest. Maybe she would drop in and see him from time to time, but he was sorry, very sorry, that their classes were now at an end.

Ma sat very still, trying hard to hold back the tears pricking her eyes. It was not fair, she thought. The one thing that was hers was being taken away. She stood up. It was all right, it did not matter. It was just a hobby, anyway she did not have time, they were about to move and when would she have time to paint with all that going on? Teacher Fu looked sad.

'Well, keep in touch,' he said as he showed her the door. Then, remembering something, he turned back into the living room and came out a few moments later with a roll of papers. 'Your paintings. How could you forget your paintings?'

'Thank you,' Ma said. She wiped her eyes with a handkerchief, then laughed. 'So much dust in the air.'

'Yes,' said Teacher Fu, 'so much dust.'

Ma cycled home through the rush-hour traffic. The impatient cars and taxis and the lumbering buses saved her from thinking more about Teacher Fu. She just kept her eyes on the road ahead and emptied her mind of everything else.

~

She was wondering in her misery what to make for supper, when she saw ahead of her a familiar shape turning the corner into the next hutong. She cycled fast until she had almost caught up with it. It was Nainai.

'Where are you going?' she called out.

Nainai stopped, turned round and stared at her. Then she turned round again and continued walking. Ma jumped off her bike and walked alongside her.

'Come home,' she said. 'It's time to go home.'

Nainai ignored her and walked faster, tapping her stick ferociously as she went.

'Would you like to sit on the bike?'

Nainai stopped, put her head to one side, and considered this proposition. Then, as Ma held the bike steady, she heaved herself up onto the back carrier and sat there side-saddle, her feet dangling well above the ground. Ma pushed off with one foot, and off they rode, Nainai holding tight, with her arms around Ma's waist and a big smile all over her face.

~

Xiao Mei, Ba and Old Wang slept most of the way back home. Tong stared at the road ahead, willing himself not to fall asleep as well. The sound of the engine changed as the van turned off the main road into the hutong.

Xiao Mei opened her eyes and looked over her shoulder. Ba and Old Wang were slumped against each other, fast asleep. Tong stopped outside their door, and it was only when he switched the engine off that they woke up.

'That was quick,' said Ba.

Tong said nothing but opened the back door for Ba to take his box out.

'Good night,' he said to Tong, 'and thanks.'

'Thanks,' said Old Wang.

'Bye,' said Xiao Mei as she climbed out of the van and walked towards their doorway. But before she got there, she remembered and turned back.

'The honey. You forgot the honey!'

Tong looked stricken. He had promised.

'Next time,' he said. 'I'll get it for you next time.'

But Xiao Mei just shrugged her shoulders and said nothing. Just at that moment Ma appeared, with Nainai sitting on the bike carrier.

'What are you doing with her on the back?' said Ba, suddenly remembering something and feeling a small wave of guilt come over him.

'I found her,' said Ma icily, 'wandering around, streets away from here. I can't believe that you went off and left her all on her own.'

'He forgot to tie her up,' said Xiao Mei.

'Take that look off your face!' Ma snapped.

'What look?'

But Ma's expression made Xiao Mei think twice about saying any more. Instead she slunk off and kept well out of the way on the rooftop until she was called down for supper.

~

After they had eaten Ma took the paintings out of her bag, the little one that Old Auntie had given her, and seven or eight of her own paintings. She rolled them up together, wrapped the roll in newspaper, tied a length of string around the whole thing, went into the bedroom, and slid the roll down between the wall and the chest of drawers, a place where no one was ever likely to look.

~

Tong drove back home thinking about the day's events and what fun he and Xiao Mei had had racing down the Spirit Way. He should not have forgotten the honey. He had promised he wouldn't. Then he thought of Mrs Chen. The van smelled bad. The next day he would give it a good clean. She would be furious otherwise. How hard it was to please everyone.

37.

The Arrest

Heavy hands clamped down on Stone's thin shoulders and lifted him up so his feet barely touched the ground. The little dog yelped, and before Stone knew what was happening, it had wriggled out of his arms and was racing down the street, its pink string lead trailing behind it.

Stone twisted round, desperate to free himself and rush after the dog, but instead found himself looking up into the grim faces of two policemen, one short and stout, the other thin with a scar down one cheek. Scar-face let go of his collar and grabbed him under one arm. Shorty grabbed him under the other, and between them they dragged him kicking and squirming to their van.

'Stand still!' said Shorty. 'Empty your pockets!'

Stone stopped wriggling and looked at his feet. Then he slowly pulled out the squashed and dripping bun and handed it over. Shorty took it gingerly and dropped it on the ground.

'And the other pocket!' shouted Scar-face.

'There's nothing there,' Stone mumbled.

They pushed him hard against the side of the van and held him there.

'Empty your pocket!'

Stone felt in his pocket and drew out one of the notes. He glanced down. It was the ten kuai one. Reluctantly, he handed it over. The two men looked at each other. One of them nodded. While Shorty continued to pin him to the side of the van, Scar-face thrust his hand into his pocket and pulled out the twenty-kuai note, which he waved triumphantly in front of Stone's face. Then, they dragged him round to the back of the van, opened the door, threw him inside, and slammed the door hard so that it locked shut. They climbed into the front, and the van moved off.

Stone was trembling all over. He looked around him. He was sitting on the bare corrugated floor of the van. There was wire mesh across the windows and the air smelled of stale sweat. What were they going to do with him? He looked out of the window trying to work out where they were going. Then his heart jumped. The little white dog was standing at a crossroads, busy traffic flowing past in both directions.

'My dog, my dog!' he cried, banging on the window that separated him from the policemen in the front. 'Let me out, let me get my dog!'

Shorty, who was driving, just laughed. Scar-face turned round and said with a smirk, 'Show us your dog licence first! Otherwise it'll be another offence!'

Stone kept banging on the window for them to stop. Then he twisted round to look out of the back window. The little dog had stepped off the pavement and was in the middle of the road, with cars streaming past on either side. There was absolutely nothing he could do. He drew up his knees and buried his head in his chest. It was all over. He and the little white dog were done for.

They must have been driving through the city for at least twenty minutes, stopping and starting at traffic lights, never moving very fast. The policemen did not seem to be in any great hurry to get anywhere. Even when the traffic was moving quickly, they drove slowly, as if on the lookout for something. Stone dozed uneasily.

Then Scar-face slapped Shorty on the shoulder. 'There!' He pointed out of the window.

Shorty pulled the van off the road, bumped up onto the pavement and came to an abrupt halt. They jumped out, slamming the doors behind them. Stone scrambled to his knees and looked out through the back window. They had stopped at a small street market. A flat-bed bicycle cart was piled high with watermelons. Next to it was another one with peaches for sale. Three women were squatting next to the carts. In front of them were vegetables spread out on cloths on the ground. As the policemen appeared, the women rushed to bundle up the vegetables in the cloths. Two men, who had been squatting near the carts, leapt up and began to push the carts away.

'You again!' shouted Shorty. He jumped in front of the watermelon cart, pushed the man to the ground, and tipped the watermelons off the cart so that they cracked open and splattered in a bright red mess all over the pavement.

Meanwhile, Scar-face had grabbed one of the women, who was screaming at him at the top of her voice, and shoved her against a railing. The peach seller abandoned his cart and raced off down the street, with Shorty in pursuit. It was complete chaos. A small crowd gathered to watch and make loud comments on what was happening, but no one intervened, neither to help the sellers nor to help the police. No one wanted to get involved.

The two policemen were now joined by three colleagues whom they had summoned to help them round up the illegal market people. Stone watched all this from inside the locked van. So he was not the only one in trouble today. Eight people had been arrested, the water-melon seller, the peach seller, the three women selling vegetables, and three more peddlers from further down the street who had been caught selling trinkets and watches. They stood in a dejected line. When the water-melon man remonstrated loudly, Scar-face shoved him hard so that he stumbled and fell to the ground.

Shorty unlocked the back door of the van and told them all to get in. The women screamed some more but the policemen pushed them, and they scrambled inside, one after the other. They scarcely seemed to see Stone, who was huddled right at the back. Then they climbed in, one after the other. Now there were eight of them in the van, Stone and seven of the sellers. Squashed at the back, Stone could hardly breathe.

The water-melon seller remained outside, still shouting. The policemen grabbed him under his arms and pushed him inside. But his legs were hanging out and though they tried to stuff them in, there was no room left and it was impossible to shut the door. The policemen stood around scratching their heads.

Then Shorty said 'Get them all out!'

Scar-face ordered the sellers to leave the van and stand in a row next to it. Stone sat quite still at the back.

'And you!' barked Scar-face.

Stone hesitated, then climbed out.

'Stand to one side,' said Shorty.

Stone did as he was told.

'Get back in the van,' shouted the policemen to the sellers. 'Now!'

The sellers climbed back into the van. Last of all was the water-melon seller. Scar-face slammed the door shut. Stone was completely ignored. The two policemen got back into the van. When he looked round, he saw the other policemen, job done, wandering off into the distance. The van revved its engine and drove off. Stone stood in a daze. He was free.

The onlookers were filling bags with peaches and gathering up any watermelons that were still intact. Stone bent down and picked up two peaches. Then, not knowing where he was or which direction he should go in, he started walking away as fast as he could, in case he was recognised and arrested again.

When he had gone far enough to feel safe, he sat down by the side of the road and ate one of the peaches. He looked around him. Behind some tall buildings shone the red ball of the setting sun. If he continued in that direction he would find himself walking west into the nearby hills. He must be on the outskirts of the city. His courtyard was in the east. So he stood up, and keeping his back to the sun, began the long trek home.

As he walked, he kept thinking about the little white dog

standing all by itself in the traffic. He feared for its safety in a way he had never feared for himself. He tried not to think about what might have happened, what would inevitably have happened. He thought about his uncle who had abandoned him at the bus station. He thought about Xiao Mei, who had been his friend once and tried to help him. But she had turned away from him as well. And about her Nainai, who had cheated him with promises of food. And how could he forget the heavy hand on his shoulder and the theft – yes, theft, because they had stolen from him – and the way they had pushed him into the van. Then he felt angry, and this anger gave him the strength to walk faster and further than anyone would have thought possible after all he had been through that day.

38.

The Meeting in the Hills

Early morning sunlight flooded the valley, illuminating one side of the hillside; the quarry, on the other, lay in shadow. Crickets chirped. Blue iridescent dragonflies hovered and darted.

The earth turned and the sun rose in the sky, shedding its golden rays on the quarry, on the pines and walnut trees. Light fell through the branches, casting dappled patterns on the ground below.

In a hole, in a stone wall, near a walnut tree, the two huangshulang slept. They scarcely heard the hum of an engine, the crunching of tyres on gravel, or the tramp of feet and the call of voices pass by on the quarry path below. To Mouse-wolf and Little Yellow these were familiar, everyday noises. In their half-sleep, forgetting where they were, such sounds did not seem odd and out of place.

The sounds came closer, feet scrambling up the hill, breathless voices, and then, from just several walnut trees away, the shuffling of feet and the slight bump of something being set down on the ground, not far from the stone wall where the two huangshulang were concealed. There was a crying noise, then the voices receded, and soon all was silent.

But it was something else that jolted Mouse-wolf and Little Yellow awake. It was the smell, a warm, pungent, overpowering but, above all, familiar and homely smell that set their noses quivering with curiosity and apprehension. Safe in their hole in the wall, they peered out and watched.

The strange huangshulang edged her way through the undergrowth, fearful, exhausted and hungry. Her ears were erect, signalling that she sensed great danger. The slippery pine needles beneath her paws, the fragrant walnut leaves, the freshness of the air, all were strange to her. Mouse-wolf could just see her as she crouched motionless under a low spiky bush, her nose to the air.

From not too far off came men's voices and a childish wailing, and the sound of feet retreating down the hillside, then a motor engine, first loud, then fading away, further and further down the hill, until all that they could hear was the rustle of leaves and the plop of unripe walnuts falling to the ground.

Mouse-wolf reached instinctively for the little red bag around his neck and felt for the reassuring shape of the jade Guanyin. When he glanced down, he saw a faint glow shining through the faded cloth. Had the glow become stronger or was it just the effect of the dappled light through the trees? Little Yellow crouched tense next to him.

'Can't you smell it? It's an old one. It's got years of smell on it.'

'Hutong smells,' Mouse-wolf said. 'Like us.' He knew what she meant. The odour that wafted up from the undergrowth was of dust and grime and overflowing rubbish bins, as out of place in this natural world as the fumes that lingered from the van after it had driven down the hill.

Mouse-wolf and Little Yellow continued to watch as the huangshulang from the hutong eased her long slim body through the grass, pausing every now and then to listen and to sniff the air. They knew she would not normally be out in daylight. But things were not as they usually were and they could tell that she was on edge, and that she was ravenous from the way she lunged to snatch at a small cricket that jumped across her path.

Now she was out in the open, beneath the walnut tree and just below the stone wall. Mouse-wolf and Little Yellow kept completely still, watching.

The hutong huangshulang paused, one paw raised in front of her chest, then drew back her mouth in a snarl, baring her teeth. At the wall, she raised herself up on her hind legs, front paws scrabbling at the stone.

Mouse-wolf and Little Yellow retreated as far as they could into the cavity between the stones; the musty odour outside was overpowering.

But then, something quite different distracted their attention. The light shining through the cloth bag was becoming ever brighter, so bright that it soon lit up the dark hole where they were concealed, as if a torch were being shone to make them completely visible to the world outside. Mouse-wolf tried to cover the bag, but it made little difference. Fierce as laser beams, the light from the jade Guanyin shone out through his paws. Blinded and confused, Mouse-wolf and Little Yellow tumbled out of the hole onto the ground, where they lay for a moment in a daze.

The hutong huangshulang leapt out of the way and stood at a safe distance, watching.

Almost immediately, Mouse-wolf picked himself up, grabbed the bag and put his paw inside. Little Yellow held her breath as he extracted the jade. The little Guanyin sat on his paw, emitting a steady, pulsating glow, changing from rose pink, to sage green, to lavender mauve, to pearly white. Now the light was glowing less strongly, becoming fainter and fainter, till, like the battery of a torch losing strength, there was almost nothing left, and in the end all that was visible was a tiny pinprick of light shining from deep within the Guanyin's breast. Mouse-wolf gazed at it and when the light was gone he put it back in the bag.

Overcoming her natural wariness, the hutong huangshulang inched forward and stretched out her paw, so that now all three of them were gathered around, marvelling at what had just occurred.

As Mouse-wolf and Little Yellow stood mesmerised, too astonished to move or say anything at all, the hutong huangshulang began to make a strange dry coughing noise, as if she had dust or a small bone stuck in her throat that she wanted to vomit up. She shook her small head from side to side, then lay down, rubbing her neck against the ground and scratching at her throat. Mouse-wolf and Little Yellow looked on in consternation.

Suddenly, she stood up on all fours, shook herself all over and emitted a final terrifying bark.

'She's trying to speak!' gasped Little Yellow.

Painfully, slowly, with many coughs and splutters and hesitations and repetitions, for the first time ever in her entire life, the solitary hutong huangshulang uttered words.

'The jade,' she rasped, 'the jade!'

Mouse-wolf grasped the bag tightly to his chest. The hutong huangshulang paused, breathing hard with the effort of speech.

'It's the girl's!'

The girl's? What girl? Mouse-wolf edged nearer.

'I saw her. I saw the jade goddess. I lived in her courtyard. It was my home. They caged me because they wanted to set me free. That was my tragedy after she lost the jade. No one asked if I wanted to go. They caught me, locked me in a box and then brought me here.' The hutong huangshulang narrowed her eyes. 'How come you've got it?'

Mouse-wolf hesitated. He had to trust her. In a few brief words he related how he had found the jade in Tiantan and how he was on a quest to return it to its owner.

The hutong huangshulang looked desperate. 'Give it to me,' she said, hoarse with the effort of talking.

Mouse-wolf put his paw around the bag and took a step back. 'No.'

'Then I'll take it from you,' said the hutong huangshulang, and lunged at the jade.

Mouse-wolf leapt to one side. 'If I give it to you, what then? It's not yours. The bad luck will just continue!'

'Yes,' said the hutong huangshulang in a whisper, 'but not if I return it to her.'

Mouse-wolf laughed uneasily. 'And how will you do that?'

But Little Yellow interrupted, her voice shaking with emotion. 'Don't you see,' she said, the words tumbling out of her mouth in her agitation, 'it was them! It was they who brought our sister here. The voices we heard of the men and a girl wailing, it was them!'

As if a signal had been given, from down the valley came the sound of distant voices and the faint hoot of a vehicle. The three huangshulang stood still, ears pricked. There was no time to lose.

As fast as they could they raced through the walnut trees and down the hill, along the narrow path and out onto the track that led to the village, where the humans were preparing to leave. When they reached within sight of the yard, the three huangshulang hid in some long grass by the side of the house and waited.

A fat young man opened the back of the van. Then he and another, older man carried some empty cages to a corner of the yard. A girl was sitting on the front seat. A man was saying goodbye to the woman just outside the house. The woman called to the men with the cages. The girl jumped out of the van. They walked back towards the house. The back door of the van was wide open.

Mouse-wolf hesitated for a moment, then pulled the bag over his neck and held it in his paws for one last time. The jade Guanyin inside was warm and glowing through the cloth. He raced to the van, leapt up into the back and pushed the bag far beneath a pile of old rags. But when he emerged, ready to jump out, he saw to his consternation that Little Yellow, fearful of being separated from him, had followed him into the van – and that the humans were returning.

In a flash, Mouse-wolf and Little Yellow buried themselves under the cloths. They felt the van shake as the door was slammed shut, and heard voices as the humans settled themselves in their seats. Then the engine started up and they were shaken from side to side as the van bumped down the road. The two huangshulang crouched under the cloths, once again with no idea of where they would end up.

~

The hutong huangshulang watched their departure, then turned and ran back up the hill, as agile and fresh as a much younger animal. At the sunlit top of the hill she stood still for a moment, then opened her mouth as wide as she could to fill her lungs with the cool fresh air. Then she looked across the dark valley. The light was fading fast. It was dusk and time to go hunting.

39.

Demolition

The demolition men arrived at dawn. A man with a sledgehammer stepped over the wooden threshold into the courtyard and looked around him. He saw the empty noodle packets on the ground, a bottle of water, and some discarded peach stones.

And then, a flurry of white fur from inside the house. A little dog rushed out and stood in the centre of the yard, looking at the man, barking furiously. The man swung the sledgehammer, just grazing the dog's back. Swearing loudly, he chased it out into the hutong. Another man appeared, carrying a pickaxe. The first man walked over to one of the rooms and looked inside.

'Nothing,' he said. 'Let's start.'

'Wait a moment,' said the second man, 'someone seems to be living here.'

A red vest was hanging from a nail on a wall A can of coke and a peach lay on the windowsill.

But the man with the sledgehammer was impatient to start the job. The demolition vehicle would be there any moment.

'I tell you, there's no one. Let's get on with it.'

But the man with the pickaxe shook his head and went back out into the hutong. The sun was up and the city was beginning to hum with traffic noises. The little white dog was nowhere to be seen.

Further down the hutong, Nainai was stepping out, shopping bag in one hand, stick in the other. When she saw the workman looming towards her with his fearsome weapon, she stopped and flattened herself against the wall.

'Old lady,' called the man, pointing towards Stone's house. 'That house up there, is anyone living in it?'

Nainai gawped at him and said nothing.

'Who's living in that house?' he said, raising his voice.

But Nainai remained silent and, never taking her eyes off him, inched herself away. The man shrugged his shoulders and muttered something under his breath. He turned his back on her, stepped through her doorway and into the courtyard.

'Anyone at home?' he called.

The noise of a chair being scraped across the floor, a door opening and then Ba, in his vest and underpants, sticking his head out. When he saw the man, pickaxe over his shoulder, he caught his breath. Surely not yet? Old Wang, hearing a voice, stuck his head out of his door and looked anxiously across at Ba. Ma had already left for work. Then Xiao Mei appeared from her room, rubbing her eyes and still half asleep.

'What's going on?'

Ba took no notice of her and, more loudly than he intended in his nervousness, cried, 'No, no, you're at the wrong house! It's not this house you want. You're far too early!'

The man with the pickaxe looked exasperated. As patiently as he could he explained why he had come.

'Oh,' said Ba, calming down, 'they left a long time ago. There's been no one living there for months.'

'That's all I need to know,' said the man, 'so now we can get on with the job.' He turned to go. 'Sorry to trouble you.'

Xiao Mei caught her breath.

'Ba!'

'What is it?'

What would she say? That she had made friends with a vagrant boy, that she'd been bringing him food, and that he had then stolen the photo that she had borrowed? Above all, that she knew he was living in the house?

Or, say nothing at all.

It seemed as if Ba, Old Wang and the man with the pickaxe were all looking at her, waiting for her to decide. But now the man was turning to leave, walking across the courtyard, another few seconds and he would be walking down the hutong to Stone's house and then it would be too late. Old Wang was sitting down under the pomegranate tree, lighting a cigarette. Ba was going back inside.

'Ba,' she said again.

But Ba had gone - and so had the moment.

'What's the matter?' said Old Wang, puffing on his cigarette.

'Nothing,' she said. 'It's nothing.'

She ran back to her room and slammed the door shut. The noise of the cicadas crescendoed in the early morning heat.

~

All day long there was the sound of banging and smashing and men shouting and the roar of the demolition vehicle as it rammed into walls and scooped up the rubble from one place and deposited it somewhere else.

Nainai stood and watched from a safe distance, her mouth ajar. She remembered a long time ago sorting out bricks from rubble, she could not recall why. Had they been building something or knocking it down? All she could remember was that the work seemed to go on forever. Not like these men. How fast they were! Just a few hours and the Li family's house was all but gone. But look, there was that little white dog sitting by the stone step that was all that remained of the entrance to the house. She hobbled over and poked the dog with her stick. It whimpered and made off, its tail drooping between its legs. Then forgetting why she had come out she turned back home.

But there was Xiao Mei running towards her, running past her, and scooping up the little dog in her arms.

'All gone,' said Nainai. 'Nothing left. Go back home.'

Xiao Mei ignored her and ran with the dog to see what was left of Stone's house, where she stood on the stone step, staring at the devastation.

The men were still at work. One of them was standing on a wall, pounding at it with the sledgehammer. The other was piling up wooden beams. The painted lintel, so admired by the foreigners, was propped up against a pile of bricks. Perhaps some money could be made out of it. A demolition vehicle, its mighty orange claw swinging from side to side, was balanced on top of a huge pile of rubble.

Then, she saw the red vest and some empty noodle packets, and a length of pink string caught under the pile of bricks. Lying on the ground nearby was the red cloth monkey. She looked down at the dog. A frayed piece of string was round its neck.

'Stone!' she cried, 'Stone!'

She dropped the dog and began to scrabble with her hands at the pile of bricks but it was no good, the bricks kept slipping down. She stood up and looked round wildly. The men had not seen or heard her. The pickaxe man was now out in the hutong. Grabbing the cloth monkey, she ran to him, waving her arms, the dog at her heels.

'Stop, stop! There's a boy in there! Under the rubble!'

The man looked at her. It was the girl from the house down the hutong. She had not said anything when he had gone round there. None of them had.

'There's no one there,' he said doubtfully. 'You told us this morning.'

'But there is!' Xiao Mei was desperate. 'There is! That's his dog. He was living there.' But when she turned round the dog was nowhere to be seen.

'Well,' said the man, 'we didn't see anything.'

'He might have been sleeping, somewhere dark. You wouldn't have noticed him, he was so thin!'

Without thinking what she was doing, she pulled at his vest. He moved aside.

'But I tell you, there was no one. Just the dog.'

'Yes, but he never left the dog alone. They were always together!'

Just at that moment a shout came from down the hutong. It was Ba.

'Xiao Mei!' he yelled, 'Xiao Mei! Come back home at once. It's not safe there.'

Xiao Mei looked up at the man.

'Look for him,' she pleaded. 'Help me look for him.'

The man shook his head. They had not seen anyone. Yet, he thought to himself, what if there had been someone there? A body would be found eventually. And that would cause a whole heap of trouble. Anyway, who would live in such a derelict place? Just some vagrant, surely. The family had moved out a long time ago. And what about their deadline to finish this job before moving on to the next one? On the other hand...? I am just a simple man, he thought, scratching his head. The last thing I want is anything that will get me into trouble.

'What's going on?' said Ba as he approached.

'Nothing,' said the man. 'She just came to get the dog.'

'Dog?' said Ba. 'We don't have a dog.'

'But Ba!' said Xiao Mei. 'What if...what if there'd been someone living there? And what if they are lying under the rubble, like in an earthquake?'

'You're talking nonsense,' said Ba. 'Of course there's no one there. And throw that dirty thing away.'

He pulled at the monkey but Xiao Mei held on tight.

'Please,' she turned to the man and mouthed one last desperate plea, as Ba, his hand firmly on her shoulder, steered her back home. 'Please do something!'

The man shrugged his shoulders. He went back into the courtyard and stared at the pile of rubble. Then he bent down, picked up a few bricks and threw them to one side. No, there was nothing there. He returned to work, stacking up window frames and planks of wood.

An uneasy feeling nagged at him all day. Could someone be lying there, crushed beneath a ton of masonry? The girl was deranged! And anyway, if there had been someone they should not have been there in the first place. Yet what if there had been? A piece of loose masonry fell at his feet, making him jump. The place was spooked. All day long he was troubled by disquieting thoughts but he kept these to himself and said nothing to the man with the sledgehammer. Better to let sleeping dogs lie. At last, as dusk fell, their job was done. He could not wait to leave.

As he walked down the hutong, he saw Ba standing in the doorway.

'All finished?' asked Ba sociably.

The man nodded.

'You'll be back here soon, I should think,' Ba went on. 'We're moving out at the end of the week.'

The man grunted and hastened his step. He would make sure he was assigned to work somewhere else.

~

That evening after supper, Xiao Mei, carrying a plastic bag, slipped unnoticed out of the house. It was almost dark and bats were swooping in the warm air, chasing after midges. When she reached the place where Stone's house had once been, she stopped. All that was left standing was a single whitewashed wall. She stepped over wooden threshold into the yard, now piled with broken masonry and splintered wooden beams. Stone, she whispered, Stone. But there was no sound, except the soft throbbing rasp of the cicadas, and traffic noises in the distance. The dog, too, had gone.

She squatted down and took from the bag a bottle of water, a packet of noodles and two peaches. She placed the two peaches by the wall, put the packet of noodles in front of them and the bottle of water next to them. Under the bottle she put a small sheet of white paper folded in half. Then she reached into the bag again and took out a stick of incense and a cigarette lighter. She lit the incense and stood up, then clasped her hands, inclined her head and mouthed a single word. A thin grey pungent skein of smoke rose into the air. She waited until the incense had burnt down to ash, then turned and without a second glance walked back home.

40.

Africa

The packing was nearly done. Boxes and cases were everywhere. Tables and chairs were stacked in piles. Heaps of rubbish were swept into corners of the courtyard. Only the beds and bedding remained untouched. These would be dismantled and packed up on the very last morning. Nainai wandered about getting in everyone's way. Old Wang, who had few possessions to pack, spent most of his time under the pomegranate tree, consoling himself with glass after glass of spirits.

In the midst of all the chaos, Ma and Ba had an almighty row, observed by Xiao Mei from her perch on the rooftop. Ma, who had done most of the packing, was particularly tense and tired. So when Ba happened to mention that Mrs Chen was lending them Tong and his van for the move, she completely flipped.

'That woman can never keep her nose out of our business!'

'But it's free, we won't have to pay a thing!' protested Ba.

'Free! Free?' screamed Ma. 'What have you given that foxy woman that makes her give you something for free?'

Ba glanced up at the roof.

'Keep your voice down,' he said, an embarrassed look on his face.

But Ma took no notice.

'Don't tell me that I don't know what's been going on all these months. And now she wants to interfere in our private business!'

'But she only wants to lend us the van, there's no harm in that,' said Ba, adding, somewhat unwisely, 'she's always been very kind.'

At that point, Ma came up close and slapped him hard across the face. Then she turned and ran back into the house, where Xiao Mei could hear her sobbing loudly. Nainai, who had been observing the confrontation, sat rocking on a stool, grinning to herself. Old Wang disappeared into his room. Ba, holding a hand to his cheek, sat down under the tree and reached for his cigarettes. For a while all was silent.

After some minutes, Xiao Mei peered down from the roof and said, 'And anyway, that van is much too small. It would have to make about ten journeys to move all our stuff.'

Ba nodded. Right on cue, his phone rang. He glanced down at the number and, quickly standing up and moving to a corner of the yard, answered the call.

'Uh....uh...,'was all Xiao Mei could hear him say. 'Uh....'

When he had hung up he glanced up at the roof. 'She says the van's not free that day, anyway,' he said forlornly. 'Tong's got to meet someone at the airport.' He paused for a moment. 'And she said Uncle Song is back in town.'

Ba went back inside. Through the open door Xiao Mei could hear Ma's loud sobs and Ba's mollifying tones.

'You're quite right,' he was saying. 'We won't use that van

after all. It's far too small.'

Ma's sobs abated somewhat.

'Why don't I leave it to you?' Ba went on. 'Perhaps you can borrow a big van and a driver from work. They've always been helpful.'

Ma sniffed and wiped her eyes with the edge of her skirt.

'Who was that on the phone?'

'Nothing,' said Ba quickly, 'just some scam or other. Well? What do you think?'

Ma nodded and sat up straight.

'Well, don't just stand there,' she said sharply. 'There's still lots more to do.'

~

Ba was very quiet that day and the next. Then he made up his mind. Choosing his words carefully, he said to Ma, 'Old Song is back. I thought I might just go over and say hello.'

Ma stiffened. 'Back?' she said. 'I thought he was in Africa.'

Then, after a long pause, while Ba waited on tenterhooks, she said, 'Well, I was sorry when he left. He was a good man. You'd better take Xiao Mei with you. He was always very fond of her.'

'Would you like to come too?' asked Ba strategically, knowing full well what the answer would be. Ma shot him a look as if to say 'are you completely off your head?' The conversation had gone very satisfactorily. Ba took himself outside and sent a text message to say that he would pay a visit the very next day.

~

Xiao Mei was lying on the roof when Ba called her and told her where they were going and that she'd better get ready right away. 'Oh no,' she thought, 'not another visit.' She was in no mood to go anywhere, least of all to visit Mrs Chen.

She stood up and looked down the hutong. Some men were standing in the courtyard of what had once been Stone's house, filling a handcart with broken window frames. Pale yellow dust hung in the air. Almost all the houses except theirs had been levelled now. Far in the distance, beyond a rubble-strewn plain, light glinted off the plate glass windows of a row of white tower blocks.

'Xiao Mei,' called Ba. 'Let's go!'

It was not worth putting up a fight. She climbed down the ladder. Ba, in a clean shirt and hair combed, and impatient to leave, barely noticed what she was wearing, a none-too-clean t-shirt and a pair of old sandals.

'We'll have a car one day,' said Ba, as they stood on the footbridge over the ring road and looked down at the traffic below. Xiao Mei shrugged and said nothing.

The same lift attendant was there when they arrived at Mrs Chen's block.

'Mr Song's back,' she said, giving Ba a knowing look. Ba straightened his collar and said nothing. They stepped inside and the doors closed behind them.

Someone buzzed on the seventh floor. The door slid open again. It was the fashionable young woman with the yapping pedigree dog. Now the dog was straining at its lead, scrabbling with its claws on the floor, desperate to get into the lift and down and out of the building.

'Going up,' said the lift attendant. The young woman frowned in annoyance, yanked the dog away, and the doors closed.

Mrs Chen's door was opened by Old Song.

'Hello,' he said to Xiao Mei, barely glancing at Ba. 'You've grown a lot!'

Mrs Chen fussed about, bringing Ba a cup of tea and Xiao Mei a carton of apple juice and a straw. Then she sat down on the sofa next to Old Song. For a while no one said anything. Then Ba and Mrs Chen both spoke at once.

'How's your work going?' said Ba to Old Song.

'Cuter and cuter,' sighed Mrs Chen, looking at Xiao Mei.

There was an awkward silence. Xiao Mei slurped her apple juice through her straw.

Old Song said, 'Business is good. We're expanding all the time. But it's hard work. Especially being on my own out there.' Mrs Chen gave a complacent smile and patted his leg. 'He's working too hard.'

Old Song went on, 'So it's a really good thing that she'll be joining me soon.'

The polite smile on Ba's face vanished.

'Joining you? Where? In Africa?'

'Yes,' said Old Song. 'We'll be leaving any day now.'

Xiao Mei glanced at Ba and felt almost sorry for him. A series of expressions appeared on his face, the main one being total astonishment. Quickly rearranging his features, he said, 'That's excellent news. Business must be flourishing.'

Mrs Chen glanced at him, fanning her face with a delicate sandalwood fan.

'Africa will be very hot. Almost as hot as here.'

'Much hotter,' said Old Song. 'You'll have to get a whole new set of clothes.'

'Yes,' Mrs Chen sighed. 'Such a lot of trouble. I'll have to spend days and days shopping.'

Ba stood up. 'Well, you are busy. We should go.'

Old Song and Mrs Chen stood up too.

'And how are things with you?' asked Old Song as he showed them the door. 'And with Xiao Mei's Ma?'

'Fine,' said Ba mournfully. 'Just fine.'

'Keep in touch,' Mrs Chen said, dabbing at her eyes with a handkerchief. 'We'll be back at New Year.'

And with these few words to console him, Ba pressed the lift button. The lift door opened immediately.

'That was a short visit,' said the lift attendant.

'Yes, it was,' said Xiao Mei, fixing her with a hard stare, as if to say 'and what business is it of yours?'.

As they exited the dark entrance into the bright sunshine, she looked up at Ba and gave his hand a squeeze.

'I wonder what Tong will do now,' she said. Ba said nothing, remaining uncharacteristically silent all the way back home.

41.

The Horse and Cart

Stone looked around, trying to work out where the police van had taken him. The only thing he was sure of was that he had to walk east, keeping his back to the distant mountains in the west. He set out, and after a while he glanced back. The mountains had receded, obscured by murky air and tall buildings. He kept an eye on the passage of the sun, but when it set all he could do was to follow the straight road, though whether his hutong lay to the north or to the south of this road, he had no idea at all.

No one he passed took any notice of him. He might have been invisible. After his encounter with the police he was glad of this. With the dog gone he asked himself why he was trying to return to the courtyard house. But in the end he had nowhere else to go, so why not? At least it gave him a purpose. The anger that had fuelled him was waning.

He stopped by a brightly lit fast food place, squatted down in a dark corner and watched the well-dressed people going in and out. Through the large plate glass windows he could see them sipping drinks through straws, unwrapping their French fries, biting into huge burgers smothered with ketchup. A warm oily smell wafted on the air.

A man came out followed by a little girl, no more than three or four years old, who was clutching a half-wrapped bun in her hands, nibbling at it as they walked. In her effort to keep up with the man she tripped on a loose paving stone and dropped the bun. She let out a wail. The man turned round, took her by the hand and pulled her away.

The burger lay on the ground. Stone ran forward and picked it up. It was still in its wrapping, printed all over with yellow 'M's. He ran his fingers over the bitten part to dust it down, then stuffed it into his mouth. Red gooey paste ran down his chin. It tasted good, sweet and satisfying. When he had eaten it all, he unwrapped the paper and licked it clean. Then he squatted down in the shadows and waited. But apart from a few dropped potato chips and a discarded paper cup half full of cola, he had no more luck. He stood up and walked away.

After a while, he turned down a dark and silent alleyway. A pile of flattened cardboard boxes lay in a small backyard. He walked in and looked around. There was no sign of anyone, so he heaped the cardboard up around him, and almost immediately fell into a deep sleep.

Some hours later, he was startled awake by a loud snuffling noise, a jangle of metal, a resounding clang of things striking a hard surface, and a warm, familiar, earthy smell. He lay there, believing for a moment he was back in the village and the cows were passing by. Then he pulled the cardboard away from his head and found himself looking up into a pair of large, long-lashed eyes. The horse shook its head and snorted impatiently. Behind it stood a wooden cart piled high with bricks, which a man was unloading into the yard. Before Stone could make another move, the man caught sight of him.

'Hey! Give me a hand with these!'

He was old and not unkind looking. Stone patted the horse on its nose and stood up. The man was grumbling to himself. He had set off with his son, but then the good-for-nothing young fellow had got a phone call and jumped off the cart, saying that he had something important to do and would be back later. That was the problem with these new phones. As people said, it was as if they were the grandfather and you were the grandson, running around at their every beck and call.

'Where did he go?' asked Stone, wishing that he had a phone too.

'You think he'd tell me?' said the old man irritably. 'I'm only his father, after all.'

Stone picked up one of the bricks and looked at it. How many of these had he moved in the past? Thousands and thousands, probably. He had never wanted to lift another brick again. The bricks were in bundles tied around with twisted straw and the old man was carrying them to a corner of the yard. The horse stamped and tossed its head. Stone picked up a bundle and followed him. Together they worked quickly and before long the cart was empty. Then the old man reached for a cloth bag that was hanging from the horse's halter and pulled out a metal tin.

'Here,' he said. He opened it and gave Stone a steamed

bun. 'You helped me a lot today. Not like that useless son of mine.'

They sat on a cardboard pile in companionable silence. After a while, the old man stood up and, slapping the horse on its side, said that he had to go. The horse put its ears back and shook its harness. Stone stood in the yard, his hands hanging down by his sides. The old man eased the horse with the cart out into the alleyway. Then he climbed up onto the seat. Stone stepped forward and asked him where he was going.

'Eastwards,' said the old man gesturing. 'That's the direction I came from.'

Pausing for only a second, Stone swung himself up onto the back of the cart where the bricks had been. The old man looked round. 'You going eastwards too?'

Stone nodded and they set off. Relieved of its burden, the horse trotted along easily, the old man cracking his whip and Stone dangling his legs over the cart's edge.

The old man turned the cart out of the alley and into the main road, keeping close to the kerb. The horse moved steadily, oblivious to the overtaking bicycles, cars and buses, every now and then tossing its head in irritation at the flies that hovered about its ears. The old man, hunched in his seat, said nothing. Stone sat for a while looking around him. Then he lay back and gazed up at the sky until his eye closed and the easy motion of the cart rocked him to sleep.

They had been travelling like this for a short while when the old man shouted something and Stone felt a bump as the horse turned into an unpaved side road and after a minute or two they came to an abrupt halt. He sat up and looked around him. On the pavement was a large pile of flattened cardboard boxes and white polystyrene packaging. Two men, one fat, one thin, were standing nearby. The old man turned to Stone.

'You can help load the cart.'

Stone got down. The men looked at him.

'Who's that?' said one of them.

'A relative,' said the old man, not looking at Stone and not moving. 'He came along to help.'

The men stood by as Stone heaved the cardboard onto the cart. The old man sat watching. The pile became higher and higher. Stone struggled to push the cardboard sheets on to the top.

'Use the ladder,' the old man said, pointing to a short wooden ladder lying on the ground. So Stone picked up the ladder, leant it against the pile, and climbed up. The load towered above him.

When almost nothing was left on the ground except for a few bundles of the lightweight polystyrene, the men stepped forward and, with much shouting, tossed the bundles onto the top, threw a rope over and lashed the load securely to the sides. The old man climbed off his seat to take a look.

'Mmm...,' he said. There was a small gap between the packaging and the edge of the cart.

'Sit there,' he said to Stone, 'and hold onto the rope to keep everything steady.'

The men laughed and the fat one said, 'Plenty of room if you're thin.'

Stone felt doubtful and edged away. The old man opened up his bag and gestured to him. 'Have another bun.'

Stone put out his hand but the old man told him to get into the cart first, then he could eat it as they went along, no point in hanging about any longer. He would have more to eat when they arrived at their destination. Stone looked at the cart. The pile of polystyrene and cardboard teetered precariously above him and the gap where he was to sit looked impossibly narrow. But hunger overcame him and he put his foot on the edge of the cart, swung his leg over the side, and crouched down in his designated space.

Handing him the bun, the old man told him to hang onto the rope and pull on it if the load looked like toppling over. Then he climbed back onto his seat, the men gave the cart a push, and the horse lumbered off, the load swaying alarmingly from side to side, until they were on the main road and travelling at an even pace.

Stone leant against the load, one hand holding onto the rope and his knees squeezed up tight against his chest. He ate the bun without much enjoyment. Every now and then he would feel the mountain of cardboard veering away from him and he would pull on the rope, but not too hard in case it fell the other way, on top of him. It was impossible to relax even for a second.

They had travelled in this manner for some distance, when a black car, blue lights flashing, hooting loudly, weaving in and out of the traffic, raced past them. The horse, usually so placid, stamped its hooves, whinnied and shied away. The old man cursed and pulled hard on the reins. The load of cardboard and polystyrene slipped to one side, dragging Stone backwards.

Still swearing, the old man stopped the cart and jumped out. When he saw what was happening he rushed round to the other side and began to push the load back. The hooting cars and taxis behind them had come to a standstill, drivers leaning out of their windows and shouting. Stone managed to twist round, and with both hands pulled hard on the rope. Slowly, as he pulled and the old man pushed, the load righted itself.

The old man wiped his forehead with the back of his hand. Breathing heavily, he said nothing except 'let's move, we're nearly there 'and then climbed back onto his seat.

Stone hesitated for a moment. He could just walk away. Or he could stay with the old man and help steady the load. He had a choice.

'Get back on!' shouted the old man.

In the end, it made no difference either way. He heaved himself up onto the edge of the cart and sat there swinging his legs. The old man shouted at the horse and they moved off.

After they had unloaded the cardboard at a recycling depot, the old man sat down for a rest and said nothing for a while. Stone sat quietly next to him. It was getting late. The old man looked at him.

'You thinking of leaving?'

Stone shrugged.

The old man scratched a sore on his leg.

'I've got to see someone. A relative, just arrived in the city.

You want to come with me?'

Might as well, Stone thought. He nodded.

That night, he, the old man and the relative, a sinewy, middle-aged man, slept in the damp basement room of a block of flats. The old man cooked up some soup on a hotplate. It was the first hot meal Stone had had for a very long time. The three of them sat in the gloom of a single electric light bulb, slurping the soup in silence.

After a while, the old man said, 'I remember coming here many years ago.'

The relative nodded his head. Stone listened. He was lying on his side on a bamboo mat, his head propped up on one hand. The other two were sitting on low stools.

The old man went on, 'It was all fields then and the road we came along was just a dusty track. There was an apple orchard just over the way. Of course, that was long before they pulled the city walls down. The countryside started outside the walls and the city was inside.'

'But now it's all city,' said the relative. 'It's hard to tell where one ends and the other begins.'

The old man nodded.

'The air was good then, clear and clean. Now you can barely see the Western Hills for smog.'

'It's progress,' said the relative. 'Everything's modern now.'

The old man sighed. Stone lay on his mat, half asleep. The relative yawned and scratched his back. The old man yawned too. For some minutes no one said anything.

Then the old man said, 'You ever see a huangshulang?'

'I saw one once,' said Stone sleepily, 'in the hutong where I live.'

The old man shook his head. 'Not the ones you see every day, they're the ordinary ones.'

The relative gave a low laugh. 'Those old stories!'

The old man leant forward, his voice dropping to a whisper.

'Wang San saw one once. Taken the shape of a child, it had. He whacked it over the head with his scythe.'

Stone opened his eyes. 'Why?'

'He had his suspicions. The child was speaking in a strange way.'

'And then what happened?'

'It was a huangshulang, of course. It shrieked and ran away, leaving fragments of a human skull all over the ground.'

He leant back complacently. 'That's what I was told.'

'Where was this?' asked the relative.

'Could have been where the railway line is now. But it was a long time ago.'

The relative laughed again.

The old man's words reminded Stone of something but he could not think what. Then it came to him. The dream about the huangshulang and the railway line and the great clanking train. He lay down, feeling troubled. What had happened next? But his eyes were closing and the image faded away. The old man and the relative lay down too. Soon, all three of them were asleep.

~

Stone remained with the old man for the next few days. The relative had found temporary work on a building site and the old man needed Stone's help. There was still no sign of his son. It was typical, the old man told him. He would disappear for a few days with some excuse and then reappear as if nothing had happened. So Stone helped the old man load the cart with bricks, or cardboard, or empty plastic bottles and deliver them to wherever they were needed. But though they crisscrossed the city, Stone never saw a familiar landmark that would tell him where his hutong was.

About three days after they first met, the old man and Stone were driving the cart loaded with glass bottles to the recycling yard. The old man said he was tired. He would sit in the back with the bottles and Stone could drive the cart. Stone felt proud to be sitting up in front; every now and then he would touch the whip to the horse's rhythmic flanks to make sure it kept a steady course. They had been to this yard several times already so Stone was familiar with the route. The old man dozed watchfully amongst the bottles. Stone reached the yard with some reluctance, hoping that the old man would allow him to drive the cart again. He leant forward on his seat and patted the horse's neck.

Just as the old man was climbing out of the back, a shout came from a brick building on the other side of the yard and a young man came running out.

'Been waiting for you for hours,' he said, irritation in his voice.

The old man said meekly, 'You better unload these bottles.'

The young man glared at Stone and shouted at him to get down off the cart. Then he turned to the old man and said, 'You crazy or something, letting a stranger drive our horse?'

Stone climbed down.

'He was just helping while you were away,' said the old man in a plaintive voice. 'How can I manage all on my own?'

'It's your fault if you refuse to learn how to use a mobile phone,' said the son, glancing down at his phone. 'Otherwise you could have just called me.'

The old man sat down, exhausted. He opened up his bag and took out the metal tin.

'Here,' he said to Stone.

Stone squatted down next to the old man and ate. The son stood over them impatiently. As soon as Stone had finished eating, the son told him to unload the bottles. When Stone had done this, the son told him to leave, he was not wanted anymore. Stone looked at the old man, but the old man looked away.

'Go!' said the son, dismissing Stone with a flick of his hand. 'Go! And there's no need to come back.'

Stone stood up. There was no point arguing with someone like that. Then he stroked the horse on its nose and left the yard, not knowing what he would do next.

The narrow street outside looked like any other. White railings separated the road from the pavement, there were scholar trees planted at intervals, and little shops selling mobile phones, electric fans, ladies' underwear, and stuffed toys. Buses, cars and taxis trundled up and down. Stone walked for a while and then leant against the railing considering his limited options. He could either walk up the street – north – or down the street – south.

Then he saw something that caused him very quickly to make up his mind. A bus was coming towards him and on the front was a single, familiar word: Tiantan. And if it was going to Tiantan, then that meant it had come from the direction of his hutong. All he had to do was to follow the bus stops on the other side of the road and eventually he would arrive back 'home'. His heart feeling lighter, he crossed the road and started walking.

42.

Leaving

'Why didn't you come with us?' Ba shouted up to the roof. 'The new place is much better than here.'

Xiao Mei looked down but said nothing. Nainai's door was open. She could see her sitting on the edge of her bed looking out into the courtyard and peering at the piles of boxes and cases. She watched as Nainai grabbed her stick and made her way into the yard and, squatting down on her stool, heaved one of the boxes towards her. It was full of winter clothes, wrapped up in plastic sheeting. She clawed the plastic away and drew out a red cardigan. This she inspected closely before laying it to one side and pulling out a pair of bright blue long-johns that Ma had knitted with great effort years and years ago. These too she set to one side. Next she found an old man's grey sleeveless jumper. She inspected it, puzzled. After this she stood up and took herself back to her room, where she lay down to have a nap.

When Ma saw the clothes lying all over the yard and Nainai's open door, she gave a snort of exasperation and bent down to put them back in the box.

'Come down at once!' she shouted, spying Xiao Mei up on

the roof. 'If you can't be bothered to help in any other way, at least sit in the yard and make sure she doesn't cause any further trouble!'

How on earth would they manage with her in a tenth-floor flat? Xiao Mei wondered as she climbed down.

~

Nainai lay on her bed and opened her eyes. She turned her face to the open door. Xiao Mei was sitting under the pomegranate tree, fiddling with her hair, twisting it round and round her fingers.

'That's me,' thought Nainai, 'waiting for Ma to come back from the melon fields. If I forget to feed the chickens again she will be angry with me.' She stared at Xiao Mei, willing her to move. Xiao Mei stood up and glanced through the open door. For a second their eyes met as if connected to each other by a single beam of light.

~

'Why is Ma always so jumpy?' Xiao Mei thought as she turned away and climbed the ladder to the roof. If Nainai left her room she would come down again; she did not need to be there all the time.

She sat on the roof looking out over the hutong. Tomorrow night, she thought, I'll be sleeping in a new space, high up in the sky. What will my room be like? What will it be like outside? And what about all the other people living there? Will they be friendly?

She had refused to see the new flat. After Stone's disappearance, she was too miserable to go anywhere. She thought about losing the Guanyin, about the white demolition sign painted on their walls, about how she and Stone had failed to get to Tiantan, and how, when she finally had got to Tiantan, poor, anxious Tong had dragged her away from the cypresses and back to the car where an angry Mrs Chen and a dejected-looking Ba were waiting for them. She thought of Nainai who was rapidly losing her mind, and of the fragile old aunts and their anxieties. She thought of Ma, always so stressed and irritable. She thought of the huangshulang whom they had banished to the wilderness. Then she thought again of Stone and the little white dog, and a heavy weight pressed down on her heart.

Finally, she thought about the dead baby. She wouldn't have known about it if she hadn't picked up the photo. Had Ma and Ba tried hard enough to save it? Had they really done everything they could possibly have done?

Nainai was right. She'd lost the little jade Guanyin and now it was her turn to be unlucky.

~

That evening Nainai sat on the stool underneath the pomegranate tree, waiting. By the stool was a small suitcase of clothes packed by Ma. 'This is yours,' Ma said. Nainai carried the suitcase outside, ready for the journey. Ba was about to pick it up but Nainai grabbed the handle and pushed him away.

'It's mine, don't touch it!'

'We're only leaving tomorrow,' he said, 'are you going to sit here all night? Here, you carry the case and we'll go back inside.'

Nainai scowled at him but she stood up and allowed herself to be guided back to her room and into her bed. Before closing her eyes, she ordered him to put the suitcase at the end of the bed near her feet. Ba stood by the bed for a few minutes, then switched off the light and shut the door. When he was out in the courtyard he slipped the bolt and snapped the padlock shut.

Xiao Mei climbed down from the roof and went to her room. Her own suitcase was standing in a corner. A clear plastic box containing her winter clothes was in another. Right at the bottom of the box, hidden amongst the clothes, was the red cloth monkey.

And then, how could she have forgotten? She pushed the bed aside, reached down for the loose brick in the wall and pulled out the little wooden box that had contained the jade figure and now contained the peach and cherry stones. Carefully she placed it inside her school bag. Then she went to bed. Ba and Old Wang were out in the courtyard talking in low voices. She tried not to think about the momentous day ahead.

~

Several bottles of beer stood on the ground next to Ba. Ma, cup in hand, came out to join them. They said little to each other.

'Ganbei,' said Ba after a while, raising his glass. 'To tomorrow!'

'To tomorrow,' echoed Old Wang raising his glass of beer
and Ma raising her cup of hot water said, 'To tomorrow!'

~

Xiao Mei stood alone in the empty courtyard. A little breeze
lifted the branches of the pomegranate tree. The doors of the
empty rooms swung on their hinges. Several beer bottles lay on
the ground. She climbed the ladder to the roof one last time
and looked out along the hutong. At the end stood a yellow
demolition vehicle. A van and a taxi were parked just below.
Ma called to her and she climbed down, walked slowly across
the yard and out over the wooden threshold.

Ba and Old Wang rode in the van. Xiao Mei, Ma and
Nainai went in the taxi, Xiao Mei sitting in the front and Ma
and Nainai in the back. Nainai stared straight ahead, clutching
a plastic bag. Ma slumped back, exhausted with the final effort
of packing.

Xiao Mei rolled the window down and looked out. Now the
van was moving. The taxi driver started up his engine and they
followed behind. Now they were passing Stone's house, or what
was left of it. A little gust of wind sprang up and blew eddies of
dust around the yard. There was a movement of something in
the shadows. Xiao Mei craned her head to look as they passed,
but it was nothing, just the play of the light. Now they were at
the end of the hutong, inching past the demolition vehicle. In
a few minutes they reached the main road where they picked
up speed and headed north to their new home.

He's not like the great big panda, thought Xiao Mei,

glancing at the scrawny taxi driver and thinking of plump, smooth-skinned Tong. The man looked as if he had been driving all night and smelled as if he had eaten raw garlic for breakfast. She looked back at Ma and Nainai. Ma, her mouth a little open, had fallen asleep, but Nainai was sitting bolt upright, holding tight to her bag, her head turned to look out of the window.

How strange it was, Xiao Mei thought. They had left forever, but it did not feel like that. The pomegranate tree, the roof, Old Wang feeding his pigeons, Ba smoking in the courtyard, Ma shelling peas, Nainai pottering around the kitchen, the huangshulang scratching in the corner - they were all there; she had just stepped out for a few hours. They would still be there, waiting for her, when she returned.

Then a different picture imposed itself: an image of dust and empty rooms, of a discarded tarpaulin and broken beer bottles; and of the heavy wooden doors creaking as Ba pulled them shut. In her mind she kept switching from one set of images to the other. It gave her a headache. She forced herself to stop thinking, and concentrated on the road ahead.

Through the window she could see the huge grey bulk of one of the remaining city gates. From behind her Nainai's voice said something and Ma gave a grunt of assent. The traffic had slowed almost to a standstill. A horse and cart drew alongside them in the cycle lane separated from the road by white railings. Xiao Mei leant out of the window. The cart was piled high with cardboard and driven by an old man holding the reins. The horse flicked its head from side to side.

'Put your head back in,' said Ma, 'or there'll be an accident.'

Soon the cause of the delay became visible. A black car had smashed into the railings. Two men were standing next to it, shouting into mobile phones. A taxi stood at an angle nearby, a large dent in its side. The driver was shouting at the men. They edged round the accident and after a short while the traffic began to unsnarl and pick up speed. The van with Ba and Old Wang was just ahead.

Tall buildings rose on either side of the road, light shimmering off their plate-glass windows. Tiny sticks of trees with infant branches had been planted all along at even spaces. 'The buildings look too big for the trees,' thought Xiao Mei, 'or the other way round.' The road was straight and the buildings converged in a single hazy point in the distance.

'It's very far away,' said Xiao Mei, turning round to look at Ma. 'How much further?'

'Not far,' said Ma vaguely.

'It's very far,' said Nainai. 'I feel uncomfortable.'

'Well, you'll just have to hold on,' said Ma. 'We can't stop here.'

Nainai sniffed and shifted in her seat.

The van was just ahead of them. Ba was leaning out of the window and pointing to the right. Nainai was wrong. They were nearly there.

They bumped down an unpaved road towards six or seven white blocks of flats, many storeys high. Beyond were several tall orange cranes and a half-built structure covered in scaffolding. The van swung left and stopped outside one of the blocks where a number of men were laying paving stones near the entrance.

'Is this it?' Xiao Mei asked, looking around her as she climbed out of the taxi. 'It's like a building site.'

Then Ba appeared. 'Let's go in,' he said.

'Where's Old Wang?' Xiao Mei asked.

'He's over there.' Ba pointed down the road. She saw him walking towards a similar building.

'Oh,' Xiao Mei said, disconcerted. 'He's not going to be with us then.'

'No, not in our building,' said Ba. 'Didn't I tell you?'

He helped Nainai out of the taxi. She looked around her.

'What is this place?'

'Our new home.' He took her arm but she pulled away and looked down at her hands.

'My bag, what did you do with my bag?'

The taxi was leaving, bumping slowly over the potholed surface. Ma ran after it and knocked on the window. The driver stopped. She opened the door and retrieved the bag. Nainai snatched it out of her hands without a word.

Xiao Mei ran ahead into the building. The entrance was dusty and the walls were covered with stickers printed with mobile phone numbers of all kinds of building and decorating services. She stood by the door of the lift staring at the panel of numbers.

'Which number are we?' she asked Ba as he came up behind her, followed by Ma and Nainai.

'Ten.' Almost at the top.

When the lift door opened, Nainai refused to go in.

'I'm not going in that cupboard,' she said in a firm voice, turning to leave.

Xiao Mei was about to say something when it occurred to her that probably Nainai had never been in a lift before. Ma took her mother-in-law's hand.

'It's all right,' she said. 'Look, we're all going in.'

The lift attendant looked at them curiously.

'What floor?'

'Ten,' said Ba proudly. 'We're moving in today.'

He pushed Nainai inside. When the doors closed and the lift began to ascend, Nainai gave a little gasp and clung to Ma's hand. The lift attendant laughed and said conventionally, 'The old lady's in pretty good health.'

Nainai said nothing but held her breath all the way up, as if willing the lift not to plunge to the ground.

They stepped out into a long dusty corridor. Ba pulled out two keys from his pocket and unlocked first the outer metal security gate and then the lightweight wooden inner door.

'You go first,' he said to Xiao Mei, and she stepped inside.

The door opened directly into the living room. The floor was covered in dust and there were marks on the newly painted walls. She ran from one room to the next, three small bedrooms, a tiny kitchen and a tiny bathroom. Then she ran to the window and looked out through the smeary pane. She was about to open it but Ma, who had come up behind her, told her not to in case she fell out. She stared through the glass at the grey sky, nothing but grey sky.

'What do you think?' said Ba. 'Not bad, is it.'

Xiao Mei turned and ran to the door, slamming it behind her. The automatic light in the corridor had gone off and the red numbers on the panel by the side of the lift were dark. Unable to see anything, she slumped against the wall and sank to the floor, where she sat sobbing, her head between her knees.

43.

Return to the Hutong

Stone walked quickly. He was his own master now. He knew – more or less – where he was going and what he would find when he arrived. He even had a friend, if she still wanted to be friends with him. He tried not to think about the little white dog.

The bus stops were far apart. There was nothing along the road that looked familiar, but every now and then a Tiantan bus would pass him so he knew he was going in the right direction.

Then he saw, with a leap of hope in his heart, something he recognised. Just ahead was the ironmonger's shop where he and Xiao Mei and the little white dog had sheltered from the rain. The sheet of metal that the wind had blown to the ground with a clang was still propped up against the wall. The same sallow young man was standing by the step, picking his teeth. Stone glanced at him as he walked past, but the young man stared into the distance and said nothing. Stone, who was used to being invisible, said nothing either. It was near here, after the thunderstorm, that Xiao Mei had taken the bus back home. Not being able to take the dog on the bus, he had walked. It had taken him about an hour.

The air was quite still and very hot. The trees cast black shadows on the ground. Stone was thirsty. If only he had money for an orange ice-lolly like the one that Xiao Mei had bought for him. Ahead was an ice-cream cart. He looked at it longingly. He squatted down nearby, watching a man buy an orange ice for a small boy who was pulling at his hand and screaming.

'If you don't stop that noise at once, I'll give it to someone else,' the man said impatiently.

The boy let out another loud wail. 'But I don't want that one. I want the other one!'

'I told you,' said the man, 'I only have enough small change for an orange ice.'

The boy stamped his foot and pummelled his father on his leg with his two little fists.

'That's enough,' said the man. 'I've had enough.'

And without another word, he walked over to Stone and shoved the orange ice into his bewildered hand. Then, before Stone could say anything, he picked up the screaming child and hurried away.

As Stone squatted by the side of the road licking the ice, he thought of the old man and the horse. He hoped he was all right and that his son had not left him again. Perhaps he would see him one day, trundling down the road with his cart piled high with cardboard, the horse snorting and panting with the effort. He remembered the son's mobile phone. If only he had one then he could call someone. He squeezed his eyes shut and tried to remember his uncle but all he could conjure up was the back of a thick neck and the pungent reek of garlic. The melting orange ice dripped onto his hand. Soon there was nothing left. He threw the stick to the ground, licked his fingers clean, stood up and looked around. He reckoned he was half way there.

The street he was on crossed a wide road with a white metal barrier down the middle, separating the flow of traffic. When he reached this intersection he could see, to his right, the footbridge that he and Xiao Mei had crossed. The tree-lined street had provided some shade but here the sun bounced off the tarmac and the plate-glass windows of the large grey buildings that lined the road. Stone wished he had another ice lolly. He walked up the ramp of the bridge. At the top lay the beggar, his one good hand stretched out in front of him holding a white enamel cup with a single coin inside. Stone looked at him, but the beggar, who had covered his head with a piece of cloth to keep the sun off, said nothing, though he rattled the cup as Stone walked past. Stone remembered the apricot and wished he had one to share with him.

Then he saw the bus stop, the very same one where he and Xiao Mei had looked at the sign and worked out that it was five stops to Tiantan. He ran down the ramp; he was nearly there. Just beyond the bus stop was the hutong he and Xiao Mei and the little white dog had walked along. He turned in, past the fruit stall heaped with peaches and melons, into the welcome shade of the dusty old scholar trees. The hutong on the next corner would be his one. He would go back to his courtyard house and wait. Xiao Mei was sure to come looking for him sooner or later.

He rounded the corner, stopped and looked ahead. He had come the wrong way. He must have turned off too early. He retraced his steps, back to the fruit stall. Then he turned round and walked back into the hutong. Sure enough, the little shop where Xiao Mei had got the packet of noodles for him was on his right, though it was boarded up now. Some way, further down on the left, was Xiao Mei's house, though the door was shut.

And ahead, on the right, was his house. Except it wasn't. Instead, what met his eyes were piles of rubble and a single white wall left standing. He stood in the middle of the hutong, heart thumping. Then, confirming his worst fears that it really was his house, or rather the remains of it, he caught sight of a limp strip of cloth hanging from a nail on the wall, his red vest, the only extra bit of clothing he possessed.

His heart thumping, he ran back down the hutong to Xiao Mei's house. Not daring to knock on the heavy double-leaf door, he peered in through the crack, fearful of going in, of being seen. The courtyard was quite empty, apart from several piles of rubbish. The door to Old Wang's room was open. He tried to look in through the small window that looked onto the hutong. It was too high, so he climbed up on a box that had been discarded by the door and peered through. The room was empty and its door was also swinging open. The family had gone.

Stone squatted down, his mind a miserable blank. He was hungry and very thirsty. He stared into the distance, saw the yellow demolition vehicle with its upraised claw, heard the shouts of men and the rumble and crash of falling walls, smelt the dusty air. In the broken branches of a tree the cicadas shrilled.

Something moved in the distance, something small and white coming towards him. He rubbed his eyes, it was just a trick of the light, surely. He stood up to get a better look, hardly daring to hope. And then it was unmistakable. The little white dog raced down the hutong and into his arms.

'You've come back,' said Stone, burying his face in the little dog's furry neck, 'you've come back!'

The dog licked his face, squirming with delight.

Stone walked back to the remains of his house to retrieve his vest. As they crossed the threshold the little dog wriggled out of his arms. It sniffed at the piles of rubble in the courtyard then trotted towards the wall. It was a moment or two before Stone noticed the two soft and slightly mouldy peaches, the perfectly intact packet of spicy chicken noodles and the bottle of mineral water. 'Xiao Mei,' he whispered to himself, 'she came back.' Then he saw the piece of paper under the bottle. He picked it up, unfolded it and read the single word written there. It was the first time he had ever received a message written specially for him.

He refolded the paper carefully and put it in his pocket. Then he unscrewed the top of the bottle and drank deeply. He ripped open the packet of noodles, sprinkled a few on the ground for the dog and ate the rest himself. After that he inspected the peaches, bit off the mouldy parts, and ate the rest. Then he lay down on his back by the wall, the little dog next to him, resting its chin on his chest. The light was fading. Bats flittered overhead in the evening air. Stone looked up at the sky, his hands clasped beneath his head, his eyelids heavy, his mind whirling with thoughts of all that had happened over the past few days.

~

The distant city noises vanished as if someone had closed the door of a room and shut them out, giving him the sensation of being enclosed within walls that were not there. He turned his head first to one side and then to the other but all he could hear was the thumping of his heart.

But when he looked up, he saw above him a faint transparent ceiling through which he could discern the pale ghostly shapes of chairs and tables, and above them another ceiling, and another room, and another ceiling and another, higher and higher, till all merged together in a mist where no detail could be distinguished.

Turning his head, he saw a door with a panel of numbers down its side. The door slid open and a man and a woman walked out, oblivious to his presence. He stood up, looked around him and saw that he was still in the courtyard; the rooms were intact, the wooden threshold and the door to the hutong were still there. Washing was hanging from a line strung between two poles. Mrs Li was sitting on a stool, sorting through garlic shoots. Mr Li was mending a bicycle. A young man was sitting on the step, washing his feet in a bowl.

No one noticed Stone, even when he stood right in the middle of the courtyard, in that space occupied simultaneously by present, past and future. Neither did they seem to be aware of the ghostly walls and ceilings that towered above them. The little white dog under his arm, he walked to the lift, pressed the button, and the door opened and he stepped inside. Mrs Li looked up for a moment then carried on what she was doing. The lift shot up. He pressed frantically at the buttons but the lift did not stop until it had reached the top and burst out into the sky. Only then did the door open.

Stone spread his arms just in time to ride an uplift of warm air. The dog tumbled on top of him. When he looked down all he could see was a thick blanket of yellow cloud and the tops of tall buildings, and in the far distance faint grey smudges that were the Western Hills. He plunged down through the clouds and, using his hands like paddles, propelled himself over the city, spread out below him like a map.

From such a height, the city revealed itself in all its forms. There was the broad highway that cut through from east to west and the ring road that followed the line of the old city wall, and the remaining great gates, and the imperial palace in the centre with its yellow roofs and red walls. And there were the secretive courtyards of the little hutongs that led off left and right like the ribs of a body. In vast open areas of wasteland were tall yellow cranes dangling loads of concrete, and massive pits the size of whole villages, which would become the foundations of new buildings. To the north he saw a spiky mass of shining metal rods like a giant bird's nest and next to it a cube of shimmering glass. And beyond those were rows and rows of tall white towers. High above were planes flying in to land. He banked and swung back south.

Now he was flying low over the long-distance bus-station, circling, looking for someone amongst the crowds that thronged the streets. The corncob seller was still standing there, her white polystyrene box of yellow cobs covered with a cotton cloth. Passengers descended from buses and streamed out in a solid flow to the main street where they dispersed in all directions. He followed the street to the east, turning his head from side to side as he flew, hoping to find what he was looking for. A little further and he came to a building site. Trucks trundled through a temporary gateway decorated with pink bunting. Two men squatted outside the gatekeeper's wooden shack.

Then he caught his breath, and was filled with hope. A big man with a fat neck, lying on the ground in the shade of the shack, mouth wide open, nostrils flaring as he breathed in and out, gleaming stomach bulging over grimy shorts.

'Uncle!' he called in desperation, 'Uncle!'

But the uncle did not stir, not until a man in a white shirt and yellow helmet strode over and shouted at him to get up. Then the uncle sat up slowly, scrambled to his feet, picked up his pickaxe and lumbered off. Stone watched him as he walked slowly down the side of a giant pit and disappeared out of sight.

~

The little white dog stood on Stone's chest licking his face. He pushed the dog away, then sat up and rubbed his eyes. He had slept all through the night and the sun was up.

Squatting on his haunches, he picked up a twig and drew a line in the dust to help him think. But the line became a circle and returned him to the point he had started from. He scribbled round and round. Then he snapped the stick in two and threw it across the yard.

He put his hand in his pocket and drew out Xiao Mei's piece of paper and once again read the word it contained. 'Sorry'. In the clear light of morning, he understood that the word marked a finality, and that there was no point in staying here any longer.

44.

Back in the City

Mouse-wolf and Little Yellow had buried themselves under a pile of cloths in the back of the van and were keeping themselves as still as possible, fearful of attracting the attention of the humans sitting in front. The smell from the hutong huangshulang's box was familiar but unpleasant, the smell of a stranger, even though she was one of them. For a while there was the sound of animated voices from the seats in front but these soon faltered and, except for the steady purring of the engine, there was silence. Petrol fumes wafted up through a rusty hole in the floor.

Mouse-wolf felt the little bag that had hung around his neck for so long. Now it was lying next to him. He took the jade figure out and stood it up. The Guanyin glowed, a faint smile on her lips.

'What will you do with it now?' asked Little Yellow.

Mouse-wolf hesitated and twisted round to scratch his leg. Then he said, 'It's done. They'll do the rest.'

'The rest?'

'It's up to them now. It's out of our hands.'

'But will she get it back?'

'Perhaps. I don't know.'

'It's up to Fate?'

'Yes, this last part is up to Fate.'

'Or up to them?'

'Both. It depends.'

'Depends on what?'

'On chance. And on whether he does the right thing.'

'She might never get it back.'

'No. But she might.'

Little Yellow fell silent. She lay down and thought about many things. She thought about the hutong huangshulang left behind in the mountains, about the chickens and the rats and the hordes of twittering mice. Finally, with a sharp pang, she thought about the crackle of yellow flames and Big Yellow trying to escape through the smoke. What had his Fate been?

The sound of the engine changed. The van was slowing down, turning. Then it stopped and the two men got out, followed by the girl. The driver opened the back door, took out the box and slammed the door shut. Not enough time to escape unnoticed. Immediately, the driver started up the engine and the van moved off.

Now the huangshulang were wide awake, wrinkling their noses and pricking up their ears. Familiar smells and sounds floated in through the driver's open window – rotting vegetables, stale cooking oil, chilli vapour, cigarette smoke, snatches of conversation and song, the hooting of cars and taxis, the rumble of buses, the pulsating of cicadas in the trees. The city was all around them.

The van stopped again. The driver switched off the engine, got out and shut the door. There was the sound of footsteps retreating down the narrow street, and then silence.

The huangshulang lay motionless, their senses on high alert. Then, in no more than the blink of an eye, one after the other they squeezed through the hole in the floor and dropped to the ground below. Mouse-wolf peered out from under the van's chassis. A bicycle went past but nothing else moved. The two huangshulang froze for a moment, then darted out. They were briefly illuminated by the light of a street lamp before they disappeared into a dark space by a wall.

45.

Tong

It had been a good day out in the mountains, Tong thought. No one had made any unreasonable demands, he had slept well in the middle of the day, and he'd had an excellent bowl of noodles at lunchtime. Most of all, it had been fun being with Xiao Mei. It was not like being with Mrs Chen, who was particular about everything and so very hard to please.

When he arrived back at the little flat where he lived with his mother near Tiantan he was exhausted and went straight to bed. The next day he took his mother to the hospital for treatment for her high blood-pressure, and for some days after that Mrs Chen kept him busy from morning to night driving her around on shopping expeditions, having her hair or nails done, or going out to the airport to meet one of Old Song's business partners. For these events he drove the car, and the van remained parked on the street. There was also one afternoon when he drove back out to the hills.

It was some days later before he had time on his hands to give the van a good clean. When he opened the back, the smell hit him. The cages and the box had gone, and all that remained were the tools, the empty crate of soft drinks and the pile of old cloths. It was days since the pigeons and the huangshulang had been there but the smell was still strong.

He opened the windows and the doors. The only thing to do would be to take everything out, get a bucket of soapy water, and wash down the interior. Mrs Chen would not like a bad smell in her van, not that she ever rode in it. He picked up the tools and put them on the back seat. He put the empty crate on the pavement for someone to take away. He scooped up the pile of old cloths and dumped them on the roof. He spent the next hour brushing and washing and polishing till the smell was almost gone and the van shone. Then he arranged the tools neatly in the back and took the bundle of cloths off the roof.

They too had an animal smell so he shook them out one by one over the road. Dust and feathers and a scrap of red fabric flew off and a few little nails scattered on the ground. But in one of the old sheets there was something else. Tong could feel it, heavy like a small pebble. He might have shaken it out and the thing would have shattered into pieces on the ground. But instead, he put his hand into the folds.

When he withdrew his hand and opened up his palm he saw, to his surprise, that he was holding a small figure carved out of some sort of smooth shiny material like opaque glass. Turning it the right way up, he peered at it more closely. She was standing, eyes cast down, one hand raised in front of her chest, the other holding a long-stemmed vase. The long-sleeved robe she was wearing fell in folds about her body. He scratched at the dirt that was caught in some of the folds. When he held it up to the light it emitted a faint glow. It must be Mrs Chen's, he thought, strange she had not mentioned that she had lost it. He put it in his pocket and resolved to phone her later in the day.

When he looked back into the van he noticed something else. The bundle of cloths had concealed a ragged hole about the size of child's hand. He would have to fix it before the rust got any worse. He sighed. It was about time that Mrs Chen thought of buying a new van but it was an awkward thing to bring up. She did not discuss her plans with him.

It was already evening when he remembered the little figure. He took it out and set it on the table as he rang Mrs Chen's number. She was abrupt with him.

'What is it? I'm busy.'

He told her what he had found.

'What figure?' she asked impatiently, her voice fading as she turned away from the phone, 'No, no, no, not that colour, the lilac one.'

He had dropped her at her friend's flat in the morning and now, it seemed, she had got herself to the beauty parlour.

'The little statue,' he said. 'I found it in the back of the van.'

'You phoned me just to tell me that?' Mrs Chen snapped. 'I don't know what you are talking about. And by the way,' she went on, 'you had better come and pick me up. I'll be done in fifteen minutes.'

Tong sighed. He picked up the keys to the car.

'I'm going out,' he called to his mother. But before he left, he took the little figure out of his pocket and hid it under his pillow. As he drove Mrs Chen back home, he did not mention it to her again.

~

Mrs Chen had a busy schedule over the next few days so Tong was fully occupied. The jade Guanyin remained hidden under his pillow until he had time to do something about it. It was not until the following Monday that he finally had a free afternoon. Mrs Chen had a cold and had taken to her bed for several days. He knew this because in the morning she had him go to the pharmacist's with a long list of medicines to buy. Her forthcoming departure for Africa was affecting her nerves, she said.

He set out with the little jade figure in his pocket. Could it be Xiao Mei's perhaps? He was not sure that it belonged to her but he wanted an excuse to see the little girl again. The song kept going round and round in his head: 'Why do I wander, wander so far?' He thought of when she had raced him laughing down the Spirit Way, so free, he thought, free as a bird. He wished he had more fun like that.

He turned out of his street and into the next one, and then headed north past the ironmonger's shop and under the footbridge. At some red traffic lights he put his head out of the window to check he was going the right way. He recognised the fruit stall on the corner of the hutong. He was nearly there. Several turns more and he knew where he was. The houses ahead had been demolished, but he saw, to his relief, that Xiao

Mei's house was still standing. He parked the van by the wall.

The heavy wooden doors swung open when he pushed lightly against them. He stepped over the threshold and walked into the empty courtyard. They had gone. He felt a pricking in his eyes.

The jade Guanyin was in his pocket. He pulled her out, turning her over and over in his fingers as he pondered what to do next. Then he sat down and set the little statue on the step next to him, and the two of them waited, gazing out over the courtyard.

A noise behind him, a snuffling, pattering sound, startled him. When he looked round he saw a white dog, standing by the door. The dog was small and friendly looking so he put out his hand and called to it. The dog hesitated, one paw lifted, and trotted over to him. He patted it on its head and stood up. There was no point in staying any longer.

He was about to pick up the Guanyin when something caught his eye and he squatted down to take a closer look. But the glowing colours that seemed to come from within the little figure – rose pink, sage green, lavender mauve – were just a trick of the light flickering through the pomegranate leaves.

The dog gave a low bark. He heard running footsteps, someone coming up behind him. He turned, was about to stand up, his hand over the jade figure.

A boy stood there, one hand on the dog's neck.

Tong slipped the Guanyin back into his pocket.

'They've gone,' said the boy.

Tong looked at him. 'Do you know where they've gone?' he

asked, already knowing the answer before the words were out of his mouth.

'No.'

Tong sat down again, feeling tired. The boy sat next to him.

'Do you have anything to eat?'

Tong felt in his pocket and brought out some chewing-gum.

Stone took it.

'Did you know the family?' asked Tong after a while.

'No.'

Tong sighed.

'Only Xiao Mei.'

Tong turned to look at him.

'You knew Xiao Mei?'

'She was my friend. But I'll never see her again.'

Tong said nothing but he took the jade out from his pocket, concealing it in his hand.

'What's that?'

Tong opened up his hand slowly.

'Is this hers?'

Stone caught his breath. He put out his hand.

'Can I hold it?'

Tong hesitated. Could he trust him not to run away with it? He closed his hand over the figure. The boy was looking at him wide-eyed.

'Please?'

Tong opened up his hand again. The jade figure stood on his palm, glowing in the light. Stone stretched out a finger and touched it. Then he brought his other hand close and scooped the little Guanyin up, cupping her in both his hands, a goddess sitting on a lotus blossom.

'Yes,' he said. 'It's Xiao Mei's.'

A little breeze blew through the pomegranate tree. Tong gazed up at the hazy vapour trails in the sky, thinking. Then he took out his phone and tapped a message. It was better not to speak to her directly otherwise she would find another job for him to do. The answer came a few minutes later. The place was quite far away.

'Would you like to come with me?' he said to Stone.

'Can I take the dog?'

Tong nodded. Stone held out the jade figure. Tong took it and put it back in his pocket. They walked to the van, the little white dog tucked under Stone's arm.

~

Stone sat on the front seat next to Tong, holding the little dog firmly. The dog did not like being in the van so Stone opened the window a little. Scrabbling with its paws against the door, the dog stood on its hind legs and stuck its nose out through the gap. Stone thought about the last time he had been in a van. He had sat in the back on the floor with no idea of where he was being taken. Now he was riding in the front, like when the old man allowed him to drive the cart. He wondered what had happened to him and if he would ever see him and the horse again.

'She was looking for it everywhere,' he said after a while.

Tong scanned the road ahead looking for a road sign. He said nothing.

'Where did you find it?'

'She forgot it in the van.'

'The van?' Stone was puzzled. 'Not in Tiantan?'

'Well, I live in Tiantan. I found it when I got home,' said Tong.

'Oh,' said Stone, 'you live in the park.'

Tong glanced at him.

'Of course not. No one lives in the park. I live nearby.'

Stone could not work it out. She said she had lost it in the park. He was about to ask another question but Tong interrupted him.

'Don't talk. I don't know these roads.'

Stone fell silent. He sat back. Perhaps she had been pretending and he had been drawn into some silly adventure. The little white dog was restless so he pulled it away from the window and put it down on the floor. The dog snuffled around by his feet.

'He can smell the pigeons,' said Tong, 'and the huangshulang.'

Stone was not listening. He was staring out of the window and thinking about Xiao Mei. Would she still be angry with him? Turning away so that Tong would not see it, he put his hand in his pocket and drew out the photo.

46.

Sweet Resiny Air

Mouse-wolf and Little Yellow hid by the wall for a short while. There was something wafting on the air that told them that not so far away was a different sort of space to the place they were in now. Little Yellow raised her head and sniffed. Mouse-wolf sensed they needed to head south.

Keeping close to the wall they set off. It was dark and the sun would not rise for four or five hours. Mouse-wolf moved quickly, Little Yellow following close behind. The streets were lined with little shops and there were many hiding places, boxes left out on the pavement, bins for rubbish, trees, dark corners and gutters. They followed the street to the end where it joined a wide, treeless, well-lit road, divided down the middle by railings. Though there was less traffic than in the daytime, there were still a few cars, mostly taxis. A horse and cart was visible in the distance, its sleepy driver slumped over the reins.

Mouse-wolf looked right and left. Barely checking to see that Little Yellow was following him, he darted across the road to the central barrier, only then turning round to see if she had followed. Then he looked out at the half of the road they still had to cross. There were more cars on this side and every now and then an overloaded truck rumbled past on its way out of the city.

The pull to the south was becoming ever stronger. For a second time, as soon as there was a gap in the traffic, and scarcely looking at Little Yellow, he dashed across the road to the other side. Only then did he glance back and saw Little Yellow still sitting by the central barrier. A car was in the distance, there would just be time. He willed her to cross. She dashed out and at that moment, the car - a black one with a flashing red light - sped past and vanished into the distance. Little Yellow was nowhere to be seen.

Mouse-wolf stiffened in panic. He ran first one way and then the other. There was no sign of her. She was gone. Like Big Yellow, she was gone. But an overwhelming instinct to keep moving south drove out any further emotions. Keeping close to the gutter, he hastened along the wide road, looking for a turning.

Now there was a different noise. A woman wearing a headscarf and white cotton mask rhythmically sweeping the side of the road came towards him. He froze, and her long-handled brush just touched him as she passed. Half-asleep as she was, she did not see him. He thought again of Little Yellow, but the thought vanished as soon as he started moving again.

Just ahead he saw what he was looking for, a southward-leading alleyway. He hurried forward, then stopped, catching his breath.

A small dark shape was sitting on the corner. It was Little Yellow, blown out of sight by the force of the speeding car. She was out of breath but unhurt.

'I'm all right,' she said.

Mouse-wolf just nodded.

The two huangshulang continued moving south. Black buildings obscured the horizon. The sky above was paler. In the distance was a long building. Its two roofs with upturned eaves, a black pearl on top of each, were silhouetted against the sky. A footbridge arced across the road. A little wind blew up. Mouse-wolf stopped for a second and raised his nose to the sweet resiny air. Little Yellow looked at him enquiringly but he said nothing and just hurried on.

By the long building Little Yellow stopped. 'Wait,' she said picking something up in her paw. 'Look.'

It was a little green jade bead. They were nearly there. Mouse-wolf stretched out his neck and sniffed.

On top of the footbridge they stopped again and looked west. The sun came up behind them, casting its bright rays on the red walls, the dark green cypresses, and the golden drop on top of the blue roof of the Temple of Heaven at Tiantan.

Mouse-wolf let out a deep breath.

'We're home.'

47.

The Return

'You are not to go out, do you hear? You don't know your way around and you'll get lost,' Ma said sharply as she left to go shopping . Xiao Mei was about to follow her into the lift.

Xiao Mei kicked the corridor wall, went back into the flat and stood by the window. She put her head under the curtain and pressed her face to the glass. Down below she saw Ma walking quickly across the yard, turning a corner and disappearing out of sight. The curtains were drawn to keep out the heat. Ba had switched the air-conditioning off because it was too expensive and Nainai complained of cold draughts. Then she sat down on her bed between the four cream-coloured walls of her room, feeling bored and disconsolate.

Through the closed door she could hear Ba and Old Wang talking in the living room. Since the windows were also closed their cigarette smoke had nowhere to go except to swirl around the room and under her door. Nainai was in her room, also with the door shut.

A flowerpot stood on the window-sill. She raked a finger through the earth. Would the peach and cherry stones ever grow in air like this? She stared through the window, tracing patterns on its dusty surface. Workmen down below were constructing a concrete-covered walkway on the patch of land between their building and the next. The ground, muddy from the last heavy rainfall, was rutted with tracks. In the hazy grey distance rose a line of white tower blocks. Cars sped past on the main road.

A van drew up outside the building. She watched it idly as it reversed into a space by the wall alongside a row of bicycles. She heard the door being slammed and voices. And saw the plump figure of the driver standing by the van, looking up at the building.

'Oh!'

She leapt off the bed, dashed into the living room, and before Ba or Old Wang could say anything, was out of the door and pressing the lift button. The lift door opened almost immediately. 'Going out?' said the lift attendant and jabbed at the ground floor button with a short bamboo stick. Xiao Mei said nothing but stood there, willing the lift to go faster.

The lift stopped, infuriatingly, at the seventh floor. The door slid open. A woman with a baby in her arms got in. No one said anything. The baby dribbled. Xiao Mei shifted from one foot to the other.

When the door opened she ran out into the dark hallway. The door to the outside was standing open, letting in a shaft of white sunlight. A round figure stood at the entrance, silhouetted against the radiance. She hesitated.

'Xiao Mei!' Tong beamed at her.

But she was looking past Tong and out towards the van.

He did not move but the dog wriggled out of his arms and ran towards her. She picked it up and stroked its head.

'Stone!' she said, her eyes wide.

'Xiao Mei!' Tong called. 'I've got something for you.' But she did not look back.

Stone stood quite still by the van. She stopped, squeezed her eyes tight shut and opened them again.

'You didn't die!'

He looked at her quizzically.

'No?'

'I thought, I thought...'

'Thought what?'

'That, that...' The words tumbled out in a rush, how she was angry because of him and the photo, how the demolition men had come to find out if there was anyone living in the house because they had seen the red vest.

'And, and...I didn't tell them that you were there.'

'Well,' said Stone matter-of-factly, 'I wasn't.'

'But, don't you understand?' Xiao Mei's voice rose. 'I didn't know you weren't there.'

They looked at each other in silence as Stone digested what she was saying. He turned his face away and stared out over the yard.

'Stone?' She looked at her feet. 'I didn't mean to.' Tears welled up in her eyes. She squatted down and buried her head in her arms, her shoulders shaking.

The dog nuzzled at her but Stone pulled it away. Then he put his hand in his pocket and dropped the photo at her feet.

'There's your photo. I don't want it anymore.'

Xiao Mei looked up at him, her face streaked with tears. The family in the photo stared up at her, impassively.

Tong came up behind them. When he saw Xiao Mei's tears and Stone's unforgiving expression, a shadow passed across his good-humoured features. He opened the van door.

'We'd better sit inside,' he said. Stone picked up the little white dog and climbed up onto the front seat next to the driver's.

'Go on,' said Tong when Xiao Mei hesitated. She climbed onto the back seat. Tong climbed in next to her. She was still sniffing.

For a while no one said anything. Stone stared out of the window. Xiao Mei wiped her face with a corner of her t-shirt. Tong looked from one to the other, wondering what had happened. The little white dog jumped off Stone's lap through the gap between the front seats and clambered up onto Xiao Mei's.

Then, after a moment's hesitation, Tong put his hand in his pocket and drew out a small package wrapped in newspaper.

'Xiao Mei,' he said. 'I found this.' He put it in her hand. Stone sat very still in the front, staring straight ahead of him.

Xiao Mei pushed the dog off her lap and turned the package over.

'Open it.' Tong looked anxious. 'Stone said you'd lost it.'

Stone shifted in his seat and turned his head.

She unwrapped the newspaper, feeling something inside. How cool and smooth it was! When she held it up to her half-closed eyes, she saw it glow through her fingers. She opened her eyes and gave a small gasp. The Guanyin smiled up at her. She looked from Tong, to Stone and back to Tong again.

'I found it. It's yours, isn't it?' said Tong, wiping his arm across his sweaty forehead.

'But..?' The words would not come out. She nodded, her eyes bright with tears.

Tong smiled in relief. 'Don't cry, little sister, don't cry!'

Xiao Mei said nothing but stared at the Guanyin for a long time. Tong and Stone looked at her. Then she looked up at Tong.

'Where did you find it?'

'At home in Tiantan.'

'Oh, you went back to the park?' Xiao Mei was puzzled, had she told him she'd lost it? As she glanced up something caught her attention in the rear view mirror. Ma with two heavy bags on her way back from the supermarket. She had to hurry.

She looked from Tong to Stone and back to Tong again. Tong wiped the sweat from his face with the back of his hand. Stone stared at her, his one eye bright in his face, dusty hair sticking up on his head. The little white dog twisted on her lap, pawing at her knees.

Xiao Mei took a deep breath. She knew what she had to do. She cupped the little jade figure in her hands. The Guanyin stood on her palms looking out at the world.

Then she stretched out her arms towards Stone.

'Please,' she said, looking away, 'take it.'

Stone looked at her with his one eye.

'Take it. Please.'

Stone put out his hand, then withdrew it and rested it on the back of the seat.

Xiao Mei looked at him directly.

'It's yours now.'

Stone hesitated, then took the little jade figure from her palm and held it to his cheek. Surprise, confusion, pleasure and again confusion passed across his thin face. After a while he gave a lopsided little smile. He said nothing.

Xiao Mei turned to Tong. 'Thank you, big brother.'

Tong sank back in his seat, a look of incomprehension on his guileless face.

'You gave it away, it was yours!'

'Yes,' said Xiao Mei. 'I did.' But she could not explain, even to herself, quite why she had done so. All she knew was that it felt right.

Tong shook his head.

She pulled at the door handle. 'I've got to go. She'll be mad at me again.' Then, turning to Stone, as she hurried out of the car, she said, 'What will you do now?'

Stone shrugged.

'He can come with me,' said Tong, 'and help me with a few things.' He remembered something and bent down to put his hand under his seat. 'Here.'

Into Xiao Mei's hands he placed a jar of honey. She murmured a word of thanks.

As she walked back slowly towards the tower block there was a sudden rush of feet behind her. The little white dog leapt up and Stone, his face flushed, thrust the photo at her, saying 'You nearly forgot it.' He stood there for a moment as if wanting to say more. For a moment his hand was on hers and then he was gone.

~

Tong revved the engine, and bumped down the rutted track and out onto the main road. He sat in forlorn silence all the way back to Tiantan and said nothing until he had stopped the van.

'You had better come in and have something to eat.'

So Stone followed him inside and Tong's mother served soupy noodles and watched with pleasure as he slurped them down, first one bowl, then another and then another. Then she made up a bed for him on the sofa and watched him as he fell asleep, the goddess clutched in his hand and the little white dog lying ever watchful by his feet.

Like all the other days that lay ahead, tomorrow would have to take care of itself.

48.

Miaoshan

Xiao Mei arrived back home expecting trouble from Ma. The door of the flat was ajar. She stood outside in the dark corridor, looking in. Old Wang had gone. Ma was taking a long narrow box out of her bag. She opened one end, pulled out a roll of paper and handed it to Ba.

'What's this?' he asked as he unrolled it.

Ma said nothing.

Ba held the scroll at arm's length. It was a painting of mountains and a river. In the bottom right hand corner was a red seal.

'That's nice,' he said. 'Where did you get it?'

'Oh,' she said, 'someone at work gave it to me. For our new flat.'

Ba looked at it more closely. 'It's an original.'

'Yes,' she said. 'It's an original.'

'Might be worth something.' He turned and looked at the wall. 'Let's find the best place to hang it.'

Xiao Mei went inside. Ma and Ba looked at her for a moment, then turned back to the painting.

'I think we should hang it there,' Ba said, 'right in the middle.'

Xiao Mei looked at the painting. Such high wild mountains and such a fierce river. And a tiny solitary stooped figure walking along a stony path.

Ba pointed at the figure and laughed.

'That's how I feel sometimes! All on my own, battling against the elements!'

'Everyone feels like that,' said Ma quietly. 'You're not the only one.'

Xiao Mei slipped into her room and pulled her school bag out from under her bed. She unzipped the bag, took out the little wooden box and rubbed it against her shorts to clean it. Then she opened the lid and looked inside at the faded red silk padding. She should have given Stone the box as well. But perhaps, after all, it was better that she kept it, to remind her of all that had happened. She closed the lid and put the box under her pillow.

Ma looked in through the door. 'Are you hungry? We'll eat soon.'

Xiao Mei smiled and sat up.

'I'll come and help you.'

Ma looked at her in surprise. 'You could put the shopping away and then wash the spinach.'

'Ma, who painted that picture?' Xiao Mei asked a little while later as she sorted through the spinach leaves.

Ma hesitated, then said, 'No one you know very well.'

She was about to ask another question but Ma had turned her back and was washing her hands in the sink. A thought ignited in Xiao Mei's mind, a tiny flicker of comprehension.

'Oh,' she said.

It was only later, when Xiao Mei was getting undressed to go to bed, that she remembered the photo. She pulled it out of her pocket and looked at it. One corner was folded down and there were dirty marks on the back. She turned it over. Something new had been added: a thumbprint made with hutong dust, where Stone had held the photo, gazing at the family and wishing they were his.

She thought of the little jade figure, now tucked away in Stone's pocket perhaps. Then she thought of something else. She went quickly into the living room and squatted down by the glass-fronted cupboard. The little picture book was, as before, on the bottom shelf.

Ba was sprawled on the sofa, watching the weather forecast.

'What are you looking for?'

'Nothing, just something to read.'

She returned to her room where she sat on the bed flicking through the pages until she found the one she wanted. Then she lay back against her pillow and read.

~

"Miaoshan said nothing, but stood quite still, her hands folded before her in prayer. Around her head hovered a radiance that penetrated the cavernous gloom. The drifting ghosts were drawn towards the light like moths to a flame.

When King Yan saw the strong, young woman standing unafraid before him he knew he had met his match. He watched helplessly as Miaoshan blessed each lost soul one by one and they floated out of the cave into the light, ready to be reborn in a new body and live their life again.

Then Miaoshan walked out of the cave and when she came to the entrance she saw the Buddha standing before her holding out a peach as a gift. He instructed her to eat it, saying that from now on she would never suffer from hunger or thirst and that she must go to the holy island of Putuo mountain.

When Miaoshan arrived at the island she stopped and stared in wonder. Who would not want to stay on this beautiful, light-filled island and leave the miseries of the world behind forever?

She thought of her father the king, whose greed for wealth was more important that his own daughter's life, of her weak mother who was powerless to protect her, and of the soldiers who loved her but whose fear of the king overrode their love, and of the lost souls drifting for all time in the underworld in their hopeless search for freedom.

Then she took a step, turned round and walked back into the world, and along her path flowers grew and the air was filled with a sweet fragrance.

She remains in this world to this very day, and is known as Guanyin, the goddess with a thousand arms and a thousand eyes, the one who perceives all sounds on earth, the compassionate one, the protector of women and girls, full of unconditional love for all people and all things."

~

As Xiao Mei came to the end, she thought of Stone. She smiled. Her eyelids fluttered and closed, and she fell into a deep and dreamless sleep.

49.

The Roof

In the weeks after they moved into the new flat, Ma and Ba became less anxious about Xiao Mei going out on her own.

'After all,' Ba said, 'once term starts she'll have to get to school by herself.'

Ma in particular seemed less stressed. Though they now lived much further away from her work, there was a metro line that took her directly to the department store. 'It's so convenient,' she kept saying, 'and I nearly always get a seat.'

Ma's artist friend at work often gave her paintings and these now hung in every room.

'I've never met an artist,' said Ba as he stuck a big red peony on the bedroom wall. 'They must be interesting people.'

'I'll introduce you to her one day,' Ma said, 'if she has time.'

Once Ma left for work, Ba began to feel restless. After staring for a while at the television, he switched it off and went down to the yard. It was an irritation that he always had to remember to take his keys, not like when they lived in the courtyard. Sometimes he took Nainai with him or, rather, he would turn round when he was at the lift and see that she had followed him out, shopping bag in hand and a determined look on her face. Once outside, he would look for Old Wang and they would settle down for a game of cards, Nainai sitting on an upturned box next to them.

Nainai had overcome her suspicion of the lift and had taken to riding it up and down several times a day. Ba was forever having to go outside and look for her. She did not go far, but would sit on a wall watching the traffic pass at the end of the road. From their upstairs balcony Ba would see her stand up and stare around her before setting off home in the wrong direction. Then he would rush downstairs and bring her back.

'When are we going home?' she would ask plaintively. 'I don't know this place.'

'She's not happy,' he said to Ma. 'I don't know what to do.'

Ma shrugged her shoulders.

'We do what we can. At least she's got us.' She thought of the two aunts living on their own with no one visiting them except her, and now Teacher Fu. She was glad she had introduced Teacher Fu to them and her painting classes could continue at the aunts' house.

Old Wang lived in the building behind. His flat was on the third floor and, because it was north-facing, had little sun. Like Nainai, he would often wander out into the yard where he would sit in the shadow of a wall. The recently planted sapling trees gave little shade. But in the evening, when the sun was low, he and Ba would squat down and play a game of cards, two glasses and a bottle of spirits by their feet. He did not often go to Ba's flat. It felt awkward having to take the lift up to the tenth floor and then ring the bell to be let in as if they were strangers and not the close neighbours that they once had been when all that separated them was a small courtyard with a pomegranate tree. He missed that. Above all he missed the pigeons and the daily routine of feeding them and cleaning out their cage. How things change, he thought. Now they are free and here am I cooped up in this box of a flat.

~

One early evening, after a night of heavy rain and not many days after they had moved in, Xiao Mei glanced at Ma to say she was taking the rubbish out, stepped through the door and walked down to the end of the dark corridor. She lifted the metal lid of the chute and dropped the bag of rubbish in, waiting for a moment to hear it fall ten floors to the bottom. None of the numbers on the lift panel was illuminated. The lift attendant must have taken a break.

Xiao Mei walked over to the stairs. But instead of going down, she went up. The floor numbers were stencilled in red on the wall of each floor. No one came down as she walked up, though she smelled cooking smells, and heard faint voices and, on one floor, the incessant yapping of a small dog. Stickers and handprints marked the walls. High on the wall up by the thirteenth floor were the faint marks of shoe soles. She wondered how they had got there.

On the fourteenth floor, which was the top floor, she stopped and looked down the dark corridor that led away from the lift. It was identical to theirs. A bicycle was leaning against the wall outside the second door on the left. Forgetting for a moment where she was, she wondered why Ba had left it there.

The stairs continued, as if the builders had just kept building staircases until they had had enough and put a roof on top of the whole thing. She hesitated for a moment, curious about where they led. She walked up.

At the top was a pale green door, not like the doors of the flats but narrower, with a padlock and a bolt. Although the padlock was locked, the hoop it was dangling from was not engaged with the hasp. She stood still for a moment and pulled on the door. It creaked open. A steep flight of dusty concrete steps rose in front of her. A cool breeze wafted down. At the top was nothing but pale sky.

She ran up the steps, stopping short of the top. A strong wind whipped her hair across her face. She stepped forward and stood on the wide wet concrete surface. Far in the distance stretched the misty ridge of the Western Hills. She walked as close to the edge as she dared and looked down. Far below, half hidden in the warm mists rising from the ground, were antlike cars and people. Beyond were clusters of white tower blocks rising up through the murky yellow air.

She stepped back and sat down, her heart racing with vertigo and the notion that there were no barriers to stop her from stepping off the side and plummeting to the ground. For a while she sat still, then turned onto her stomach and, careless of the wet surface, crawled back to the edge.

The sky to the west was turning a fiery orange, fading upwards into pale lemon, olive green, deep cyan blue. In the distance she saw planes with their black vapour trails flying in to land in the east, and below them highways with moving ribbons of red and white light.

She turned over to lie on her back and in the tattered flags of golden clouds she thought she saw a smiling face and a thousand waving arms. As if in acknowledgement of a benign presence, the high white beams of two distant searchlights swept the starless sky. Xiao Mei sighed. It was magnificent.

50.

Top of the World

The morning sun streamed in through Xiao Mei's window. She sat up and listened to the silence. The television was off. They were all out. She took a steamed bun from the kitchen, made sure her key was in her pocket, and shut the front door behind her. When she got to the end of the corridor she saw, to her irritation, Nainai standing by the lift. She had followed Ba out but he had not seen her behind him and had gone. She grabbed Xiao Mei by the arm.

'Now we can go out together,' she said, a purposeful look on her face.

'I'll take you home.' Xiao Mei turned back to the corridor as she bit into the bun. But Nainai held her fast with her dry little hand.

'I don't want to go back there. I want to go out.'

Nainai's eyes were bright. Xiao Mei hesitated for a moment and pressed the lift button. The door opened. 'Fourteen,' she said. The lift attendant raised her eyebrows. Xiao Mei said nothing. 'Going up,' said Nainai.

The lift door opened. Xiao Mei took Nainai's hand in her own and led her to the foot of the stairs. They climbed slowly,

Nainai stopping for breath half way up. When they reached the top Xiao Mei pushed the door open. Bright sunlight flooded down the cool dark stairway. Nainai shut her eyes tight. Xiao Mei helped her up the last step and onto the roof. She stood motionless for a few seconds, holding tight to Xiao Mei, then opened her eyes.

'Look, Nainai.' Xiao Mei let go of her hand and took a few steps across the dazzling white surface. Then she walked almost to the edge and gazed down onto the miniature world far below. Toy cars crawled along the road. A diminutive horse and cart stood motionless in the yard. Two small figures sat in the shade of a wall, playing cards. A tiny woman with a bag walked towards the building and disappeared out of sight. Xiao Mei waved down at them but they did not see her.

She felt a hand grasping hers. Nainai was still out of breath. Still holding on to her she lowered herself towards the floor and sat down with a bump, her legs crossed. 'That's better,' she said, wheezing with the effort.

Xiao Mei sat down next to her. They gazed out. The blue-grey ridge of the Western Hills was so clear they could almost see the trees. There was the needle-like television tower, its golden, bubble-shaped observation deck gleaming in the sun, and the sparkling lake nearby. Streets and alleys crisscrossed in straight lines from east to west and north to south, dividing the centre of the city into squares and rectangles filled with low grey roofs; in the very heart of this lay a vast grey space where tiny red flags fluttered; north of it were red walls enclosing a series of courtyards and the yellow-roofed palace buildings. Way over in the east rose clusters of high-rises; tall orange cranes stood in squares of bare yellow earth, moving their arms slowly through the air. The bowl of sky above was cloudless and blue. Faint sounds drifted up from the yard below, a shout, the revving of a car engine.

They sat in silence, lost in their own thoughts. After a while, Nainai stuck her arms out on either side.

'We're like pigeons!'

Xiao Mei laughed and put her arms out too.

'Maybe even pigeons don't fly so high! We're aeroplanes!'

'Higher than our roof back home!' Nainai giggled.

Xiao Mei nodded.

'But don't go up there,' she said, her voice becoming sharp, 'or you'll fall off and then who will get blamed?'

She looked sombre. 'You never know when bad luck will strike.'

Xiao Mei took a deep breath.

'Nainai, you know the jade Guanyin you gave me?'

Nainai was hunched up, her arms wrapped around her chest.

'Would anything bad happen if I didn't lose it but just gave it away?'

Nainai looked up at her, her chin tucked into her jacket.

'That old thing! Why should I care what you do with it?' She clamped her mouth shut.

'But...?' Xiao Mei frowned. 'You said...'

The old woman tilted her face to the breeze, her eyes closed, her lips slightly parted in a faint smile, her hands tucked into her sleeves.

Xiao Mei shook her head. She gazed up at the sky. But she had given the jade to Stone and that felt right.

They had been sitting like this for some while when a commotion behind them roused them from their thoughts. Ba's head appeared through the door; he stepped out onto the roof, soon followed by Ma and Old Wang.

'They're here!' shouted Ba over his shoulder. Xiao Mei and Nainai turned round. Ma ran towards them, out of breath.

'You worried the life out of us!'

Old Wang nodded, his face creased into a smile. 'We were looking for you everywhere.'

'We thought you'd been kidnapped!' said Ba dramatically. 'You hear about such things all the time!'

'Don't be stupid,' said Ma, 'why would anyone want to kidnap them?' But her face showed her relief.

Xiao Mei looked from one parent to another. Nainai was struggling to get to her feet. Xiao Mei put out her hand. Nainai grasped it and they stood up together.

'Look,' said Old Wang. They turned in the direction he was pointing. A flock of pigeons was diving and soaring in the sun, splinters of light catching on their wings as they turned. They watched as the wheeling flock descended over the crisscross of hutongs, hovered for a moment over one spot, circled and then swept back up. Old Wang's face drooped. Ba put his hand on Old Wang's shoulder. Ma put her hand in Ba's.

Xiao Mei and Nainai stood together next to them. Ba looked out at the city spread below them and at the wide sky above, then turned to Nainai.

'Well, what do you think? Not bad, is it?'

Nainai narrowed her eyes against the glare of the sun and stretched her arms above her head.

'Top of the world,' she said, giving a wide, toothless smile, 'top of the world!'

Top of the world? Xiao Mei wrinkled her nose. Gazing out over the magnificent new city, she pondered Nainai's words, but this time was unable to work out what she really felt about it all.

Epilogue

Big Yellow shook himself hard. Golden sparks showered off his fur into the dark smoke-filled air. His eyes watered and reddened. His ears were deafened by the crackling, hissing, popping roar of the fire as it consumed the bone-dry timber window frames.

'Big Yellow! Big Yellow!'

The voice seemed to come from a very great distance.

'Big Yellow!'

The voice receded further and further away. Then he heard it no more.

He felt his body distending and evaporating in the intense heat, till all that remained of blood, bones and fur was a shimmering huangshulang outline. He shook himself again, stood up on his hind legs, and stepped out of the burning heap. He was growing all the while, so that now he could see over the wood-pile, over the houses, over the dark hutongs. He cast his eyes in all directions, paused for a moment, and strode out across the city.

As he passed down the silent wide streets, the shining plate-glass windows of the tall buildings reflected a towering black shape, arms swinging, ruby-red eyes scanning the horizon.

When he came to the high grey wall surrounding Tiantan park, he leapt lightly over and wafted through the pines, till he arrived at a patch of moon-soaked grass and two slim black cypress trees.

In the shadows of the trees he paused, exhaled a deep breath – and was gone.

THE END

Mouse-wolf

Acknowledgements

Many thanks to my writing group – Ianthe Maclagan, Yvonne Lyon and Helen Newdick, without whose practical support and encouragement I might never have finished; and to all my friends who so helpfully read and commented on the novel at its different stages.

Many thanks to Patricia Wells who introduced me to James Harrison at Oxfordfolio; and to James for his enthusiasm and for making the whole thing happen.

Many thanks to Weimin He for his wonderful illustrations that perfectly capture the spirit of Beijing.

Many thanks for the support of my family: Bao (Colin Kailin), Susan and her family, Stephen, Lili and Sonya.

And above all, thanks to Ning, who had unwavering faith in the book, and to whom I read the whole story through from start to finish, and who was never too tired to hear endless discussions about huangshulang!

This article was an inspiration:
On the Cult of the Four Sacred Animals (四 大 門) in the
Neighbourhood of Peking by Li Wei-tsu Folklore Studies,
Nanzan University, Japan. Vol. 7 (1948), pp. 1-94
https://www.jstor.org/stable/1177454?seq=1#page_scan_
tab_contents

I found the Malcolm Bradbury quotation here:
http://www.suttonelms.org.uk/imison2010.html